Two Hearts United Beneath the Desert Moon

"My friend Prince Khaldun would have me believe that every marriage in Kamar Ginena is enchanted. Shall we believe him about that?" Michael said.

"It makes a lovely story," Mallory returned.

"Ah, a skeptic. You don't believe that if we kiss beneath the moon, our lives will be entwined for eternity?"

She wanted to tell him that her heart already belonged to him, but she dared not.

He bent his dark head and touched her trembling lips, ever so softly. She sighed, drawing closer to his hard body. His hand moved up to cup her face, and he turned it toward the moon. "I believe I'm enchanted already. You are beautiful, Lady Mallory DeWinter."

Mallory curled up in Michael's arms and he saw mischief dancing in her eyes. "So this is what it feels like to have a legend make love to you."

Also by Constance O'Banyon

Forever My Love
Song of the Nightingale
Highland Love Song

Available from HarperPaperbacks

Desert Song

Constance O'Banyon

HarperPaperbacks
A Division of HarperCollins*Publishers*

This is a work of fiction. The characters, incidents, and dialogues are products of the author's imagination and are not to be construed as real. Any resemblance to actual events or persons, living or dead, is entirely coincidental.

HarperPaperbacks   *A Division of* HarperCollins*Publishers*
10 East 53rd Street, New York, N.Y. 10022

Copyright © 1994 by Constance O'Banyon
All rights reserved. No part of this book may be used or reproduced in any manner whatsoever without written permission of the publisher, except in the case of brief quotations embodied in critical articles and reviews. For information address HarperCollins*Publishers,*
10 East 53rd Street, New York, N.Y. 10022.

Cover illustration by Pino Daeni

First printing: June 1994

Printed in the United States of America

HarperPaperbacks, HarperMonogram, and colophon are trademarks of HarperCollins*Publishers*

❖ 10 9 8 7 6 5 4 3 2 1

This is gratefully dedicated to you, my readers. Many of you I know through your letters, many I have met in person, and some I will never meet. But we know each other all the same. You are the reason I spin my tales. Your warmth has touched me in so many ways. Thank you for your wonderful support and encouragement.

Desert Song

Cairo, Egypt—1845

Raile DeWinter, the duke of Ravenworth, moved out of the bedroom of his rented quarters when he heard his valet arguing with someone at the front door.

"If you wish to see His Grace, you must wait until morning. He's retired for the night," Oliver said imperiously, barring the person's way.

"I'm not asleep, Oliver," Raile said, wondering who would be visiting this late. The man was out of his view because he stood in the shadows. "Come forward so I can see you," Raile ordered, his eyes narrowed.

Reluctantly, Oliver stepped back and allowed the man to pass into the room.

The stranger wore a black robe and a white turban. He had a black patch over one eye that gave him a sinister appearance. "Effendi," he said, bowing subserviently. "I want but to deliver a letter to you from my esteemed master, Sheik Sidi Ahmed."

Raile looked the man over, then took the letter from him and began to read.

English Lord,

It has come to my attention that you are searching for certain individuals. I want to aid you in your mission because these men are dangerous to us who love peace. I can help you if you will meet me at an appointed place. Understand that I do this in peril of my own life. If you are interested in my information, come at once with the man who delivers this letter. He can be trusted, and I have anticipated your needs, so you will travel in comfort. Tell no one about this meeting, or it will not take place.

Raile raised his head and looked at the guide speculatively. "You know what's in this letter?"

"Only that I am to take you to my master if you agree to go."

"I don't know your master."

"He knows you, O exalted one."

Raile had no choice but to meet with this sheik. He had been in Cairo for eight weeks, trying to discover who was arming rebellious Bedouin tribes and inciting them against the British. But the Egyptians were suspicious of foreigners, and this was the first time he had been contacted with an offer of help. He was uneasy, but could think of no reason why he shouldn't trust this man. "Very well, I will accompany you. But I should first contact the British consul."

The man bowed. "Sorry, please, illustrious one, but my master instructed me not to guide you if you tell anyone."

"Very well. Oliver, pack only what I can carry in one valise."

Oliver had been with the duke for thirty years. He'd served him faithfully in the war against Napoleon, and when the duke had been wounded at Waterloo, Oliver had devotedly nursed him back to health. He would not let the duke go into the desert without him.

"I'm coming with you, Your Grace," Oliver said, with a look that dared the foreign guide to object.

Raile's lips twitched. "Of course you are, Oliver."

It seemed Sheik Sidi had thought of everything. Besides two guides, there were three servants to see to Raile's comfort. Under Oliver's direction, the servants set up camp each night with quiet efficiency.

Each day they traveled farther and farther from Cairo, until at last they stopped at a small oasis. Raile began to wonder if Sheik Sidi Ahmed really existed.

Raile stepped impatiently from beneath the awning of his tent. Looking past the small oasis where three tents dotted the sand, he raised his hand to shade his eyes against the scorching Egyptian sun.

His two guides had ridden off early in the morning and should have returned hours ago. How long did it take for them to arrange a meeting with Sheik Sidi Ahmed?

Raile's jaw tightened in anger. "Oliver, what am I doing in the middle of the Sinai Desert without benefit of guide and with no notion how to get back to Cairo? There are any number of men that Her Majesty could have chosen— why did she choose me?"

"Because, Your Grace, she knew you were the only man for this mission," the faithful retainer said with pride.

"A dubious honor," Raile replied cryptically. "Damn," he swore softly. "Where are they?"

He watched grimly as a gathering cloud of dust swirled in the distance, filtering slowly upward toward the sun. The storm would hit soon. Already the wind was whipping grains of sand and whirling it into Raile's face, stinging his eyes and blistering his cheeks.

"We're in for a fierce blow, Your Grace," Oliver, observed with growing concern. "If the guides don't return soon, they'll be caught in the sandstorm."

"If I knew the way back to Cairo, I'd leave now," Raile fumed.

"I'll ask the other men if they have any notion when the guides will return," Oliver said, hurrying toward the servants' tent. He returned a short time later. "Something odd has happened, Your Grace. The servants aren't in camp, and they took their belongings with them. Strange we didn't see them leave."

Suddenly a gust of wind struck with such a force it ripped one of the guy ropes away from the tent, causing one side to collapse. Raile and Oliver grabbed the rope, securing it firmly to the stake.

Oliver had to shout to be heard above the wind. "I rather like the Sinai Desert, Your Grace."

Raile glanced up at the cloud of dust that was quickly descending on them. "I find little to admire about this cursed place."

"It's so pristine and quiet," Oliver said reverently. "It makes me feel close to . . . I don't know—it seems almost sanctified."

Raile gave Oliver a disparaging glance, as if he questioned his man's sanity. "When that storm hits, you'll most probably retract your opinion. Your only thought will be how to breathe."

Oliver tightened the last knot and looked at their hand-iwork with satisfaction. "I believe this should hold it, Your Grace."

"We'd best seek shelter. The storm's about to hit."

Raile entered the tent and tossed aside the burnoose he'd worn to protect him from the sun. "I'm wondering how much longer we'll have to remain in this hellish country. Already we've been here for over two months, and I still don't know who is arming the bedouin."

"When our guides return with Sheik Sidi, he'll be able to help you, Your Grace," Oliver said encouragingly.

"I'm not even certain there is a Sheik Sidi, Oliver. I may be on a fool's mission."

Raile turned to the camp table and lit a lantern. He wondered what his wife, Kassidy, was doing at the moment. He didn't want to be here; he only wanted to return to her. Not that she needed him—God only knew she was a most capable woman, but perhaps she missed him, too.

He picked up a miniature of his wife and stared at it for a long moment. He felt a deep aching need for her—he longed for the sound of her voice and most of all the musical sound of her laughter.

Dropping down on a cot, he reached into his breast pocket and withdrew the letter he'd received from her just before leaving Cairo. Apparently she was concerned about their son, Michael, and there must be cause since Kassidy wasn't one to worry needlessly. He reread the letter, trying to decide what to do about Michael when he returned to England.

My Dearest Raile,
How long the days seem without you. I pray each night for your safety, and for your speedy return to

me. I received a letter from Arrian today and her health is good. You should be a grandfather within the month. I wish I could be with her, but so much requires my attention here at Ravenworth, and Scotland is so far away. Michael came home last week but stayed only three days. Raile, I believe it's time our son took on more responsibilities. I have insisted that he spend the winter at Ravenworth. Perhaps here, we can bend his mind to important matters, and he'll be less inclined to squander his life in frivolous pursuits.

Raile folded the letter and placed it back in his pocket, glancing up at Oliver, who was closing the flaps on the tent.

"I believe it's time I took my son and heir in hand, Oliver. Perhaps it was a mistake to allow him to reside in the London town house. He's too much a favorite with the ladies, and that crowd of young people he's connected with have no aim in life other than having a good time."

Oliver smiled. "As I recall, Your Grace, you were much the same in your youth."

"I suppose. But Her Grace is worried about Michael."

Oliver had a great respect for the duchess. "Then there would be a reason to worry, Your Grace."

The tent rattled and shook as the full force of the wind hit. The flap blew open, and it was dark as pitch until Oliver relit the lantern. "I'll just go and check on the horses, Your Grace. They seem to be restless."

Raile watched Oliver leave. If this meeting with Sidi wasn't fruitful, then he planned to return home at once. He frowned as he glanced at his travel clock. It was nearing evening, and still the guides hadn't returned. Most probably they had been forced to hole up until the storm abated.

At that moment the flap of his tent was thrown open and five men in dark robes entered. At first Raile wasn't concerned, thinking they must be the sheik's men. But when one of them leveled a gun at him, Raile instinctively dove for his holstered revolver, which was lying draped across a folding chair.

He never heard the shot that hit him so hard he was propelled backward from the impact. Sudden weakness drove him to his knees, and he fell face forward.

Kassidy's picture had been knocked to the ground, and one of the men crushed it beneath his boot.

"Kass . . . idy." Raile groaned, reaching his hand for the miniature of his wife—it was out of reach.

Raile fought against the black tide that threatened to swallow him, but he was soon engulfed in a dark void.

The black-robed man with a patch over one eye turned Raile over with his foot. "You fool," he said to his companion, "you killed him. Sheik Sidi will have you beheaded for this."

Blood ran from Raile's wound and was soon absorbed by the sand—he moved no more.

Two men lifted him and carried him out into storm. One of them spoke with uncertainty. "We shall take his body. Our lord will want proof of his death."

The other man asked with concern, "Is his man dead? Sheik Sidi wanted no one left alive to tell what happened here today."

A third man, who held the horses, nodded at Oliver's dead body that was impaled by a lance against a palm tree. "The English servant is dead, but he gave a valiant fight. He will talk to no one—he is food for the jackals."

Raile's limp body was thrown over a horse, and the black-robed men led him away from the oasis. They were soon swallowed up in the howling storm that sounded very like a woman's scream.

Chapter 1

London

The room was dark but for the lone candle that flickered on the shiny surface of a round mahogany table. Twelve fashionably dressed people were seated at that table, and the silence was so pronounced that even the rustle of a taffeta gown drew attention. All twelve pairs of eyes were riveted on the old Gypsy woman dressed in black with golden coins dangling from her headdress. In a trance, she rocked back and forth while she waved a gnarled hand over a crystal ball.

Just outside the circle of light, Lord Michael DeWinter sat with a cynical expression on his face. He half smiled as the fortune-teller predicted wealth and happiness for Lady Lenora Reeves. Lenora already had the wealth, and she always glowed with happiness. Why not? She was spoiled and pampered by her mother and father—a beauty with many gentlemen vying for her attention. But Lord

Michael was not one of admirers. He found her too inexperienced for his taste and her conversations rather dull.

Lady Samantha, who was more to Lord Michael's liking, rose from her chair and approached him, smiling. "Come, Michael," she cajoled, taking his hand and urging him to come to the table. "Join us. It's all done for our amusement. Allow the Gypsy to tell your fortune."

Lady Samantha wore her dark hair pulled straight back from its widow's peak and secured with a pearl clip. Her eyes were dark brown, her skin creamy and flawless.

"Hardly my idea of entertainment," Michael said with a morose expression on his face. "That woman can no more see into the future than you or I. She makes her fortune by predicting what naive fools want to hear." He nodded toward the table contemptuously. "Observe how your guests hold on to her every word—I must congratulate you on such a successful party," he said mockingly.

Lady Samantha was crushed. She had planned this evening just for him. She was desperately in love with Lord Michael. She was certain she would have loved him even if he hadn't been born the only son of one of the most powerful families in Britain. He was tall and broad shouldered. His hair was almost as dark as hers. There was a dangerous, exciting power that emitted from him. When he entered a room, everyone watched him. And when he left a room, it became strangely empty.

Now, as she looked into his cold, green eyes, Lady Samantha saw no evidence of the love she desired. She had realized long ago that she would have to break through a tight reserve to reach his heart. She was jealous of every woman who flirted and fawned over him. She envisioned herself as his wife, and no one was going to stand in her way.

Thus far, Lord Michael had not committed to any

woman, and Lady Samantha was determined that when he did, it would be to her.

Michael glanced back at the table where the fortune-teller held her audience spellbound, and he almost envied them their jovial mood. Nothing interested him for long, and this dinner party was becoming tedious.

"Michael," Lady Samantha said pleadingly, "I planned this evening just to amuse you. You can't know what I had to do to get Madame Zambana to attend my gala." She shuddered. "Imagine if you will, I personally rode to her house on Swinton Street to engage her for tonight. Madame Zambana has been the rage ever since Lady Wilhelmina used her to entertain her guests at a garden party last spring."

With a resigned sigh, Lord Michael rose to his full height and moved to the table. After he was seated beside Lady Samantha, he watched the old Gypsy wave her hands over a crystal ball and gaze into the depths as if she saw that which others could not see.

Madame Zambana smiled at Lady Garnet, who stared back at her with wide-eyed innocence. "You will obtain your heart's desire. The man you love also loves you. The two of you will live in wedded bliss, have many children, and grow to an old age together."

"Is it Charles?" the young girl asked, looking shyly at the man beside her.

The Gypsy pointed a bony finger at Lord Charles Bonnom. "That is the man who will be your husband," she said in a mysterious voice.

Lord Michael sneered as he watched Lady Garnet beam at the man she had been betrothed to for two years. Everyone knew Lady Garnet and Lord Charles were to be married in June. The old fortune-teller had certainly made no great revelation in predicting their union.

The Gypsy finally turned her attention to Lady Samantha, staring at her for a moment and then glancing down at her crystal ball. The gold bracelet on her wrist jingled as she waved her gnarled hand over the shimmering orb. The old woman hesitated before she gave her next revelation. "You will never obtain that which you desire. The man you wed will never have your heart, and the man you love will never be your husband."

Lady Samantha gasped and shrank visibly. "I don't believe you," she said in a trembling voice. "You cannot possibly see what will happen just by glancing into that silly little glass ball."

The old woman raised her dark eyes and shook her head. "I see many things that I do not tell because it is not good to know too much of the future. What I tell you tonight will come to pass."

Lady Samantha's mouth formed a pout. "Tell Lord Michael's fortune, and let's hope you find a more favorable prediction for him."

Madame Zambana looked up into scornful green eyes. She stared at Lord Michael so long that the others at the table began shifting in their chairs, but Lord Michael merely stared back at her unflinchingly.

"You are a handsome one," Madame Zambana said with a toothless grin. "Many women of high and low birth have vied for your notice. But, my handsome young man, all their attentions have become commonplace to you."

"Tell us something we don't know," Lord Grussom said tauntingly. "Lord Michael would have all the women and leave us with none."

The Gypsy continued as if she had not heard the interruption. "You will soon meet a woman that will not be so easily won, and you will suffer much before you are tamed, my comely one. Take particular notice of any woman you meet with hair like flame."

Lord Michael merely raised a dark brow.

The Gypsy continued. "You will take a long sea journey within a fortnight."

Lord Michael yawned behind his hand. "I can assure you I have no intention of leaving England until spring. My mother has suggested that I spend the winter at Ravenworth." He glanced at Lady Samantha. "As you know, my mother's suggestions are more like commands."

The old woman shook her head. "Nonetheless, you will embark on a long sea voyage. Beware, for you shall know betrayal as well as great friendship. Trust not a one-eyed man, and avoid a man of high rank who is of Turkish descent."

Lord Michael grinned, thinking this woman was quite entertaining after all. "A journey at this time might be quite amusing. It would certainly take me away from the doldrums of spending the winter months in the country."

The Gypsy waved her hand over the crystal ball and stared long into the smoky depths. Her dark eyes suddenly turned colorless like a swirling mist. "The black feather of disaster has fallen at your feet, young lord. Much trouble for you—much trouble. Someone close to you is in grave danger, perhaps dead."

There was a gasp from one of the ladies and a murmuring of voices. Suddenly the fun had gone out of the evening.

Madame Zambana's tone became urgent, and she caught Michael's hand. "You will not know winter this year, for you will travel to a land of warmth and sand. It would be best if you heed my words, young lord, for there is someone who needs you." Her eyes became piercing, and she looked deeply into Lord Michael's eyes. "You should go home."

Michael pried her hand from his and looked into eyes that were glowing with sincerity. He reminded himself that the Gypsy was acting a part and had put on a good performance. Why then did he feel this uneasiness in the pit of his stomach? Why had her predictions struck fear in his heart?

Without another word, he rose to his feet, tossing a few coins to the old woman. "You are most entertaining, madame. But you missed your calling—you should have been on the stage."

The Gypsy gathered up the coins and held them in her hand. "You do not believe what I have told you, but you will soon know that I have spoken the truth. Remember my words."

He laughed and bowed stiffly. "I'll consider your warning."

"That is all I ask."

Lord Michael turned to the others. "I take leave of you." To Lady Samantha, he added: "A most enlightening evening."

"Must you go?" she asked with disappointment etched on her face.

"Yes, I must. I'm to meet Lord Walters at my club. Fortune has been kind to me of late. I promised I'd give him a chance to win back his money."

Lady Samantha accompanied him to the door and waited for the butler to bring his hat. "You don't believe that old woman, do you?"

"No," Lord Michael said adamantly, "and you shouldn't put any trust in her words either."

"Will I see you at Lady Milan's party tomorrow night?"

He became impatient to leave. "Of course."

She watched the butler close the door behind Lord Michael, feeling empty inside. If only she could tell him how much she loved him. But she knew if she ever declared her love, Michael would turn away from her as he had from many others. No, she had to be cleverer than those women who threw themselves at his head. She would be patient and wait for him to come to her.

When Michael was seated in his coach, the Gypsy's warning rang in his head. No, he would not believe her—she was just an old woman who preyed on peoples' hopes and fears for profit.

He tapped his gold-tipped cane on the top of the carriage and called to his driver. "To my club."

As the horses clopped along the deserted street, he thought of Lady Samantha. He supposed he would one day ask her to marry him. Yes, they would deal quite well together, he thought with no particular exhilaration. He had to marry someone, and she was more acceptable than most of the others. At least she didn't bore him.

Michael's thoughts turned to his family. Perhaps it wouldn't be so tedious spending the holidays in the country. By Christmas his father should have returned from Egypt and they would hunt together. There was no one he admired more than his father, and no one he loved as much as his mother. His sister, Arrian, had married a Scottish chieftain. Since Arrian was expecting her second child, she wouldn't be coming to Ravenworth this winter. But no matter—perhaps he and his father could go to Scotland for a bit of hunting.

He leaned his head back and closed his eyes. His mother and father had a marriage everyone envied. Arrian and Warrick were deeply committed to one another. What was wrong with him? he wondered. Was there a woman who would make his eyes soften as his father's did when he looked at his mother? Perhaps he was incapable of love. He certainly didn't like clinging females. He shuddered at the thought of spending his life with a woman who would demand his entire attention.

Again he thought of Lady Samantha. She never made demands on him. Perhaps next spring he would ask her to become his wife.

The carriage stopped at his club, and he ascended the steps, hoping to find amusement in gaming with his contemporaries. Still, in the back of his mind the old Gypsy's warning haunted him.

After spending the better part of the night at his club playing cards, Lord Michael climbed into his coach and directed the driver to take him home.

A warm sun bathed the wet cobblestone streets with a soft golden glow as his crested carriage turned the corner and stopped before a three-story town house. Four prancing grays stomped their hooves, impatiently tossing their shimmering manes, while the coachman kept a steadying grip on the reins.

The street vendors were already about, selling their wares. "Lavender, buy my sweet-smelling lavender." A woman sang out her melodic chant as she moved through the more fashionable part of London, hoping to sell her flowers. "Lavender for your lady—lavender."

An outrider dressed in green livery jumped from his high perch and hurriedly lowered the steps and opened the coach door, speaking respectfully to Lord Michael. "Do you require anything further, m'lord?"

"No. Go to bed, Simmons."

Lord Michael yawned sleepily as he climbed the steps. Another long, dull evening, he thought, longing for his bed.

The door of his town house was thrown open, and his valet, William, rushed toward him, his usual calm manner forgotten in his anxiety. "Her Grace is inside, m'lord. She's been here since midnight. She seems most distraught. Your aunt, Lady Mary, is with her."

"Mother and Aunt Mary here at this hour?"

"Yes, m'lord, and they've been waiting all night for your return. I sent Horace to Lady Samantha's, thinking you'd still be there, but he was informed you'd already left."

Michael's path was suddenly blocked by a woman selling lavender. Absently, he thrust a shilling at her and unconsciously took the flowers she pushed in his hands.

"Thank ya', sir. Thank ya' kindly," she said, biting the coin to make certain it was genuine, and smiling when she was satisfied with its value.

Lord Michael pushed past the woman and hurried up the steps. His mother would never arrive in the middle of the night unless something was amiss. His first thought was that something was wrong with his sister, Arrian. Perhaps the birth of her child had not gone well.

He rushed inside, calling his mother.

Chapter 2

er Grace, the duchess of Ravenworth, had heard her son's carriage arrive and was waiting for him in the door-way of the drawing room.

Michael went to her, searching her face and seeing the distress reflected in her eyes. He took her hand, finding it cold to the touch.

"Mother, what's wrong?"

She shook her head, unable to answer, and he drew her into his arms, causing the clump of lavender to fall to the floor to be trampled beneath his boots. Trepidation surrounded his heart as he felt her tremble. His mother was a woman of great courage, and he knew something terrible had happened.

"It's Arrian, isn't it?" he asked, fearing to hear the worst.

Kassidy lingered in her son's arms, drawing on his strength and hoping to find the courage she needed to tell him what had occurred. At last she pulled away, and green eyes stared into green eyes. "Your sister gave birth to a daughter and they are both well."

Her eyes were shining with tears, and Michael couldn't remember a time when he had seen her cry.

His great-aunt, Mary, came to him, and he saw sorrow in her eyes. "I'm afraid it's your father, Michael. Your mother has received grim news concerning him."

Kassidy moved out of her son's arms, but kept a tight grip on his hand. She hesitated to speak, as if she couldn't form the words. "Michael, I'm so . . . frightened. Your father has disappeared. I'm told he was abducted, but they don't know by whom. The prime minister fears for his life. Her Majesty has also expressed her concern for your father's safety."

"I advised Raile not to go to that barbaric country," Lady Mary stated emphatically. "I knew nothing but trouble would come from such a dangerous mission."

Michael guided his mother gently across the room and seated her on a chair. Dropping on his knees before her, he took her small hands in his. "Tell me everything," he urged.

Kassidy took a deep breath. "As you know, your father reluctantly agreed to this trip to Egypt. You know he doesn't like to go anywhere without me."

Michael tried to be patient and not give in to the fear that gnawed at his insides. "Yes, I know. I received a letter from him just after he arrived in Egypt, and then another letter a fortnight ago. I've heard nothing since."

Kassidy didn't want to cry, but now that she was with her son, she could no longer be brave, and tears spilled down her face. "He'd written me a note that was found in his room. He said he was going into the desert to meet with a man who promised to help him find the persons who were arming the bedouin tribes. He was hopeful that he would be home before . . . Christmas." Her voice broke.

Michael glanced from his mother to his great-aunt. "When Father left, it was my understanding that he was only going to Cairo to confer with the viceroy about whoever it was that is arming and inciting the border tribes. He should have been in no danger."

"It sounded so simple when he was trying to convince me it was his duty to go." Kassidy rose to her feet and turned to the window. "I don't know why your father went into the desert alone, or who he went to meet." She glanced up at the ceiling as tears continued to fall. "Why, Raile, why?" she cried.

Lady Mary looked at Kassidy with growing concern. Kassidy and Raile had been inseparable. Lady Mary grieved for her niece.

Michael went to his mother, hiding his own fears from her. "What's being done to locate father?"

Kassidy made a hopeless gesture. "Her Majesty has assured me that they are doing everything they can. She promised me that if your father is alive, he will be found."

"Why should anyone think my father is . . . dead?"

Kassidy swallowed hard. "A messenger delivered to the British consul in Cairo a bloodstained shirt, claiming it was your father's. It had his initials on the pocket. They sent it to me to identify. There's no doubt it's your father's shirt."

Michael swallowed a painful lump. "You know Father would never do anything foolish. If he went into the desert, he was well prepared for anything that might happen. Whoever abducted him must know his importance and would see the folly of harming him. Has there been a demand for money?"

"No." There was a gleam of hope in his mother's eyes. "Do you think that's why he was taken? We'll pay anything to get him back."

Michael pressed a kiss on her cheek. "I believe it's a possibility that we may yet receive a ransom demand. What else can you tell me?" he asked gently.

"Nothing, except . . ." Again tears gathered in her eyes. "Dear, faithful Oliver was killed by those monsters. His body was . . . run through with a spear. He . . . they . . . buried what remained of him in the desert."

Rage was building inside Michael, but he had to control his anger, for his mother's sake. Oliver had been more like a member of the family than a servant. "Why would anyone want to harm him?"

His mother dabbed at her eyes. "I imagine that dear little man tried to protect your father. He was like that, you know."

"The fact that they haven't found . . . Father's body is encouraging." Michael walked to the window and looked unseeingly out at the lavender woman moving down the street. "I'll not rest until I find out who has done this. God help them when I do. He went to Egypt to aid those people." Closing his eyes, he tried to empty his heart of anguish before he turned back to his mother. "Has no one claimed responsibility for Father's disappearance?"

Lady Mary supplied more information since his mother was having difficulty controlling her grief. "Your father wrote me that most of the bedouin tribes don't feel they owe their allegiance to any nation, and that they recognize no borders. His one concern was that if they were being armed they might unite into one army and there would be another bloody civil war in Egypt. I suppose whoever is responsible must have seen your father as a threat."

"Yes, but who?" Kassidy asked.

"Someone must know the identity of the man Father went into the desert to meet. Is there no one in authority in Cairo?" Michael demanded.

Kassidy shook her head. "It doesn't seem so. There is only the British consul. He has little authority and must answer to Egypt's viceroy. In the last letter I received from your father, he was not impressed with the man."

Anger snapped in Michael's eyes. "Someone has to know something. I'm going to Egypt myself, and *I'll* find out what happened."

"That's what I want you to do, Michael," Kassidy said hopefully. "If your father is alive, bring him home." Her lower lip trembled. "If he's . . . dead, bring me his body. I will not rest until I have my husband."

Michael pulled her into his arms, feeling her tears soak through his shirt. "I'll find him, Mother, and I'll bring him home to you, I promise."

She seemed to collapse against him. He lifted her into his arms and moved out of the room and toward the stairs. "You are going to bed. When did you last sleep?"

"She has slept but little since she received the news." Lady Mary said, moving up the stairs beside them.

Michael climbed the stairs with his light burden, carrying her as tenderly as he would a baby. If only his sister, Arrian, were there, she would know how to comfort their mother. He was helpless against her tears and grief.

He glanced down at his mother and watched her dark lashes close, and she seemed to relax, if only for the moment.

Lady Mary rushed into the bedroom before him and turned down the coverlet. When he laid his mother on the bed, her eyes fluttered open.

"I wouldn't ask you to go, Michael, if I didn't know

you are probably the only person who can find your father. No one will search as diligently as you. You will not give up until you find him, will you?"

"I will find him," he assured her.

"Take care of yourself, Michael. I don't want to lose you, too. I couldn't go on if I lost you both."

He kissed her cheek tenderly. "I'll be back, and I'll have Father with me. And take heart, Mother—if Father were dead, wouldn't you know it in your heart?"

She smiled slightly. "You know that about us?"

"I have always known the two of you shared an unusual bond."

"He is alive, Michael—I feel it in the depth of my heart. But knowing him as I do, I also know that his primary concern is about us and not his own safety. It would be just like him to do something foolish to anger his captors."

"Have you sent word to Arrian?"

"Yes, I felt your sister had a right to know. But I urged her not to come since she just gave birth."

"That won't stop her," Michael said with assurance. "She and Warrick will come."

"Yes," Kassidy agreed, "she will come."

He pulled up a chair and sat beside her. "Sleep now, Mother, and let me do the worrying for both of us."

"Yes," she said, closing her eyes wearily. "I can rest now."

Michael stared at her for a long moment. She was still the most beautiful woman he knew. Her face was surprisingly unlined; her golden hair was laced with silver, but it only added to her beauty. He could feel her heartbreak, and he knew what she was suffering. He must not fail her or his father.

After his mother had fallen asleep, Michael stood and

motioned for his great-aunt to accompany him into the hallway.

"Your mother should sleep all day now that she's seen you, Michael. There was nothing I could do to calm her until she reached you."

"Will you remain with her until I return?"

Lady Mary linked her arm through his, studying his careworn face. "Of course, dear boy, and as you pointed out, Arrian and Warrick will be here soon. You can go to Egypt with the assurance that we shall all take care of your mother."

In that moment Lady Mary saw something in Michael that reminded her of his father. There was a hardness in his eyes and a determined set to his chin. Like Raile, Michael had never known fear and that troubled her. "Michael, don't do anything foolish. The fact that you were champion of your class with rapier and pistols won't help you in Egypt. Keep yourself out of danger."

Michael kissed the cheek of the authoritative little woman he'd adored all his life. She was the matriarch of London society, outrageous and clever, but she was also capable of taking command when trouble threatened.

"I suspect Mother will draw heavily on your strength in the weeks to come. Can you be strong for her?"

"Of course I can. But I'll be glad when Arrian and Warrick arrive. Your mother will need her family about her. Arrian's children would help cheer her, and the new baby would surely be a welcome distraction."

Michael felt the unfamiliar sting of tears, and he quickly turned away to hide his weakness from his great-aunt. "I am frightened, not for myself, but for my father," he finally admitted. "I tried hard to convince mother that he's alive, but you and I both know he may be—" He could not say the word.

The perceptive little woman moved to face him and pressed her cheek to his. "I know, Michael—I know what you are feeling."

"I mustn't think like this," he said, straightening his shoulders and gathering his strength. "I'll need a clear mind if I'm to help Father."

"Put your fear aside and do what you must," Lady Mary said encouragingly. "When do you leave?"

"I'll go now to instruct William to pack my trunk. I leave within the hour for Southampton, where I'll take the first available ship to Egypt."

She gripped his arm. "Be extremely careful, Michael. The men who took your father are dangerous. Don't do anything rash or foolish. I'll expect you and your father home soon."

"I don't know how long this will take, Aunt Mary, because I won't come home without my father."

"You will write and keep us informed?"

"Every chance I get."

She tried to regain her composure and gave him a forced smile. "I'm counting on you attending my spring gala, you handsome rogue."

He hugged her. "I'll try my damnedest, Aunt Mary."

Her eyes glimmered with tears, but she managed to put on a calm face. "I don't want to have to explain to all the females why you aren't at my party. Don't disappoint me."

"If it's at all possible, I'll dance with you at your gala."

Chapter 3

Sussex

*L*ady Mallory Stanhope burst into the sitting room, her blue eyes wide with excitement. "Mother, Father, are you here?" She looked around the room for her parents, but saw no one but her cousin, Phoebe, who was sitting in a straight-back chair near the window, a letter crumpled in her hand. Automatically, Mallory's back stiffened and the enthusiasm went out of her face.

"Mallory, that is no way for a lady to enter the room," Phoebe Byrd chastised her absently.

Mallory searched her cousin's eyes. Evidently something was occupying her thoughts, for the admonishment was merely perfunctory.

Phoebe Byrd was her mother's spinster cousin, and was what the neighbors secretly referred to as a "poor relation." She was in her forties, but looked much older. Tall and birdlike, she was always fussing about, straightening a picture, dusting a table, polishing the banisters. She was strict and demanding, always insisting that Mallory act like a lady.

Cousin Phoebe had come to live at Stoneridge House when Mallory was five years old. Soon afterwards, Mallory's parents had begun their travels and left Mallory in Phoebe's care. Mallory respected her cousin and looked to her for guidance. It was Phoebe's hand that had dried Mallory's tears as a child, and it was Phoebe who had nursed her when she was ill. Though only a paid companion, she was the only mother Mallory had ever known.

"I beg your pardon, Cousin Phoebe. I thought I heard a carriage pull in the drive while I was dressing, and I was sure it was mother and father. Their letter said they would be arriving today."

Phoebe didn't answer at once, but looked down at the letter in her lap. Ten years since Tyler and Julia had seen their daughter—ten years of thoughtless neglect that she had tried her best to hide from the child. How did one explain to a young girl that her parents didn't love her? That as far as they were concerned, since she hadn't been born a boy, she might as well not have been born at all?

At last, she said, "It wasn't your parents, but merely a messenger delivering this letter."

With a rustle of skirts, Mallory moved across the room and knelt down beside her cousin, clasping the frail, wrinkled hands in hers. "What is wrong?" Mallory asked in concern. "It isn't Mother and Father—there hasn't been an accident?"

Phoebe looked on Mallory with controlled affection. The girl didn't know it yet, but she was a beauty, and

Phoebe feared for her future. Her skin was smooth and flawless, her auburn hair sparkled as if it were on fire. Her features were lovely, and her violet blue eyes were so brilliant that one could see the color from across the room. Mallory was slender, and each movement was graceful as if she'd practiced, but gracefulness came naturally to her.

"Oh, no, child," Phoebe reassured her. "Your mother and father are enjoying perfect health." She couldn't keep the bitterness out of the last words.

Mallory looked searchingly at her cousin. "They're not coming, are they?" Years of loneliness and disappointment were reflected in her voice.

"No, child," Phoebe said gently. "They had to return to Egypt. It seems that there is some dispute with the Egyptian government over ownership of artifacts your parents have found, and they have all been confiscated. I don't really understand it, but your parents were quite concerned, and they've already set sail."

Mallory's eyes were glimmering with tears. "But they were in London for weeks, Cousin Phoebe. They should have sent for me." Her shoulders drooped. "They didn't want to see me," she said forlornly. "They didn't, did they?"

"Nonsense! This letter is full of their sorrow at not being able to see you." Phoebe wove her half-truths for the girl's sake. "They also sent their loving wishes and congratulations for your birthday, along with this present," she said, indicating a large box wrapped in brightly colored paper.

"May I see the letter?"

Phoebe smoothed out the crumpled sheet, that merely contained instructions from Mallory's parents that their tenants were to grow oats instead of barley in the coming season. She quickly folded it and put it in the pocket of her dress. "You know it is impolite to read another's correspondence, Mallory."

But Mallory wasn't fooled. She knew that whatever the letter contained, it wasn't love and best wishes for her. Phoebe was trying to protect her. She felt suddenly dejected and lonely.

"Here, child," Phoebe prompted. "Open your gift. I know your birthday isn't until tomorrow, but go ahead."

Without enthusiasm, Mallory complied. She carefully unwrapped the pink paper, taking care not to tear it. She stared at the white box, wondering what it contained. The label was from a shop in Paris. "They have sent me a gown or perhaps a bonnet," she said as enthusiasm crept into her voice.

Eagerly, she lifted the lid, her eyes shining with anticipation. But when she saw what was inside, her lower lip trembled and she raised hurt eyes to Phoebe.

"What is it, child? Show me what they sent you," Phoebe urged.

Mallory lifted a stylishly dressed doll from the box and held it out for her cousin's inspection. "It's my eighteenth birthday, and my mother and father gave me a doll. Don't they know I'm a young lady now and I don't play with toys?"

Phoebe tried to disguise her anger. It would have been better if they had not sent anything, she thought, as her heart broke for her charge. She took the doll from Mallory and straightened the stiff white gown. "It's beautiful," she said, trying to sound lighthearted.

Mallory stood, her eyes blazing with anger. "Give it to one of the village children. I don't want it."

"You'll change your mind."

Mallory turned away from the doll as if the sight of it offended her. "No, I won't ever change my mind. I never want to see it again."

Phoebe sighed as she replaced the doll in the box. "I know a little girl who would love to have this. I doubt she's ever had anything half so nice."

"Then give it to her. I'm going to ride Tibor."

Mallory raced her gelding across the meadow, her eyes on the fence just ahead. It was high, but she had been training Tibor for months, and she felt he was ready for the jump.

"Come on, boy," she said close to his ear, "you can do it, I know you can."

With little urging on her part, the horse lunged forward as if he had wings. The wind kissed her cheeks as horse and rider sailed over the fence, landing safely on the other side.

Mallory patted the horse's sleek neck and spoke softly to him. "I knew you could do it. You were magnificent!"

Her attention was drawn to the wooded area where she heard someone approaching. When she glanced up to see their neighbor, Sir Gerald Dunmore, emerging from the woods, she straightened her back in displeasure. Of late, he always seemed to know where to find her and when she was alone. Why was he pursuing her when he was a married man? she wondered. She detested him, but nothing she could say would convince him of that fact.

"That was superb, Lady Mallory. There's no disputing that you're the best horsewoman in Sussex."

"I wasn't aware that I had an audience, Sir Gerald," she said coldly. "I would prefer that you inform me ahead of time when you plan to come to Stoneridge."

He merely grinned at her rebuff. "If I had informed you that I wanted to pay a call on you, you would have found a reason to be absent."

He was tall, with sandy-colored hair and blue eyes. Mallory knew that many women found him attractive, but she did not. She loathed him for the shameful way he trifled with other women, giving little thought to his poor wife.

"I do hope Lady Dunmore is enjoying good health," Mallory said pointedly. "She did not accompany you today?"

Sir Gerald merely shrugged. "You know I'm alone. Little my wife cares where I take my pleasure as long as I don't bother her."

"I would rather not hear you speak disparagingly about Lady Dunmore. I like her, and she deserves better."

"Why not pity me? You don't know what it's like to be married to a woman with a cold disposition. Twelve years we've been married." His eyes raked Mallory's body to fasten on the swelling of her young breasts against her tight-fitting riding habit. "I've often imagined how you'd warm a man's bed on a cold night, Mallory."

She stared at him in horror. "How dare you? You're deplorable."

He appeared undaunted by her rebuke. His voice became silky. "Perhaps I am, but I could do things to you that would leave you begging for more."

She whirled on him, her eyes darkening in rage. "Get off my father's land. You aren't welcome here."

He merely laughed. "Not very hospitable this morning, are you? Never mind—sooner or later I'll break down your defenses."

"Never! What must I do to convince you that I don't even like you?"

His eyes burned into hers with naked desire. "It's been my experience with women that they often say no when what they really mean is yes."

"You think too much of your charms. I find you offensive and without honor."

"Honor is just a word invented by fools who were too afraid to say what they really feel. I believe, given the right circumstances, you would be more than amiable to me."

Tibor chose that moment to perform his antics. He tossed his mane and pranced about, causing Mallory to devote her full attention to quieting the spirited animal.

Sir Gerald's eyes followed Mallory's every graceful movement. As she attempted to gentle her mount, her hat flew off and dark auburn hair spilled down her back. He ached to possess her. He was determined to have her, no matter what. He had been very tolerant with her, but no more. Today he would take her, with or without her consent.

Mallory slid off her horse and walked to the bramble bush where the wind had blown her hat. Before she could poise it on her head, she was grabbed from behind. She spun around to face Sir Gerald.

"Take your hands off me!" she demanded.

His eyes rested on her heaving breasts, and he felt a strong need to crush her in his arms. "You always turn away my advances, but there is no one here to stop me from taking what I want."

Mallory was suddenly afraid, but she was determined not to allow him to see that fear. "Release me," she said bravely. "Your wife will hear about this if you don't leave me alone."

His grip only tightened. "Why do women pretend they don't want a man's kiss, when all along they ache for it?"

"Don't you care about your wife?"

"I can't even abide to be in the same room with her. Have pity on me and give me what I crave."

"I don't know what kind of woman you think I am, Sir Gerald. But I'm outraged that you would take such liberties with me. If my father were here, he'd kill you for touching me."

"But he isn't. The whole village knows that your parents have never been concerned for your welfare, m'lady. Since your father began acquiring artifacts for British museums, he and your mother only care about traveling the world for treasures, leaving their greatest treasure unguarded." He touched her hair and she drew back. "Your mother and father don't give you a thought, while I can't get you out of my mind."

"You insult me."

"You know I speak the truth, m'lady. Now, if you were nice to me, I'd never leave you alone. I know your father has left you practically impoverished. Most of the servants have gone, and those who remain are too old to look after you properly. Under my protection, you would want for nothing. I would shower you with fancy gowns and expensive trinkets."

She was disgusted by his vile suggestion. "How dare you make such a lewd offer to me. I'm a highborn lady, and not some guttersnipe."

He slid one hand behind her head and the other about her shoulders, bringing her closer to him. "It's because you are highborn that you appeal to me. I will have you, Mallory, make no mistake about that."

Her heart was thundering with fear. "I'll scream."

He smiled. "Go ahead. No one will hear you."

She struggled to be free of him, but his grip only tightened. "What do you want of me?"

His eyes settled on her lips. "I think you know. Can you guess what it feels like to have a man make love to you, Mallory? I've watched you grow into a beautiful young woman, and I've lain awake at night aching to touch you."

Fear robbed her of her voice, and she could only stare at him in disbelief.

He dipped his head, and his lips covered hers in a suffocating kiss. She pushed against him, and tried to turn her head away, but he persisted. She froze when his hands moved up the bodice of her gown.

At last she was able to move her head enough to escape his kiss. "You monster," she said, rubbing her hand across her lips. "You vile, unprincipled monster!"

He only smiled. "When you struggle like that, it only excites me more. Now I shall excite you."

"Surely you aren't saying that you would . . . that you would force me to . . ."

His eyes gleamed with something she couldn't define. "I believe we understand each other."

She decided to try reasoning with him, at least until she could think of a way to escape. "Why would you want me? I've had no experience with a man. Surely you could find a woman much more willing than I."

He studied the fine details of her face—her upturned nose, her finely arched eyebrows, eyes so blue a man could get lost in them. Her innocence only aroused him more. "You are unaware how your beauty can tear at a man's guts. Ask of me what you will, and it's yours. I'll do anything to possess you."

"I ask you to let me go."

He stared into her eyes. "Anything but that," he said harshly. Then his wet lips pressed against hers, making her stomach churn sickeningly.

Sir Gerald was beyond reasoning, and Mallory felt bile rise in her throat as his lips moved down the curve of her neck. His hand was fumbling with her gown, and she realized that he was raising her skirt. When she tried to pull away, she heard the fabric rip. Pain shot through her body as he shoved her to the ground, his weight crushing her.

She knew what she must to do. She still held the riding whip, and her fingers tightened over the silver handle. Using all her strength, she wedged her elbow between them enough so she could roll out from under him. She quickly gained her feet and turned to run.

Sir Gerald ran after her, and when he caught her, he whirled her around. Before he realized what she was doing, Mallory struck him across the face with her whip.

He cried out in pain and grabbed his cheek. She saw her chance to get away, so she went flying toward her horse.

He muttered a loud curse, and she could hear him running after her. Fear gave her the strength she needed. She grabbed Tibor's reins and led him forward quickly. She leaped on the fence, and lifted herself into the sidesaddle.

Sir Gerald was nearly upon Mallory when she urged her horse into a run. After she was safely out of his reach, she halted and glanced back down the hill. She felt great satisfaction when she saw him dab blood from his face with his handkerchief. Mallory was glad she had drawn blood.

He raised his clenched fist at her. "You'll pay for this, Mallory. You'll see—you'll pay."

"You are mistaken. Let this be a warning to you, Sir Gerald. If you ever touch me again, you'll get a lot worse than a lashing from my whip."

"No one stands between you and me except that

crazed old spinster cousin. She can't keep me away from you."

Mallory spun Tibor around, riding down the hill toward the stables. Her heart was beating so fast she could hardly breathe. She had endured Sir Gerald's insults and innuendoes for over two years, but today was the first time he'd been so bold as to try and force himself on her.

Riding into the interior of the stable, she was assisted from her horse by the aging coachman. Bill would be no help—he was much too frail to take on Sir Gerald, and she dare not involve him in this anyway.

Today she'd escaped Sir Gerald's advances, but would she be as fortunate the next time? She could think of no one to turn to for help.

Mallory was still shaken from the encounter. She had to tell someone what had happened, so she went in search of Cousin Phoebe.

Mallory was so distraught that she didn't notice the carriage in the driveway. The sun was waning, and candles flickered in the entryway as Mallory rushed into the house. Seeing warm light spilling into the hallway from the formal sitting room, she ran in that direction.

Bursting into the room, she blurted out, "Phoebe, Sir Gerald—"

Phoebe was on her feet, immediately interrupting her. "No, Mallory, Sir Gerald isn't here. But you may greet Lady Dunmore."

Mallory stared at Sir Gerald's wife with trepidation. "Lady Dunmore," she said, gathering her composure, "how delightful to see you."

Sir Gerald's wife stared at Mallory, and there was comprehension as her eyes narrowed with anger.

Phoebe had also understood the situation and spoke up

quickly. "Mallory, go to your room immediately and change out of your riding habit. You've torn it again, and I don't know if we'll ever get the mud stains out." She turned to Lady Dunmore. "I have tried to make a lady out of Mallory, but she insists on spending most of her time on horseback. It's a thankless task to try to make a lady out of a girl who'd rather run wild."

Lady Dunmore took in Mallory's disheveled appearance, her torn and muddy gown, her tangled hair. "It could be that she's up to more than riding. I'd look to her morals, Phoebe. When a girl has her kind of beauty and also has a wild streak in her, no woman's husband is safe."

Mallory bit back an angry retort as her cousin ushered her out of the room. She wanted to shout at Lady Dunmore to look to her husband's behavior, but Phoebe silenced her with a glance and shoved her toward the stairs. "Go to your room," she told Mallory in a sharp voice. "Make yourself presentable before you come downstairs again."

Mallory slowly climbed the stairs, feeling dejected. She would get no help from Cousin Phoebe. Most probably she'd get a dressing down and be blamed for the whole incident.

After she stripped her gown off, she stood before the mirror assessing herself. Was she beautiful? Everyone seemed to think so. But beauty was only a curse to someone who didn't have the protection of a father.

Chapter 4

ady Dunmore took a sip of tea before she spoke to Phoebe. "You should be more strict with that one. Mallory has become the talk of the village with her wild and undisciplined ways. No decent man would ever offer her marriage."

Phoebe sat down, her anger smoldering close to the surface. "You should look to your own house before you try to clean mine, Winifred. As for Mallory, no one is of a sweeter nature. Her wild ways, as you call them, are nothing more than the behavior of a lonely young woman who has to fill her days riding horses when she should be attending balls and having fun."

"She's too pretty for her own good," Lady Dunmore said pettishly. "Nothing good comes from a young woman who attracts men the way she does."

"Perhaps the fault lies with the man, and not with Mallory."

The woman's gray eyes snapped with indignation. "What do you mean by that, Phoebe Byrd?"

"I mean that your husband chases everyone in skirts. Don't deny it. But if he's harmed Mallory, I'll not let it pass. You'd do better to keep him closer to home."

Lady Dunmore came to her feet. "You're a fine one to talk. No man has looked at you in years, if they ever did. You're just jealous because I have a husband and you don't."

"Winifred, I much prefer my life to marriage to a philandering husband like Sir Gerald."

Winifred gathered her shawl, glaring all the while at her hostess. "I'll never step one foot in this house again, Phoebe Byrd. This is what happens when one befriends a person beneath one's station."

Suddenly Phoebe's eyes became sympathetic. "I pity you, Winifred, your life can't be easy."

"Don't pity me. You are a nobody who lives on the charity of others. I have a fine house, a husband, and three daughters."

"I don't accept charity, Winifred—I earn my own way."

"I give you this warning, keep that little strumpet away from my husband, or I'll see that her name is blackened in the village."

Phoebe shook her head. "Don't you realize, Winifred, that everyone in the village knows your husband for what he is? And as for Mallory, she is a sweet girl whose only crime is being born beautiful. Take your anger and lay it at the feet of your husband, where it belongs."

To Phoebe's surprise Winifred's shoulders drooped and her eyes clouded with tears. "I'm sorry for my harsh words, because you have been a friend to me. I know in my heart what you say is true. I've always known about Gerald's women but as his wife, I'm expected to look the other way when his eyes wander." She glanced up at Phoebe. "If you are wise, you will keep Mallory under lock and key. She's not the first young girl he's lusted after. Up to now, the objects of his interest have all been village girls who have been only too willing to tumble into bed with him for a few shillings."

Phoebe's mind was troubled. "Mallory isn't a village girl, as your husband is aware. It's time I did something about her situation. She is an innocent and shouldn't have to deal with a man like your husband."

"You go too far, Phoebe. I'll not allow you to insult Gerald."

"I'll do more than that if you don't keep him away from Mallory."

Winifred moved to the door. She knew her husband's shortcomings, but she would not allow someone else to criticize him. She sailed out of the room and out of the house, climbing aboard her waiting carriage. She could no longer look the other way. She must now go home and confront her husband. It was time she reminded him whose money allowed him to enjoy his pursuit of pleasure.

Mallory sat on her window seat, staring out into the gathering dusk. She waited for the sound of footsteps, knowing that when Cousin Phoebe came, she'd be outraged. She'd never be able to convince Phoebe that what had happened was Sir Gerald's fault.

When Phoebe did come, it was with a quickness that took Mallory by surprise. She looked up into dark eyes that were strangely soft.

"Did that man hurt you, my dear?"

"I . . . no." Mallory came to her feet. "I'm sorry about what happened with Lady Dunmore, but—"

"You're not to worry about that. We have more immediate problems to discuss."

"If it's about my riding habit, I—"

"No, dear child. What I have to say should have been said long ago."

Mallory stared at Phoebe as if seeing her for the first time. She had always considered her a cold and unfeeling woman, who cared for her cousin's child out of duty and nothing more. Could she have been mistaken?

Mallory watched as her cousin scooped up her torn riding habit and stared at it with contempt in her eyes. "He did this to you, didn't he?"

They both knew to whom she was referring. "Oh, Phoebe, he was beastly." Mallory ran trembling fingers through her tangled hair. "He . . . kissed me, and when I escaped, he said next time I wouldn't get away from him. Why is he doing this to me?"

"How long has this been going on?"

"The first time he approached me was last spring at the Mathersons' party. That night he led me into the garden. I didn't see anything incorrect in his manner. But when he pushed me in the arbor and tried to kiss me, I slipped past him and ran back to the party."

Phoebe folded Mallory's riding habit and placed it neatly on a chair. "I can't tell you how bad I feel about this. Why didn't you come to me before now?"

"I . . . thought you would blame me."

"No, child, I wouldn't have blamed you. I know you too well to think that you would encourage a man like Sir Gerald."

Mallory could hardly believe that Phoebe was taking her part. "He frightens me."

There was distress in the older woman's eyes. "You were left in my care, and I've failed in my duty."

"It isn't your fault. He . . . that man . . . is—"

"We both know what he is. The question is what to do about him."

"He is a truly evil man. He warned me that you couldn't keep him away from me."

"Unfortunately, I fear he's right. He knows I dare not go to the magistrate and make accusations against him because your reputation would be ruined." Her lips tightened. "It's time your father and mother took on their responsibility. They must, before it's too late."

Mallory's eyes brightened. "Do you think they'll soon be returning to England?"

"Unfortunately not. They will be in Egypt for at least two more years."

Mallory tried to hide her disappointment. "What will become of me?"

Phoebe sat down beside Mallory, deciding it was time to tell her the truth. "I've heard your parents tell you often enough that they wanted a son to inherit the title and lands, and that as a daughter, you were a disappointment to them."

Mallory had learned to live with the pain of knowing her parents didn't want her. "Yes, they have always made that clear."

"I remember your eighth birthday when your mother explained that she gave you the name Mallory because they'd chosen it for their son. I wanted to cry with you when she told you how difficult your birth had been, and how it was your fault that she could never have another child."

"I remember that day, Phoebe. I felt so guilty—I still do. But for me, they could have the son they wanted."

"I believe not having a son was the only time your mother failed at what she had her mind set on, Mallory. But I want you to understand it wasn't your fault."

"I've always felt as if I belonged to no one, and no one belonged to me. Sometimes I have a difficult time remembering my father's face, and my mother is little more than a blur."

"That's understandable since you haven't seen them in ten years."

"They do send presents," Mallory said, as if gifts were some proof of their love. "I suppose they just forgot that children grow up."

"Yes," Phoebe agreed, wishing she could tell Mallory that sending presents was the way her parents eased their guilt for forsaking her. "We must make them realize their mistake. They must see that you are now a young lady and need their guidance."

"But how can we do that? Will you write them?"

"No, I'm going to do something I should have done years ago," Phoebe said with calm determination. "You are going to Egypt to live with them."

Mallory stared at Phoebe. "Do you mean it?"

"I do. This is no life for you. You should be attending parties and meeting young gentlemen of your station."

Mallory shook her head. "Mother and Father won't want me with them."

"They are your parents, and it's time they remembered that."

Excitement stirred within Mallory. "I have always wanted to see Egypt."

"And so you shall. I have a friend who will be joining her husband there, and she leaves in four weeks. I'll send word to her and ask if she'll consent to be your chaperon on the voyage."

"But what about you?"

Phoebe reached up and touched Mallory's cheek in a rare show of affection. "I inherited a small cottage from my father, along with a modest income that will meet my needs. I'll sit in the sun and tend my garden. But I shall miss you, dear child."

Mallory realized in that moment that her cousin did care for her. She took Phoebe's hand in hers and was gratified when her cousin didn't pull away. "I will miss you, Cousin Phoebe. You were always a steadying influence in my life."

"If that's so, then I have not failed."

"When will I leave?"

"As soon as possible."

"Suppose Father and Mother are angry when I arrive and send me back?"

"They may very well try. But when they see how charming you are, they'll be proud to show you off as their daughter. I'll write to them today and tell them to expect you."

"Cousin Phoebe?"

The older woman gave her a smile. "Yes, Mallory."

"I truly will miss you."

Phoebe cupped Mallory's chin in her hand and looked into the young girl's eyes. "I'll think of you every day, and imagine you basking in a warm Egyptian sun."

"I never thought you loved me."

"That's my fault, Mallory. I come from an unloving family and haven't been able to show my feelings as I would have liked. But always know that I have cared for you in my heart, and I'll always want what's best for you."

"You taught me many things, Phoebe. You piqued my interest in reading, and instructed me in the ways to behave as a proper lady."

"I wanted you to have every advantage. If it seemed to you at times that I was demanding, it was only that I wanted you to be armed with knowledge. It's time for you put childish antics aside and present yourself to the world as Lady Mallory Stanhope."

"I promise not to disappoint you, and I'll try to remember everything you taught me, so I'll be a credit to you."

"You have never disappointed me. I see in you the makings of a truly fine lady."

Phoebe stood, and moved to the door. "Now I'll write those letters. Until you leave, I want you to remain close to home."

Mallory nodded. She had no intention of being alone with Sir Gerald again.

She turned to look out the window. Darkness covered the land, and she felt an ache that she would soon be leaving the only home she'd ever known. She had no illusions that her father and mother would welcome her to Egypt, and that was the deepest hurt of all.

Autumn was in the air, and the weather was crisp and clear. Time passed slowly for Mallory. She was bored staying in the house, but she dared not ride Tibor, lest Sir Gerald be waiting for her.

Phoebe had decided to engage a village seamstress to make Mallory lightweight gowns for the hot Egyptian climate. There was satisfaction in her eyes when she talked about sending the bill for the gowns to Mallory's father.

One morning Mallory was called into the salon. When she entered the room, she saw a stranger having tea with Phoebe. Her cousin motioned her to sit beside her.

"Mallory, this is Mrs. Wickett. She and I were girls together. She has agreed to be your companion on the voyage to Egypt."

The rosy-cheeked woman with a rounded body and soft

gray hair beamed at Mallory. "M'lady, I can't imagine why a lovely girl such as yourself would want to leave England for such a barbaric land. But I'll be glad for the companionship all the same. It's such an arduous voyage."

Reality hit Mallory, and it left her breathless. She was actually leaving her home. It was somehow frightening, and yet, exciting at the same time.

"Since my parents moved to Egypt, I have read books on Egyptian history. It is an exciting country, is it not?"

"I would hardly call it that." Gloria Wickett sniffed. "It lacks any modern conveniences, the people are surly to foreigners, and the climate is abominable."

"I'm looking forward to seeing the Nile and the pyramids," Mallory confided.

"Well, m'lady, I do admit the pyramids are a wondrous sight. As for the Nile, it's only a muddy river that often overruns its banks."

Mallory was not listening to Mrs. Wickett. She was thinking of her parents and hoping they would welcome her.

Chapter 5

The village seamstress arrived at Stoneridge House with her sewing basket in hand. She worked frantically, stitching a new wardrobe. Poor Mallory was measured and fitted for hours on end. She paid little attention to the gowns and allowed Phoebe to choose the styles and material from the seamstress's limited supply.

When the task was at last completed, Mallory looked at her new wardrobe with a heavy heart. Not only were the gowns wrong for her coloring, but they were hopelessly out of date. Worst of all, they looked as if they had been sewn by a village seamstress.

But Mallory put her disappointment aside and concentrated on the voyage to Egypt. She was caught up in the magic of the moment, and happiness sang in her heart. At times she almost believed she would be welcomed by her parents.

* * *

Saying good-bye to Cousin Phoebe had been more difficult than Mallory had anticipated. To leave all that was familiar to her was like tearing out part of her heart. She threw her arms around her cousin and fought back the tears. "I shall miss you, Phoebe. I wish you were coming with me."

Phoebe patted her awkwardly. "Nonsense, child. You'll be far too busy to miss me. Go along with you now. And don't look back, Mallory—don't ever look back."

Reluctantly Mallory climbed into the buggy that was to take her to the crossroads where she would take the public coach with Mrs. Wickett. When the buggy started, she glanced back at the house. No, she would not cry. A new life was waiting for her in Egypt, and she must not be sad.

When the coach pulled away from the crossroads, Mallory looked out the window for a last glimpse of Stoneridge. The red bricks were faded to a soft pink, and even from there it looked run-down. The house was shrouded in fog and was soon lost from sight. Mallory had a feeling she'd never see Stoneridge again. She was facing the unknown and realized for the first time that her old life was gone forever.

The docks were bustling with hurried activity as a press of humanity went about appointed tasks with practiced certainty. Work crews for the Peninsula and Oriental Steam Navigation Company hurriedly stowed mailbags and luggage in the hold of the paddle steamer, *Iberia,* which was to put out to sea with the evening tide.

Mallory watched the dockworkers shoulder her trunk and carry it up the gangplank. Her mind was on the voyage, so she didn't see the coach approaching from behind her. The morning shower had left pools of water on the cobblestone street, and when the wheels of the coach sped by, Mallory was sprayed with muddy water.

Angrily she stared after the coachman, who hadn't even bothered to apologize. She was further enraged when the man inside the coach tipped his hat at her, and she stared fleetingly into sardonic green eyes. She bit back her anger, wishing she could give that man a dressing down. She hurried across the street, dodging several other carriages.

Climbing the steps to the Dauphin Inn, where her traveling companion waited for her, she turned back to see the coach moving toward the docks.

Mrs. Wickett was peering out the window and had witnessed the incident and she shook her head sympathetically. "What an unfortunate accident. Your gown is surely ruined."

"The arrogance of that man," Mallory said, her anger still smoldering. "He showed no concern at all that his coach splashed me."

The cheerful matron ushered her into the vestibule where they would wait until word came to board the *Iberia*. Gloria Wickett studied Mallory's dark gray traveling gown. "If you can get to it before it drys, you may be able to remove the stain."

Mallory dabbed at her muddy gown with a handkerchief. "Today is the first time I've worn this gown. It was the only one I liked out of my new wardrobe."

"M'lady, 'tis a pity. The driver of that carriage should be horsewhipped. It just shows that it isn't safe for a woman traveling without the protection of her husband. Now, when I was younger, men had more respect for women, but that's no longer the case."

Mallory stared out the window as the black carriage

pulled up to the dock and stopped in front of the *Iberia*. It never occurred to her that the man she had glimpsed through the coach window might be a passenger on the same ship she was taking.

Mrs. Wickett peered over Mallory's shoulder, staring at the ship with concern. "I do so dislike traveling by sea, but I haven't seen my dear Horace in two years. The only thing that would induce me to make this voyage is to be reunited with him."

Mallory brushed at her gown but saw the stain was hopelessly set. She turned soft blue eyes on the woman. "I'm sure Sergeant Wickett awaits your arrival with great anticipation."

"Indeed he does. I only consented to remain in England until our last two daughters were settled in worthy marriages. That being accomplished, I'm now free to be with my husband."

"I can imagine how difficult it's been for you and Sergeant Wickett to be separated for so long."

"Indeed it has." The little woman glanced at Mallory's gown. "Perhaps you should find some water and dab on the gown, m'lady. Or," she remarked indecisively, "you could wait and let it dry so you can brush at the mud." Her mind moved on to other matters as she fanned herself with a tattered newspaper. "I do declare, the weather is unseasonably warm for this time of year."

"Yes," Mallory said automatically, "and I'm told Egypt will be even warmer."

"It'll be sweltering. You'll have to remember to cream your face every night, Lady Mallory. The hot dust just takes the skin right off you. You dare not go out without benefit of bonnet and parasol."

"Tell me about Egypt," Mallory said. "I've read about it

extensively, but that's not the same as talking to someone who has been there."

Gloria Wickett shuddered. "I'll never understand those people's strange customs. I've seen hostility in their eyes when they look at us English. Horace says it's a sinister land—and make no mistake about it, they resent foreigners, especially the military. You'd think they would be grateful that we're there to help them. They'd never have defeated the Turks without our aid."

"And yet Mehemet Ali is Turkish and he's viceroy of Egypt."

"Well, who can explain those people. One day you're their friend, the next day they'll knife you in the back."

Mallory tried to push her apprehension aside. "I'm sure I will enjoy it once I'm settled with my father and mother."

"I've never had the pleasure of meeting Lord and Lady Stanhope, but I know they are accomplished in their field of antiquities, and I've heard they made many great discoveries for our museums."

Mallory could have told Mrs. Wickett that she knew little about her parents or their activities, but she remained silent.

Gloria Wickett glanced at Mallory with curiosity. Although she had been friends with Phoebe, she knew little about her young cousin. On the coach ride to Southampton, Gloria had been able to assess Lady Mallory's character and found her to be a delightful young lady. And she'd been a most amiable companion.

"Look who that is!" Gloria Wickett exclaimed, glancing out the window at the man who stepped out of the carriage that had splashed Mallory. "It can't be—but yes—it's he! Do you suppose he'll be accompanying us on the voyage?"

The man was apparently someone of great influence because everyone seemed to be scurrying about to do his bidding. Mallory couldn't see him well from this distance, but he was tall and moved with the imperious air of one who felt his importance.

"Who is he?" Mallory asked, trying to get a closer look at the man. She felt only vexation toward him and his driver.

"Why, m'lady, surely you know him—everyone knows the duke of Ravenworth's only son."

Mallory shook her head. "I don't know of him, nor do I care to make his acquaintance."

"He's Lord Michael DeWinter, son of the duke of Ravenworth. Such a fine gentleman. Look how he's allowed to board before anyone else. Horace always says money and power will tell. I'm sure that Lord Michael had no notion his carriage splashed you or he would have apologized."

"Oh, he saw me all right," Mallory said, wishing she could tell that "fine gentleman" what was on her mind.

"M'lady, Lord Michael's something of a legend in London society. It's hard for me to believe you haven't heard of him, you both being titled."

"I'm not a member of London society."

The older woman's eyes glowed. "He's dashing, handsome, and has a different lady on his arm every day, or so they say. He'll one day come into a great fortune. I've heard his mother, the duchess, is an intimate friend of Her Majesty."

"You are acquainted with him?"

"Goodness me, no. I don't associate with the nobility, but I certainly know *of* him. My Horace says that the duke and duchess of Ravenworth are the only aristocrats that he respects. His Grace fought bravely under

Wellington and was awarded the Order of the Garter, along with other honors. Surely with a man like that for a father, Lord Michael is a most worthy gentleman."

Mallory's eyes followed the man who walked leisurely up the gangplank. She noticed how everyone gathered around him as if they hoped to please him. A duke's son. Well, she was not impressed—bad manners were bad manners, no matter what the rank.

"I'll surely be introduced to him," Mrs. Wickett continued. "I can't wait to write Phoebe and tell her we sailed on the same ship with a member of the DeWinter family."

Mallory's lip curled with contempt. She doubted the man would give poor Mrs. Wickett a glance. Certainly he appeared to be more concerned with his own comforts and needs than with being courteous to others.

Mrs. Wickett smiled with delight. "Look, the other passengers are now going aboard. Come, m'lady, you are in for a great adventure after all."

Since the *Iberia* was a mail ship, it offered very little in the way of comfort to its passengers. Mallory's cabin was located under the quarterdeck and was cramped and cheerless. There was a bunk, a washstand, and her trunk, which had been placed at the foot of the bed, leaving scant room for her to move about. Mrs. Wickett's room was next to hers and similarly cramped.

Mrs. Wickett had informed Mallory that the captain's cabin was located in the aft of the ship along with the larger cabins that were reserved for important passengers. Of course, Lord Michael would occupy one of those.

Hoping to accustom herself to the swaying of the ship, Mallory braced her back against the wall while trying to remove the muddy smudges from her gown. She brushed the material with a stiff-bristled brush, then dabbed at it with a damp cloth, but she could not remove the stain.

She sat down on the lumpy bed and stared at her ruined gown, knowing it was destined for the rag heap. She folded it and put it at the bottom of her trunk. Perhaps some of the material could be used to trim another gown.

As night gathered, Mallory lay in her dark cabin feeling alone and friendless. She was going to a mother and father who wouldn't want her. She thought of the doll they had given her for her birthday. When Cousin Phoebe's letter arrived, they would be expecting a child.

Mrs. Wickett appeared at her door dressed for dinner, and looked disapprovingly at Mallory's robe. "My dear, you aren't ready. We've been invited to dine with the captain tonight. This is an honor."

"I'm just too weary, Mrs. Wickett, and want only to go to bed early."

"I'm sure Lord Michael won't be dining there, if that's what's worrying you. He'll probably have dinner in his cabin," Mrs. Wickett said.

"I haven't given that man a thought," Mallory said. "I must meet him soon enough, but I don't feel up to it tonight."

"Very well, m'lady, I'll have the steward bring you something light to eat."

After Mrs. Wickett had departed, Mallory lay back on the bed and stared at the swaying overhead lantern. She tried to visualize what her father and mother looked like, but they were only shadowy memories.

She felt as if her life were spinning out of control and

she was unable to predict what would happen next. Her blue eyes hardened. It was Sir Gerald's fault that she had to leave England. She was determined to make herself as unattractive as possible. She had no desire to encounter another overzealous man like Sir Gerald.

Later, Mrs. Wickett knocked on the cabin door to relay the events that had taken place at dinner. She had endless praise for the captain's table.

"Although this is only a mail ship, and far from the luxury one would expect of a proper passenger ship, I found dinner a delight." She gushed about Lord Michael, who had indeed dined with them tonight. "He actually spoke to me," she said, her eyes shining. "He even asked if I found my quarters comfortable—can you imagine that?"

After Mrs. Wickett departed, Mallory went to the small porthole, staring out at the stars that twinkled in the ebony sky. She was lonely for the only home she'd ever known. And she missed Phoebe.

She searched for the North Star, as she had as a child. When she located it, she smiled and imagined herself back at Stoneridge riding her horse over the green hills.

Chapter 6

aptain Eustace Barim had served in the Royal Navy for thirty years before retiring to a small farm with his wife. After the first year, he had found farming tedious, and his wife too demanding. That was why he became the captain of the mail ship, *Iberia*. He was a tall man with a weather-beaten face, wrinkled from too many hours of sun and salt air. He was always popular with crew and passengers because he had a ready wit and an engaging manner.

After the evening meal, Michael sat with the captain and the only other Englishman aboard, Mr. Alvin Fenton, a banker from London.

The glass of brandy the captain had given Michael went ignored, as did the unlit cigar. His mind was on his father, and he was impatient to reach Egypt so he could begin his search. Sir Robert Peel, the prime minister, had given him letters to present to the viceroy of Egypt, Mehemet Ali, in hopes that he would aid Michael. He reached inside his

breast pocket to make certain the papers were still there—
he never let them out of his sight.

Michael became aware of the heavy silence and
glanced up to find the captain and Alvin Fenton staring
at him. "I beg your pardon, were you speaking to me?"
he asked.

Captain Barim poured brandy into his own glass before
he spoke. "I merely asked about your family yacht, the
Nightingale. I've heard she's a fine ship."

"Yes, she is. The *Nightingale* has been in my family
since I was three years old. My father had her refurbished
last year. I've made many voyages on her. Captain Norris
always said I cut my teeth on the railing. It's certain that
my sister and I carved our initials there."

Captain Barim nodded in approval. "I'm nothing but a
seafaring man, myself, your lordship. Although the *Iberia*
is not a ship of the line, you'll find she's fast."

"I've been impressed thus far," Michael said graciously.
He was having a difficult time making polite conversation
when his mind was on his father.

"Since she's been fitted with engines, we'll be reaching
our destination in ten days," the captain said with pride,
"rather than the two weeks it took previously."

"I'd heard how fast she is, although it's hard to comprehend such speed," Alvin Fenton said. "I would like to
see the engines when it's convenient."

"It would be my pleasure to show you about whenever
you say." The captain looked at Michael. "I'd be happy to
show them to you as well, m'lord."

"Thank you. I'd like that."

Captain Barim looked pleased. "Tomorrow, then."

"How many passengers can you accommodate,
Captain?" Michael inquired, more to keep the conversation light than from curiosity.

"We've carried as many as twelve, but this voyage we have only seven. Besides you and Mr. Fenton here, there's three Arabs and two English ladies. You've met Mrs. Wickett, who is joining her husband's garrison at Cairo. There's also Lady Mallory Stanhope, who I believe is joining her parents."

"Lord Michael, what I can't understand is why you would be going to Egypt alone if you are on a hunting excursion," Mr. Fenton questioned. "Unless you are meeting a larger party?"

Michael had decided it would be prudent to keep his father's disappearance a secret, so he had fabricated a story of game hunting to explain his visit to Egypt. "Yes, I'll be joined by others once I reach my destination."

"But surely India would have been more ideal for hunting than Egypt," the man persisted. There are tigers and other large game animals that you won't find in Egypt. Also, we have garrisons there that would provide you with all you require. In Egypt there is only a small army post."

Michael swirled the amber liquid around in his glass before answering. "Yes, but you see, I'm not interested in hunting in India."

"But why not?" Fenton pressed.

Michael took a sip of brandy, then put the glass on the table and raised cold eyes to the presumptuous man. "What I seek can only be found in Egypt." He stood up to take his leave. "Captain, Mr. Fenton," he said with a nod to each, "if you gentlemen will excuse me, it's been a long day."

Both men watched him move to the door. "Then what do you hunt?" Mr. Fenton asked insistently, willing to cross the bounds of politeness to have his curiosity satisfied.

Michael's green eyes flickered. "I hunt not for pleasure but for exigency," he said.

He walked out of the cabin, leaving his companions staring after him.

"Lord Michael's a secretive one," Captain Barim said, putting his thoughts into words.

"I say he's not going to Egypt on a hunting expedition, as he'd have us believe," Mr. Fenton declared. "A man of his station would never go abroad without a valet to attend him. No, he's up to something mysterious—I wonder what."

The captain rubbed his chin. "Who can say? Whatever his reasons, I wish him well, but I'm afraid Lord Michael will find the Egyptians a suspicious lot with little love or trust for we English."

Fenton nodded in agreement. "I noticed the three Arabs on board are a brooding lot. They are watchful and silent behind those white kaffiyeh. I tried to engage one of them in conversation, but he merely stared at me with those great dark eyes and pretended he didn't understand English."

Captain Barim moved toward the door, hoping to put a stop to Mr. Fenton's speculations. "They don't bother me and I don't bother them. They pay like everybody else and are therefore entitled to the same courtesy." He looked pointedly at his guest. "I'm sure Lord Michael won't appreciate anyone meddling in his affairs."

But the man was not to be deterred. "Don't you find that the aristocrats are a strange lot?"

The captain halted in his tracks. "In what way, Mr. Fenton?"

"Take Lord Michael, for instance. I have the feeling he thinks I'm beneath his notice."

"Well, I'll tell you, Mr. Fenton, if you were surrounded by people whose only task is to see to your comfort, and if your family was one of the oldest and most respected in England, I suspect you'd also appear proud."

"That may be, but his lordship isn't being honest with us. I know enough about human nature to detect when someone is hiding something."

Captain Barim opened the cabin door and waited for his guest to precede him. "If you'll excuse me, I have the early watch."

Mallory woke early and quickly dressed so she could take a turn about the ship before the other passengers rose.

The sun was just rising above a watery horizon when she stepped on deck. The only people about at this hour were two crew members who were swabbing the deck. She stepped around them and moved leisurely along, enjoying the fresh breeze.

She paused at the railing to watch the waves build and splash against the ship. Continuing her walk, she stopped to inspect the lifeboats that were secured with rope and covered with canvas. By now she had come full circle so she could return to her cabin.

Suddenly she gasped and sputtered as someone threw saltwater into her face. She almost lost her footing and had to hold onto the railing to keep her balance. Her eyes were stinging from the salt, and she was temporarily blinded.

The poor sailor hadn't seen Lady Mallory as he dashed water on the deck to wash the suds away. He was just wondering how he'd explain himself when Lord Michael came up behind him and grabbed the bucket from his hand.

"Fool, why don't you watch what you're doing?" Michael admonished the poor man.

Mallory rubbed at her eyes and then turned angrily on

the man who held the bucket. As her vision cleared, she recognized the same mocking green eyes she'd seen once before. "My lord," she said icily, "is it your lot in life to make my life miserable? Do you derive some satisfaction from ruining my gowns?"

He dropped the bucket and it clattered to the deck. "But—"

He had never seen eyes that color of blue, and they were sparkling with anger. Her damp red hair lay plastered to her face. The wet bodice clung to her and made her gown transparent. "I—"

"Save me your apologies. I think you are the most despicable man, with an unconventional sense of humor. Why don't you leave me alone?"

He could only stare at her. He could not defend himself, for if he did, the crewman would probably be reprimanded by the captain. He watched the woman turn on her heels and head angrily down the steps to her cabin.

Michael's jaw set in a grim line. What was the matter with that poor, pathetic girl? Did she really believe he was capable of such an ungentlemanly deed? He exchanged a glance with the crewman who was the real culprit.

"I'll tell the lady that it was my doing, m'lord."

"Don't bother. I have a feeling she wouldn't believe you."

When Mallory reached her cabin, she stripped off her wet gown and hung it over her trunk. She grabbed up a towel and began drying her dripping hair. Had that man no sense of honor? she wondered. She should report his conduct, but she doubted the captain would do anything to a man with Lord Michael's influence. She detested Lord Michael—in her mind he was no better than Sir Gerald. Why did he take such delight in humiliating her?

*   *   *

Mrs. Wickett was complaining of a headache, so Mallory convinced her to take a turn about the deck, certain that the fresh air would be good for her.

When they stepped onto the deck, Mallory drew in a deep breath, allowing the salt air to fill her lungs. Mrs. Wickett dabbed at her face with a damp handkerchief, but her color was better.

The sea was at a flat calm, and the sun was obstructed by heavy clouds. It looked as if it would rain before the day was over.

Mallory tucked an errant red curl beneath her bonnet and stopped at the railing to watch a school of playful dolphins weaving in and out of the water.

A dagger of sunlight pierced the clouds and fell upon the sea, painting it crimson and reminding her of silk rippling in the wind. She gasped at the lovely spectacle.

"It's breathtaking, isn't it?" a masculine voice spoke behind her. "The sea is like a woman and never wears the same face twice. It's always intriguing and mysterious."

Mallory knew before she turned to face the man that it would be Lord Michael. She raised her chin haughtily. "I beg your pardon, sir, were you speaking to me?"

Michael stared into frosty blue eyes. He was unaccustomed to having a woman annoyed with him. He had not really intended to engage her in conversation, but it somehow seemed impolite to pass her by without speaking. "Forgive me if I appear bold, but on shipboard, especially one this small, it's foolish to stand on formality. I am Michael DeWinter." He bowed slightly. "I believe you have a misconception about me."

"My encounters with you always seem to end in disaster for me," Mallory answered. "I do not wish to make your acquaintance."

"I know I appeared guilty this morning. I can only ask you to forgive me."

Mrs. Wickett beamed. "It's always good to see you, m'lord. I told Lady Mallory I couldn't believe you would dash her with water."

He bowed slightly to the little woman, making her smile even brighter. "I'm encouraged by your belief in me."

Even dressed informally in tan-colored trousers and a white ruffled shirt, Mallory thought he was the essence of how the son of a duke should look. He was tall and trim; his features were classic and aristocratic. He was undeniably handsome.

"I know what you did." Mallory said, turning away and glancing back to sea.

"If you would allow me to—" He paused, knowing he could not explain without involving the poor seaman.

She tossed her head and glared at him. "See, you can't explain, can you? You know I saw you with the bucket in your hand."

She was dressed in a simple burgundy gown and a black bonnet trimmed with dried blue flowers. She was pretty, he thought, but he knew many pretty girls—this one did not appeal to him. Michael could see wisps of red hair poking from beneath the brim of her bonnet—he'd never been partial to red hair.

"I find myself unable to explain what happened, my lady. If only you would—"

"I don't wish to hear anything you have to say, my lord."

He looked past her in exasperation, thinking she didn't deserve his consideration. Never had he met a more disagreeable young woman. "Then please forgive the intrusion, Lady Mallory. I'll wish you a good day."

She turned her back on him and stared out to sea. He had attempted to apologize for his actions and she suddenly felt guilty for behaving so discourteously. What did it matter? They would never meet again after this voyage, and she intended to avoid him whenever possible.

"M'lady," Mrs. Wickett said in shock. "How could you speak so to his lordship? He was attempting to apologize."

Mallory drew in a deep breath of salt air. "I don't care to hear anything he has to say." But she did turn to watch him walk away. His back was straight, his head held at a proud tilt. She wondered if he ever smiled. Surely if he did, he would steal a girl's heart.

She turned back and stared silently out to sea. After a while, she had the feeling someone was staring at her. Glancing up, she met the dark eyes of a man wearing a white robe and a matching burnoose.

The man bowed to her slightly, his eyes never leaving her face. He was obviously a passenger, perhaps an Egyptian returning to his homeland. But why was he watching her so intently?

She turned back to the railing, but she could still feel his eyes on her, and it made her so nervous that she dropped her sunshade.

When it clattered to the deck, the stranger rushed forward to retrieve it for her. "With your fair skin, you will need this, Lady Mallory," he said in cultured English.

On closer inspection, she saw that he was younger than she'd thought. The man bowed, and then moved away before she could find her voice.

"Well, did you ever!" Mrs. Wickett exclaimed indignantly. "How dare that man speak to you. He was much too familiar. He spoke your name."

Mallory could find nothing disrespectful in the man's manner. "I suppose everyone is aware of our names."

"Well, we shan't welcome the company of the likes of him. I do believe he admires you. We just can't have that. I'll speak to the captain about his actions."

Mallory touched the older woman's arm. "It is a matter of little importance. Besides, his manners were above reproach. You will not speak to the captain about him. It would only cause him trouble."

Mrs. Wickett wanted to insist, but the determined look in Lady Mallory's eyes made her reluctantly agree. "I'll let it go this time. But if he speaks to you again, I shall certainly inform the captain."

Mallory leaned over the railing, watching the foamy spray fan out from the ship. She had already forgotten the incident.

Chapter 7

he night was balmy, and the stars were reflected in the gentle waves, giving the illusion that sea and sky were one. Michael stood on deck, hesitating to enter his cabin. With a troubled mind, he watched silvery foam ride on the waves.

His insides were tied in knots, and he gripped the railing until his knuckles whitened as questions pounded in his mind. What had happened to his father? Would he be able to locate him? What if his father was dead—how would he accept that? How would he tell his mother?

Michael's attention was diverted by the sound of scuffling. He glanced across the deck, trying to see past the shadows cast by the rippling canvases. He heard a muffled cry and moved quickly to the foredeck to investigate.

He saw three men locked in combat. It didn't take him long to assess the situation. It was the Egyptians, and it appeared that two of them had banded together to overcome the third. One of the men held their victim in a tight grip, while the other raised his arm, and in a flash, Michael saw light reflect off the blade of a knife.

Without stopping to think, Michael rushed forward to grab the attacker's arm, holding it in a firm grip. Moments passed as a life-and-death struggle ensued between the two of them—the assailant had turned his rage on Michael. The blade of the knife came dangerously close to Michael's throat, but he gained the advantage and thrust the Egyptian from him.

Suddenly both assailants turned on Michael. He managed to slip out of one man's grip, but the man with the knife lunged forward, burying the blade in the fleshy part of Michael's arm.

With renewed determination, Michael gripped the man's arm and slammed him into the bulwark. The man groaned in pain and crumpled to the deck.

Michael then turned to engage the other assailant, only to see the man move out of his reach. The second attacker jumped to his feet, and they both darted into the shadows.

Michael quickly dropped down to examine the injured man, who was having trouble catching his breath. "Are you hurt?" he asked.

The man answered him in a gasping voice. "They . . . tried to choke me . . . I am but winded. I would now be dead if it were not for you. I owe you my life."

"Nonsense," Michael replied, reaching out his hand to assist the man to his feet. By now blood had soaked through Michael's shirt and he could feel the pain of his wound.

"You are injured," the Egyptian said with concern. "I will help you."

"It's but a scratch and can wait until we report this incident to the captain."

At that moment, a noise drew their attention. Michael looked toward the sound of hurrying footsteps and watched in disbelief as one of the attackers slipped over the railing and dropped into the sea! Horror registered in his mind as the second man also leaped into the dark waters.

"My God, they must be demented," Michael cried out as he ran to the rail of the ship. He could see nothing but inky blackness.

He turned to the other man, who had come up beside him. "It's too late to save them from drowning," Michael said grimly, "but we must inform the captain at once."

The Egyptian put his hand on Michael's arm. "I would ask that you not say anything about this. As you said, those men are now beyond help. I know that they were sent to slay me or die in the attempt. Since they failed, they had no recourse but to end their lives."

"What kind of men are they that they would deliberately drown themselves?"

The man merely shrugged. "For them, it was better to die than live with the disgrace they would have faced if they had returned and I still lived."

Michael was feeling lightheaded from his wound and staggered to rise. "Perhaps the wound is more serious than I thought."

"I will get the ship's doctor for you."

Michael waved him aside. "No, I'd sooner be in the hands of a butcher. I'll not have that man tend me. I've heard too many horror stories about seafaring doctors."

The Egyptian nodded in understanding. "Then perhaps you will allow me to assist you. I am quite capable of treating your wound."

Michael agreed. Already he had lost a lot of blood, and a feeling of weakness made him stumble. With the assistance of the Egyptian, they made it to his cabin before Michael collapsed on the bed.

The stranger removed Michael's coat and ripped the shirt sleeve. He was silent while he examined the wound. "It is deep, and it is a miracle his aim was not accurate. Allow me to go to my cabin and get my medical kit. I'll only be gone a short time."

Michael closed his eyes, trying not to think about the pain. He reached for one of his shirts and tied the sleeve around his arm in an attempt to stop the flow of blood.

Soon the Egyptian reappeared. With the expertise of a man who had treated injuries before, he cleansed the wound and applied some strange-smelling herbs. Deftly, he bandaged Michael's arm in clean white linen, then stood back, observing his handiwork with satisfaction.

"It was a clean wound and should heal nicely, Lord Michael."

Michael took a good look at the man. His white robe was disheveled and soiled from his encounter with the assassins. He'd lost his burnoose in the struggle. His complexion was swarthy, but he had finely chiseled features.

"You have the advantage over me. You know me, but I don't know your name."

The Egyptian bowed, touching his forehead and mouth, his dark eyes suddenly cautious. "My name is Khaldun Shemsa, and I owe you my life. The knife that you took was meant for me. I will always be indebted to you, Lord Michael, and I shall never forget your bravery."

"You have determined enemies, Khaldun Shemsa. Are you certain you don't want to report this to Captain Barim? He will soon begin to question the men's absence, and I'm sure he'll come to you, since they are obviously from your country."

"Obvious to the English, perhaps, but the men who attacked me were Turks, not Egyptians. I beg you to say nothing of the incident. It is imperative that I reach my home with all possible haste, and if this matter is brought to the attention of the authorities, I will be detained for an indefinite time." He looked into Michael's eyes. "There is much turmoil in my tribe. Even now, I am uncertain whether our enemies have taken control and slain our leader. Otherwise, why would the assassins so boldly attack me on an English ship? I fear those I love may be in great danger."

Michael somehow believed the Egyptian. "I understand your concerns better than you think."

"Then you will say nothing?"

"I will say nothing," Michael agreed, "because I, too, have no wish to be detained by questions."

Relief plainly showed on the Egyptian's face. "You are most unusual for an Englishman. I never expected one of your race to put his life in danger for me."

Michael smiled faintly. He couldn't help but like the man. "You are most unusual for an Egyptian, Khaldun Shemsa. Where did you learn to speak English so well?" Michael asked, eyeing the man speculatively.

"I attended your Oxford University for two years and am on my way home. My two escorts were found dead before I left London. I knew then that someone was stalking me, but I could prove nothing. Your captain would send me back to England if he knew about the murders of my servants. I tell you this because I trust you, Lord Michael, even though I cannot say why."

Michael flexed his sore arm and winced in pain. "I will keep your secret, and share mine with you, because I feel I can also trust you. My father went to Egypt at the request of your viceroy. He is missing, and we don't know if he's alive. If there is any advice you can give me that might help me locate my father, I would be most grateful."

Khaldun was silent for a moment as he considered Lord Michael's words. "I will do all I can to help you find your father. Until I contact you, perhaps it would be best if we pretended we didn't know one another. I would not like my enemies to become yours. There could be other Turks hiding on this ship, posing as members of the crew."

Michael flinched when the Egyptian propped his wounded arm on a pillow. "I know little of your country and would welcome anything you can tell me."

"I will do what I can, for we are as brothers since your blood was spilled in place of mine."

"You will excuse me if I rest now. I find I'm very fatigued."

"Tomorrow you should re-dress the wound. I shall leave the herbs and bandages with you. I will not come to you again, lest I put you in danger." Khaldun handed Michael a bottle of green liquid. "If it pains you during the night, take some of this."

Michael could only nod. "I would advise you to look to your own health, Khaldun. As you said, there may be others on board who wish you dead. It would be wise for you to sleep lightly."

"I will be more careful." Khaldun lowered his eyes. "I cannot say why anyone would want to harm me since I am only the son of a humble tailor."

Michael stared at the Egyptian, knowing he was not being truthful now. His speech and manner of dress were not in keeping with a son of a tailor. And a man of humble background did not go all the way to England to attend Oxford.

Khaldun touched his forehead and bowed. "Sleep well,

my new friend. *Allah ye'tik,* may God go with you in your search for your father."

"May God help us both," Michael said with growing weariness.

After Khaldun departed, Michael closed his eyes. He had been foolhardy tonight. If he had been killed, who would have continued the search for his father?

Outside Michael's cabin, hostile eyes peered out of the shadows, watching his door. After hearing someone approaching, the man left hastily to be swallowed up by the night.

Since the night Michael had saved Khaldun's life, the Egyptian avoided him when they would chance to meet. One morning, Michael awoke to find that a note had been shoved under his door. It was from Khaldun.

Lord Michael,
I have reason to believe I am being watched, although I cannot say why. I know that my cabin has been searched. So for your safety, I will continue to pretend we do not know each other. Do not think I have forgotten that you saved my life. We shall surely meet again, and I will come to you if you ever need me.

The note was unsigned. Michael still wondered why anyone would go to so much trouble to kill Khaldun. His instinct told him there was more to the Egyptian than he would have people believe. But then Michael also had his secrets, and like Khaldun, he might have his enemies.

At that moment, there was a knock on the door and

Michael opened it to find the first mate standing there with his hat tucked under his arm. "Begging your pardon, m'lord. The captain wondered if you would do him the honor of dining with him tonight. All the passengers are to be included in the invitation."

Michael had been having his meals brought to his cabin because he didn't want anyone to notice that he'd been injured. Now he could at least move the arm without too much pain. "Inform the captain I shall be glad to dine with him."

Thus far, there had been no inquiry about the two men who had jumped overboard. Michael was sure that the captain was beginning to wonder what had happened to them. He suspected that everyone at dinner tonight would be questioned about the missing Egyptians.

He would keep Khaldun's secret because he didn't want to be entangled in a web of intrigue.

Mallory parted her hair down the middle and arranged it in the French finger curls that were so in vogue. She slipped into a powder blue satin gown with bows on the sleeves and all about the hem. When the seamstress had made this gown, Mallory hadn't liked it, and she still didn't. Poor Cousin Phoebe could not have known it was shamelessly out of style.

Mallory lifted her hand mirror and stared at her image. Oh, well, there was nothing she could do about her appearance. She might be considered a beauty in the country, among the locals, but to a man like Lord Michael, who was accustomed to polished beauties, she would seem plain.

On a whim, Mallory quickly removed all the ribbons that adorned the gown and added a small cluster of silk lilacs to her hair. The gown might appear simple, but at least it wasn't garish.

With a resigned sigh, she worked her hands into her wrist-length white gloves, hoping no one would notice they had been mended at the fingertips.

Chapter 8

he sea was rolling gently as Mallory and Mrs. Wickett were greeted by Captain Barim. He looked very distinguished in his blue uniform with gold trim and epaulets.

"Good evening, Lady Mallory. Nice to see you, Mrs. Wickett. So glad the two of you could join us this evening." He ushered them into the cabin where the table had been laid with a white tablecloth and sparkling silver and china.

He presented them to his officers and then turned toward the banker. "Lady Mallory, may I present you to Mr. Fenton?"

Mallory acknowledged the introduction with a smile. Next, the captain turned to the Egyptian. "Lady Mallory, this is Mr. Shemsa. He's returning to his homeland after going to school in England."

Mallory recognized him as the man who had retrieved her sunshade. "How do you do, Mr. Shemsa?"

He was dressed in a flowing white robe and matching head covering that was tied with a black cord. His skin was dark and his eyes even darker. He bowed respectfully to her, but not before she saw his eyes widen with unmasked admiration.

She moved away from him, knowing the moment she'd been dreading had arrived. Mallory could hear Mrs. Wickett talking to Lord Michael. Then it was her turn, and she stood before him, her eyes raised to his face. How handsome he was, dressed formally in black. There was mockery in his eyes as Captain Barim presented her.

"Now, Lady Mallory," Michael said, "we have been properly introduced." He extended his arm to her. "I believe you are seated next to me."

Unwilling to create a scene, she reluctantly placed her hand on his arm. Apparently he was enjoying her discomfort. Did he think she would so easily forgive him for his pranks?

He held the chair for her, and she sat down, folding her hands demurely in her lap. Mrs. Wickett had been placed on Captain Barim's right, and the Egyptian, Khaldun Shemsa, was across the table from Mallory.

When they were all seated, Captain Barim turned to Mallory. "M'lady, it falls to me to apologize to you about an incident that happened several days ago, but has only come to my attention today."

She looked at him, puzzled. "I can't think what you would have to apologize to me for, Captain."

"It's about the drenching you suffered."

Her eyes went to Michael. "I don't hold you responsible for the bad manners of your passengers."

The captain looked mystified. "Passenger? No, m'lady. A member of my ship's crew came forward this morning and admitted what he had done. I have reprimanded him severely, and he will be punished."

Mallory's mouth flew open and she looked at Lord Michael, too humiliated to meet his eyes. "Please, Captain, I would consider it a favor if you wouldn't punish the poor man on my behalf."

"As you wish, m'lady. You have a kind and understanding heart."

Mallory straightened her spine when she heard Lord Michael choke back laughter.

The first course had been served before she finally turned to him. "I ask your pardon, m'lord. I did you a great wrong."

His lips twitched in an almost smile. "It was a natural mistake. I admit I did look guilty holding the bucket. I can't imagine why you would think I'd throw water on such a charming young lady, though." He laughed. "A young lady with such a charitable disposition—and how did the captain phrase it—with a kind and understanding heart?"

Mallory chose to ignore his attempt at humor. "Nonetheless, I beg your pardon."

"I accept."

Mallory was glad when Captain Barim called for everyone's attention. "I regret that I must ask questions of all of you while we are eating. But it seems I have a bit of a mystery on my hands, and I'm hoping one of you might have seen or heard something that will help me in my dilemma."

"What is it?" Mrs. Wickett asked, her eyes round and expectant.

The captain cleared his throat. "Well, it seems we have lost two passengers."

"Surely you jest," Mrs. Wickett declared. "How does one go about losing passengers at sea?"

"In that is the mystery, madam. Two Arab gentleman, Mr. Senosiris and Mr. Burlos, have simply disappeared. They haven't slept in their cabins in days, and no one has seen them. I have had the ship searched from stem to stern, and they are not aboard."

Michael and Khaldun merely exchanged glances.

"Surely there is only one alternative," Mallory commented with horror.

"I agree, m'lady," the captain said. "They must have gone overboard. But there is a puzzle as well. The weather has been calm, so they could not have been washed overboard. Say one of them fell, I could accept that, but both—I hardly think so."

"I feel certain I have solved your dilemma, Captain," Mrs. Wickett said with confidence. "One of the gentlemen fell overboard; the other jumped in to save him, and they both drowned."

"I have considered that." The captain looked at each of his guests in turn. "Did any of you see or hear anything that would help?"

There was no answer, so the captain looked regretful. "In all my crossings, I've never lost a passenger. I'll have to answer to the port authorities for this. I'm afraid this will delay my return trip for weeks."

Again Michael and Khaldun exchanged glances. If they had admitted their knowledge of the incident, they would also be delayed.

Mallory was so distressed about the poor men who had apparently drowned that she hardly tasted the filet of salmon that was served with a rich cream sauce.

She was very aware of Lord Michael, because his presence was overpowering. Everyone at the table seemed to defer to him, and most of the conversation was directed at him.

"Lady Mallory," Captain Barim said, at last turning to her. "Mrs. Wickett has informed me that you will be joining your parents in Cairo."

"Yes, I am, Captain."

"I'm slightly acquainted with your father. You must be very proud of the work he's done."

Mallory could hardly admit she knew little of her father's work. "Yes, I am, Captain."

Michael looked at her with new understanding. "Your father is Lord Stanhope? I've heard of him. He acquires artifacts for the museums, does he not?"

She glanced down at Lord Michael's tanned, well-shaped hand resting on the white tablecloth, and her breathing seemed to close off. Raising her eyes, she met his green glance and found humor dancing there. "Yes, my lord, he does."

"I met your mother and him last summer at a garden party in London. Were you also present?"

"No, my lord." Mallory hadn't known her parents had been in England the previous summer. The pain of that knowledge tore at her heart. Why hadn't they come to see her if they had been in London?

"My parents travel a great deal," she said at last. "I don't often get to see them."

Michael could sense her discomfort. "We shall be seeing more of each other, Lady Mallory, because I will also be traveling to Cairo."

She had just taken a bite of salmon and had to swallow before she could answer. "I understand that Cairo is a crowded city, my lord. I doubt our paths will cross."

He raised an inquiring brow, wondering why she was still so hostile toward him. "Nonetheless, we shall probably meet again, Lady Mallory."

She glanced at the Egyptian across from her and found

he was staring at her. "I look forward to living in your country and learning many of your customs, Mr. Shemsa."

"You will like my country, my lady, and I know my country will like you."

She warmed to his cordiality. There were so many questions she had about Egypt. "I'm fascinated, not only by your past, but your present as well."

Khaldun's dark eyes swept her face. "I would be most honored to help you understand the history of my people. Do you perhaps speak my language?"

Captain Barim intervened, drawing the Egyptian's attention. His young passenger evidently didn't know that a female shouldn't converse familiarly with an Egyptian. Their culture was such that the man would mistake politeness for encouragement. "Since there are so many different sects and languages in your country, that would be an extraordinary undertaking. Even the most proficient linguist and scholar would have trouble with them all, Mr. Shemsa."

"That is so, Captain. There is a great diversity among my people."

Mallory, unaware that she was doing anything wrong, asked, "Is it true, Mr. Shemsa, that your country has considered building a channel that will link the Mediterranean and the Red Sea?"

Khaldun looked pleased. "You are very knowledgeable, Lady Mallory. It is indeed a project that has been debated over the centuries. But I fear it would be a very costly endeavor, and many doubt that it will ever come to pass."

Mallory placed her fork beside her plate and gave her full attention to Khaldun. "I read that when Napoleon invaded your country, his engineers came to the conclusion that the Red Sea was higher than the Mediterranean, thus making the task impossible."

"That was their conclusion, Lady Mallory. Engineers have debated that issue for many generations. It is my hope that the canal will one day be built, to the advantage, not only of Egypt, but of the rest of the world as well."

Michael saw the admiration in Khaldun's eyes as he looked at Lady Mallory. Was she mad? Didn't she know that by talking to Khaldun, she was sending him the message that she was interested in him as a man? She was too young and inexperienced to realize the danger of her actions. He decided to stop her before she went too far.

Michael spoke in a soft voice so only Mallory could hear. "Lady Mallory, it's inconceivable to me that you know so much about Egyptian affairs and so little of their customs. You should not invite Mr. Shemsa's attentions."

Mallory stiffened with indignation. Stormy blue eyes met piercing green eyes. She answered quietly, so no one would overhear. "What I do or don't do is no concern of yours, Lord Michael. And I certainly have not solicited your advice."

"You're right, of course, my lady. My intention was merely to keep you from making a mistake." His eyes hardened. "If you are wise, you will heed my warning."

Mallory came to her feet, unable to endure his interference a moment longer. All the gentlemen rose, while Mrs. Wickett looked on puzzled.

Mallory addressed her comments to Captain Barim. "Thank you for a lovely evening. If you will excuse me, I have a dreadful headache and wish to go to my cabin."

Mrs. Wickett was reluctant to leave such admirable company, but she had a responsibility to Lady Mallory. "Shall I come with you?"

"No. You haven't yet had dessert. I'm just going to my

cabin to lie down." Mallory smiled at the other guests, all but Lord Michael, and left the cabin.

She stood at the railing, drawing in gulps of air until her temper cooled. After long reflection, she admitted that it might not have been prudent for her, an unmarried female, to have engaged Mr. Shemsa in conversation. Lord Michael seemed to have enjoyed pointing out her mistake. That man was insufferable!

Her thoughts turned to the disappearance of the two Arab men. Could they have drowned? She shivered as she looked into the inky black sea. What a horrible way to die.

"You are feeling better, Lady Mallory?" Khaldun asked, coming up beside her.

There was no moon, but a lantern swung in the breeze, so she could clearly see the concern in his dark eyes. "Much better." She couldn't tell him her headache had been a fabrication so she could leave an intolerable situation. "The fresh air has helped ease the pain."

The Egyptian stood silently beside her, and feeling uneasy, she was about to wish him good-night, when he spoke: "I was in your country for two years, attending your Oxford University."

"My father also attended Oxford in his youth."

"It was not my wish to leave Egypt, but my father insisted that I have an English education. Two years is a very long time to be away from one's home."

She could sense a sadness in him and decided to disregard Lord Michael's warning. "Surely you made friends who helped you be less lonely?"

"There were several students from my country. But I made little contact with the English students." He smiled slightly. "I'm sure we were an oddity to them since our ways are so different."

"I will know how you felt when I reach Egypt, for I shall be the stranger there."

He smiled. "My country will willingly welcome such a beautiful lady."

She tensed at his unwelcome compliment. But he was unaware of her discomfort. "You are the first English woman I have spoken to other than the maid who made up our rooms each day." His dark eyes sparkled with humor. "She had a grandson my age."

"And now you are returning home."

"Yes. Home to an uncertain future."

"I must go in now," Mallory said nervously.

"Please allow me a moment to speak to you." Khaldun reached out his hand to her and let it drop. "I just wanted to tell you that you have a rare gift for making a man feel important."

She withdrew several steps.

"I don't mean to frighten you. I should not have spoken, but this might be my last chance to tell you how I feel. I have watched you, and I knew there was a sadness about you. I wanted to see if I could help."

"We are strangers, and you mustn't say this to me, Mr. Shemsa."

He seemed not to hear her. "I have never seen a woman with hair like fire. To be near you would be like living with sunshine."

She now realized Lord Michael had been correct with his warning. "Please excuse me."

He bravely clasped her hand. "Don't go."

"The lady has asked to leave, Khaldun. Release her hand."

Mallory turned to an angry Lord Michael. "I was only . . . he didn't—"

Michael reached for her hand and turned her toward

her cabin. "Leave now, Lady Mallory. And I hope you have learned a lesson tonight."

She scurried down the companionway, her heart beating in her throat. She was so ashamed, and so sorry for her actions. Poor Mr. Shemsa was not to blame—the fault lay with her. He must have thought she had been encouraging his attentions. Oh, how would she ever face either man again?

Michael stood beside Khaldun, sensing his confusion. "Lady Mallory is an innocent, Khaldun. She's young, she doesn't understand your customs."

The Egyptian shook his head regretfully. "I realize that now. But she is so beautiful, and she was so sad. Is it wrong for one human being to reach out to another?"

Michael realized that Khaldun was as innocent in his way as Lady Mallory was in hers. "Have you a woman waiting for your return?"

"Yes, but she is not of my choosing. I have never met her. She was destined for me from the time she was born. It is the way of my people."

"My country was once the same as yours. Now marriages of convenience are rare, although they still occur occasionally."

"I have heard that my intended bride is fair to look upon, but this is always said by parents, to keep the bridegroom from objecting if she is ugly. I feel horror thinking about her. She is of the Sawarka tribe, and their women often tattoo their faces. Can you imagine living with a woman who disfigures her face?"

Michael was glad to move the conversation away from Lady Mallory, but he felt a little horrified himself. "No, I can't imagine that. I've thought little about marriage. I suppose someday I'll have to take a wife."

"You will choose your own wife." Khaldun's shoulders

slumped. "For a brief moment I envisioned myself with Lady Mallory as my second wife. Yasmin will, of course, have to be my number-one wife."

"An Englishwoman would hardly agree to such an arrangement. You have lived in London where a man can have only one wife."

"I know that I made a mistake with Lady Mallory. Would you be so kind as to convey my apologies to her?"

"I'm sure there will be no need of that."

"But I ask it of you all the same. I want her to know I meant to honor her and not to be disrespectful."

"I'll tell her."

"Do you not think she's a beauty?" Khaldun said regretfully.

"I hardly noticed. She is too young for me. Another thing I have never admired is red hair."

Khaldun smiled at his friend. "She is a rare and delicate flower. But she is so much more than she seems. Inside she has the burnings of a woman, but she does not yet know it."

"Are any of us all we seem?" Michael commented with a searching glance.

"We all have our secrets, Lord Michael. But should you have trouble when you reach Cairo, I shall know it at once and come to your aid."

Michael stared out at the darkness, unable to see the sea or the sky. He thought it highly unlikely this Egyptian could help him in what he must do.

allory received a letter from Lord Michael, which she tore into tiny pieces. Was there no end to that man's arrogance? How dare he take it upon himself to apologize for Mr. Shemsa. He never missed a chance to goad her—this was only his way of pointing out that he'd been right and she'd been wrong.

"Insufferable," she said, slamming the lid on her trunk. Well, at least they would be leaving the ship today.

Later, Mallory stood on deck beside Mrs. Wickett as they both watched the *Iberia* cut her engines and rely on her sails to take her into the deep waters of Aboukir Bay.

"A colorless country," Mrs. Wickett remarked, waving her hand toward the small fishing village that existed in the shadows of the city of Alexandria.

"Everything is brown, brown, brown. There is no color, no personality."

Mallory didn't agree. She stared in wonder at the tall mosques and domed buildings. She was only sorry there would not be time to explore the ancient capital of Egypt before boarding the boat that would take her down the Nile to Cairo.

"You have to admit the Mediterranean is very blue," she said breathlessly. "It makes one long for a swim."

Mrs. Wickett looked at her as if she'd lost her faculties. "Certainly not! It would be unthinkable for a properly brought up English girl even to contemplate such an action. Swim in the Mediterranean, indeed not."

Mallory was saved from answering when two crew members began tying off the sails and Captain Barim brought the *Iberia* into port. The sound made by the lowering of the anchor was a welcome one to Mallory. She would be glad to place her feet on solid ground.

Mallory felt a burst of excitement that was tempered with fear of the unknown when the gangplank was lowered into place and the crew bustled about performing last-minute duties. Cargo was brought up from the hold and wheeled toward waiting wagons that would take them to their final destination.

"There—there's my husband," Mrs. Wickett beamed. "Lud, he's grown a beard." She waved frantically. "He looks distinguished, does he not?"

"Indeed he does," Mallory agreed, looking at Sergeant Wickett as he must seem to his wife, and not as the heavyset man he looked in his red uniform.

"Come, m'lady, he'll be impatient to be on his way. We must not dally."

As Mallory stepped forward, she came in contact with a lean, hard body, and Lord Michael steadied her.

"I beg your pardon, Lady Mallory."

She looked into those cool eyes and knew his mind was not really on her, but on whatever it was that had brought him to Egypt. There was something mysterious about this man, something that thrilled and intrigued her. As she stepped away from him, she realized she would never know what mystery he hid behind those expressive eyes. Even though he predicted they would probably meet in Cairo, she doubted she would ever see him again. But it would be a long time before she would forget him.

"I hope your stay in Egypt is all you hope it to be, m'lord," Mrs. Wickett said, as she took Mallory's arm and steered her down the gangplank. To Mallory, she whispered, "If you weren't so young, my dear, he would be such a match for you." She babbled on good-naturedly, for there was no harm in the little lady. "You are very presentable, and I daresay that, had the two of you met in London, you would have had a better chance to become acquainted."

Mallory's first footstep onto land was jarring. After being on shipboard so long, her legs didn't seem to want to obey her. Mrs. Wickett, seeing her dilemma, smiled understandingly. "The feeling will soon pass when you get your land legs. It's always a shock when experiencing it for the first time."

When they reached Sergeant Wickett, husband and wife hugged perfunctorily, and Mallory would have thought them indifferent to one another if it weren't for the softness in their eyes when they embraced.

Afterward, Mallory was presented to Sergeant Wickett, and she found him as amiable as his wife. Deciding to give the two of them a moment alone, Mallory walked a few steps away and stared at the flurry taking place on the waterfront.

Her eyes narrowed against the bright sunlight reflecting off the blue Mediterranean. In the distance, she could hear the sound of the Moslems being called to morning prayer. Suddenly, she caught movement to her left, and turned to see Khaldun Shemsa dart behind a cart. His actions were mysterious, almost covert. When she moved toward the cart, he had disappeared. Was everyone in Egypt so perplex?

Mallory forgot about the Arab's strange behavior and stared at the sights around her. She could see a busy thoroughfare in the distance, filled with throngs of people. There were camels, sheep, and two-wheeled carts that were pulled by donkeys. This was a world like nothing she could have imagined. She watched women, shapeless in their black garments, their faces covered but for their eyes. What kind of people were these who hid their faces and lived their lives in secret except when they were in their own homes? It would be interesting to learn more about them.

Mallory was soon seated in a cart beside Mrs. Wickett, while Sergeant Wickett instructed the porters to place their trunks in the back. At last they were on their way down the clay-packed streets, the driver of the carriage weaving in and out of the heavy traffic.

Mallory's first view of the Nile River came unexpectedly. The carriage turned a corner, and there the muddy, winding river was spread out before them, shimmering in the sun.

She was helped from the carriage by Sergeant Wickett, and they were soon aboard the small barge that would transport them to Cairo. The barge was crowded with a press of humanity, and there were even goats and sheep in a cordoned-off area. The smell was offensive, and she turned her face into the wind—she would not get sick—she would not.

As they got under way, Mallory could feel the heat like a heavy hand pressing in on her, which, combined with the unpleasant smell of the animals, made her stomach heave. With a trembling hand, she untied the ribbon of her bonnet and leaned her head over the side of the boat.

"This is the most difficult part," Sergeant Wickett assured her, detecting her condition. "Alas, I fear you will find this leg of the journey most uncomfortable. We will be forced to sleep on deck. But I will try and make you as comfortable as possible. I have brought supplies and bedrolls."

She smiled at him. "I feel better now. It's just the heat."

"Egypt hasn't a fit climate for a gentle-bred English-woman." Mrs. Wickett snorted. "Didn't I tell you so, m'lady?"

By midafternoon they had left the coastal fishing village behind and started the journey that would snake its way through a fertile farmland and into the very interior of Egypt. The meeting with her parents lay ahead, and Mallory could only guess at her reception.

She imagined her mother counting the hours until she arrived. She had half hoped that her parents would greet her when she stepped off the *Iberia*. Of course, they would be too busy to come all the way to˜Aboukir. But that didn't mean they wouldn't be glad to see her.

Michael glanced across the deck of the barge and nodded at Mrs. Wickett. He watched a gust of wind rip the straw bonnet from Lady Mallory's head and miraculously drop it at his feet. He retrieved the bonnet and walked toward her, extending it to her on his fingers.

"You had better tie the ribbon beneath your chin, or next time, it may be blown overboard."

"Thank you," she said, feeling embarrassed for fear he would think she had deliberately lost her bonnet to gain his notice. "I'll tie it now, and it won't happen again."

For the moment, he was fascinated by the sun reflecting on her dark auburn hair that had come tumbling down her back almost to her waist. Why had he not noticed before how lovely she was? The small sprinkle of freckles across her nose somehow bespoke a spirited young girl with little care for her outward appearance. How different she was from Lady Samantha, who was always so meticulously groomed.

He turned his attention to the distant horizon, and his mind raced ahead to his meeting with the British consul in Cairo. Perhaps they'd had word of his father by now, perhaps they had even located him.

"Lord Michael, I'd be pleased to present my husband, Sergeant Wickett," Mrs. Wickett said, glad for a chance to show her husband the illustrious nobleman she had become acquainted with.

The two men exchanged greetings. "Sergeant, perhaps you can explain some things to me about this country. I'd be very interested in your views."

"You must join us for lunch, and the two of you can talk," Mrs. Wickett offered, unwilling to be left out of any conversation involving Lord Michael. "My husband brought a basket of food, and there's plenty here for all of us."

Michael smiled at the woman who reminded him in some way of his own Aunt Mary. "I'd be delighted to join you, Mrs. Wickett."

The resourceful little woman found a secluded area among grain barrels and wooden crates. With Mallory's help, she turned a crate into a table. Mrs. Wickett spread out her provisions, which consisted of cheese, bread, oranges, and dates.

The two men were deep in conversation, so Mallory was able to observe Lord Michael without him being aware of her interest. Because of the heat, he'd asked permission to remove his coat, and it was thrown carelessly across a barrel. She could see that the white shirt fit snugly across his wide shoulders. His gray trousers molded to the length of his long, muscled legs. Dark hair curled at the nape of his collar and fell carelessly across his forehead. His brows were dark and winged above long lashes. His skin was browned from the sun, enhancing the brilliant green of his eyes.

Mallory quickly lowered her head when Lord Michael glanced at her. She could feel the fever of a blush spread over her face at being caught watching him.

"And you, Lady Mallory," he inquired, "is Egypt everything you'd hoped?"

She lifted her head to meet the mockery in his eyes. "I will reserve my judgment until we reach Cairo."

"I feel sure your parents eagerly await your arrival," Sergeant Wickett assured her. "I have been to Lord Tyler's residence on several occasions. You'll be quite comfortable there. It's easy to find since it's right across the street from El-Azhar University. It has high walls that surround a magnificent garden filled with citrus trees and date palms."

"Have my mother or father spoken to you about my arrival?"

He smiled apologetically. "You'll have to understand that I don't see them socially. My visits to their residence are of an official capacity."

Mallory fell silent, and Sergeant Wickett turned his attention back to Lord Michael. She was suddenly struck by a feeling of homesickness and longed for the cool climate of England.

The English passengers paid no heed to the three men swathed in black robes. Dark, hostile eyes watched Michael's every move. They observed his interest in the woman with the red hair and decided among themselves that when they reached Cairo, they would also have the woman watched. They knew it would not be wise to approach their quarry with the Inglizi sergeant on board. The time would come when they would find him alone— then they would strike.

The sun had long since disappeared beyond the muddy banks of the Nile before Michael took leave of Sergeant Wickett. Mrs. Wickett had skillfully curtained off a section of the deck so she and Mallory could have privacy while they slept.

It was cooler now, and Mallory was exhausted. As soon as she lay upon her bedroll, she fell fast asleep.

Her sleep was disturbing because she dreamed of haunting green eyes that probed to the very depths of her soul. It didn't matter that there could never be anything between Lord Michael and her, her dreams were her own and no one would ever have to know that her heart beat faster every time she thought about him.

Before dawn, Mallory was awakened by Mrs. Wickett. "Dear, I thought you might like to freshen your appearance. We are just coming into Cairo."

As she washed from a jug of water, Mallory felt the boat bump against the pier. Hurriedly, she brushed her hair and secured it to the back of her head. Her clothes were hopelessly creased since she'd been forced to sleep in them, but there was no place to change into a fresh gown.

As she emerged from the curtained-off area, she secretly hoped to see Lord Michael once more, but he was not among the waiting passengers, so he must have already departed. She would always remember their encounters, even their disagreements, with fondness.

As the donkey cart rambled over the uneven streets, Sergeant Wickett informed Mallory about the points of interest. "Look, just there," he said, glad to display his knowledge of the city, "see the tall, Byzantine-style mosque that sits atop the great citadel? The one that towers above the rest?"

Mallory glanced at the silver domes that gleamed in the noonday sun. "Yes, I see it."

"That's the Citadel of Cairo. It was planned by the great Saladin, himself." Wickett smiled. "You have no doubt, Lady Mallory, heard of the great Saladin, who defeated our Richard the Lion-heart in the Crusades?"

Mallory nodded eagerly, engrossed in his story. "Yes, of course."

"Saladin took many Crusaders as his prisoners and forced them into labor to make Cairo an impregnable city. That is, in a way justice, is it not?"

Mrs. Wickett was not so magnanimous. "Had our solders captured that man, I'm certain he would have been sent to the Tower and lost his head."

Mallory watched the sights in fascination. Her eyes followed a tall man wearing a black robe and white turban, who carried braided strands of garlic over his shoulder. His voice called out, hawking the prized spice that the Egyptian women used to season their food.

The streets were so crowded with humans and animals that they made slow progress, but Mallory didn't care— she relished each new sight and sound. She was feeling truly alive, enjoying a freedom that she had never experienced before. She was going to love Egypt, she was sure of it.

Chapter 10

*M*ichael *arrived at the British* consulate and was immediately shown into a small, cluttered office. Behind an imposing desk was a life-size portrait of Queen Victoria.

Michael was greeted by a little man who kept taking out his watch and checking the time, and Michael concluded that this act was performed more out of nervousness than a need to know the correct time.

The man stared anxiously over the brim of his thick glasses. "I'm sorry, m'lord, but the consul is away from Cairo and I don't know when he'll be returning. He's gone to London."

Michael's eyes narrowed. "Then who might you be?"

"I'm the vice-consul, Thomas Abrams, at your service, m'lord.

"Can you help me?" Michael asked.

"If you mean about your father, I don't have any new information about him. But be assured that his lordship will take up the matter with the queen."

"It seems to me that my father's cause would have been better served if the consul had remained in Egypt instead of conferring with the queen in London."

"Well, as to that, I don't know," the man sputtered. "Perhaps I can be of help to you."

Michael leaned forward, placing an impatient hand on the polished desk. "Mr. Abrams, how can you possibly help me?"

"I've been left in charge of your father's case. However, I don't know what anyone can do to find him."

Michael gave him an imperious glare. "You are the third person I've seen today, and none of them could tell me anything about my father either." He stood, towering over the man. "I'll not deal with an underling—do I make myself understood? Unless you can provide me with the information I need, I'll find out on my own."

If the man took offense, he still spoke to Lord Michael with respect. "We found your father's servant, and buried him. But there was no clue as to your father's whereabouts. How can you find a man when it seems that the desert sand just swallowed him up?"

"Mr. Abrams, you must understand I will not leave until I know all there is to know about my father. Just what has this office done to locate him?"

"We've talked to the viceroy, Mehemet Ali, and he assures us everything is being done to locate your father. He's a good man and will do what he can to help."

"Well, if neither you nor the viceroy know where my father is, or who's responsible for his disappearance, then you're not doing enough."

"Now, see here, m'lord—"

"No, you see here, Mr. Abrams. I want some answers and I want them now. If you can't get them for me, as I told you, I'll find someone who can."

Abrams removed his glasses and anxiously wiped them with his handkerchief, feeling inadequate in dealing with the earl. Why had the consul chosen this time to leave the country? he wondered. "I'm sure if the consul were here, he could tell you no more than I have, m'lord. But you must understand that I have no authority to help you in a matter concerning Egyptian policy."

"Then I'll ask for an audience with the viceroy. Damn it, someone is going to give me the answers I seek, or I'll bring so much trouble down on your head, you'll never be able to free yourself."

Looking into angry green eyes, Abrams never doubted for a moment that Lord Michael would do just as he threatened. He searched his mind for a solution to the dilemma. Surely he would lose his position and be sent back to England in disgrace if he made a wrong decision. "I'll attempt to arrange an audience with Mehemet Ali, but it won't be easy. Come back this afternoon, and I'll know if he will see you. However, I doubt he'll be able to tell you more than I have."

The cart came to a halt in front of an imposing wall that looked more like a compound than a private residence. "This is your parents' house," Sergeant Wickett announced.

Mallory glanced at the high walls, feeling raw panic. She would soon be with her mother and father—would they welcome her or look on her as an incumbrance?

"Shall we come in with you, m'lady?" Mrs. Wickett offered.

"I'm sure you two have many things to do, while I must become reacquainted with my parents. I do hope to see you both very soon." She reached forward and hugged the woman who had been her companion. "Thank you for your pleasant company. You made an otherwise tedious voyage bearable."

Mrs. Wickett smiled with pleasure and then looked doubtful. "Are you sure you'll be all right if we leave? We could come in for just a moment."

Already the native driver was unloading Mallory's trunk under the guidance of Sergeant Wickett.

"Don't worry about me," she said, hoping she sounded more confident than she felt. She climbed down from the cart. "Good-bye, Mrs. Wickett."

Sergeant Wickett was giving instructions to the driver, who opened the gate and placed Mallory's trunk inside the compound.

"Take care of yourself, m'lady," Sergeant Wickett said. "My wife is most fond of you."

"Thank you for everything, Sergeant. I shan't forget either of you."

When she heard the cart move away, Mallory stood undecided inside the high compound walls. Down a curved pathway, she saw the residence. She took her courage in hand and moved toward the imposing front doors.

A servant wearing an immaculate white robe opened the door to Mallory. He spoke to her in English. "May I help you, madame?" he inquired with a smile.

"I'm Lord Tyler's daughter. I believe my father and mother are expecting me."

The servant looked puzzled for a moment. "If his lordship and her ladyship were expecting you, they failed to inform me, my lady."

Mallory was tired, hot, and thirsty and she had no desire to stand at the door conversing with the man. "What's your name?" she asked pointedly.

He smiled broadly. "I am called Safwat, my lady."

"Well, Safwat, take me to my father at once."

He stood aside and allowed her to enter. "I am sorry, my lady, but his lordship and her ladyship are not at home. Further, my lady, they are not even in Cairo."

She stood in an arched hallway with mosaic walls, feeling no kinship with her new surroundings, and wanting to cry. "Where are they?"

"I only know they took ship down the Nile. They did not inform me of when they would be returning or where they were going." He cast her a sympathetic glance. "I am sure they would not have gone had they known you were arriving."

She glanced on the hall table and saw a stack of letters. Rifling through them, she found one from Cousin Phoebe unopened. This was not the welcome she'd envisioned. Her heart ached and she felt yet another rejection. But her mother and father had not known that she was coming when they left. That at least was a comfort.

"I am very weary," she told the servant. "Have you a room for me?"

He bowed respectfully. "I am most happy to meet his lordship's and her ladyship's honored daughter, and I will be most happy to serve you. My good wife will show you to your room, and I shall see to your belongings."

Mallory was shown to her quarters by Safwat's wife, Inna, who it turned out could speak no English. She was given a suite that was beautifully decorated in bright yellows. It was certain her parents did not suffer from lack of funds. She remembered how poor Cousin Phoebe had been forced to economize just to put food on the table, and felt betrayed.

As Inna unpacked her trunk, Mallory pushed open a latticework door that led onto a balcony. Here, in this hidden luxury, far from the bustle and noise of traffic, she settled into her new home with a heavy heart.

Later, in the cool of the evening, Mallory walked in the courtyard that was filled with tropical plants of brilliant colors. There were also orange trees and olive trees with exotic birds perched in the branches. One would never suspect from the other side of that wall that a paradise existed inside.

Mallory did not know that in the tall branches of a cypress tree, treacherous eyes carefully watched her every movement.

Michael stood before Mehemet Ali, meeting the insolent gaze of the Turkish viceroy of all Egypt.

"Lord Michael, I want no incident with your country, for we have only a fragile understanding between us," Mehemet said with a curl of his lip.

"Do not mistake me for a diplomat, Your Excellency. I only came to find my father, and I seek your help because I hoped you could tell me how best to proceed."

Mr. Abrams, who had accompanied Michael, started to speak, but the viceroy silenced him with the wave of his hand. "We have heard nothing new of your father's disappearance. It saddens us that he may have fallen prey to foul means in our country. But understand it is not our responsibility."

Michael gritted his teeth. "You must understand that I have to know, one way or the other, what happened to my father."

"Are you aware of your father's mission?"

"Not in detail. I know only that I won't leave without him."

Green, defiant eyes bore into brown, imperious eyes,

and the brown eyes looked away first. Mehemet reached a jeweled hand into a bowl, selected a sugared date, and popped it into his mouth. "Your father knew he walked into danger when he chose to come here. He should not have gone into the desert without my protection." His eyes hardened even more. "Did your government send the son to complete the father's mission?"

Michael heard Abrams gasp, and knew the little man was having an attack of nerves. But Michael realized that the viceroy was playing a game of strategy and intimidation. "You are viceroy of all Egypt. Why would you need my help? I have not the power or the knowledge of my father," Michael stated with assurance. "And I don't have Her Majesty's ear."

"Your queen would like to see one of her choosing on the throne of Egypt."

Michael looked the man in the eyes. "If that were so, Your Excellency, you would already have been unseated."

Grudging respect glowed in the viceroy's eyes. "You are a bold one. I have heard it said that your queen is not entirely pleased with me because I don't grovel before her like many of my confederates."

"I do know Her Majesty cares little for kowtowing." Michael's eyes didn't flinch, because he knew they were still playing a game that he would lose if he showed any weakness. "But that is not why I'm here. I only care about my father. Make no mistake about it—I'll find him, Your Excellency. I would like to have your help, but I will find him on my own if I must."

The viceroy suddenly smiled. "I have little doubt, Lord Michael, that if your father can be found, you'll be the one to do it. But I tell you in all honesty, I know nothing about his disappearance. Please assure your queen that we are doing everything we can to find him."

Michael bowed and stepped back a pace, knowing the viceroy's flowery phrases were hollow promises. "As I said, Your Excellency, I'm not a diplomat. Send your own messages to Her Majesty. Perhaps you can convince her that you know nothing about my father's disappearance."

Without looking back, Michael turned on his heels and walked out of the chamber.

Abrams moved beside him with jerky little steps. "That man's insufferable," he muttered. "You played a dangerous game when you sparred with him."

"Yes," Michael answered, "but I found out what I wanted to know. He has no knowledge of my father's whereabouts. If he did, he would have told me."

"How can you know that?"

"For all his bragging and swaggering, he very much wants to remain an ally of Britain."

"He didn't appear to care about Her Majesty's patronage."

"What you heard was the crowing of a frightened man. He knows the seriousness of my father's disappearance. He wants my father found almost as much as I do."

On the carriage ride to the inn, Abrams studied Lord Michael. At first he'd thought of him as just another wealthy nobleman making demands and expecting everyone to obey his commands.

He now realized this man was highly intelligent, and determined to find his father. God help those who got in his way, Abrams thought with growing admiration for the young earl.

Chapter 11

ichael settled into the rooms his father had occupied while in Cairo. He had gone through his father's belongings several times, and nothing seemed disturbed. Nor was there anything to indicate where Raile had been going or with whom he was meeting when he went into the desert.

Michael searched his father's trunks and discovered he had taken very little with him when he left.

He paced the floor, feeling heartsick and discouraged. He was in a strange country where no one seemed to know or care what had happened to his father. For the first time, Michael was afraid that he might never find him.

He wouldn't allow himself to believe his father was dead—but where would he begin his search? There was no clue, nothing to follow, but someone had to have the answers. He would remain in Egypt until he found out what he wanted to know.

He hadn't slept in days, so he lay upon his father's bed and fell asleep without even removing his boots. His dreams were filled with images of his father that were suddenly replaced by the old Gypsy fortune-teller. Her words echoed over and over in a nightmare. *Someone close to you is in grave danger.*

He awoke suddenly in a cold sweat. Sitting up, he saw from the glow reflected through the window that it was after sundown. He'd been asleep for hours, but he didn't feel rested. Wearily, he stood and stretched his body. He would return to the consulate to see if there had been any new developments, although he expected none.

As Michael crossed the street and walked down a narrow alleyway, his thoughts were on his mother. If this waiting was difficult for him, then it was a hundred times more difficult for her.

There was a bright moon, but it didn't touch the corners of the alleyway, so he didn't see the man creeping along behind him, staying well out of view. He moved down an even darker alley that was deserted.

Ordinarily, Michael's senses would have been alert, but he was worried and preoccupied. When he heard a rush of footsteps, he glanced behind him, but he did not see the assailant who buried the knife in his back. He only felt searing pain as he fell to his knees.

It took all his strength to pull himself to his feet. He managed to stagger out of the alley and across the street to the British consulate. He pounded weakly on the door, and when no one answered, he realized that everyone had left for the day.

Michael began to feel dizzy, and he knew he was about to lose consciousness. He suddenly remembered Sergeant Wickett explaining to Lady Mallory where her parents lived. He prayed he'd have the strength to make it there before he lost consciousness.

It had been a week since Mallory had arrived at her parents' home. She had still received no word from them, so much of her days were spent in solitude, reading in the cool garden. Tonight she was restless and moved down the pathway toward the pond that shimmered in the moonlight. She was near the back of the garden when she heard a scratching noise.

Moving closer to the gate, she listened more intently. There it was again. Now she heard a groan, as if someone was in pain, and a whispered plea came out of the darkness.

"Let me in, I'm injured."

Without thinking, she threw the heavy bolt and the gate swung open. She saw the man crumpled on the ground and bent to touch him. Raising his face to the moonlight, she saw it was Lord Michael and he was apparently unconscious. Running her hand down his back, she felt something hot and sticky—it was blood!

"Lord Michael," she cried, "you're wounded."

Jumping to her feet, she raced down the path, calling Safwat. She had to get help at once.

Between the two of them, Mallory and Safwat managed to get Lord Michael to the cottage across the garden that was kept in readiness for visitors. After they got his unconscious body on the bed, laying him on his stomach because of his wound, Mallory sent Safwat for a doctor.

She stared at Lord Michael's pale face in the flickering candlelight, wishing she had the skills to help him. With his eyes closed, he was not so imposing; in fact, he looked vulnerable and almost boyish.

When the doctor finally arrived, he was a dirty little man, wearing a robe that must have once been white, but was so filthy it was hard to tell. When Mallory spoke to him, he shook his head, indicating he spoke no English. He quickly examined Lord Michael and told Safwat to ask the lady about the stab wound.

Mallory shook her head. "I know nothing about how it happened. Can the doctor help him?"

"He says so, my lady. We must first remove his clothing."

Mallory watched with horror as the doctor opened his medical case and displayed instruments that were dirty and rusted.

She quickly stepped between him and Lord Michael. "Safwat, tell him his services will not be needed—I want him to leave now!"

The servant looked confused. "But my lady, he is a comprehending doctor who can help your friend."

"Is there no English doctor in Cairo?"

"I know not of one, my lady."

She glanced at the doctor, who had a surly expression on his face. Her eyes dropped to his hands, and she saw dirt beneath the fingernails.

"Tell him I will treat the patient myself," Mallory said firmly. "Ask the doctor what I should do."

For a moment, the two men argued in Arabic, and the argument ended with the doctor stalking out and throwing heated words over his shoulder at the insolent Englishwoman.

Mallory ignored him. "Safwat, I want you to fetch the doctor who treats the English residents—where is my father's doctor?" she demanded.

The Egyptian was thoughtful for a moment. "The lord's doctor is military. The post is many hours from here."

Mallory was becoming desperate. "Can you and Inna help me?"

"I am not good with the sick, my lady. And it is not permissible for my wife to treat a man."

In horror, Mallory realized that only she could help Lord Michael. For a moment, she looked at him, feeling very inadequate. Gathering her strength, she set her chin determinedly.

The first thing she must do was stop the bleeding. "Bring boiled water and clean bandages—I'll want a sharp knife—hurry," she directed the servant.

Safwat immediately ran from the room to carry out her instructions. Meanwhile, Mallory rolled up her sleeves, feeling sick. She wasn't sure how to proceed, but anything she could do would be better than what the Egyptian doctor would have done with his filthy instruments.

Safwat returned a short time later with her father's medical bag. The servant watched as she nervously ripped Michael's shirt open with a knife.

Mallory shuddered at the sight of oozing blood. Carefully at first, she cleansed the wound. She could see that it was deep, and hoped it would not require stitches. She applied salve and bound him with a tight bandage. Not knowing what else to do, she sat beside his bed, changing the bandages as often as needed. Once she was satisfied that the bleeding had stopped, she pulled a sheet over his back and turned to Safwat, who had not left her side.

"There is nothing more I can do for him," she said wearily. "I only hope I did enough."

"All is in the hands of Allah," Safwat said earnestly. "Would my lady like me to sit with the wounded Inglizi?"

"No, get some sleep, Safwat," Mallory replied, brushing a tumbled curl off her forehead. "I'll remain with him throughout the night in case he needs anything."

She would do all she could to keep him alive.

Michael awoke in a strange room, wondering why he was lying on his stomach. When he tried to move, pain ripped through him and his head fell back against the pillow. He licked his dry lips, trying to remember what had happened. He blinked his eyes and looked at the room—it was unfamiliar to him.

Turning his head, he saw that a woman sat near his bed, but his eyesight was bleary, and he could only make out her shape. Apparently she was asleep, for she did not speak to him.

Michael attempted to turn to his back, but the agony was too great. He groaned and closed his eyes until the pain subsided. What had happened to him? His head was spinning, and he felt as if his shoulder was on fire. Just before he closed his eyes and drifted off, he felt a cool hand on his brow and heard the woman speak soothingly to him.

Mallory watched Michael with concern. He was feverish, and that worried her more than the wound. She leaned back in the chair, her eyes sweeping his face. He was indeed a handsome man, but so complicated. Who had done this terrible thing to him? And why had he sought her help?

She reached out and touched his cheek, and he suddenly grabbed her hand, holding it in a tight grip. "Who are you?" he asked in a low voice.

"It's Lady Mallory," she said, clasping her hand around his. "You came to me, remember? You are in no danger here—you are safe."

"Lady Mallory. Yes, I must make it to her . . . only one I know in Cairo. So weak can't make it to . . ."

He released her hand and relaxed against the pillow. She quickly applied a cold compress to his head, for he was still too hot. She must bathe him all over to cool his fever. She thought of asking Safwat to help, but quickly discounted that notion—the servant had not proven to be competent.

With a resigned sigh, she pulled the sheet away. At first she avoided looking at him, but she knew she would have to put her modesty aside if she was going to lower his fever.

She dipped the cloth into the cool water and bathed his face. She then carefully washed his back, taking care not to touch the bandage. She felt a strange sensation as her cloth slid over his naked skin. She had never realized men had so many muscles. She dampened the cloth and pressed it across his forehead.

When the task was completed, Mallory stepped back and looked at him, feeling an ache deep inside. He was so beautiful to look upon. For this moment, he seemed to belong to her.

Suddenly his eyes opened, and his usually lustrous green eyes held a glazed look. "Mother, I'll find him. . . . If I die trying, I'll bring Father back to you." He groaned and closed his eyes, but his tortured rambling continued. "It's dark, I can't see. No one to help me. Father . . . you aren't dead . . . you can't be. Someone came out of the shadows. Been hurt—can't die until I find you, Father. Must find . . . Lady Mallory before I die—she'll get word to Mother. . . ."

Tears of pity rolled down Mallory's cheeks. Now she better understood why he'd come to Egypt. It had something to do with his father. She touched his cheek and spoke softly. "You will recover, my lord. You will yet find your father."

"I'm dead." Michael groaned. "I failed . . . failed."

"No, you haven't failed. You will find your father. And I won't let you die."

Throughout the night, he would drift into a troubled sleep, only to awaken and desperately try to get out of bed. Because he was so weak Mallory managed to restrain him.

She bathed him twice more, and just before sunup, his fever broke and he fell into a peaceful sleep.

Exhausted, Mallory rested her head against the back of the chair and fell asleep herself.

No one in the compound heard the man slip over the high wall and drop into the garden below. He adjusted the patch over his blind eye and slunk across the garden, heading toward the only light. Silently, he flattened his body against the cottage, then moved forward to glance into the room. The Inglizi was supposed to be dead, but he was lying on a bed, being tended by the woman they had been watching.

He stared for a long moment at the woman, his eyes taking in her delicate beauty. Surely she belonged to the Inglizi. He had never before seen a woman with hair the color of a desert sunrise.

He considered entering the cottage and making certain that his quarry died. But he decided against it, because he would be forced to kill the woman as well.

If the Inglizi lived, he would have to emerge one day—and Ali Hitin would be waiting for him.

Chapter 12

ady Mary handed Kassidy a cup of hot tea, and looked at her niece with troubled eyes. "Dearest, try not to worry. Just because you've not heard from Michael is no cause for alarm. It's my belief that he's been so actively seeking Raile, that he's had no time to correspond with you."

"Oh, Aunt Mary, what have I done by sending my son into danger? I know now that Raile would not have approved. I should have gone to Cairo myself."

Lady Mary had just taken a sip of tea and almost choked. When she could catch her breath, she looked at Kassidy in disbelief. "You can't be serious. Raile certainly wouldn't want you in Egypt. Just think about the joy you will feel when they both come back." Lady Mary lowered her head so Kassidy couldn't read the distress in her own eyes. "Perhaps by tomorrow you will receive word from Michael. Let's just wait and see."

Suddenly the door burst open, and Arrian rushed to her mother. The two embraced while Kassidy cried on her daughter's shoulder. "Oh, Arrian, why did you come? You should still be in bed after giving birth to the baby."

"She's here because she's stubborn like her mother," a masculine voice said. Her daughter's husband, the laird of Glencarin, pulled Kassidy to her feet and brushed her cheek with a kiss. "We both wanted to be here. Is there any word?"

"Nothing. Oh, Warrick, now Michael may be missing. We haven't heard from him since he left. It's my fault if I've lost my husband and my son."

Warrick put comforting arms around his mother-in-law, trying to absorb her pain. "When did Michael leave?"

"A fortnight ago," Lady Mary offered. "I told Kassidy he'd write when he had the time. And lord only knows when the mail would reach us if he had written."

Warrick nodded. "Let's give him another week, and if we haven't heard from him by then, I'll go to Egypt."

Kassidy clutched at his shirt. "No, I will not lose another member of my family to that cursed land. Promise me you will not go, Warrick."

Arrian took her mother's hand, thinking she'd never seen her so distraught. "Come with me upstairs, Mother. Little Grant has talked of little else but seeing his grandmama. And you have a new granddaughter who wants to meet you. Did you know her name is Kassidy?"

Kassidy smiled through her tears. "Oh, yes, I must see the children." She rushed toward the stairs, and Arrian embraced her aunt.

"I've never seen Mother like this. I'm frightened, Aunt Mary."

Warrick turned to Lady Mary. "Is the situation as grim as it appears?"

"I fear so, Warrick. I try to keep Kassidy's spirits up, but I'm having a hard time being cheerful after all that's happened. Thank God you brought the children, that will help her."

Michael awoke slowly, blinking at the sun shining through the crack in the curtained window. With effort, he raised himself up on his elbow and turned on his side to glance around the room. Vague memories stirred in his mind, but he was slow to comprehend all that had happened. Before he could question his situation further, the door opened and Lady Mallory entered.

"You," he said, jerking the covers over his bare chest. "How did I get here?"

She placed a tray on the table beside his bed and smiled at his embarrassment. "No need to be modest with me, because necessity has forced me to be your nurse. And as to how you got here, you'll have to tell me. I found you outside my garden gate. You had been stabbed."

He shook his head to clear it. "Stabbed? But who would do—"

"You don't keep very good company, Lord Michael. You might consider changing friends."

He looked Mallory over carefully. She wore a dark green gown and her hair was hanging in curls to her waist. Surely if the goddess Diana had come to earth, she would not be more lovely. "You tended my wound?" he asked, thinking of his state of undress.

"I had no choice. The doctor that came to treat you

was none too clean, and I sent him on his way. I noticed that you have another scar on your upper arm. It's healed, but it can't be too old. Why are people trying to harm you?"

"I'd rather not say." He flexed his arm and winced in pain. "How long have I been here?"

She handed him a napkin, which he took without question. "Two days and nights, and I'm sure you are hungry by now."

"I could use a drink," he admitted.

She handed him a glass of sweet lemonade, which he gratefully took and drained immediately. "Thank you," he said, looking at the tray. "What other tidbits have you for me? I find I am indeed hungry."

"I made my Cousin Phoebe's chicken and rice. She swears it can cure almost everything."

Michael took the bowl she handed him and raised the spoon to his lips. "Mmmm, this is good. So the lady cooks. What else can you do?"

"Play doctor to errant young men who turn up on my doorstep."

He looked into laughing blue eyes—he hadn't realized she had a sense of humor. He watched her move around the room, straightening a lampshade, pulling the curtains aside, and opening the window to let in a cool breeze.

"Sit and talk to me while I eat, Lady Mallory. I'd like to hear more about you."

She stood at the foot of the bed, her hands clasped demurely in front of her. "There isn't much to tell. I lived in the country with my Cousin Phoebe. She sent me here to live with my mother and father."

"Where are your parents?"

"As you may have surmised, they have gone away. I'm all you have."

"So you're country bred. I guessed as much. You have that healthy appearance about you."

She glared at him. "Just what do you mean by that remark?"

"Nothing, except you don't have that polish and sophistication that London society demands."

When he saw her eyes sparkle with anger, he hurriedly added, "I have no particular liking for refinement in women. You somehow remind me of my sister."

Was he deliberately being cruel? she wondered. Was she no more than a gauche country girl that he could hold up to ridicule? "If by that you mean I would find no pleasure in splashing an innocent pedestrian with my carriage, then you're right—I'm not sophisticated, and I'm glad."

"What carriage—you have me confused. Am I supposed to know what you are talking about?"

Mallory walked to the door. "You should not overeat. I'll send Safwat for the tray. Since you are mending nicely, he will now dress your wound and see to your needs."

"Wait, I—"

"Good day to you, Lord Michael."

The door slammed behind her. He was puzzled. Why had she been so angry with him? Well, he had never understood women, and he certainly didn't understand this one. He supposed he should have been more gracious to her. After all, she probably had saved his life.

"Red hair and temper," he muttered, taking another bite of tender chicken, "apparently they go together." He had no liking for a woman who couldn't be reasonable and was always putting a man on the defensive. He'd never met a woman like this one.

*   *   *

Mallory moved through the garden, breathing in the fragrant scent of the many exotic plants. Girlishly, she plucked a large yellow blossom and tucked it behind her ear. Then she moved onto the edge of a huge pond and looked at her reflection in the shimmering water. She did so detest her plain chocolate-colored gown. If only her mother would return, she might buy her more appropriate ones.

Suddenly another image appeared in the pond. Lord Michael had come up behind her. Turning quickly, Mallory lost her balance and toppled into the pond. Sputtering and gasping, she regained her feet. With her wet gown clinging to her body, and water streaming down her face, she glared at the cause of her mishap.

Michael couldn't hide his amusement. He reached up and plucked the blossom from behind her ear. "I'm sure there's an easier way to water this flower. Do you realize that I've seen you wet as often as I've seen you dry?"

"And why do you suppose that is, Lord Michael?" Mallory asked him icily.

"Surely you cannot blame me for this dunking."

She refused his offered hand and stepped out of the pond. "Aren't you supposed to be in bed?" she asked in an angry voice.

"And miss the spectacle of you tumbling into the pond. Not me."

She stood before him, bedraggled and dripping. "If you cause your wound to bleed again, Lord Michael, I promise that I won't help you, but I'll call the Egyptian doctor back and let him practice his medicine on you. I'll even hand him the rusty instruments myself."

His lips twitched. "Bloodthirsty when you're wet, aren't you?"

Mallory saw nothing amusing in the situation. "Did your mother never teach you manners?"

"Alas, she did, but I have not heeded all of her teachings. Here," Michael offered, "allow me to help you into the house lest you have another misadventure."

Mallory's eyes blazed. "Thank you, no. I am perfectly capable of making it on my own."

Michael watched her turn away and move toward the house with as much dignity as she could muster. His laughter rang out, and he realized that he hadn't laughed in a very long time. Lady Mallory was proving to be most entertaining.

He glanced about the walled garden that had been his sanctuary in his time of need. She had taken him in, nursed his wounds, and asked no questions. Surely that set her apart from most women he knew. She really did somehow remind him of his sister, Arrian.

Safwat led Lord Michael into the informal dining room, where a servant was setting two places at the table.

"Where is Lady Mallory? Michael inquired.

"She will be here shortly and asks that you excuse her tardiness."

Michael smiled to himself. She was probably late because she had to dry her hair after falling into the pond.

Suddenly, she appeared at his side, smelling of fresh flowers and reminding him of England. "Forgive me, my lord, for being late."

He held the chair for her and sat opposite her. "I want to thank you for your kindness to me in tending my wound, and your hospitality," he said with sincerity.

"I'm sure you would have done the same in my place," she said, on the defensive. "I'm also sure you are thinking that an unmarried girl in England would never entertain a gentleman at dinner while her parents were away from home. But you will have to admit that these are rather unusual circumstances."

"I do admit that, and I appreciate your position. But this isn't England, is it, Lady Mallory?"

She looked at him suspiciously, as if expecting hidden meaning in his innocent remark.

Michael's eyes settled on her long, delicate neck. There was something different about her tonight and it took him a moment to comprehend what it was. She wore her hair swept up to the top of her head, in a style that made him realize she was attempting to look older.

If she but knew it, she was lovelier in her plain, gray cotton gown with its simple lace collar than most women were when they dressed in their finest silks and satins. He really must have hurt her when he told her she was unsophisticated, but he had meant it as a compliment.

"My gratitude is most sincere, Lady Mallory. If ever I can be of service to you, you have but to ask."

She lowered her eyes and watched as Safwat served the main course. "I find myself worried about you, my lord. After you leave here, I hope you will be careful."

"And I have concerns about you, Lady Mallory. Egypt is a dangerous place at this time. Do you know when your father will return?"

Her lower lip trembled as if she were trying to keep from crying. "No. I haven't heard from my parents."

"I would suggest if he does not return soon, you go to

the British consulate and ask them to find you a suitable companion so you can return to England."

"I have nowhere to return to, my lord." She glanced up at him. "Are you sure you're feeling well?"

"Yes, you were an excellent nurse. I'll be leaving after we've dined."

She stared at him for a moment, knowing she didn't want him to go. "I would not like to see you open your wound."

"I can assure you that I'm perfectly well." To demonstrate, he raised his arm. "See, no pain."

"You never did explain to me how you got that other wound."

He smiled. "Let's just say I collided with another knife on board the *Iberia* one night."

She reached out and touched his hand. "I don't know your story, but I do know you have enemies. Promise me that you will be careful in the future."

He smiled, taking her hand in his and raising it to his lips. "I can assure you I'll be alert from now on, my ministering angel."

Mallory withdrew her hand. "Most people would say I was more devil than angel."

"And why is that?"

"Because I have the devil's own temper," she admitted.

"Ah, so you have."

She glanced at him, her eyes blazing, but his laughter cooled her anger.

"I'll still call you my angel."

Her expression became serious. "You were out of your head with fever one night, and you talked about your father."

"What did I say?" Michael insisted.

"I inferred from your delirium that your father is missing here in Egypt."

"Yes," he said, reluctant to discuss the matter with her.

"Surely you aren't going to attempt to find him without help. Already you have suffered two mishaps."

His expression hardened. "As I told you, I will not be taken unaware another time."

"Can you not wait until my father returns? Perhaps he can help you. He knows about Egypt."

"No, I cannot wait."

Mallory was silent for a moment, then raised her eyes to his. "What will you do?"

He wiped his mouth and laid his napkin aside. "I don't know, but I must leave now." He stood and stared down at her. "How can I ever thank you, my lady?"

"By keeping safe," she answered, rising.

"Will you let me out through the garden gate?" he asked. "If someone is watching, I don't want them to see me leave."

She nodded. After they walked down the path to the gate, Michael stopped and turned to her. "Promise me you won't go out alone?"

"I won't. One of the servants is always with me when I leave the compound. Do you think your enemies know you are here?"

"I can't be sure. But I hope I haven't put you in danger. My enemies are faceless and nameless—they could be anywhere and anyone."

Mallory felt an aching emptiness surround her heart. "Will I hear from you again?"

Without a word, he swept her into his arms and pressed his lips against hers. Mallory melted against him, feeling as if she couldn't breathe. He quickly released her and stared into her eyes for a long moment. "I believe we shall meet again, my angel."

Before she could answer, he had walked out of the gate

and blended into the shadows. She wanted to call after him, but she merely closed the gate.

For a long moment, she stood there with her back braced against the wall, her heart breaking.

Then, for reasons she could not understand, Mallory began to cry.

Chapter 13

ichael had gone once more to see the consul, only to find he had still not returned from England, so Michael had been forced to speak with Abrams. He left, angered by the man's incompetence and wondering where he could turn for help.

When he arrived back at his quarters, Michael again went through his father's letters and papers, but found nothing that would indicate where the duke had gone or with whom. He was discouraged because he didn't know what to do next.

"I'm sorry, Mother," he said, sitting on the edge of the bed and burying his head in his hands. "You had faith in me, and I have failed you."

When the knock fell on the door, Michael yanked it open. Seeing a man dressed in black flowing robe, and a patch over one eye, he vented all his frustrations on the stranger.

"What in the hell do you want?"

"Effendi, I've come as a friend."

"I have no friends in this cursed country."

"You are mistaken, effendi. My master has invited you to his camp. He begs that I say to you, to come and dine with him and your father."

Michael grabbed the man by the robe and yanked him forward. "Do you take me for a fool? If my father was with your master, he would have written to me or come himself."

"He could not come, effendi. He has been cursed with the desert fever—too much sun. He is just now able to sit up. Will you come?"

Michael looked at the man suspiciously. "Of what tribe are you?"

"Of the Mutullib bedouin, effendi."

"I know little of your desert tribes, but I do know that effendi is a Turkish title of respect, is it not?"

The man rolled his one good eye. "You are too shrewd, effendi. My mother was Turkish, so I adopted many of her manners and words."

"What does my father look like?"

"Like you, effendi, but older. He is of your tall height."

Michael tightened his grip on the man. "What color are his eyes?"

"Not green like yours, effendi. Your father's eyes are dark, effendi—dark like an Arab's."

Michael released him, fearing to hope. This must be the opportunity he had been waiting for.

"When do we leave?"

"At once, effendi. I have all the provisions and a horse for you to ride."

Michael nodded. "How many days' journey to your master's camp?"

"Six days, no more, effendi."

"Then let's get started."

The one-eyed man grinned and motioned with his hand. "All is in readiness, effendi. Follow me—follow me."

For three days Michael and his four guides rode into the desert. Scorching sand, borne on the eternal winds, stung his face, while the sun blistered his skin and cracked his lips.

Endlessly they rode, and Michael had to admit the desert ponies were of hearty stock and carried a man easily across the sand.

He glanced about, noticing that only the hardiest plants clung to life in this wasteland. They passed colossal limestone figures left over from some long-forgotten pharaoh. Now they merely cast broken shadows on the lifeless valley of sand.

That night, as they made camp, Michael ate the unidentifiable meat that the one of the men handed him. He thought it best not to ask what it was—he didn't really want to know.

"When do I see my father?" Michael asked of the one-eyed man, who seemed to be the only one of his companions who spoke English.

"Two more days, effendi. No sandstorm, so we make good time—good time."

Glancing up at the full moon, Michael restlessly left the camp. He stood on a sand dune that gave him a glimpse of the surrounding desert. Over the next dune was another and another. A man could wander forever in this nightmare of sand.

In the distance, he heard a jackal howl. Perhaps the desert wasn't barren after all—there was life for those who knew where to look for it.

As he walked back to camp, his footsteps disappeared in the ever-shifting sand. He had the feeling this land could swallow a man and he'd never be heard from again. Was that what had happened to his father—would it happen to him?

When he went to his tent, Michael fell exhausted upon the sheepskin that had been provided for him, but tonight he kept his pistol close at hand. He still didn't trust these men, for they were acting secretively and were often huddled together, casting furtive glances his way.

He fell asleep, only to dream tortured dreams. He was back in London and the old Gypsy woman was predicting his future. She had warned him that someone near him was in danger. She had also warned him to beware of a one-eyed man. Suddenly he sat up, his eyes searching the darkened tent. Ali Hitin had only one eye. Michael shook his head in disbelief.

No, it was impossible—no one could foretell the future. But why, then, had many of the things the old woman had said, come to pass? He slept lightly, awakening at each noise. He would not think about the old Gypsy. Ali Hitin was going to lead him to his father, just as he said he would.

Michael was still in a sleep-drugged state when he heard the sound of bloodcurdling yells. Grabbing his pistol, he raced out of the tent, only to be confronted by several black-robed bedouin.

He aimed his pistol with the intention of defending himself, but before he could fire, his four guides were shot. Ali Hitin lay face down in the sand, twitched convulsively, then moved no more. There was no doubt they were all dead!

In the confusion, Michael's pistol was wrestled from

his grip by two men. He realized there was no reason to put up a fight, he was hopelessly outnumbered.

He stood facing the man who appeared to be the leader, waiting for a bullet to pierce his body. But the bedouin merely motioned toward a horse, indicating that Michael should mount.

Michael thrust his foot in the short Arab stirrup and swung his long leg over the horse. He glanced at his guides—poor devils had never had a chance. He wondered why he'd been spared. Perhaps his captors had something far more terrible than death waiting for him.

He spoke to the man who appeared to be the leader. "Why have you done this?"

The man merely yelled out an order, and Michael's reins were yanked from his hand and his horse led forward. So he was a captive. He could not guess where they were taking him, and apparently they would not tell him.

In two days, he would have been reunited with his father. Frustration turned to anger. Who were these men who had so mercilessly slain his guides?

Michael stared straight ahead as they rode into the night. The moon had dropped low on the horizon as their tireless horses climbed sandy mounds as high as mountains. There was nothing here to guide a man, no landmark, nothing to gauge distance. How could these men find their way in the desert? he wondered.

The sun was just painting the sky with a golden hue when they appeared to leave the desert behind. Now the terrain became craggy, and they rode into a valley that was dominated by huge granite cliffs. After an hour, an oasis opened up to them. Surprisingly, there was a large river-fed lake and many palm groves.

In the distance, against the highest granite cliff, was a

large village. Several men stood atop thick walls and waved their rifles in greeting. Wide gates swung open to admit them, and they rode through on cobbled streets.

The village was just stirring to life, and Michael paid scant attention to the sun-dried brick houses they passed.

"Where is this place?" he demanded of the man beside him, and received only a shrug for his trouble.

He was totally unprepared for the huge limestone and granite palace that rose above the other buildings. It was built in the Greek style, so out of keeping with the usual villages and towns he'd seen thus far in Egypt.

Michael didn't need to be told that this town was not on any map.

As they made their way toward the palace, many of the men began to disappear, most probably going to their homes. When they stopped at the palace steps, only one of his captors remained. He dismounted and motioned for Michael to do the same.

Two guards stood before the ornate doors, and when Michael's companion spoke to them, Michael was quickly ushered inside.

"You wait here," his captor said, speaking to Michael for the first time in English.

Michael soon found himself alone in a huge anteroom. He walked to the window of intricately carved lattice-work. He could see children playing in the streets, women balancing water jars on their heads, and men going off to their farms. These didn't seem like violent people.

Glancing around the room, he saw that the great doors were arched and set with semiprecious stones. Whoever ruled this valley was in possession of great wealth.

At last his guard reappeared. "My prince will see you now."

Michael walked silently across the pink marble floors toward jade green doors that swung open at his approach. The man who had accompanied him did not enter the room, but bowed and departed.

Across the vast room with high dome ceiling, Michael saw the prince standing in the shadow of an arched window. Silently, the man motioned him forward. Michael's footsteps were noiseless as he moved across the red Persian rug.

The prince still hadn't come out of the shadows, and all Michael could see was a white robe and a well-manicured hand with a huge ruby ring.

"Why have you brought me here?" Michael demanded.

"To save your life, my friend."

Michael was shocked when Khaldun stepped out of the shadows. "But you—you can't be the—"

Khaldun bowed his head and smiled before clasping Michael's hand. "My brother, I have had you watched since you left the boat. I was sorry that my men were too late to save you from the attack in the alleyway, but they waited to see that you were safely inside Lady Mallory's home."

"I don't understand."

"When it was reported to me that you were riding into the desert with men from the Mutullib tribe, I knew your life was in danger."

"But how—"

"The Mutullib are ruled by my uncle, Sheik Sidi Ahmed, and they have no liking for Inglizi, er . . . English. Sidi is my mother's brother, though my mother considers him unworthy. You see, he is dead to her because he sides with the enemies of Egypt."

"Is he Turkish?"

Khaldun nodded. "As is my mother. But she honors my

father and his beliefs. My uncle bestows his loyalty on the radicals who would divide this country. They would like to see Egypt fall."

"But the men who guided me into the desert assured me that they were taking me to my father."

"This I do not know for sure. It could be that they know where your father is being held. But I do know you would not have left my uncle's city alive."

"Is it possible that your uncle holds my father captive?"

"I do not know the answer to that, but I shall find out for you."

Michael understood many things now—why the men had tried to kill Khaldun on the ship. "It seems I owe you my life."

"There will be no talk of what is owed between us, for you are as a brother to me. Does not a brother help a brother?"

"It's fortunate for me that you had me watched. I suppose in my eagerness to find my father I forgot to be cautious."

"Even now I have my spies looking for your father. The desert sand speaks to my people. We will find him. But we will talk of this over breakfast. You must be famished."

Shortly afterward, Michael sat across the low table from Prince Khaldun. He took a drink of the strong, dark coffee and smiled. "Why didn't you tell me who you really were?"

"It was my father's wish that I hide my identity since there would be those who would try to keep me from reaching my home. As you saw, our enemies found me anyway. I would be dead but for you."

Michael saw sadness in Khaldun's eyes. "How is your father?"

"He was gravely wounded while on a hunting expedition. We cannot prove if the deed was done maliciously, because the man who fired the shot killed himself before my father's men could stop him. The physicians hold out very little hope that my father will recover, for his wound is severe."

"Could it have been your uncle's treachery?"

"That is what I believe, but as yet, I have no proof."

"Why don't we go to your uncle and demand answers?"

"Patience, my friend. I must warn you that my uncle barricades himself inside a great fortress. If your father is his prisoner, it will not be easy to rescue him."

"Nothing has been easy since I arrived in your country."

The prince smiled slightly. "That is not all true. You were reunited with the beautiful Lady Mallory."

"Under unfortunate circumstances."

"Is she not of your heart?"

"If you are asking if I love her, the answer is no."

"Then I am free to seek her out, am I not?"

Michael was thoughtful for a moment. He had a strange reluctance to lie to Khaldun, but it was necessary—Khaldun must not think there could ever be anything between him and Mallory.

"I'm hesitant to speak of an emotion that is yet so new to me. My love for Lady Mallory has not yet been put into words."

Khaldun looked disappointed for a moment, but then he smiled. "You Inglizi have no fire in your blood. Perhaps it is because you come from a cold country, devoid of the desert heat."

Michael nodded. "Perhaps."

Prince Khaldun looked at his friend, taking in his appearance. "If you want the desert to reveal her secrets to you, Michael, you must appear to be as one with her."

"I will do anything you think necessary to find my father. Will you help me?"

"I can, and I shall. First, you must sleep. Then we will see about having you properly clothed. It would be good if you were to train in Bedouin warfare. You must also think like a Bedouin and not be too trusting of others."

"Yes, I see what you mean. I followed those assassins as trustingly as a newborn lamb being led to the slaughter."

"You have much to learn of our ways, my friend. But there will be those who are eager to teach you."

At last Michael had tangible hope that he would find his father. "I'm impatient to learn anything you can teach me. I now know that I came to your country ill equipped."

"It is good that you know this. But the desert yields her secrets slowly. If your father is still alive, he will be alive when you are better prepared to rescue him." Prince Khaldun clapped Michael on the back. "All will be well, my friend. We will leave it in the hands of Allah."

Chapter 14

ichael found it difficult to curb his impatience. Time had little meaning to these desert people. Three weeks had passed since he'd arrived at the hidden kingdom, and he was still no closer to finding his father than he had been in Cairo.

Michael had not been idle. Each morning he was up early, tirelessly training. He practiced with the best warriors of the Jebeliya. His wounds had healed, and his sword arm was becoming strong. He had been a student of the greatest fencing master in Europe, and those skills now served him well. He used his agility and knowledge in the daily contests. In no time, he could wield a scimitar and split a melon from the back of a galloping horse.

The day of his most glorious triumph came when he beat the Jebeliya champion three bouts in a row. Thus he was honored as the new champion. Michael was also learning that Khaldun's people were generous with those they liked, for that day he won the bouts, the whole tribe cheered, but no one louder than the defeated champion.

Michael adapted easily to the native dress, which was not as confining as his English clothing. His robe and headdress were black, the kaffiyeh held in place by three golden cords befitting a man of his high rank. He exchanged his heavy English riding boots for the lighter Bedouin boots, which were more suitable for the desert.

The city of Kamar Ginena, which, translated, meant moon garden, had been built seven hundred years earlier by the Jebeliya. Many of the tribe were descendants of freed slaves, and on rare occasions, children were born with blue eyes and light-colored hair.

Michael discovered that the Jebeliya were also fierce warriors and were feared by most of the bedouin tribes. Few ever challenged them, and no one entered their city without permission. They had great pride and loyalty, and were devoted first to the tribe and second to their families.

The city itself was fed by twelve underground springs and bloomed like a beautiful garden. Food was plentiful there, and what couldn't be grown or made in the city, was acquired from the caravans that passed on the route three days' journey to the south.

Michael had become friends with Yanni, the fierce captain of the guard. Yanni taught him many ways to survive in the harsh desert, and how to live off the land if he was ever lost.

When Michael heard that Yanni was preparing to make the journey to meet a caravan, he volunteered to go along. Khaldun agreed that Michael was ready for his first excursion into the desert.

Khaldun and his escort rode with them until noon the first day. When the prince turned back to the city, he smiled and raised his hand. "Yanni, bring back my friend in one piece." His laughter rang out. "And see that he doesn't scar his pretty face, or the women of our city will weep."

There was a strong comradery between the twenty black-robed men that rode silently across the desert. On they rode in silence as the ever-shifting wind covered all traces left by their horses' hooves.

Michael's muscles were hard, his sword arm true, and he had a confidence he'd not had before. He was a warrior, trained, molded, and honed by the fiercest fighting men in the world. There was no fear in his heart, and no feat he would not attempt.

The first night, they set up camp behind a huge sand dune, the black tents blending in with the night sky. Guards were posted on top of the dunes so they could observe anyone who might approach from any direction. In some ways, Michael thought these bedouin were like children, laughing and enjoying life. That night they sang songs and joked among themselves. By then Michael had learned enough of their language to laugh at their jests.

By daylight on the third day, they were nearing the caravan trail. Before they topped a hill, Yanni held up his hand, and the men came to a silent halt.

"My ears tell me there is trouble," he told Michael. "Can you hear the sounds of battle?"

Michael shook his head, but listened until he did indeed hear the clashing of swords. Without an issued order, each man drew his sword, and urged their horses up the hill and over the top.

Michael rode beside Yanni, his sword ready, his jaw set with determination.

It took only a moment to assess the trouble. The caravan was small, with just thirty camels, and the merchants were hopelessly outnumbered by their assailants.

The black-robed Jebeliya came charging down the last sand dune, their swords clashing with those of the attackers.

Although they were outnumbered, the tide of battle was soon turned in favor of the powerful Jebeliya. At one point, Michael found himself surrounded on all sides by the enemy. He swung his sword with precision—attack, withdraw—attack, charge. Sweat blinded him, and blood made the sword slippery in his hands. He yielded his sword with a vengeance—slashing, cutting, unaware of anything but the battle that raged.

He was no longer the pampered English lord. All semblance of civilization had been stripped from him as he fought, to kill or be killed. There was no fear in his heart, and no remorse for the men who fell beneath his sword.

Soon someone came up behind him, and he swung to meet the foe. "Have done, my friend." Yanni laughed. "Can you not see that you have won the day?"

In a daze, Michael looked down at the dead enemy strewn on the ground at his feet. Today was the first time he had taken a human life, and he suddenly felt sick inside. At the time of battle, he'd thought only of surviving. Now he had time to consider his actions. He turned away from the tribesmen who were stripping the dead of their possessions.

"The first time is always the hardest," Yanni told him with great insight into what he was feeling. "But do not waste your sympathy on these dung beetles, they are of an enemy tribe. They are of the same tribe that brought you into the desert when I rescued you."

"Prince Khaldun's uncle's tribe?"

"Sidi has the loyalty of many tribes, and this one has no honor. They prey on caravans and think nothing of killing for profit."

The leader of the caravan came forward, bowing several times before Michael, and holding out a small open chest, filled with gold coins. Michael didn't understand what the man was saying, so he turned to Yanni to translate.

The captain of the guard laughed and took the chest, placing it in Michael's hand. "He calls you Akhdar 'em Akraba, the green-eyed scorpion. He says your sting is deadly and your name will be feared by all that hear it. He begs you to take this small token of his gratitude."

Michael shook his head and pushed the chest away. "Tell him I don't want his gratitude or his treasure."

"You must take it, to refuse would be an insult to him." Yanni laughed. "This poor excuse for a man will tell everyone how the green-eyed scorpion saved his caravan. By the time he reaches Cairo, you will be legend."

Michael reluctantly took the chest and placed it in his saddlebag. He then dismounted and walked a little way from the caravan, praying for a breeze to cool him and carry away the stench of death. Uncapping his flask, he dashed water in his face and took a deep drink.

He didn't feel like a legend. He only hoped he wouldn't be sick.

Drawing in another deep breath, he felt the heat scorch his lungs. When he was able to face the others, he walked back down the hill to his horse. If the Jebeliya knew what he was feeling, none spoke of it.

While Yanni traded with the caravan, Michael sat beneath a makeshift tent he'd constructed by draping his flowing robe over his sword. He was aware of the many glances of respect that were cast his way, but he didn't feel he deserved the admiration. He could only wonder what his father would think of him if he'd witnessed the battle.

Michael was glad when the transactions had been

completed and they were on their way back to Kamar Ginena. He had learned something about himself today— he was capable of killing without mercy. He only hoped he never had to do it again.

Michael would never know how it had happened, but news of the battle had preceded the returning heroes, and the people of the city lined the roadway, cheering as they entered the gates. Long after Michael had entered the palace, he could still hear the people chanting, "El Akraba the scorpion, the scorpion."

Khaldun was not among the throng that welcomed them, so Michael surmised the prince must be out of the city. He went directly to his room in the palace and bathed, scrubbing away the blood, but he could not rid himself of the disgust he felt for what he had done.

Michael lay back on the bed and closed his eyes. He'd become as ruthless as any bedouin that roamed the desert. He was no better than Sheik Sidi Ahmed.

Hearing a knock on his door, he moved off the bed and opened it to find Khaldun's body servant. "My prince has asked if you will accompany me to the royal quarters. The king desires to meet you."

Michael pulled on his robe and followed the servant, happy that Khaldun's father was well enough to receive a visitor.

He was led into a room were sunlight poured through stained glass, sending sparkling prisms dancing against the white walls.

Prince Khaldun came forward to greet Michael and escorted him to the man who was propped against pillows on an arched divan. Michael knew the veiled woman beside him would be Khaldun's mother, the queen. The king was pale, and his eyes were drawn in pain.

"Welcome, Lord Michael, friend of my son," he said in

a surprisingly boisterous voice. "Since you are a brother to my son, that makes you a son to me."

Michael stood before the man, knowing he had been great in his time, because power still emanated from him even in his weakened condition.

"You do me honor, Your Majesty."

"We were told of your actions in defending the caravan, and your exploits will be spoken of for many years to come." He smiled, easing the harshness of his expression. "I am told they have placed a title on you."

"It would seem so, Your Majesty. But I felt no pride in what I did. Condemn me for speaking frankly, sire, but I feel only shame."

The king shook his head. "It is well that you feel this way. A man should never grow so hardened that he finds pleasure in the taking of a life. Although many do, even some among my people." The king shifted his weight and grimaced in pain. "However, I would ask you to put your remorse aside because the same people you killed are indeed the people who hold your father captive. They are ruthless and shameless. You need not mourn their passing."

Michael's eyes widened. "You know where my father is being held?"

"Our spies tell us of a tall Englishman who is imprisoned at Caldoia, the stronghold of the traitor, Sidi Ahmed."

Michael tried to speak, but he had to catch his breath before he found his voice. "Are your spies certain it is my father?"

"I am assured it is the duke of Ravenworth."

"Is he well?"

"Of this I have no knowledge. But I do not think even Sidi would dare harm so important a man."

"I must go there at once, Your Majesty. I must try to reason with Sheik Sidi and ask him to release my father."

"No! This you cannot do. Do I not know that my brother-in-law would like to capture you also? Did he not already try and fail?"

"Then what shall I do?"

"You will bide your time. We will find a way that is the least dangerous to your father. I warn you, if we are precipitate, my brother-in-law will most certainly kill your father."

"I have been patient, Your Majesty, and I will continue to be so, if you think it best. Just to know my father is alive is more than I hoped. I must send word to my mother at once."

"Yes, you must write your mother. But before you leave, may I present my queen to you? She wishes to thank the man who saved our son."

Michael stood speechless as the queen rose and threw off her veil. She was dressed in yellow silk, with dark hair and dark eyes. She must once have been a great beauty, for she was still a handsome woman. "I am . . . honored to know . . . you, brother of my son," she said haltingly. "And I am . . . grateful to you that I still have a son." Keeping her face uncovered, she sat beside her husband and smiled at Michael.

Khaldun kissed his mother's cheek and joined Michael. "My mother does not speak English, but she learned these words so she could say them to you."

"I am greatly honored," Michael said, bowing respectfully before the queen. He had heard enough about Moslem customs to know that a man who was not a family member would never be allowed to see the faces of their women, and especially not the face of a member of the royal family.

The king spoke again. "We honor you further, Lord Michael, as a father honors a well-loved son. From this day forward, you will have the privilege of dining with our family, addressing our women, and sitting in our presence."

Michael was filled with emotion when he glanced at Khaldun. He saw pride in his friend's eyes, and he knew their bond went beyond friendship. They were truly like brothers.

"There is another reason you are here tonight. I would ask a favor of you, Michael," Khaldun said expectantly, as if he were going to ask something of great importance.

"Anything you want from me, you have only to ask."

"My bride, Princess Yasmin, will begin her journey from Sawarka in one week. I would be pleased if you would lead the honor guard to escort her here."

Michael recalled Khaldun talking to him about his distaste for the marriage that had been arranged for him as a child. He could see the misery in his friend's eyes.

"I will be pleased to bring your bride to you, my friend."

The king smiled. "Go and make preparations, my sons. I will see Khaldun married before I die." His face softened as his eyes met his wife's. "What a celebration we will have at this long-awaited wedding. At last our family will be united with the family of my old friend, Sheik Hakeem."

It was much later, when Michael walked with Khaldun in the garden. There was distress in the prince's eyes as he paced back and forth.

"My father is old and does not understand how I feel. His love for my mother was so great that he took only her as a wife—I believe I shall have many wives," he said bitterly. "The first time I marry to please him. The rest of the times I marry to please myself."

"Khaldun, perhaps you will love this woman who is to be your wife."

"I already told you that the Sawarka tribe, to which my bride belongs, often tattoo their faces. They are also nomadic and very restless, moving from one place to another when the grass gives out for their sheep and camels. I fear I shall never love as you love the Lady Mallory."

"I don't—oh, yes—well, there are different kinds of love, Khaldun," Michael said bracingly.

"Yes, there is the love I have for my mother and father, and there is the love they expect me to feel for a woman that I have never known, a woman who will sit beside me all my days. Maybe I shall order her never to remove her veil in my presence. Even when I must take her to my bed." He was thoughtful for a moment. "Especially when I must take her to my bed."

Michael found it hard not to laugh because he knew his friend was being serious. "Why don't you tell your father that you don't want to marry Princess Yasmin?"

"Because life without honor is useless, and it is better to die than live without honor. My father gave his word to her father, Sheik Hakeem—my father's word is the same as mine."

"I don't understand how marrying a woman you have never seen could be called honorable."

"Let us not dwell on unhappiness, my friend. Let us not be gloomy today. Let us instead celebrate your victories."

In that moment, Michael remembered another prediction the old Gypsy woman had made in London. She'd told him he would know great friendship. In this, too, she'd been right.

Chapter 15

Mallory was growing weary of her solitary life. The only one who spoke English in the house was Safwat, and his knowledge of the language was limited.

She had gone to the consulate and spoken to Mr. Abrams, but he had no notion of when her parents would be returning. She inquired if he had heard from Lord Michael, but he had not. In fact, he was certain his lordship was not in Cairo. The only advice the man could give her was to return to England since she was unchaperoned. No one understood her predicament.

So the endless days stretched before Mallory. Each night, she ate a solitary dinner and spent another evening alone. She had reread the three books she'd brought with her several times. She had been excited when she found several books and manuals in her father's office, but they'd turned out to be a disappointment since they were written in Arabic.

Mallory's thoughts turned to Lord Michael. She wondered if his wound had healed properly, and if he was taking care of himself. She still feared for his safety.

Mallory received a letter from Mrs. Wickett. It seemed she and her husband were returning to England. Sergeant Wickett had received a promotion and would be stationed in Bath. Mallory had the strongest urge to write and ask if she could accompany them.

But then, where would she go when she got back to England? Cousin Phoebe had already moved to the house her father had left her, and couldn't support another person on her small income. Mallory knew that she couldn't return to Stoneridge with Sir Gerald lurking about. No, it seemed she must stay in Egypt and wait for her parents to return.

On her daily walk, Mallory had just reached the pond at the edge of the garden, when a black-robed man approached her. She noticed the gate leading to the alleyway was open, and drew back, her heart pounding. The robe did not disguise the man's wide girth. His beard was dark, and his eyes were almost black.

"Who are you?" Mallory asked through trembling lips, her eyes darting back toward the house and safety.

"A thousand pardons, lady, I did not mean to frighten you," the man said ingratiatingly.

She considered calling out for Safwat, but he was too far away to hear. Bravely, she faced the intruder. "You have no right to be in my father's garden. What do you want here?"

"Lady, I'm sent by one who knows you. He begs that I bring you to him right away."

"My father sent you?"

"No, lady. I was sent by Akhdar 'em Akraba. He has asked that you come to him at once."

Mallory looked at him suspiciously, and took a frightened step backwards. "I know of no one by that name."

"Perhaps you know him by the name of the green-eyed
scorpion."

"If you don't leave at once, I'll call for help. I don't
know you, or the person of whom you speak."

He held up his arms. "Lady, he's the Inglizi you know
well, the son of the great lord."

"Lord Michael?"

He grinned. "That is right, lady. The lord is hurt and
needs your assistance."

She still didn't believe him. "Then why didn't you come
to the front and ask for me in a proper manner?"

"The lord has many enemies who want to see him
dead, lady. He is gravely ill and trusts only you to treat
him."

Mallory was undecided. "Where is he?"

"Two days' ride across the desert. We must hurry, lady,
he needs you."

"I'll just inform the servants of my intentions. We can
trust them."

"No. You must come with me now and no one must
know. The lord is in much danger. His fever is high, and
he calls out for you."

Mallory wasn't certain she could trust this man. But
why would he come for her unless Michael had sent for
her?

"I have a fine horse for you to ride and the supplies we
shall need. You will come at once?"

Before she could answer, Safwat appeared down the
walkway. "My lady," he called. "My lady, you have correspondence from your father."

Mallory turned back to speak to the black-robed Arab,
to find that he had disappeared. The only evidence that

he'd been there was the unlatched gate swinging back and forth on its hinges.

At that moment, Mallory was sure that the stranger had been trying to lure her away from the safety of her father's home.

"Safwat, did you see the man who was talking to me?"

He looked puzzled, and then noticed the unlocked gate. "You were alone when I arrived." He moved to the gate to discover the lock had been broken, and his brow furrowed with worry. "I will have a new lock placed on the gate right away. I believe that since you saved the life of the young lord your movements have been watched. It may be dangerous for you to walk in the garden alone."

Mallory raised her head, her blue eyes shining with anger. "I will not be a prisoner in my parents' home. And I'll not whimper in a corner like some frightened animal. No one is going to frighten me."

"It is wise to know when to be frightened, my lady. It is my duty to keep you safe until your mother and father return."

She smiled at Safwat and followed him to the house. He was right, of course, she must not take chances. After all, she was a woman in a strange land, with no one to protect her.

When she entered the house, Safwat handed her the letter from her father. She quickly opened it and began to read.

Mallory,

Word has reached your mother and me that you are in Cairo. I cannot imagine what Phoebe was thinking to send you to us without our permission. As you have, I'm sure, already gathered, Cairo is no place for a young girl. Your mother and I shall return within two weeks, and at that time, we will discuss what is to be done with you. We had thought a nice girls' school in London is where we should place you. Until we return, it would be best if you remained inside the compound and obey Safwat and Inna.

Mallory read the letter a second time, with a heavy heart. They still thought of her as a child. Her father's letter had been cold and dispassionate. He hadn't even bothered to sign his name.

"Safwat," she called, hurrying to her room.

He came into the hallway. "Yes, my lady?"

"Have the carriage made ready. I'm going to the British consulate to speak to them about my passage home."

"Yes, my lady. But if someone is watching you, would it not be better for my wife to dress you in something of hers so you will escape detection?"

Mallory considered his suggestion. If the man who had broken into the garden was still watching the house, it might be wise to disguise her appearance.

"I believe your idea is sound. Please ask your wife to come to my room, and I'd appreciate borrowing her apparel."

Safwat nodded at her good judgment. "It will be safer for you that way."

When Mallory saw the lovely red robe with gold embroidery at the hem, she realized that Inna had offered her finest garment. When Inna helped her dress and belted the waist, she draped the long black burka over Mallory's head. The woman smiled happily as she showed Mallory how to pull the bottom part over her lower face, so that only her eyes would show.

When she looked in the mirror, Mallory nodded in satisfaction. "Even my Cousin Phoebe wouldn't know me in this." She turned to Safwat's wife. "Thank you."

Inna smiled and nodded, backing out of the room.

Mallory suddenly felt a surge of excitement throb through her body. Nothing like this could ever have happened to her in England. She could go about the streets of Cairo just like the other faceless women, and no one would know she wasn't one of them. Why hadn't she thought of this before?

Thomas Abrams glanced up at the Arab woman who entered his office. "Who allowed you in here?"

Mallory dropped the veil and watched the color drain from his face.

"Lady Mallory—but what—surely you haven't taken up the native dress!"

"I had to talk to you, and I found it necessary to come in disguise." She watched his eyes widen, and then his lips thinned in disapproval.

"This should not be permitted, Lady Mallory. What will your mother and father say when they return?"

"But my reason for wearing native dress is a sound one." She explained to him how the man had come into her garden and tried to lure her into the desert.

"This is intolerable. I intend to lodge a protest with the viceroy this very day. When an English woman isn't even safe in her own home, it's time to take action."

"I don't think that will do any good, Mr. Abrams. What I don't understand is why the man went to so much trouble to trap me."

"Who will ever understand these people?" he said pettishly. "They have no love for us English. We try to educate them and teach them a better way of life, and what do we get for our trouble?"

"Mr. Abrams, the Egyptians were a great civilization when we were still running around in animal skins. I hardly think they need our guidance."

He looked at her as if she'd lost her senses, but merely snorted his disapproval. "Nevertheless, one of them tried to abduct you, you can't deny that. I can't think what the consul will do about this when he returns. I would advise you to remain indoors until your father and mother return. Meanwhile, I'll post two guards to watch the house."

"If you wish." She moved to stand beneath the picture of the queen. "I'm concerned about Lord Michael. Have you still had no word from him?"

"Nothing. You'd think he'd have the courtesy to keep us informed of his whereabouts. I, for one, will be glad when the consul returns, so he can take command. Lord Michael is arrogant, undisciplined, and most unappreciative. I did all I could to locate his father, but did he thank me? No, he only accused me of incompetence."

In this, Mallory was inclined to agree with Lord Michael. The man was certainly incapable of representing the Crown. He had no liking for the people he had been sent to serve. It was no wonder the Egyptians didn't like foreigners, if Mr. Abrams was any indication of the disrespect they endured from the English.

"I must return home now. You will inform me if you hear anything from Lord Michael?"

"The only thing I've heard, and I'm not inclined to believe it, is that he's gone native. Rumors persist that he's something of a legend, and the Arabs call him Akhdar 'em Akraba."

"The green-eyed scorpion," Mallory said.

"Yes, how did you know?"

"Because the Arab who came into my garden referred to Lord Michael by that name."

"Astounding. I don't know what to make of this."

"I am going home now, Mr. Abrams," Mallory said, moving to the door.

"Very well. I'll have the soldiers at your home by sundown, m'lady."

As Mallory stepped into the coach, she didn't see the man huddled in the shadows, or the signal he gave to three men pulling a vegetable cart down the street.

At that moment, the horses reared on their hind legs, bringing the carriage to a sudden halt. Mallory glanced at the vegetable cart that was overturned in front of them. She thought nothing of it, until a man jumped at Safwat and shoved him into the street. A second man climbed into the coach beside Mallory.

He held a knife at her throat and muttered a quick command. "Do not call out, lady. Do exactly as I say."

She recognized the man who had confronted her earlier in the garden. "What do you want?"

"It is not for you to ask," came the sharp reply. The man made no attempt to be polite. "You will do only what you are told."

"But, why do—"

"Do not speak!" he ordered.

The carriage sped away, and after many twists and turns down narrow streets, they entered a courtyard where heavy gates closed behind them.

"My father will hear of this," Mallory said, in what she hoped was a calm voice, for she was terribly frightened.

"You will be well out of Cairo before your father hears of your fate." The man roughly tied a scarf over her mouth and smiled in a satisfied manner when he was certain she could not speak. He then pulled her headdress in place so no one would see she had been gagged. "That will keep you silent, Inglizi woman."

She was jerked from the carriage and hurried to a waiting horse. The man lifted her onto the saddle, and two other riders closed in around them. The gates were flung open, and they rode through the streets of Cairo, heading toward the desert.

Mallory realized their plan had been carefully thought out and perfectly executed. She dared not think about what they wanted with her.

As they rode away from the city, she glanced back over her shoulder. She had faith that Safwat would go to the British consulate for help, but she couldn't find comfort in the knowledge that Mr. Abrams was her only hope of being rescued.

Even that faint hope diminished when they reached the desert and were soon lost in a wasteland of sand dunes.

Chapter 16

ichael rode at the head of fifty Jebeliya warriors. They passed by scrub-covered sand dunes, sighting an occasional oasis where they would rest from the heat and fill their waterskins. At night they slept beneath the stars. When they reached the hottest part of the desert, they slept during the day and traveled by night.

For four days, they moved steadily toward the coastal mountains until at last the sand dunes changed to craggy cliffs. They traveled fast, but on the homeward journey, it would take longer, because many in the wedding party would be riding camels and not the swift Arabian steeds favored by the Jebeliya.

Michael guided his horse through a deep valley, his eyes riveted on the highest point of the mountain. They rode past an abandoned monastery and into the high mountains, where the nights were cold and the days were as hot as the inside of a furnace.

By the eighth day, they encountered several riders, who welcomed them with high-pitched yells and by joyfully firing their rifles into the air. This was to be their escort to the Sawarka camp.

As they entered the camp, Michael saw groves of cypress and tamarisk trees. It was hard for him to comprehend how a race of people could survive for centuries in this isolated and hostile land. But they had more than survived, they were thriving.

As they moved on through the camp, the exuberance over their arrival mounted, and many people rushed forward to greet them with welcoming smiles. Michael saw pride on the faces of the Sawarka bedouin, a trait that he was to encounter over and over in this land.

When he dismounted, he was led to a huge black tent in the center of the encampment. He came face-to-face with a bejeweled man with a ready smile and a twinkle in his dark eyes. Michael knew this was Princess Yasmin's father.

"Welcome with honor, Akhdar 'em Akraba," Sheik Hakeem greeted him. "We have heard much about your cunning. Enter—enter, and relieve your hunger and satisfy your thirst. You have come far. Rest in my home."

When Michael entered the tent, he found to his surprise that it was larger than it appeared from outside. His feet sank into a rich Turkish rug, and there were low gilded tables and velvet cushions on which to recline.

"Sit, sit," Sheik Hakeem offered. "We will converse while we eat."

When both men were seated, Hakeem clapped his hands, and three veiled women immediately appeared through a curtained-off area, bringing food and drink. While they ate, Hakeem spoke about the glowing tales he'd heard of the green-eyed scorpion.

"I believe I should inform you that the accounts are

greatly exaggerated. Every time the tale is repeated, it grows in magnitude. I can assure you I am neither a warrior nor a hero."

Hakeem waved Michael's denial away with a jeweled hand. "Are not all heroes part fantasy in the mind of less brave men? We need our heroes, Akhdar 'em Akraba." His dark eyes settled on Michael. "I know why you have come to our land. There is much talk about a great one being held by Sidi Ahmed. This is your father, is it not?"

"Yes. Do you know if he still lives?"

"It is difficult to smuggle information out of Caldoia, but it is said that the Turk, Sidi, guards his prisoner well."

Michael stared out the tent opening to the desert beyond. "I will find a way into Caldoia—this I swear."

Hakeem stroked his beard thoughtfully. "Perhaps in this I can help you. My bedouin are allowed in Caldoia if they remain only in the marketplace. Of course, they always take Sidi a gift of great value and leave the city before sunset."

Hakeem saw Michael's hopeful look, and continued, musingly. "It would be dangerous for me to smuggle you inside." When he saw Michael's face fall, he smiled and clapped Michael on the back. "You will find that my bedouin like danger. Would the green-eyed scorpion care to venture forth with my bedouin?"

This was what Michael had been waiting to hear—a way into the forbidden city. "I will consider it an honor to ride with your people. But I would not want to put men at risk."

"Risk adds spice to an otherwise dull life. I would rejoice if I could tweak Sidi's nose."

"I could go immediately after I have delivered your daughter to Prince Khaldun."

"Not so hasty, my young friend. First, preparations must be made, that will take time. Also, do you remember I mentioned we must provide Sidi with a valuable gift?" He shrugged. "I have recently married off my eldest daughter, and now my youngest is to be married. Poor father that I am, to pay bride's price for two daughters. I can hardly be expected to present a gift to Sidi as well."

Michael smiled. "If you will allow, I shall provide the gift."

Hakeem's eyes sparkled. "And do I not have a gift that will widen Sidi's eyes? You must see this." He reached behind him and brought out a carved wooden box. Flipping it open, he handed it to Michael. "I will sell you this for a mere trifle."

Michael looked at the knife crafted of turquoise and silver and smiled at the cagey old fox. "How much?"

"Whatever you think is generous."

Michael laughed aloud and reached into the pouch about his waist. He counted out ten gold pieces, and Hakeem nodded in approval. "It is sufficient. Your generosity is second only to your bravery, green-eyed hero."

Michael stared at the old thief with growing respect. "And your wit is only surpassed by your cunning."

Hakeem smiled. "I have a feeling the stories about you are not all that exaggerated."

Again, Hakeem clapped his hands, and a lone veiled woman appeared from behind the curtain. She was dressed in white silk that shimmered in the lantern light.

"I was told, green-eyed one, that you are considered like a brother to Prince Khaldun."

"That is so."

"I was also told you were honored by seeing his mother unveiled."

"This also is true."

"Then behold the face of your brother's wife—behold my daughter, Yasmin." He motioned to the woman, and she dropped the veil.

Michael looked into the softest brown eyes he'd ever seen. They were so luminous he could read the innocence in their depths. Her hair was as black as midnight, and ebony braids entwined with golden ropes. Michael saw that Khaldun's fears had been groundless—Yasmin's face had not been tattooed. She was so lovely, Michael could only smile.

"My brother is a most fortunate man."

Yasmin coyly ducked her head. She had never seen an Inglizi, and she hadn't known that a man could have green eyes. "Can you tell me about my husband? It is said that he honors you above all men."

"I can tell you that Prince Khaldun is loyal, a good warrior, and an imposing prince."

"Yasmin!" her father scolded. "Do not bother our guest with your silly chatter." His words were harsh, but his eyes were soft. He hugged his daughter. "When this one goes, she takes her father's heart with her. I would give her only to a prince."

Michael thought she was indeed a bride worthy of a prince.

"Leave us now, daughter. Lord Michael and I have much to discuss."

After she had taken another quick glance at the man with the green eyes, she moved behind the curtains.

Hakeem leaned toward Michael. "How would you like to go with my men on a raid of a bedouin village that supports Sidi? The devils struck at my cousin's camp ten days ago, and they slaughtered innocent women and children."

"I would be honored to accompany you. But when?"

"We shall strike in the morning. There will be no interference in your duty to Prince Khaldun since you shall return before the wedding party departs for Kamar Ginena."

Michael nodded, knowing the old fox was testing him. "I will go with you, but only if your men do not harm women or children."

"I will instruct them not to do so, but they will take what spoils they can."

"That is acceptable."

"Excellent! You must rest now, for we leave in two hours' time."

"You do understand why I must get to Caldoia without delay?"

"I do. But it is ambitious to face the devil in his lair without being prepared. There are many of the bedouin tribes that would gladly give their lives to see him dead. He is of the Ottoman Turks, and would see all desert dwellers enslaved. He has slowly armed the warlike bedouin so they can rise against us."

"I know. It was my father's mission to discover who was inciting war. Is Sidi Ahmed the one who has been shipping guns into Egypt?"

"He is the one. He once offered us guns, but only if we would fight as his army. I refused him, as have many other tribes. Still, he gathers a large army. Those who accepted his guns are massing in numbers. I believe they will first come against those of us who have opposed him. You can see why it's dangerous for you to go into Caldoia. And you can see why we're prepared to help you."

Michael stood. "I'll bide my time until I enter Caldoia. But don't make me wait too long. If my father is there, every day must be hell for him."

"The guards at the gate look for anything and anyone suspicious," Hakeem warned. "They will surely be looking for you, green-eyed one. But enough of this, for you must rest now. I'll have my servant show you to your tent."

Michael hadn't realized how tired he was. He lay back on the soft lambskin and was soon fast asleep.

He was awakened some time later by a smiling Yanni. "The others are ready to go on the raid. They wait only for you, Lord Michael."

The Sawarka hit the enemy camp just before daybreak. The guards at the outpost had been quickly eliminated, so they were unable to raise an alarm. Hakeem's men rushed the camp, catching the tribe still sleeping.

Michael had thought he'd come only as an observer, but he soon found himself in the heat of the battle. He swung his sword true, and fought like a man possessed. All he could think about was that this tribe was the enemy, they were the tools of Sidi, the man who held his father prisoner. In his mind, every enemy slain was a strike for his father's freedom.

At the end of the battle, bodies littered the camp. Hakeem had kept his word, and none of the women or children had been harmed. They had been allowed to scatter into the desert to hide.

Hakeem had one of the survivors brought before him, because a plan was forming in his mind. The Turks were a superstitious lot, and he would plant a grain of fear in their minds that would grow into a legend. "Ride to your Turkish master and tell him and all his people that the green-eyed scorpion has made him an enemy. Tell the people how Akhdar 'em Akraba's

powers allowed us to come into your camp and overcome you without one casualty because his magic protected us."

The man stood before Hakeem, quaking, his eyes darting about the crowd of faces, looking for the green-eyed
devil. "Kill me now. I do not wish to look upon the face
of the scorpion," he cried.

Michael did not know that Hakeem had used him to
strike fear into the enemy. He dismounted and watched
what he thought was an interrogation of a prisoner. He
was astonished when the man trembled and dropped to
his knees as Michael's eyes met his.

"Surely I have looked upon the face of death!" the man
cried. "I beg you to kill me quickly."

To Michael's surprise, the man crawled to him and
buried his face on the ground. "Mercy, oh, green-eyed
one—have mercy."

Michael jerked the man up and glared at him. "As you
showed mercy to the women and children you have mas-
sacred?"

Hakeem smiled, seeing that the man was now wild
with fear. Unknowingly, Michael had furthered his
scheme. He ordered his men to place the prisoner on a
camel and send him into the desert.

"He will spread the news of your victory today, my
friend," Hakeem told Michael.

"It was not my triumph, but I have slain my father's
enemies."

"Our prisoner will tell of your magic, and that is what
is important. This tribe will think long before attacking
me or my friends."

Michael was not certain what the wily Hakeem would
do next. He liked the old sheik, but he did not completely
trust him.

* * *

Michael remained in the Sawarka camp for two more days, while preparations were made for the bridal journey. In that time, he became acquainted with a way of life that he'd never known existed. The men were continually holding contests, mostly with swords and on horseback. The women seemed to do all the work, while the men trained as warriors.

He doubted that any of Sawarka bedouin could read or write, and yet they had a knowledge about life that was not in any book.

Since coming to the camp, Michael's excitement began to grow. At last he had hope of finding his father. He and Hakeem made plans to enter the city of Caldoia soon after the wedding.

"You should know, Lord Michael, that we cannot just ride in and take your father to freedom. There must be war, and we don't even know the location where your father is being held. We must know this before we attack."

The night before they were to depart for Kamar Ginena, the sheik presented Michael with a gift, a black robe and sword of the Sawarka tribe.

"If you are like a brother to Prince Khaldun, you are like a son to me." He took a huge emerald from his finger and handed it to Michael. "This is to remind you that you are as one with my people." He smiled and clapped Michael on the back. "All who see this ring will know it as mine. Those in Caldoia who see it on your finger will accept you without question as one of my bedouin."

"I cannot take this," Michael insisted. "It's far too valuable."

"Nothing is as valuable as friendship."

Michael had learned much in the Sawarka camp—most of all he had learned to respect the old sheik. While Hakeem had tricked him into buying the silver knife, he had given him a gift of a much greater value.

A rooster crowed, announcing the impending dawn, and already the heat was punishing. Clansmen emerged from their tents to prostrate themselves on the sand for morning prayer.

The camp was filled with the sound of children's laughter as they rose from their beds to begin their appointed chores.

This simple people knew a peace that many would never encounter or understand. If Michael had not gained the friendship of Khaldun, he would never have known this world existed, and he certainly would not have been allowed to walk among them as a trusted friend.

The whole camp turned out to wish the travelers a happy journey. The heavily guarded caravan moved away from the encampment carrying gold, jewels, and the most precious jewel of all, Prince Khaldun's bride.

Slowly, they wound their way past granite hills, and into the ocean of sand. Tirelessly, the camels left their tracks in the desolate wilderness.

As the sun reached its zenith, the desert was strangely silent, but for the tinkling of bells that decorated the camels.

At night, the women's tents were set up within a ring of safety, while the tents of the men were outside that circle. Michael had no contact with the women, except for Yasmin's serving woman, who kept him informed on how the princess was faring.

When the caravan was a day's journey from Kamar

Ginena, Prince Khaldun rode out to meet them. He greeted Michael with enthusiasm, but kept casting furtive glances at the tent that Princess Yasmin occupied.

From behind her filmy veil, Yasmin watched the prince with anxious eyes. She had heard he was fair to look upon, but she could not see his face. She glanced at her servant. "Surely he sits his horse well."

"I see he does, Princess Yasmin."

"He appears to be very tall."

"He sits tall on his horse," the servant agreed.

"If only I could see him, talk to him. I have loved him for so long, but until now he has been faceless. Oh, Abba, I do so want to see his face."

At that moment, Khaldun turned his head, and she saw his finely chiseled features. "Abba, he is beautiful. Will we not have beautiful children?"

"That is so, my princess."

Yasmin lowered her head. "He is too handsome to have only one wife. He will surely take many wives after me."

"That is his right, but you will be head wife and the princess. The lesser wives will honor you, as will Prince Khaldun."

"Yes," Yasmin said sadly. "But I want more than honor, I want his heart."

Michael sat in the shadow of the campfire, staring at his friend. "Well, aren't you going to ask me?"

Khaldun tossed a stone in the fire and watched the sparks fly. "Ask you what?"

"I told you I have seen the face of your bride."

Khaldun's eyes showed his anger. "It isn't right that you should see my bride before me."

Michael suppressed a smile. "It was her father's decision."

"It should not have happened."

Michael became serious. "Princess Yasmin's thoughts were only of you."

Khaldun stood and walked away from camp, and Michael followed him. "The bridegroom squirms," Michael observed.

Khaldun turned to his friend. "You must tell me, I can wait no longer. Is her face tattooed?"

Michael laughed. "I can assure you, it is not. I believe the moment you see her, you will lose your heart, because she is very fair."

"She is passingly pretty?"

"More than passing, I would say."

"I cannot meet her until my father presents her to me."

"That will be tomorrow night. Not so long to wait."

"Do you not yearn for your lady love?"

"I, er, have hardly had time to give her a thought."

"If I loved the one with the red hair and the blue eyes, I would think of nothing but her."

Michael laughed. "Thoughts of another woman could be dangerous when your bride is nearby."

"You are not jealous that I think Lady Mallory is the most beautiful woman I've ever seen?"

"I'm not. Although I believe you exaggerate. She is pretty and she has much spirit, so I suppose you could call her beautiful."

"I say she is beautiful."

Again Michael smiled. "As you wish." Someday he would have to tell his friend that he'd never lost his heart to Lady Mallory, but not until Khaldun was safely married to Princess Yasmin.

allory licked her dry lips, craving a cool drink of water. Didn't these Arabs ever stop? Didn't they ever get thirsty?

Her hands were tied in front of her, and she had to hold on tightly to keep from being unseated from the horse.

They had been riding for three days, stopping only to rest the horses every few hours, and then they would lift her back in the saddle. Each day took her farther from civilization.

At first she'd kept demanding to be released, but one of the men had struck her hard across the face and ordered her to remain silent. After a while, she found it easier to comply. Her eyes were almost swollen shut, and she longed for a cool compress to soothe the pain.

At last they came to an oasis, and she was lifted from the horse and shoved onto the sand. She crawled toward the spring and cupped her hands, raising water to her lips. One of the men grabbed her by the hair and pulled her back.

"Do not drink fast. I will not have a sick woman."

She nodded and eased herself away, taking small sips of water. Once she had satisfied her thirst, she dunked her head in the water, washing the sand from her hair and face.

Mallory looked about her, wondering if the men meant to feed her. One was tending to the horses, and one had walked up on a sand dune, apparently as a lookout. She stood up and stretched her aching muscles. At least she had satisfied her thirst and it was cooler here.

She sat down and braced her back against a date palm and closed her eyes. She was so exhausted that she immediately fell asleep.

When the caravan entered Kamar Ginena, the whole city turned out to greet them. Children ran along beside Princess Yasmin's camel, strewing flower petals along the path. The Jebeliya women smiled and tried to peer past the silk covering for a glimpse of her face.

Prince Khaldun looked more like a man who was about to be executed than a bridegroom. Michael had every confidence that when his friend saw the princess, he would not be so downcast.

When they reached the palace, the princess's bodyguards led her inside and away from curious eyes.

Princess Yasmin entered a world like none she could have imagined, and her heart was filled with joy.

The night finally arrived when Khaldun's bride would be presented to him at a family banquet. The next day would be the wedding, and already there was celebrating in the streets.

Khaldun paced the floor of his bedroom while Michael watched him with a smile on his lips. He couldn't resist baiting the prince.

"I can see why you might be worried since you will be spending the whole of your life with this woman you have never seen."

Khaldun stopped before Michael. "I have already made a decision. After a decent interval of, say, a month, I shall take two other wives, and they will be of my own choosing."

"I, for one, wouldn't want to be burdened with more than one wife," Michael stated. "I have found the female of the species to be jealous and possessive."

"I will not permit such jealousy. A husband must be master of his own house."

"You have much to learn about women, my friend. It's my belief that they are born with the ability to complicate a man's life."

"Does Lady Mallory complicate your life?"

Michael was thoughtful. "Most assuredly. But I also have to admit that without her help, I would probably be dead. I call her my angel."

"You have not said when you and Lady Mallory will marry. If you love her, should you not make her your wife as soon as possible?"

"My only goal at the moment is finding and gaining my father's release. Until that is accomplished, I want no woman in my life."

Michael picked up Khaldun's red-and-silver robe and held it while he slipped into it. "I believe we should go now. You don't want to be late for your own wedding banquet."

"I would rather not go," Khaldun said with despair showing in his eyes. "Tell me again that her face is not tattooed. It is most important that you speak the truth—if she is ugly, admit it so I can be prepared."

Michael tried not to laugh, and he pretended serious-ness. "You will soon see for yourself."

"I must know before I see her, so I will not shame myself and my father by turning away in disgust."

"Her face in not tattooed, and she is most pleasing to the eye."

"You would not say this if it were not true? You would not try to spare my feelings?"

"I would not," Michael assured him. "Let us join the banquet, so you can determine her worthiness for yourself."

The great hall was filled with dignitaries who had gath-ered from neighboring tribes to join in the festivities.

Michael, seated at the high table next to Prince Khaldun, was glad to see that the king looked so well. The ruler was in a jovial mood and kept everyone laugh-ing at his wit.

Yasmin, draped in shimmering gold, sat silently beside her father. Because of her veil, no one could see that her eyes never left the prince's face.

Michael noticed that Khaldun ate little, often looking at the woman wearing the veil.

"The bridegroom is showing his nervousness," Michael whispered to him, enjoying himself. "What happened to the fearless warrior who faced danger without flinching? Can one small woman steal your bravery?"

The prince merely lowered his head, feeling even more miserable. "I sit within throwing distance of my bride, and yet I do not know her, nor do I wish to know her."

"You will meet her after you dine. Perhaps that's why you prolong the meal."

"I would rather feel the bite of a scorpion than see what is behind that veil."

*   *   *

Khaldun and Yasmin stood before their fathers, both staring straight ahead and not at each other. The only people present in the great hall were family members and Michael.

At last the king took Princess Yasmin's hand and placed it on Prince Khaldun's. He felt his son stiffen and knew what he was feeling. "It is allowed that the two of you may be alone for a brief moment, so you can become acquainted. The moon is bright and the sweet smell of hibiscus fills the garden. Walk there, my children, and talk with each other for the first time."

Khaldun looked down at the dainty hand in his and wanted to fling it away. His bow was rigid. "Shall we walk in the garden?" he asked stiffly.

A soft voice answered breathlessly. "Yes, please."

They moved out the door while the two fathers smiled and nodded their heads. "Soon we will have grandchildren to comfort us in our old age," the king said with feeling.

Sheik Hakeem hooked his thumbs in the sash around his waist and looked with pride at his friend. "I already have seventeen grandchildren."

"Ah, yes, my friend, but I have only one wife, while you have four. And I have only my son and his two sisters, while you have seven sons and sixteen daughters."

"Yoo, but none are as dear to me as my little Yasmin."

Yasmin could see the anger in Khaldun's eyes, and it pierced her heart. She had not thought that he might not want to marry her. Perhaps he loved another and resented the fact that she was to be his number-one wife.

"The garden is lovely. Kamar Ginena is truly a moon garden and wondrous to behold. I have never seen anything as magnificent as the palace. I will be happy to live here with you, Prince Khaldun."

He dropped her hand. "You will not miss your nomadic life?"

"Since I was seven, and my mother told me that I was to become the bride of a great prince, I have dreamed of this time. I am happy to be here."

"You have an advantage over me, Yasmin, you know what I look like."

"Then it is time you looked upon my face. I have also been afraid of this moment, fearing you would not like me."

She reached up and removed the gold tassels that circled her head and slowly raised the translucent veil, while Khaldun stood transfixed.

First he saw the full lips and then a delicate nose. He caught his breath as he looked into deep brown eyes that were shining and soft. Her brows were gently arched. His heart stopped beating, and he could only stare at her.

"I feared you would think me ugly." She ducked her head. "I realized today that you do not love me as I love you."

He reached out his hand and raised her chin, while his heart swelled with pride in her beauty. Oh, she was an enchanting creature. "You love me?" he asked in wonder.

"I cannot remember a time when I did not love you," she admitted shyly. "At first I loved you as a child loves an older brother, then I loved you as a woman. Please say I have not disappointed you."

"No, Yasmin, you have not disappointed me. I consider myself a very fortunate man to have you as my wife."

Tears gathered in her eyes. "If this were not true, you would not say it, would you?"

He cupped her face in his hands. "You have my promise there will only be truth between us."

As he bent his dark head and gently kissed away her

tears, he felt her small body tremble. His heart was singing—was it possible for love to come so quickly? he wondered. Already the memory of the flaming-haired Lady Mallory was fading from his mind.

The wedding was private, with only close friends and relatives in attendance.

"Two great families joined together," Hakeem said with pride.

"Our friendship is sealed for all time," the king said. "If ever the Sawarka is attacked by enemies, or are in any trouble, the Jebeliya will come to your defense."

"That is also true if you are in trouble. Let it be a vow between us since the same blood will run in the veins of our grandchildren from this union."

In a bed draped with translucent silk, Princess Yasmin came to her husband. He took her hand and gently pulled her to him.

"I tremble at the thought of holding you in my arms," he said, brushing his face against her sweet-smelling hair.

Yasmin had yearned for this night for so long, now that it was here, she suddenly lost her shyness. She pulled away from him and slowly and deliberately removed the silken gown, allowing it to drop from her fingers.

He stared at her, unable to speak as she took his hand and placed it on her face. "My body and my mind were formed so they would give you pleasure. I will never turn away from you, and you will always have my heart."

He was filled with her loveliness. His hand moved over her soft skin that was the color of golden honey. "Yasmin, I could never have imagined that you would be this beautiful."

"I always wanted to be pretty for you. Everything I learned was to please you." She moved his hand down her neck to her breasts. "Do I please you?"

He closed his eyes, his heart too full to speak.

"Feel how my heart is beating?" she whispered, wishing the tears had not gathered in her eyes. "It beats so hard I can scarcely breathe."

His hand began to circle her breasts, but she pulled it away and slid it to her smooth stomach. "I was built to receive you and to bear your children."

Khaldun felt love so strong it frightened him. Gently, he pulled her against his body, and she melted against him. "Your mouth," he murmured, "was made for my kisses."

"Yes," she said, as they both drifted onto the marriage bed.

Chapter 18

ichael was in the stables with Sheik Hakeem, making plans to leave for Caldoia within the week. He was to pose as a Syrian merchant, and Hakeem's men would accompany him.

"You must enter the city on a camel," Hakeem said, leading one of the humped animals out of the fenced area where they were kept. "If you are to pass as a merchant, you must look the part."

"I have ridden a camel on occasion, but I find it uncomfortable," Michael said, looking with aversion at the beast. "I have no liking for the animal."

"And he has no liking for you. But have no fear, my friend. By the time you reach Caldoia, your backside and the camel's hump will be well acquainted." His eyes became hard. "I await the day we bring Sidi down."

"If my father is his prisoner, I will find him. I don't know how, but I will."

"Again, I would ask you to be patient, my young friend. We who oppose Sidi are growing stronger with each passing day. We have little time to find and free your father. For the war will soon begin. You must gain your father's release before the battle, or he will surely be killed. Sidi will want no proof left that he held your father captive."

Michael thought of the impossible task that lay before him. "We don't even know exactly where he is being held."

"Does not your religion say that the earth was created in one week? Surely you can deliver your father in twice that time. Let us pray that Allah will be on our side."

Hakeem turned his attention to Prince Khaldun, who was hurrying toward them. "It's time my son-in-law emerged from the bedroom. I thought we would never see him again. My little Yasmin has surely found favor with him, Allah be praised."

Michael frowned, seeing the worried look on Khaldun's face—something was wrong.

Khaldun hurried to him and clutched his robe. "I have grave news for you, Michael."

"Has something happened to my father?"

"No. It is Lady Mallory."

Michael stared at his friend. "What has happened to her?"

"While I had my men watching you, I also had two men watching Lady Mallory. I feared your enemies would become hers. It seems I was right."

"Tell me what's happened," Michael asked urgently. "Where is she?"

"She was captured by my uncle's men."

"But why?"

"These are questions we will ask when we find them.

Ali and Fizal followed the men into the desert until they were certain where they were taking her. Fizal stays near them, while Ali came to report to me."

"Where are they taking her?"

"They ride in the direction of Caldoia. I do not have to tell you what will happen to her if she falls into the hands of my uncle. She is very beautiful and will be treated far differently than they treat your father."

"Have they hurt her?" Michael asked grimly.

"Ali says not. But they are as low as the sand flea and would have harmed her except they fear my uncle's wrath. I am sure their orders were to bring her to him unharmed. Ali does say they do not often feed her and that they seldom give her water."

Michael clenched his fists. He could not bear to think of Mallory in the hands of those murderous thieves. "We must go after her at once."

"Yes," Khaldun said. "If we hurry, we can intercept them before they reach the city. I know a way over the mountains that will save two days."

"Let's leave immediately," Michael said.

"We must first choose the men we will take with us, then we will need supplies. They will not escape us," Khaldun assured him. "But one does not go into the desert unprepared."

"I will ride along with you," Hakeem said, smiling. "I will enjoy a good fight. I do not think we will need anyone but the three of us and your man Ali to guide us."

Michael raised his face to the scorching sun that was like a blazing, white-hot fire in the sky. How long someone with Mallory's delicate skin could endure the blistering heat, he could only imagine.

"Let us make haste," he urged. "We can't be certain they won't harm her."

* * *

Mallory hung her head, allowing her long hair to shade her face. She was so hot and thirsty, so tired. She had ceased caring about where her captors were taking her. If only she could have a drink of water and a shaded place to sleep. She closed her eyes, imagining she was at Stoneridge, riding across cool, green meadows. In her mind, she stopped beside the sparkling pond that divided her father's land from Sir Gerald's, and drank deeply of the water.

But harsh reality brought her back to the present. She called out to her tormenters. "Water, please. I must have water. I am so thirsty."

One of the men came to her and pushed a waterskin at her. When she eagerly reached for it, he pulled it back, laughing at her attempt. "Beg me for the water," he said, grinning.

Mallory tossed her head and looked at him. "I would die of thirst before I begged you for anything."

His eyes became hard, and he clamped her wrist painfully. "You will not be so haughty when Sheik Sidi has you in his grip." The man ran his hand down Mallory's cheek. "My master has a preference for women with pale skin." He took her chin in his grip and turned her face from side to side. "I must admit you are a rare jewel. He will pay us much for you because you are the woman of the Akhdar 'em Akraba."

"I don't know what you're talking about. I am no one's woman. I don't even know the man of whom you speak."

"You talk with a false tongue. Did I not see him go into your house and remain until you healed his wound? You must be his woman."

Mallory knew he was talking about Michael, but she

thought it best to pretend ignorance. "Where are you taking me?" she demanded.

"It will do no harm for me to tell you. We are going to Caldoia. Until Sheik Sidi Ahmed returns and decides your fate, you will be placed in one of the cells in the west tower, where the great Inglizi lord is imprisoned. If you think the desert is bad, wait until you are locked in that rat-infested pesthole."

Mallory turned away, her eyes wide with apprehension. She was certain that the man spoke of Michael's father. Her suspicions were soon confirmed.

"I think the green-eyed scorpion will come when he learns we have you. He will come for you, as well as his father."

She blinked her eyes, hoping she had not been too long in the sun to comprehend his meaning. She asked, "You have Lord Michael's father?"

"Have I not said so?" He seemed to take pleasure in boasting of his plans. "We have baited the trap for the green-eyed one you call Lord Michael. You will be the bait that will draw him to us. They say that his magic is very powerful, but my master will conquer him. Sheik Sidi has offered much gold to the man who captures the green-eyed devil."

"I told you I am not his lady. I hardly know him. He will not come for me."

"Do not take me for a fool, and ask no more questions. It is enough that you know that the scorpion will soon be my master's prisoner and suffer the death of a thousand stings."

He released Mallory, and she fell back on the sand, but quickly scrambled to her feet, facing him defiantly. "I'll see you in hell before I help you capture Lord Michael."

"We do not need your help, lady, to lure your lord into our trap."

She turned away from him, feeling sick inside. "He will not be as easily fooled as you think."

"No, but he will be crazed when he learns we have you, and this will make him act rashly, I think."

She closed her eyes and huddled against the rough sheepskin blanket. What the man didn't know was that Michael would not come after her—no one would. She would be lost forever with no one to care. She thought of Michael's father, who had been in the grip of such an unscrupulous man, and feared for him.

London

Kassidy ripped open the letter from Michael while the rest of the family watched anxiously. In a clear voice, she began to read.

"Dearest Mother,
It is with a light heart that I inform you that Father is alive. He is being held prisoner by a man named Sheik Sidi Ahmed. I have many friends here in Egypt who are willing to help me gain his release. I am well and find much to admire in this land. I ask for your prayers for Father and myself. If God in his infinite mercy sees fit, we shall all soon be reunited. Take care of yourself and do not worry if you do not hear from me for a time.
  Your loving son,
    Michael"

Tears swam in Kassidy's eyes, and Arrian ran to her and took her in her arms. "He's all right, Mother, Father's alive! Soon they will both be home."

"Yes," Kassidy said, her voice trembling with emotion. "Soon they will be home." She moved to the window and pulled aside the draperies, watching the snow drift earthward. "But they will not be home for Christmas."

"Then perhaps for the New Year."

"There is something different about your brother, I can feel it in his words."

"What is different?" Arrian asked puzzled. "And how can you tell that from a letter?"

"I don't know. It's as if he were another person."

Arrian took her mother's hand. "Come, dearest, let us dress warmly and go for a ride. Perhaps we can stop at the church and say a prayer for Father and Michael."

"Yes," Kassidy said in desperation. "Let us do that now." She looked at her daughter, who had been her strength through this ordeal. "I shall also give thanks that I have you, Arrian." She looked at her son-in-law. "And you, Warrick—what would I have done without you?"

Michael lay prone on a sand dune that gave him a view of the camp where Mallory was being held prisoner. He raised the spyglass to his eyes and scanned the area. "How many did you say there were guarding her?" he asked, glancing at Khaldun.

"Three."

"I see only two. And there is no sign of Mallory."

Khaldun pointed to the small black tent. "I believe she will be within that shelter."

Michael glanced toward the sun that was just going down, and it looked as if the desert sky was on fire. "We should hit them just before morning. There will be only a half-moon tonight, and our black robes will help us blend into the darkness."

Khaldun smiled. "You are thinking more and more like an Arab every day. How will you function when you return to London?"

"I've wondered that myself. I am not the same man I was when I came to Egypt."

"I have noticed this also, my friend. You have a strength and courage that will never leave you. They were always a part of you. You just never had need of them before."

Mallory huddled near the far wall of the tent, watching the two men roll out their blankets upon the sand. She trembled to think what was in their minds when they looked at her with leering smiles.

Each day it grew harder and harder to climb into the saddle. Her wrists were rubbed raw from the ropes that bound her, and her garments were nothing more than filthy rags. Her hair was hopelessly matted, and she doubted any amount of brushing would remove the tangles. She closed her eyes, thinking how luxurious a bath would feel.

If only she could sleep, for in sleep there was forgetfulness. But the misery of her situation robbed her of rest. At last, she did drift off, but by then it was almost morning.

She was jarred from a deep sleep by a bloodcurdling yell. Had she dreamed it? Surely nothing human could make such a sound. She scrambled to her knees, trying to see into darkness. She heard the men stirring and murmuring among themselves. It was apparent they were as puzzled by the disturbance as she was.

As much as she feared her captors, she feared the unknown more. She huddled in the darkness while Sidi's men grabbed up their rifles and faded into the shadows.

She could hear gunfire, cries of pain, and then silence. Trembling, she waited, too frightened to move. At last a dark figure entered the tent, and she clamped her hand over her mouth to keep from crying out.

"Lady Mallory, are you here?"

She recognized Lord Michael's voice. "Oh, thank God you came. They said you would, but I didn't believe them."

Michael felt her brush against his body, and he led her out of the tent. He quickly cut the ropes from her wrists. It was too dark to see her face, but he knew she must have lived through hell.

"Come," he said, leading her to a horse. He felt her tremble and then stumble, too weak to walk. Lifting her in his arms, he put her on his horse and climbed on behind her.

Hakeem gripped the arm of the man he'd caught trying to sneak away. The prisoner's eyes rolled in fright. "Who are you?" he asked.

Hakeem smiled as he played on the man's fear. "Better you should ask who found you, even in the desert." He swung the man around to face Michael, who was more concerned with Mallory than Hakeem's captive. "That, you dung heap, is the green-eyed scorpion. Go tell your master that he will soon be coming after him."

"He is a devil!" the man cried. "How could he find us?"

"The desert speaks to him." Hakeem shoved the man to the ground, tossed him a waterskin and ordered him to remove his boots. "You are but one day's walk to the lair of the devil—go and warn him that his time on this earth is over if he does not release the Inglizi."

There was sudden hope in the dark eyes. "You will allow me to live?"

"If you can make it to Caldoia, you may live."

"How can I walk without boots? The sand will burn my feet."

"Then run before the sun comes up. If you die, it will be no great loss."

Mallory fell back against Michael, too weary to think. She closed her eyes and buried her face against his robe.

"You are safe," he said soothingly. "No one will harm you now."

"I want to go home," she whispered. "I want to return to England."

"And so you shall," he assured her.

They were soon joined by the others, and Mallory was surprised to see Khaldun Shemsa, the Egyptian from the ship. "But how did he get here?" she asked Michael.

"It seemed we were in the presence of royalty and didn't know it, Lady Mallory," Michael told her. "Meet Prince Khaldun, my very good friend, and yours, too, it would seem. Without his help, I would never have known where to find you."

She tried to smile, but was too weary. "Thank you," she murmured, instantly falling asleep in Michael's strong arms.

The prince looked up at Michael and saw softness in his eyes. Yes, his friend loved the flaming-haired beauty. "It was good that we found her, and none too soon. We are but a day away from Caldoia."

"Yes," Michael agreed, brushing sand from Mallory's face, and holding her gently in his arms. He noticed the bruises on her face, and his grip on her tightened. "I wish I could kill them again. If anyone else tries to harm her, there is nowhere to hide that I won't follow."

Khaldun stared at his friend. Michael did not seem to know that Sheik Hakeem fueled the growing legend of the green-eyed scorpion to frighten the Turks, but he was not so sure that the legend was not becoming true.

Michael was a man like no other, an enemy to fear and a friend to trust. His fame was growing with each day. When the Turk reached Caldoia, his version of what had happened today would only add to Michael's growing reputation.

Chapter 19

The sun rose high in the sky, but still the small party did not slacken its pace. They had to put distance between themselves and Caldoia before Sidi sent soldiers to search for them.

Mallory awoke once, and Michael urged her to go back to sleep. Her eyes drifted shut, for she felt safe at last. She wasn't sure if she was dreaming, but if she was, she hoped never to awaken.

Michael stared down at her, his eyes dark with anger. Her face was red and blistered. Her hair was tangled and knotted. She had certainly lost weight, and he could only guess what she had suffered. She was dressed in an Arab dress, but it was so dirty he could hardly tell its color. He thought of the spirited young girl he'd first met on board the *Iberia,* and was furious that she had been brought to this state.

"Has she spoken of her captivity?" Khaldun wanted to know.

"No. She's too weary to talk. Have you seen her wrists? They are bloody where the ropes cut into her."

"We can stop when we reach the other side of the mountains. Sidi's men will not find us there since the pass is known only to my people. Then you can doctor Lady Mallory's wrists."

"She needs a long rest."

"Perhaps you should take her back to the palace slowly, but I must ride swiftly to the city and inform my father what has happened. Hakeem will come with me, for we must finish preparation for the battle. I know a place where you can set up camp—there is a spring, and it is on the warm side of the mountain. I will send Fizal back to you with supplies, and he will guide you home when Lady Mallory has rested."

"Yes," Michael agreed reluctantly, thinking of his father. "I will wait with Lady Mallory while you prepare for war." He dropped back so he was even with Hakeem. "I will reach the city as soon as possible. Will you wait for me?"

"Fear not, my friend, my men will not enter Caldoia without you beside them."

Michael looked down at the sleeping woman who had caused him so much trouble. If not for her, he would already be on his way to Caldoia. But what else could he have done? If she hadn't helped him, she would never have become a pawn in this deadly game.

Mallory awoke and sat up quickly. Her eyes were round with fear as she tried to remember where she was. Glancing at her wrists, she saw they were no longer bound, but were bandaged instead. In the back of her mind was a faint memory of being rescued by Lord Michael, but surely it had only been a dream.

No one seemed to be around, but there were three horses hobbled nearby, grazing on the grass that grew from the side of the slope.

She heard footsteps behind her and spun around to see Michael walking toward her. She stood up on wobbly legs. "I didn't dream it—you did find me."

When she would have lost her footing, he steadied her. "Perhaps you should be careful until you regain your strength. You have been through so much."

"How long have I slept?"

"Two days."

"I don't know what those men wanted with me. They kept saying that"—she dropped her voice—"that I was your woman and you would come after me."

"Don't think about them." He moved inside the tent and returned with a bundle, which he handed to her. "Khaldun's wife, Princess Yasmin, sent this to you. It should contain everything you need. Perhaps you would like to bathe in the stream."

"Oh, yes, please." Her eyes widened when she looked up at him. "Are we safe here?"

"Yes." He pointed her in the direction of the stream. "Stay in the shallows, the water is quite swift."

Some of Mallory's old spirit returned when she tossed her head. "I can swim."

"Even so, stay in the shallows. I don't fancy going for a dip in my clothes. That's your role."

She smiled slightly. How different he was from the first time they had met. Then he'd been arrogant, cold, and distant. Now he walked with the assurance of a man destined for greatness, a man of courage, a man who would let nothing or no one stand in the way of what he wanted. His face was changed, older somehow, his stance more certain. He had the proud walk of a veteran warrior and raw energy flowed from him. The black robe fell to the tip of his desert boots. His burnoose covered his hair and was thrown carelessly over his shoulder.

"Have I said thank you for rescuing me?"

Michael's features softened. "I can remember a time you treated my wound and cared for me without questions. I have no need of thanks, Lady Mallory."

"But I will always be grateful for what you did. I can't allow myself to think what would have happened to me if you hadn't found me."

"You should bathe now," he said gently. "When the sun goes down, it grows quite cold here." He turned away, and she watched him enter the tent. With an inward sigh, she walked toward the stream.

Soon Mallory was working the perfumed soap into her hair. How wonderful it felt to submerge herself in the cool water. Reluctantly, she waded ashore and dried herself with a soft towel. She silently thanked Princess Yasmin because she'd thought of everything.

Mallory dressed herself in a soft turquoise robe and belted it at the waist. She then sat on the grassy bank of the stream and brushed her hair. It took her several minutes to work out the tangles, but soon her hair curled about her face and fell spiraling down her back.

Slowly, she walked back to camp and found Michael waiting for her.

He watched Mallory walk toward him in silence. The sun was behind her and reflected off her red hair, making it appear as if it were on fire. How young she looked in the robe that accented, rather than hid, her curved body.

Was it possible that every time he saw her she grew more lovely?

"It feels glorious to be clean," she proclaimed, reaching her arms up as if to embrace the day.

Michael averted his eyes, because he hadn't been around a woman in many weeks, and he didn't like the way he was feeling about Mallory. "Are you hungry?"

"Indeed I am." She sat down on a rug and smiled up at him. "What I wouldn't give for my cousin Phoebe's Yorkshire pudding." She cocked her head to the side in thoughtfulness. "Isn't that strange—I never liked it before now."

Michael picked up the satchel that contained food. "Let's see what bounty Khaldun has sent us."

Mallory watched him lay out the meal. "What is that?" she asked, wrinkling her nose at the dried meat.

"It's quail. We have almonds, dates, and figs. This is a feast."

She smiled. "Let's pretend we are sitting down to a well-cooked English meal, and afterwards we shall walk in the cool evening breeze."

Michael's eyes grew reflective. "I haven't thought of Ravenworth in a long time. In the past, I enjoyed living in London. I find the country appeals to me now. I wonder if I'll ever like the crowded city again?"

She took a bite of the quail which was quite delicious. "I have always preferred the country. Of course, I know so little about London."

"I could have guessed."

"Michael, the men that held me captive referred to you as the green-eyed scorpion. And I'd heard you called that once before. Why is that?"

He shrugged. "Everything is exaggerated here in the desert."

"Perhaps the Egyptians embroider stories because their lives are so uninteresting."

"If you believe that, you don't know the Egyptians. They have a kind of serenity that we British have never acquired. They laugh easily and will just as easily cry with a friend."

"You like them, don't you?"

"Yes, I do. Prince Khaldun is the best friend I ever had. He would risk his life for me, and has."

"Well, I don't like them. Not after I was abducted by them."

"They weren't Egyptians," he said dryly, "they were Turks. It was Egyptians who rescued you—remember."

"Oh. I didn't mean to sound ungrateful."

Michael leaned back and watched her tear meat off the bone and put it in her mouth.

"I just want to go home, wherever that may be."

"You shall as soon as I can arrange it. It is dangerous for you to remain here. Your father will surely agree with me."

Mallory glanced up at him. "When will you return to England?"

"Not until I find my father."

"Is there any hope of that?"

"I would have been in Caldoia now, if I hadn't had to go after you. It seems you can't stay out of trouble."

She heard the accusation in his voice. "I didn't ask you to come after me. Of course, I'm glad you did. If you hadn't, I would now be imprisoned with your father."

Michael grabbed her arm and made her look at him. "What are you saying? Did they tell you where my father is being held?"

She searched her mind, trying to remember the man's exact words. "Yes, the man who captured me said something about putting me in a cell in the west tower where a great Englishman is being held."

There was urgency in Michael's voice. "Are you certain they said the west tower?"

"Yes, I am. Is that important?"

"I should think so. How do you know they were speaking of my father?"

"Because they said he was the father of the green-eyed scorpion."

Michael jumped to his feet, his eyes shining with hope. "At last I know where to find him!" He pulled her to her feet and hugged her tightly. "You're wonderful! You just told me what I needed to know." He smiled, and her heart stopped beating. "All I have to do now is get into the west tower."

Mallory stared at him as if he'd lost his mind. "I wouldn't think that would be an easy feat to accomplish. You might as well have said you'd walk on the moon."

His eyes became piercing. "No one can stop me now. I will take my father out of that place."

She touched his arm. "Oh, Michael, I fear for you. The man bragged about how they were setting a trap for you. Don't go blindly into that evil city."

"I would expect them to try to capture me, but it won't be as easy as they believe."

"But Michael, those people have no concept of what's right or wrong. And they do not value human life. They would think no more about killing you than they did about capturing your father."

He seated her on the blanket and sat down beside her. "Let's not speak of that now. There is something else I want to talk to you about. I had a long time to think while you were sleeping."

"I know, you want to send me back to Cairo."

"No, that's not it. I think we should be married as soon as possible."

She looked at him as if he'd lost his mind. "You can't be serious."

"I am indeed serious. I don't think you realize the consequences of your being kidnapped."

"What do you mean?"

"The alarm will have been raised by now, and everyone will know you were taken by force. By the time the next boat docks in England, everyone there will know about your abduction."

"I fail to see—"

"Just listen to me. Your reputation will be ruined. Do you know what that means?"

"I don't care. I did nothing wrong."

He glanced away from her when he asked the next question. "Did those men—did they . . ."

"If what you are trying to ask is if they ravished me, the answer is no. They were too frightened of someone named Sidi to touch me."

"Thank God. But your reputation is ruined all the same. People will believe what they want to believe. I don't think you know the magnitude of this, Mallory," he said. "Accounts of your abduction will be in all the newspapers."

She lowered her head, at last understanding. "I don't consider it your place to make a respectable woman of me."

"You still don't understand. I feel responsible. Those men believed you were my woman, or they never would have abducted you."

"But I don't hold you responsible for what they did." Mallory wondered why she felt like crying. "You are not obligated to marry me."

"Damn it, I am. If I hadn't come to you when I was wounded, you would never have been compromised."

She glanced at him through veiled lashes. He was everything a woman would want in a husband. When he touched her, she felt all funny inside. But she had too much pride to marry him under such circumstances. "I will not marry you."

He looked at her in exasperation. "It doesn't have to be a real marriage. I always knew I'd have to marry someday, and it might as well be you as someone else."

"How charitable of you. What woman could refuse such a heartfelt proposal?"

Michael stood up and pulled her to her feet. "My mother and father married without love, and their marriage has been the envy of everyone who knows them. Out of that marriage grew a great love. We do like each other—at least I like you."

She looked into his eyes. "Are you saying that if I marry you, you might grow to love me?"

He felt he should be honest with her. "No, I'm not saying that. I'm not sure I'm capable of loving a woman." He touched her cheek. "But if you will do me the honor of becoming my wife, I'll make you a good husband."

Oh, she wanted to say yes, for she was beginning to realize that she cared a great deal for him. No one had ever expected her to make such an advantageous match. Even her mother and father would be impressed if she married a DeWinter.

"I'm sorry, Michael, but I must refuse."

"You have no choice. If you won't think of your own reputation, think of mine. All England will soon know that you and I have spent nights alone together."

"How?"

"Trust me, they will know. I will ask you again if you will marry me? And don't forget about Prince Khaldun and his people. They have a very strong sense of morality. They will expect us to be married." He smiled at her. "Khaldun already believes that you are my lady."

"Why?"

"Because he fancied himself in love with you. I had to convince him that you belonged to me."

"He did? I never guessed."

"How could you not know?"

Mallory turned away. "I'm sorry if by any fault of mine he was misled."

Michael came up behind her. "Khaldun is happy now. But I wonder if he will ever forget you completely."

"I like him. He seems an honorable man."

"I hadn't thought—is there someone you love in England?"

"No, there is no one."

She turned back to him. "Surely there is some woman in London who would make you a more suitable wife than I?"

Lady Samantha's face came to him, and he dismissed her. She had hardly crossed his mind since he'd left England. He thought of Mallory's adventurous spirit and how bravely she had met danger. Was there another woman with her courage? "There is no one. Doesn't it seem to you that we would deal quite well together?"

Mallory was weakening. "Where would we find someone to hold the ceremony here in the desert?"

"Just leave that to me."

"But I didn't agree—"

"You will, Mallory, you will. You must."

"I'll have to think. Right now, all I want to do is sleep."

She moved into the tent, and Michael watched the gentle swaying of her hips. He felt the blood running hot in his veins, and he knew he desired her.

But there was another reason he wanted her—a reason he could never share with her. She would only despise him if he told her the real truth.

Chapter 20

*M*ichael *was sure Mallory* would never understand how urgently he needed a wife. If his father was killed, and if Michael was also killed in the conflict with the Turks, there would be no male heir to inherit the duchy. The DeWinter name and Ravenworth would pass to a distant relative.

Long after Mallory had fallen asleep, Michael sat staring into the darkness, trying to decide what he must do. His mind was set. They must be married immediately.

He closed his eyes, feeling like the vilest creature on earth, for he would shamefully use Mallory for his family's sake. He would marry her, and desperately attempt to impregnate her before he left for Caldoia. If he got her with child, he could only hope she would bear his son.

He heard the horses stirring and knew that Fizal was bedding them down for the night.

Michael entered the dark interior of the tent and felt around until he found his bedroll. He had been sleeping in Mallory's tent so he would be close by if she needed him. Wearily, he lay down, thinking she would be well enough so they could resume their journey in the morning.

"Michael?"

"Yes, Mallory."

"I've been considering your proposal, and I can't marry you."

"Why can't you?"

"We don't love each other."

"Does that matter?"

"It does to me. I always thought I'd marry for love."

"A much overrated sentiment. I can think of many reasons for a man and woman to marry, and love is the least of those reasons."

"I don't agree. There must be a man somewhere whom I will love and who will love me in return."

"The woman's argument. Men don't feel love the same way a woman does, Mallory. You would be better off if you married for companionship. In any case, we don't have much choice. We both have reputations to protect."

"Will you ride with the bedouin when they wage war against Sidi?"

"Yes, I will, Mallory." He felt heavy with guilt that he was so shamelessly willing to arouse her sympathies. But he had to, it was his duty to his family. "Can you not find it in your heart to make a man going off to war happy?"

She choked back tears, glad it was dark so he could not see her cry. "I don't understand."

She heard him move closer to her, and she stiffened when he lay beside her. "Have you ever wondered what it would be like to be with a man, Mallory?"

"Yes," she admitted with honesty. "I have wondered. I grew up in the country, so I'm not as innocent as you might think."

"But you have never known a man's touch?"

Her voice came out in a painful whisper. "No." She reconsidered. "Well, that's not quite honest. There was a man who lived near us, a Sir Gerald Dunmore. He did put his hands on me once. But I struck him with my riding whip."

Michael chuckled. "I can't imagine a man trying to steal a kiss from you if you had a whip in your hand. It's a notion that would make me tremble with fear."

"Well, Sir Gerald won't ever attempt to touch me again."

Michael's hand brushed up her arm. "Mallory, would you send a warrior off to war without your soft kisses on his lips?"

She understood only too well what he was up to. "I know what you're doing, Michael. You are taking unfair advantage of me."

He reached out and touched her hair, allowing his hand to drift through the silken curtain. "Possibly. I had rather hoped I could appeal to your woman's heart."

He pulled her head to rest against his shoulder. "Since we left the *Iberia,* our lives have become entwined. I have come to admire you. I find your kindness refreshing, and you are fearless when danger strikes. I like those qualities in a woman."

Mallory nestled her cheek against his neck. "I have no money of my own, Michael. I fear you would have no monetary advantage in marrying me."

He smiled, thinking how guileless she was. "That's only another advantage for me. I must confess to being extremely wealthy and, therefore, would be able to give you everything you should desire." Suddenly he was serious. "I want to make you happy, Mallory. Give me that right."

She could feel his breath stirring her hair. She wanted to pull away and she wanted to stay. His arm slid around her shoulder and he held her to him. "Sweet Mallory, won't you have me for your husband?" He brushed his lips against hers and heard her sigh. "You want to be my wife—you know you do."

"I . . . can't."

He caught her chin and brought her face around to him. Dipping down, he covered her lips in a kiss that was soft, then deepened it to a passionate kiss when he felt her hands move around his shoulders. "Say yes," he demanded.

"Yes," she said breathlessly. "Yes, Michael. I will marry you, but I want you to know that your money means nothing to me. It would not matter if you were a pauper."

"Dare I hope you marry me for myself?" His words came out as a jest, but she could feel a tenseness about him as if he were anticipating her answer.

When she didn't reply, he shrugged. "No matter, we will be just as married as if we loved one another passionately."

Mallory was afraid to speak, for fear she would cry. She turned her face into his chest, loving the feel of his arms around her.

Michael held her to him for a long moment, feeling a great protectiveness toward her. This was a new emotion for him. He had to put some distance between them while he still had the willpower to resist her.

"I'm getting the best of the bargain, Mallory. All men will envy me for my beautiful wife."

"You don't have to tell me I'm beautiful. I know I am nothing compared to your lady friends in London."

"You have a beauty those women could never hope to obtain. It's a gentle beauty that sneaks up on a man when he least expects it, and has him caught before he can wriggle away."

She was skeptical. "I don't care for pretty speeches. And we both know that no woman would catch you unless it suited your purpose."

He laughed uneasily. She knew him better than he'd thought. "I will take your beauty with me into battle, and use your wit for my armor."

She was disappointed when he untangled her from his arms and stood up. "I think it would be wise if I joined Fizal on his watch tonight."

"Do you expect trouble?"

"Only the kind that lures a man into the silken web of a woman's arms." He stood over her, and she could almost feel his piercing gaze. "I'm glad you agreed to be my wife, Mallory. I hope you never have reason to regret it."

She heard him leave, and she was suddenly lonely without him. She didn't know what had driven him to ask her to marry him, but it wasn't love and it wasn't to save their reputations.

Mallory tried not to think about the danger he would soon face. She would be his wife, if that was what he desired, and she would give him anything else he wanted from her.

Mallory thought of Cousin Phoebe and wondered if she would approve of her union with Michael DeWinter. Yes, she would like him.

She could still feel the warmth of his body and the turmoil of emotions within her own body. What would it feel like to be Michael's wife and have him unleash that passion he'd kept such a tight rein on tonight? She ached with awakening desires that had lain dormant within her, waiting for the right man to bring them to life.

She gasped at her own daring thoughts, and it was a long time before she fell asleep.

The next morning when Mallory awoke, Michael and Fizal had already broken camp. As soon as she came back from washing in the stream, the tent had been disassembled and the packhorses loaded. After she'd eaten the dried meat Michael had given her, they rode down the mountain.

Fizal went on ahead, while Mallory and Michael galloped abreast. He was strangely silent, his gaze continuously sweeping the area, and she knew he was alert to any trouble that might come.

How different he was from the man he'd been last night when he'd asked her to marry him. He seemed cold and indifferent, and she could sense that he wanted to reach their destination as soon as possible. There was an urgency about him that she did not understand.

Her chin went up, and she averted her head. She would not be the one to break the silence between them.

They stopped only to rest the horses, and at those times, both Michael and Fizal were watchful.

At last, she blurted out, "Are we being followed?"

Michael handed her a waterskin. "There is always that danger. Sidi would give much to have my head, especially now that I have taken you away from him. By now, he will have sent men to search for us. We must make it to Kamar Ginena before nightfall."

After taking a drink, Mallory handed Michael the waterskin. "But Prince Khaldun said only his people knew of this mountain pass," she reminded him.

He took a deep drink and hooked the waterskin on his saddle. "The desert has many tongues, and we cannot be sure in what direction they will wag."

Mallory stared at him, as if seeing him for the first time. There was nothing of the English nobleman about him. He was more like an Arab, and that somehow frightened her. She remembered when those green eyes had danced with humor. Now they were watchful, hard, and somehow cruel. She shivered, wondering what had happened to change him.

She mounted her horse and stared ahead. "You do not have to slacken your pace because of me, my lord. I can keep up with you."

He nodded. "That's good, because we are coming out of the mountains, and if we are going to be ambushed, here we are the most vulnerable."

The swift Arabian horses never slackened their pace as they emerged from the mountain pass and entered the barren, inhospitable desert.

Michael shoved his robe aside and placed his hand on the gun that was strapped around his waist, while Fizal cradled his rifle across his arm.

Dark clouds loomed in the distance, and when the clouds passed overhead, it began to rain. Mallory was grateful for the cooling shower. But it soon dissipated, and the puddles rapidly disappeared into the thirsty sand.

When they neared the farmlands, several Jebeliya warriors rode out to meet them. They crowded around them, laughing and talking to Michael in their language. Mallory saw the admiration in the dark eyes when they looked at Michael, and she realized that they had a great respect for him.

As they neared the gates of the city, Prince Khaldun

rode forward and conversed with Michael in quiet tones. He then turned to Mallory.

"My brother, Lord Michael, has given me the privilege of speaking to you, Lady Mallory. My wife, Princess Yasmin, eagerly waits to help you prepare for your wedding." He smiled widely. "It is Allah's wish that you and my brother should be husband and wife. You are truly worthy of this great man."

Mallory could only stare at him. "Thank you," she murmured, her eyes searching Michael's.

As they rode through the gates of the city, Mallory moved her mount closer to Michael. "Surely we are not to be wed here?"

He glanced down at her and spoke as if he were conversing with a child. "You must understand that I have no time to travel to a city where we might find a Christian minister. We will be married in the tradition of the Jebeliya. Have no fear, the marriage will be binding."

Mallory was having doubts that she wanted to marry him. Last night in the dark tent, he had been so kind, now he appeared cold and indifferent. He appeared as uncivilized and hard as any of the men that surrounded them.

"Are you certain we must marry?"

"I thought we had that settled."

"Yes, but—"

"Cover your face," he urged. "Quickly."

In confusion, she drew her headdress across her face, wondering if he intended her to live like an Arab woman. Well, she refused, she thought stubbornly. But she kept her face covered all the same.

Mallory was amazed by Kamar Ginena. It was modern and pristine. She had never expected to find a civilization so advanced here in the desert. She had thought all Bedouin were nomadic and lived in tents.

She raised her eyes to the palace and wondered what manner of people the Jebeliya were that they had carved a kingdom out of the wilderness.

When they dismounted at the palace steps, Michael turned to Mallory. "I have been informed that our wedding will take place tonight. Have you any objections?"

"Yes! Surely that is too soon."

"I will be leaving for Caldoia before daybreak tomorrow. The desert people, who are loyal to Prince Khaldun, are already massing along the eastern wall of the city."

She wanted to cry out to him and beg him not to go with them into battle, but she kept her silence. He must try to rescue his father. "Is Caldoia a walled city like this?"

"I am told it is even more of a fortress."

She stared into Michael's eyes and found him watching her as if he expected something of her. "I will marry you tonight," she agreed, knowing she would rather have only one night with him than a lifetime with any other man.

Mallory had been bathed and perfumed. Her hair was braided and entwined with jasmine blossoms. Princess Yasmin, who spoke English haltingly, supervised the servants, lending her help and advice whenever needed.

The princess motioned Mallory to the bed, where many veils and gowns were spread out for her choice.

Yasmin looked at the English woman and found her beautiful, if a little too pale. Her eyes were as blue as lapis lazuli, and the flame in her hair was wondrous to behold. "You are truly worthy to be the wife of the lord Akhdar 'em Akraba," Yasmin said in admiration.

"You call him by that name also?" Mallory asked in confusion. "I thought it was only his enemies who addressed him so."

Princess Yasmin smiled. "The name was given to him by those who witnessed his brave deeds. He is a very noble man, a warrior of great courage. He is feared by our enemies and loved by my people. It is because of him that we shall defeat Sidi in his own fortress."

Seeing that Mallory looked troubled by talk of the impending battle, Yasmin picked up one of the gossamer robes and held it out to her.

"I was married in the crimson, noble lady. But if you do not prefer crimson, perhaps you would like the gold?"

Mallory reached for a white robe and held it in front of her. "It is customary in my country to marry in white."

"But the white is so ordinary," Princess Yasmin protested, picking up a white veil and draping it about Mallory's head. Suddenly, she nodded in approval. "Your beauty is such that you do not need adornment. But allow me to give you something that I treasure, so you will always remember this day."

She reached up and unhooked the necklace she wore and handed it to Mallory. "This was given to me by my father on my twelfth birthday."

Mallory looked at the delicate chain that was adorned with tiny golden hearts. "I cannot take this from you. You must treasure it greatly."

"If you give away something you treasure, you give true friendship. It is my deepest wish that you accept this from me, as a remembrance of my friendship for you."

"But we hardly know one another."

"The great lord is my husband's truest friend. I would like to be considered your friend."

Mallory looked into gentle brown eyes and saw sincerity glowing in their depths. She removed the pearl ring that adorned her finger. "Only if you will accept this from me. It was my grandmother's, and I have treasured it."

Yasmin smiled brightly as she slipped on the ring. "This will never leave my finger. We are friends now, are we not?"

Mallory took Yasmin's hand and squeezed it. "We shall certainly be friends, Your Highness. Will you fasten the necklace about my neck? I will wear it at my wedding."

The princess was delighted. "You will be happy with the green-eyed one and bear him many sons."

Tears filled Mallory's eyes. "Not if he dies trying to rescue his father."

Yasmin's kind heart ached that she had been the cause of such distress to her new friend. "It is said the great lord is invincible and cannot be slain by his enemies," she said reassuringly.

Mallory felt overwhelming fear for Michael. "That is a misconception. Michael will bleed and die like any other man. I myself treated his wound when he was stabbed by Sidi's men."

"I do not know about such things. I only know what the people believe. They see him as one who will deliver them from the evil Sidi."

"Why is Sidi so feared?"

"He enslaves the tribes to make them follow him. If he is not stopped, his numbers will grow until he controls all the desert tribes."

Mallory frowned. "I fear for your people, and I fear for Lord Michael. I believe he will be in the most danger."

"Allah will protect him because his cause is noble," Yasmin said confidently.

Mallory saw no reason to remind the princess that many men with noble causes had died in battle.

Chapter 21

ichael stood before the Moslem imam in a private chamber of the royal family. The only other person in attendance was Prince Khaldun, who stood to his right.

A guard opened the door and Michael turned to watch Mallory move toward him, her eyes on his face. Beside her walked Princess Yasmin.

Michael caught his breath at the lovely vision in white that seemed to float toward him. As Mallory walked, the veil flowed about her, and when she reached his side, he smiled down at her and took her hand.

The imam spoke Arabic, so Mallory did not understand the words. Once Michael whispered that she should repeat the words, *"aiwa, na'am,"* which she did with difficulty. Then a little later Michael repeated the same words.

Mallory felt Michael's grip tighten on her hand, and she had the feeling God had guided her footsteps to Egypt so she could become his wife.

The ceremony continued, and Mallory stared at the holy man, wishing she could understand his words. On he spoke, requiring little response from Michael or her.

Michael understood the Arabic words very well, and he wondered what Mallory's reaction would be if she knew what she was promising.

"This woman will obey her husband in all things," the imam said as he placed his hand on Mallory's veiled head. Mallory, not understanding, just smiled sweetly at Michael.

"The man will be master of his house," the holy man continued, "and the woman will make no decision without his guidance."

Michael returned Mallory's smile.

The imam then asked Michael, "Have you a ring to give this woman, since it is required in your Christian nuptials?"

Michael removed his signet ring and handed it to the imam, who said a prayer over the ring and handed it back to Michael.

Michael slipped the ring on Mallory's finger, but it was so big she had to keep it in place.

"I will give you a ring that is more appropriate when we reach England," he whispered.

Mallory looked at Michael in a daze. This was not what she had envisioned as her wedding. She had not understood one word the holy man had uttered.

The imam continued. "This man and this woman will walk through life with hearts and hands entwined. She will bear his children, and he will provide for her." He bestowed a smile on each of them.

"*We- 'alekum es-salam warahmet Allah wabarakatuh.* And peace and God's blessing be upon you."

Michael smiled down at her. "It's done, Mallory. I am your husband."

"Yes," she whispered, still in a daze, because she didn't feel married. "It's done."

Prince Khaldun clasped Michael's hand while he smiled at Mallory. "You can see that love blooms here in Kamar Ginena. There is an old legend that says, if lovers kiss beneath our moon on their wedding night, they will be united in their hearts forever."

Michael raised Mallory's hand to his lips, his eyes dancing with mirth. "Shall we believe the legend?"

"My lord," Mallory said in a slight show of humor, "it would seem too many legends are born in this country."

Yasmin pressed her cheek to Mallory's and whispered, "May you be as happy as I am."

Michael linked Mallory's arm through his. "You will excuse me if I take my bride away. We have only tonight before I leave."

Khaldun put his arm around Yasmin, and they watched Michael lead his new wife from the room. "There is something troubling those two, but I believe they will find true happiness if they but look for it."

He glanced down into his wife's eyes that were shining with love. "Allah has given me a woman with a true heart, and I find I am a most fortunate man."

"My happiness lies in seeing you happy," she said, pressing her face against his chest.

"I think I shall never love another. My heart is too full of you."

Yasmin knew something that Khaldun thought he had kept hidden. "But you have special feelings for the flaming-haired wife of your friend."

He held Yasmin to him. "You see too much with those beautiful eyes of yours. I will admit to you that I once thought myself infatuated with Lady Mallory. I now honor her as my friend's wife and nothing more." He saw doubts in her expression and he laughed. "There is no reason for you to be jealous of any woman. I pledge to you this night that I shall never take another wife."

Yasmin stared at him in wonder. "Do you speak the truth, my husband?"

"Like my father, I want only one woman in my life. You are that woman."

Yasmin's heart was soaring with happiness. She had never expected to win Khaldun's heart, and she had certainly never expected that she would be his only wife. Now she would not have to share him with other women. She would not have to lie awake at night aching because he was making love to another.

"I will make you the best wife a man can have," she vowed.

"In the short time we have been married, you have filled my life with your sweetness. I am a most fortunate man."

Yasmin thought her heart would burst with happiness. The man she had loved for so many years loved her in return. A tear trailed down her cheek, and he gently wiped it away.

"This is a night for reflecting, Yasmin, for we do not know what the future holds."

"You speak of the war?"

"I do. You know, Yasmin, that death is a black camel who comes to everyone's door."

She placed her fingers to his lips to silence him. "Then let me make you forget about tomorrow, if only for a few hours."

He lifted her in his arms and carried her to their chamber. "I can think of nothing but you, Yasmin, when you are in my bed," he said, unfastening the golden pin that held her gown in place.

*   *   *

Michael and Mallory had been given the bride's quarters that were on the ground floor. It was spacious and decorated all in white. There was a wide door that led into a private garden, where fragrant flowers filled the night air with their glorious scent.

Michael led his wife into the garden, and they were both aware of the beauty that surrounded them.

"My friend would have me believe that every marriage in Kamar Ginena is enchanted, Mallory. Shall we believe him about that?"

"It makes a lovely story."

"Ah, a skeptic. You don't believe that if we kiss beneath the moon, our lives will be entwined for eternity?"

She wanted to tell him that her heart already belonged to him, but she dared not. She glanced up at the heavens, thinking she'd never seen the night sky so black, yet so full of shimmering stars. When she looked back at him, the stars seemed to be reflected in his eyes.

Michael pulled her into an embrace. "Perhaps we should test the enchantment theory on the chance that it might have some merit."

She realized he was toying with her emotions, but it didn't matter, all that mattered was that they were together tonight. Tomorrow he would be gone. Perhaps she would never see him again!

He bent his dark head and touched her trembling lips ever so softly. She sighed, drawing closer to his hard body. His hand moved up to cup her face, and he turned it toward the moon. "I believe I'm enchanted already. You are beautiful, Lady Mallory DeWinter."

"Mallory DeWinter," she said in wonder. She closed her eyes, feeling the essence of him moving throughout her mind. Yes, she loved him, she must have loved him since their first meeting on the *Iberia*.

Michael smiled. "You make quite a vision dressed as an Arab woman. But you look more like an angel with that flaming hair—" He seemed to freeze for a moment, then he wrapped her hair around his hand, staring at it as if transfixed.

"Michael, is something wrong?"

He was remembering the old Gypsy's words. What had she said about a woman with flame in her hair? He couldn't recall her exact words—had she said he would love a woman with hair like flame?

"Michael?" she repeated as he stared at her in bewilderment. "What is wrong?"

He smiled. "Nothing, I was just remembering something someone once said to me." He pressed her scented hair to his face. "Yes, you are my angel."

He took her hand and led her into the bedroom, where he pulled her into his arms once more. "I wonder if heaven allows flaming-haired women to be angels?"

When she didn't answer, he continued. "No," he said, running his eyes over her hair and giving her a heart-rending smile. "The temper that goes with the red hair would probably prohibit you from obtaining wings."

"We both know that I am not an angel."

He touched her cheek. "I would not want an angel in my bed. Rather I would have a hot-tempered beauty with fire in her veins." He touched his lips to her brow. "Do you have fire in your veins, Mallory?"

His question required no answer. He stepped back a pace and removed his outer garment. "We have so little time together, Mallory, I cannot woo you as you deserve."

With trembling fingers, she removed her veil and placed it over a chair. But now feeling uncertain, she could only look to him for direction. He smiled and came to her, his hand unfastening the tie that held her robe. In a whoosh of silk, it fluttered about her feet.

Lately, he had begun to envision how she would look standing before him in all her naked glory, but nothing prepared him for her flawless beauty. Seeing the shyness in her eyes, he blew out the candles one by one, slowly bathing the room in ebony softness.

He sat down on the bed and took her cold hand in his. Pulling her forward, he pressed a kiss on her breasts, first one and then the other.

When he heard her sigh with pent-up emotions, he lifted her onto the bed and lay down beside her. "The pity is that we may only have this one night, Mallory."

Her voice quivered. "Yes."

By now their eyes had become accustomed to the darkness, and he reached up and ran his fingers through her hair, unbraiding the silken strands, causing the jasmine blossoms to fall about them in a rain of fragrant petals.

Mallory's eyes held a look of uncertainty, and he ran his finger across her mouth. "There is nothing for you to fear, Mallory. The joining of our bodies is but another commitment of the marriage ceremony." His lips toyed with the tips of her eyelashes, and his voice came out in a deep tone. "I will make it pleasurable for you."

Slowly he drew her body against his, and he felt her stiffen. "You aren't frightened of me, are you, Mallory?"

She buried her face against his shoulder. "No, I'm not frightened, not of you."

He closed his eyes, savoring the feel of her silken body. He felt compelled to rush, to plant his seed in her, but this was her first time, and he curbed his impatience. If only they had more time, he could be certain that he would send her to Ravenworth carrying his child.

Mallory was vulnerable to Michael because she had only recently realized she loved him, and she wanted to pour out all that was in her heart. She was well aware that the love was all on her side, for he spoke only of enchantment, and feelings, but not love.

Mallory felt the same desperation in him that she had sensed when he'd first asked her to marry him.

He ran his hand over her body, drawing her ever tighter against him.

The sadness of their situation filled her eyes with tears. If this was to be their only night together, she wanted desperately to have his child. In a bold move that took him by surprise, she took his face between her hands, bringing his lips down to hers.

Her voice was unwavering as she spoke. "If this is all we will have, Michael, then let me imprint myself on you so you will remember."

Shaken by the intensity of the desire that raged through his body, Michael roughly turned her over, pinning her to the bed with his body, sliding her legs apart.

"You go to my head like wine," he murmured, nipping at her ear and sending delightful shivers through her body.

Her silken arms slid around his neck, and he lowered his head, kissing her softly, as the heat smoldering in his body intensified. His mouth ground punishingly against hers. All he could think about was the bliss that was only moments away. His body would know Mallory's, and he would attempt to empty life into her.

His fingers slid over her breasts, until he saw her eyes shine with passion. His lips drifted over her face with tantalizing kisses. At last she turned her head, offering her trembling lips, which he willingly took.

With each sigh that escaped her lips, the blood ran

hotter in his veins, and he was having difficulty controlling his primitive, unbridled urges.

Slowly he eased into her, feeling her tight hot flesh close around him. He shut his eyes, willing himself not to rush. Michael trembled with the control he was exercising over himself. He realized that her virgin body was not ready to receive the full force of his passion.

Mallory held him to her as he filled her and made her heart sing. The desert breeze brought with it the sweet scent of the garden, and among the jasmine blossoms that had fallen from her hair, their bodies joined.

When his body trembled and erupted, she clung to him, wishing she could hold him like this forever.

He kissed her lips and found that her face was wet with tears. "Have I hurt you?" he asked, stroking her gently.

"No, not hurt. It was . . . just that I was so much a part of you. I never knew you could be so close to another person."

He stared at her, wondering why he felt this tenderness, this fullness in his heart. Why was there a thick lump in his throat making it impossible for him to answer her?

He held her tightly against him, knowing they might soon be parted for all eternity. What was this emotion she aroused in him? He did not care to examine these new feelings, because he had to let her go before morning.

Mallory curled up in his arms, and he saw mischief dancing in her eyes. "So that is what it feels like to have a legend make love to you." She smiled. "Well, Akhdar 'em Akraba, I now believe the legend is more reality than fable."

Michael shook with laughter as he crushed her in his

arms. "I see that you are going to be a most disrespectful wife. Will you not show me the respect deserving of a legend?"

Her eyes suddenly flickered, and she touched her lips to his. "Oh, yes, I will show you respect. What is it that the green-eyed scorpion desires?"

"You," he whispered. "I desire you."

Mallory willingly came to him, and he took her again and yet again. As morning approached, his lovemaking became more desperate. Each time Michael reached for her, Mallory came willingly into his arms.

Neither of them knew that they were of the same mind: he wanting to plant his seed in her so the DeWinter line would continue; she wanting him to impregnate her so she would have something of his to cling to should he not return.

Michael eased himself out of bed and stared for a long moment at Mallory, who had given him a night such as he'd never known. Her sweetness had touched him as no woman ever had, and he was tempted to go back to bed and take her to him once more.

With a resigned sigh, he tiptoed out of the bedroom and lit a candle in the small sitting room. He sat at the gilded desk and removed a piece of paper from the drawer. In a bold hand, he began to write.

Dearest Mother,

This is to introduce you to the former Lady Mallory Stanhope, who is now my wife. You will find her sweet of nature and gentle in mind. Take her to your heart, as I have taken her to mine. Make her your daughter. If God is merciful, she may bear the next DeWinter heir. Today I ride with an army of thousands in the hope of rescuing Father. I feel your prayers are with me, and I will need them to sustain me through the coming days.

Your loving son,
Michael

Michael placed the letter in his belt, thinking he must be sure to give it to the king and ask him to see that it reached his mother.

He took out another sheet of writing paper and sat for a moment. Leaving a message for Mallory was much more difficult. His heart was full of emotions he was not yet able to put into words. Dispassionately, he wrote, then folded the page and propped it against a candlestick so she would be sure to find it.

Michael paused at the bedroom door and resisted the urge to wake Mallory so he could have her blessing before leaving. He slipped a burnoose about his head and moved down the corridor. The sun would be up in two hours, and they would have to be well on their way before then.

Chapter 22

*T*he sun seemed to burst through the morning
sky with radiant pinnacles of light. Michael
rode at the head of the bedouin forces,
beside Prince Khaldun and Sheik Hakeem. Each man's
thoughts were on the battle ahead, and the women that
they had left behind.

Their number increased rapidly as they moved past
friendly Bedouin villages. Camels and horses trekked side
by side, their riders silent as they massed into an army.

By midday, the blistering sun hit the desert like heat on
an anvil, and their numbers had now swelled to over a
thousand. When the heat became unbearable, Prince
Khaldun called a halt at an oasis, where each man was
left to find his own shade.

Prince Khaldun then called the leaders of every tribe to
his side so they could best make their strategy. In no time
at all, arguments broke out as each man was sure his own
idea was the best.

At last, Michael held up his hand. "I have a plan that might work." All attention was riveted on him, and the Bedouin leaders respectfully waited for him to speak.

"As you know, I have to locate my father and bring him safely out of Caldoia before you strike. Those of you who have been to Caldoia have told me that the city is virtually impregnable. Unless we can get men on the inside of the walls, it would be folly to pit our full strength against Sheik Sidi Ahmed. He would like nothing better than for us to attack in force."

"That is so," Hakeem said, nodding his head in agreement. "But every man here is willing to die for this just and worthy cause, if Allah wills. They desire to rid the desert of this traitorous Turkish scourge."

"What is your plan?" Khaldun asked Michael.

"Actually, it isn't my plan at all. It was implemented effectively by an American general when he was fighting against my country."

"Did this American general win the war?" Hakeem asked with interest.

"Most assuredly. General George Washington led our commander to believe he was going to a certain city, when in fact he turned his troops and went in a different direction. Our British general, Lord Cornwallis, was duped into leaving strategic positions undefended and assembling his troops where he thought General Washington was going to strike. The war was lost because of this duplicity."

Hakeem's crafty old eyes surveyed the men who surrounded him. It was a good plan, but the sheiks would follow Lord Michael only if they were convinced he had support. Hakeem knew he would have to use the legend against his own friends, for their own good, of course. "I like it—I like it! It is a plan worthy only of a great general, or, the green-eyed scorpion."

The others began to mumble among themselves, while Prince Khaldun smiled knowingly at his father-in-law. "The Hakash, who are allies of Sidi, live to the north. We could make a great show of going in that direction," the prince said.

One of the lesser sheiks was skeptical. "It is a good plan, and one Sidi would not know about. But my concern is the danger of splitting our forces."

"That is a real danger," Michael admitted, "and this is not foolproof."

Hakeem sighed in exasperation. The green-eyed one was losing them. "I see no other way to lure the camel from his dung heap," he said fervently. "Now, Akhdar 'em Akraba, tell us more about this remarkably ingenious plan."

Michael's eyes met Hakeem's, and the older man just stared at him innocently. But Michael knew what the wily old fox was doing. "Since you ask, Sheik Hakeem, this is what I believe we should do," Michael said, taking his sword and drawing a line in the sand. "We send half our forces to Hakash, to draw Sidi from Caldoia, while the rest remain hidden here."

"Yes!" Hakeem shouted, infecting the other sheiks with his enthusiasm.

"The caravan route is nearby, is it not?" Michael asked.

"It is but a day's ride to the north," Khaldun answered.

"That is good," Michael said. "Should Sidi's spies see the dust when you send for the men to join the main force, they will believe it is a caravan."

Hakeem nodded in approval. He had known the green-eyed one would come up with a good plan, he had just needed prodding.

"It will work," Khaldun said. "I believe it is such a fresh idea that Sidi will never suspect a trap until it's too late."

Hakeem's dark eyes brightened. "I will send Abu, who is known and trusted in Caldoia, to spread the false information that we are about to attack Hakash."

"Are you certain we can trust him?" Michael wanted to know, since he would be putting his life, and his father's, in Abu's hands.

"I would trust him with my life." Hakeem shrugged. "Even if he is caught and tortured, he will not give away our plan. I know he would die rather than betray me." The old sheik beamed. "This will work because it is brilliant. If only I had thought of it first."

Khaldun shook his head. "Do not be too quick to celebrate. The walls of Caldoia are high and well guarded, and there will still be a sizable army inside the city."

"If Abu does his duty, he will be able to open the gates for us. But if he does not, the whole plan may fail," one of the sheiks warned.

"I will go with him," Michael said. "I have to free my father before the attack."

Khaldun nodded. "I will not try to stop you. If it were my father, I would do the same. But I must warn you to be careful. Your eyes will give you away at once. And they will be expecting you to try to free your father."

Michael took his knife from its sheath and cut a strip from his robe. He then gritted his teeth and cut a long slash across his arm and soaked the cloth in his own blood, while the others watched in amazement. "Before I enter the city, I will tie this about my eyes, and Abu will tell everyone who asks that I have a head wound." His eyes went to Hakeem. "At least now I won't have to ride your damned camel."

"It may work," Khaldun said, fearing what might happen to Michael if his identity was discovered. "Be on guard, my friend. I do not want anything to happen to you."

"If I have not joined you in three days, go ahead with the attack, because it will mean I have failed," Michael said.

"Don't forget that Abu must open the gate," Hakeem reminded him.

Michael looked at his two friends, and then allowed his eyes to drift over the hundreds of loyal men that had gathered to do battle. Many of them he would never meet, and yet he owed them more than his life. "I pray to God that the three of us will soon be reunited."

"May Allah make it so," Hakeem said.

"And may your father be among our numbers," Khaldun added.

Mallory awoke to find it was midmorning and Michael wasn't beside her. She slipped out of bed and ran to the garden, hoping he would be there—but he wasn't. After a thorough search of the quarters, she realized he was gone. He hadn't even awakened her to say good-bye.

When she entered the sitting room, Mallory found the letter Michael had left. She could tell by the long strokes of the pen that it had been written in haste.

Dear Mallory,

It is difficult to leave you so soon after our marriage, but you know how important it is that I find my father. I have left instructions that you are to be escorted to Cairo without delay. Prince Khaldun has left one of his most trusted guides as your escort.

The man will see you safely to your mother and father. You are to meet him in the north courtyard after breakfast. Please do not delay your departure. I want you away from Kamar Ginena before war explodes around you.

How could Michael be so cold and distant after what had happened between them last night? How could she return to her father's house as if nothing had happened? At least if she remained here, she would have news of the war.

With a heavy heart, she packed her few belongings while trying to ignore the panic that was building inside her. What if something happened to Michael? It could take weeks for her to receive word in Cairo.

A servant entered, carrying a tray with Mallory's breakfast. "Where is the north courtyard?" she asked hurriedly. The woman merely shook her head, not understanding her words. When the servant departed, Mallory went in search of her guide. There had to be something she could do to help Michael, there just had to be.

After asking several people directions, Mallory was finally able to locate the man who was to be her guide. He was packing supplies on a horse, and he looked up as she approached.

"Lady, my name is Fizal. I am to be your guard. Are you ready to leave?"

"Fizal, will it be just the two of us going to Cairo?"

"Yes, lady, but you will be safe with me. I will protect you with my life."

"How well do you know the city of Caldoia?"

"Very well, lady. I have many friends there. My cousin, Jabl, is a night guard at the tower."

"Have you told Prince Khaldun or my husband about your cousin?" Mallory asked.

He shook his head. "I am but a humble servant, and it is not permitted to speak to the great ones without permission."

"Can you take me to Caldoia?"

His face visibly paled. "Oh, no, lady. To do this thing would be to forfeit my life. I was told to take you to Cairo, and this I must do."

"You must help me, Fizal. My husband is in grave danger because he will attempt to break into the prison to rescue his father."

He shook his head. "He cannot get to his father, lady. The guards will shoot anyone who comes near the prison."

"Will your cousin betray you?"

"No, lady. He is of my blood."

"Then you will take me there, and convince your cousin to help us."

"No, lady. I cannot take you to that evil place. It is unsafe for an Inglizi woman."

"I will dress as a serving woman and cover my face. We must hurry, Fizal."

He looked doubtful. "Will not the green-eyed one want Fizal's head for taking his woman into danger?"

"I will tell him I insisted, so he can hardly blame you for following my orders."

"I will do it if you ask it of me, lady. But I think the green-eyed one will put an end to my poor, miserable life when he discovers what I have done."

"I'll meet you here in an hour," she said, turning toward the palace.

When she reached her bedroom, she found that the serving woman was waiting for her, concerned because Mallory hadn't eaten. It took several moments for

Mallory to make the servant comprehend that she wanted to trade clothing with her. At last the woman nodded her head in understanding, clearly delighted to exchange her plain cotton robe for one of silk.

Mallory hurried to the courtyard, where Fizal would be waiting for her. She wore a black robe and a head covering that was decorated with silver coins. With each step she took, it made a jingling sound.

Mallory wondered what Yasmin would think when she realized that she had left without saying good-bye, so she left Michael's letter as explanation. Hopefully, everyone would conclude that she had returned to Cairo as he had directed.

She was soon mounted and rode through the city streets beside Fizal. No one questioned them, and they passed unchallenged through the gates and to the desert beyond.

Mallory was glad her veil shaded her face against the uncompromising sun. Every muscle in her body seemed to ache, and she wondered if there was an end to this sea of sand.

They passed a tribe of Bedouin who showed little interest in them. Her veiled gaze traveled over the faces of the men, and she noticed their skin was like worn leather.

"They have a harsh life, Fizal."

"The land demands it of them." He spat. "When their sheep overgraze the land, they move to other lands. They are like the shifting sands, always restless, ever moving."

That night, when they stopped to make camp, Mallory was too exhausted to eat the food Fizal offered her. There was a small pond filled with spiky reeds that was shaded by date palms and short scrub bushes. She dipped her hands in the water and drank deeply, then washed her face.

Fizal had raised a small tent for Mallory and made her a bed of soft sheepskin. As soon as she lay down, she fell asleep. She did not know that Fizal sat up guarding her throughout the night.

Michael could see great earth-colored domes rising into the sky, and he knew that they were approaching Caldoia, so he tied the bloodstained bandage around his head and allowed Abu to lead him to the city.

They were stopped at the gate, and Abu spoke to the guard. "My brother has had a bad accident and needs medical attention."

The guard looked at the injured man. "You had better seek help for him soon. It appears to be a bad injury."

"I will do that, my friend."

"From where do you come?" the guard asked.

"I am of the Hakash. And I am most troubled."

"Why is that?"

"As I was bringing my brother here, I saw many men riding toward my village at great speed. They were of the Sawarka and Jebeliya tribes."

The guard's eyes widened. "Are you certain of this?"

Abu continued to spin his lie. "I can tell you on my mother's life that I speak the truth."

"Then I must alert the captain of the guards. He has been expecting an attack, but he thought it would be here."

"I do not know about such things. I only know I saw a large gathering of an army and they were going toward the Hakash. I am worried about my family."

"Take your brother to the physician, but make yourself available. I am sure my captain will want to question you."

"I shall be easy to find."

"Pass through," the guard said.

Both men breathed a sigh of relief as they entered the gate. Michael saw charms and dried bones hanging from a pole. "It's to ward off evil spirits, lord," Abu whispered. "The Turks are a suspicious people." He smiled slyly. "Even so, I had no trouble making the guard believe my tale. We can only hope that he is as convincing as I when he tells it to his captain."

"We may not have much time, so we must locate my father as soon as possible. I suggest we separate. If they discover my identity, you will be in danger."

Abu shook his head. "My master told me to stay with you. Your trouble will be my trouble."

Michael was grateful for Abu's loyalty. "Do you know where the tower is located?" he asked.

"I am not familiar with that part of the city, lord. I will make inquiries at the market."

They entered a narrow passageway where carts and stalls lined the walls. There was a strong odor of fly-infested meat and fish. He saw baskets of vegetables, leather goods, and cooking utensils lining the street.

They dismounted, and Abu paid a young boy to look after their horses. He led Michael into a coffee house, where apparently the local men gathered to play backgammon and smoke. They were served coffee, and Michael found it very strong and laced with sugar, but he forced himself to drink it anyway.

They had just been served chicken soaked in heavy oil, when they heard the sound of many horses riding through the street. Someone burst into the coffeehouse, chattering excitedly, and a great commotion started.

Abu smiled innocently and whispered to Michael, "It would seem the jackal took the bait. Those are Sidi's elite guards, and they are leaving the city with him at their head. Apparently, Sidi's most loyal ally, the Hakash, are under attack, and he is on his way to aid them."

Michael laughed. "You are a genius, Abu. It's apparent you were trained by the great Hakeem."

Prince Khaldun and Sheik Hakeem flattened their bodies on the slope of the sand dune, watching Sidi and his men ride past at a fast pace.

"The green-eyed one is clever and the Turk is a fool," Hakeem stated scornfully.

Khaldun glanced over his shoulder toward the enemy stronghold. "I only hope Michael can locate his father and make it safely out of Caldoia before Sidi learns he's been fooled."

"May Allah make it so."

Michael took a sip of his now-cold coffee. "The sun will be going down in another hour, and then we can leave. It will be easier to move about undetected after dark."

Abu glanced out the window and noticed that several guards were fanning out in different directions, pounding on doorways and questioning the residents. "This could mean trouble for you, lord. They may be inquiring about us."

"We had better see if there is a back way out of here," Michael said, jumping to his feet.

They moved quickly down the stairs, through a smoke-filled kitchen, and out the back door that led them right to four guards.

"Run, lord, I'll hold them off!" Abu cried.

"We stay together," Michael said, drawing his pistol and firing at one of the guards.

By now five others had arrived, and Michael was just going down from a heavy blow to the head, when he saw one of the enemy fire his gun point-blank into Abu's face. There was no doubt faithful Abu's wound was fatal.

"No!" Michael cried as the world went black.

He was unconscious when one of the men ripped the bandage from his head and forced his eyes open. "It *is* him, Akhdar 'em Akraba. Our master will reward us well."

"Sheik Sidi has ridden out with the guard. What shall we do?"

The man in charge was undecided. "It's too late to reach our lord tonight, but send your fastest rider to intercept him."

"What will we do with the green-eyed one?"

"Put him in the cell with the other Inglizi."

allory swallowed her fear and pulled
the veil over her face as they approached
Caldoia.

Fizal gave her an encouraging look. "Do not worry,
lady. You will be safe with me."

A stalwart guard with a suspicious expression halted them at the gate. His dark eyes were hostile, and
his voice was deadly calm. After Fizal talked to him
for some time, the guard reluctantly waved them
inside.

"Lady," Fizal said, looking apologetic, "a thousand pardons, but it was necessary to tell the guard that you are
my wife."

Mallory smiled. "If it got us inside, it was the correct
thing to do. It was clever of you to think of it."

His dark face creased in a frown. "I should not have
brought you here, lady. The guard told me they have

tightened security at the city gates because Caldoia is at war with the Sawarka and the Jebeliya."

"The war has started already," Mallory said fearfully. "We must hurry and find my father-in-law." She glanced back at the guard suspiciously. "Why do you suppose he allowed us inside?"

"I told him we were visiting my cousin, Jabl, and he is acquainted with him, so he allowed us to pass. We were fortunate to enter when we did, lady, because they are preparing to fortify the city."

For a moment, Mallory considered leaving while they had the chance. It was frightening to know that they would be trapped in Caldoia. They had managed to get inside the city, but they had no plan of escape. She took several big gulps of air and turned to Fizal.

"Take me to the tower, at once."

"But, lady, it is not safe. Would it not be better if I took you to my aunt's house while I seek my cousin?"

"No," she said stubbornly. "If there is to be a battle, we must free my husband's father at once."

His eyes widened with fear. "This is a dangerous thing you ask of me. If we are discovered, it would be death for us both."

Mallory tried another approach. "Fizal, in the battle that is about to take place, your friends and family from Kamar Ginena are the ones who will be fighting against Sheik Sidi. If we can free my father-in-law, we will be fighting Sheik Sidi in our own way. Although we are only two people, we can strike at his heart and wound his pride."

His eyes suddenly glistened. "Yes, we can do it, lady."

"I am glad you agree."

"But will you not allow me to take you to my aunt, until I can speak with my cousin?"

"I can see the wisdom in what you say, Fizal. I will agree to stay with your aunt, but only until you can speak to your cousin, and no longer."

Michael awoke, feeling as if his head was about to explode, and he flinched at the pain that shot through him when he attempted to rise.

"Careful, Michael."

He blinked his eyes, trying to focus them in the dark. "Father, is it you . . . or am I hallucinating?"

"I'm real enough, Michael. But what in God's name are you doing here?"

Michael choked down the lump that came to his throat, and he reached out and grabbed his father's hand. "Thank God you're alive!"

Raile pressed a cloth against the lump on his son's head. "If you can call this living. Do you think you can stand?"

"I believe so."

Raile aided his son to his feet, and they stared at each other for a long moment. Michael noticed that his father was clean-shaven and appeared well groomed, so apparently his captors hadn't treated him too badly. On closer inspection, he saw that his father looked older, there was more gray at the temples, and he was also thinner.

After getting over the shock of seeing his son dressed as an Arab, Raile studied Michael's face and found a new maturity—but there was more: There was a sense of confidence and strength about him and a cynical twist to his lips. His eyes no longer danced with humor as they once had, but were seeking and distrustful.

Raile wondered what had happened to his son to change him. But there would be time to talk of that later. "Does your head hurt?" he asked at last.

"It's sore as hell, Father, but I'm no worse for it."

"What happened? Why are you here?" There was a reprimand in his father's voice.

"I'm here because you are, Father. And as to what happened, I can't be sure. A friend helped me enter the city, but apparently I was expected, and Sidi's soldiers found me. We were set upon in an alleyway. My companion was killed, and I was knocked unconscious."

Raile's voice was stern. "I wasn't asking how you got into Caldoia. I want to know what you're doing in Egypt. Surely you now see the folly of your actions."

Michael was puzzled. "You should have known I'd come. Weren't you expecting me?"

"I hoped you would not become embroiled in this tangled web of intrigue." Raile motioned for Michael to be seated on a chair, and continued to apply a damp cloth to his head. "I certainly didn't want to see you imprisoned with me."

"As you might know, Mother is frantic over your disappearance. She won't rest until you have returned to England."

Raile's expression softened at the mention of his wife. "How is your mother?"

Michael could be nothing but honest. "She is only half alive without you. I have never seen her so distressed."

"Tell me about the family, what they are doing. Thinking about each of you is all that's kept me from going out of my mind all these months."

"Arrian had a daughter just before I left England. Mother had word that they were both doing well."

Raile smiled in wonder. "A granddaughter. That gives me another reason to escape this hell. I'm worried about your mother, though."

"I'm sure Arrian and Warrick are helping to keep

mother's hopes alive. Then there's Aunt Mary. You know her—she'll take everyone in hand. I'm sure you needn't worry, Father."

"Dear Aunt Mary. I even miss her." Raile tossed the cloth aside and examined the lump on Michael's head. "I suppose you'll live—at least until our jailer decides what's to be done with us."

"Don't give up. I have friends who may yet rescue us."

Raile looked skeptical. "More than likely, they'll find themselves imprisoned with us."

"Not these friends. They are powerful and resourceful. Do you know anything about the city of Kamar Ginena or the Jebeliya who live there?"

"I know that there's a rumor that such a city exists somewhere in the desert. I'd also heard it was more fiction than fact."

"It exists. Prince Khaldun, whose father rules the city, is a friend. He saved my life and helped me locate you."

"I still don't see how he can help us. The walls of Caldoia are very high, and they are well guarded."

"What you don't know, Father, is that there's a war brewing. Many of the bedouin tribes have banded together to help Prince Khaldun drive Sheik Sidi Ahmed out of Egypt. Their numbers have swelled into a powerful force. At this moment, Sheik Sidi is rushing into a trap. If Prince Khaldun is successful, Sidi may never return to Caldoia."

"I've learned something about this city's defenses since being a prisoner here. It won't matter how large a force attacks Caldoia, because no one will be able to breech the walls. And no matter what you think, Michael, Sidi will not be so easy to kill. He surrounds himself with an army of bodyguards who will gladly give their lives to protect him." Suddenly Raile's voice became sad. "Have you any word of Oliver?"

Michael lowered his head, unable to meet his father's eyes. "He was killed the night you were abducted. I'm sorry, Father."

Raile was silent a long time. "I was afraid of that. I can't imagine life without Oliver. He was with me for so long that he anticipated my needs before I did."

"I know, Father. We'll all miss him."

There was a long, poignant silence between them. At last, Raile spoke. "So, you've found me, Michael. Is it too much to hope that you have a definite plan on how we should get out of this hellhole?"

"I don't know what will happen now that I'm a prisoner, too. I had only two days to rescue you before Khaldun attacks."

"You have fallen into the hands of an evil man, Michael. He's kept me prisoner here because it satisfies him to think that by holding me, he is holding sway over Her Majesty."

Michael stood up and flexed his aching muscles. "Have you been ill-treated?"

"At first I was kept in a small cell without light, and with only some kind of weak, putrid broth to eat. But after a while, I was brought here, and allowed to have my own clothing. The food I'm now served, while not particularly appetizing, is at least palatable."

Michael looked about the cell for the first time. It was clean and had a carpet on the stone floor; there was a bed, two chairs, and a table. A lantern hung from a wooden beam and gave off muted light.

He managed to smile at his father. "While this may be considered lavish quarters in Caldoia, I prefer the humblest cottage in Ravenworth."

Raile dropped down on the narrow bed, looking suddenly dejected. "I kept myself sane by remembering every house, every stream and tree on Ravenworth. I tried to imagine what your mother was doing, how you were faring in London, and if Arrian had given birth to a girl or boy."

Michael sat beside his father. "You will yet be reunited with Mother, and you will soon hold your new grand-daughter in your arms."

Raile wanted to be as optimistic as his son, but he had been in this purgatory so long that he had lost hope. His deepest regret was that his son was now a prisoner with him.

"In allowing yourself to be captured, Michael, you have given Sidi a weapon to use against me. He has tried different methods to break me, but he has failed thus far. Now he may think he can bend me to his will by threatening me with your life. And he probably will defeat me by using you."

"What does this madman want from you, Father?"

"To humble me."

"Why would he want to do that?"

"Perhaps it makes little men feel big when they can crush others under their heel. I have become something of a challenge to him, and his obsession is to hear me beg for mercy."

"Then neither of us will satisfy his obsession," Michael said with feeling.

Raile assessed his son. "You have changed, Michael. I look for the boy and see only the man."

"Yes, I have changed in many ways."

"There is something about you that I can't define."

Michael raised his head to meet his father's eyes. "Since arriving in Egypt, I have killed men, and I have stared death in the face many times. There is nothing I wouldn't have done to find you, and there is nothing this man, Sidi, can do to me that will make me fear him."

"Don't be too sure, Michael. You have never met a man like this one." There was urgency in Raile's voice. "Don't allow him to break you, Michael, for he will surely try, and if he does, he will tire of you and . . . those he tires of, he kills."

Michael managed to smile. "I'm a DeWinter. If he couldn't break you, he will never humble me."

Raile's eyes swept across his son's face, thinking that Kassidy would be proud of the man Michael had become.

They both fell silent. At last, Michael decided to bring some levity into their conversation. "There is another new member of our family besides Arrian's daughter."

Raile looked puzzled. "How can that be? Surely Aunt Mary hasn't remarried at her age?"

"No, it's not Aunt Mary. You see before you a new bridegroom."

"What?"

"Don't ask me how it happened, because I'm not sure I know all the reasons myself."

"So," Raile said unenthusiastically, "you finally married Lady Samantha. I always thought you would."

"No, I didn't marry Lady Samantha. My bride is a precocious, fearless little redhead that I kept tripping over ever since I left England. I believe you will approve of her though, Father."

It had always been Raile's fondest wish to see his son married. But since Michael would one day be the duke of Ravenworth, it was imperative that he had made a proper match.

"Who is this woman who was able to convince you to give up your reckless ways?"

"She was Lady Mallory Stanhope."

Raile frowned. "Stanhope . . . Stanhope? That name sounds familiar, but I can't think why."

"You would have had no occasion to meet Mallory, Father, because she has lived in the country all her life."

Raile's eyes searched his son's. "I suppose her reputation is above reproach?"

"Oh, yes, of that you can be certain. She came to Egypt to be reunited with her mother and father. It seems they find artifacts for British museums."

"Oh, yes, I have heard of them, but I don't know them personally." Raile shook his head as if trying to absorb what Michael was telling him. "This was certainly sudden. I'm eager to meet this wife of yours."

"And so you shall. You will find that Mallory is like no one you have ever met." Then he smiled. "But that's not exactly true—perhaps she's something like Arrian, but with a temper."

Raile chuckled. "Heaven help you if that's so, because you'll have no control over your life. I'd say she sounds more like your mother."

"I'm not sure how deep my feelings go for her," Michael said, knowing he couldn't tell his father the real reason he had married.

Raile clapped his son on the back. "You must have had strong feelings for her, or you would never have married her. I watched you as you spoke of her just now, and I saw something in your eyes that's never been there before. Congratulations, Michael, I'm looking forward to meeting my daughter-in-law." Raile fell silent and his expression became grim. "If we ever get out of this prison."

"Have faith, Father. Prince Khaldun will breech the walls of this city and free us. He will not stop until Sidi is either dead or driven from this land."

"I wish I had your confidence."

Michael said nothing, because he didn't want to face the doubts that were beginning to gnaw at him.

He and his father were trapped, and could do no more than wait for others to free them.

Chapter 24

Mallory threw back the heavy veil as she walked with Fizal in the small garden at the back of his aunt's house. Although his aunt spoke no English, she welcomed Mallory with smiles and bows. The small woman with soft brown eyes kept a clean house, and was busily polishing her furniture, or scrubbing the floors on her hands and knees. She reminded Mallory of Cousin Phoebe.

"My aunt and uncle are happy to have you as their guest, lady."

"Do they understand who I am, and why I'm here?"

"They know only that you are a great lady with trouble. And that you are Inglizi."

"Even so, if it was discovered that they gave me shelter, they might be punished. I would not like to be the cause of any reprisals against them."

Fizal spat, his eyes rolling in his head. "Have no fear, lady. They would sooner see Sidi's bones bleaching in the desert sun than do a kindness for that Turk. My family has many reasons to despise that wicked man."

"But your cousin, Jabl, is one of his guards. Surely he is loyal to Sidi?"

"One must eat, lady, even if one eats from the hand of the devil."

"You must go at once to talk to your cousin. Beseech him to find out all he can about my father-in-law. I believe if we don't help him soon, it will be too late."

"I will hurry, lady, and do as you bid, but I still fear the danger for you."

"Do not think of that. Are you certain your cousin will help me?"

Fizal's eyes narrowed with anger. "He will do anything to strike out at the Turk who killed his wife and son as they crossed the road one day. They were run down by Sidi's horse, and he didn't even slacken his pace or inquire about their injuries. Jabl will certainly help us in this."

"I pray it is so."

"You must promise that you will remain here until I come for you, lady," Fizal insisted.

"You have my word that I'll wait here for you. But don't make me wait too long."

"I will not return until I know something about the great Inglizi."

Together they moved toward the house. At the door, Fizal paused is if he were having trouble with something he wanted to say to Mallory. At last, studying his feet, he spoke. "Would it not be better if you allowed my cousin and me to try to free the Inglizi? I will be blamed if harm comes to you."

"Fizal, don't try to talk me out of this. Come for me when you are ready."

He looked at her with troubled eyes. "Yes, lady."

She placed her hand on his arm, and he looked into her eyes. "I can never thank you for all that you are doing. Even if we don't succeed, I'll always be grateful to you for helping me try."

"It is good to serve a great lady." He grinned widely, showing crooked teeth. "Even if I lose my head when the prince and the lord find out what I have done."

Two days had passed since Michael was taken prisoner and placed in his father's cell. They waited for word of a rescue, but none came. The guards who served them were surly and silent, until that evening, when two of Sidi's personal guards entered the cell.

"You'll come with us," one of the guards said, grabbing Michael and shoving him toward the door.

When Raile tried to intervene, he was struck with the hilt of a sword, and staggered backwards. Michael attempted to go to his father's defense, but two more guards rushed forward and forcibly pushed him out of the cell.

Michael was led down several flights of stairs, through dark corridors, and finally to a heavy iron door. A key was inserted, and he was shoved inside so hard he almost lost his balance.

The sight that met his eyes would have made even the bravest man recoil. A sickening stench permeated the air. Chains were attached to the rock walls, and there were several bloodstained tables. Weapons of torture hung from rusted racks. It was obvious this was a place of great evil.

He was clapped into chains and slammed against the wall. A man dressed in a black robe that was edged with silver embroidery appeared as if from nowhere.

"So, Akhdar 'em Akraba, you are in my hands at last. How foolish of me to waste effort trying to capture you, when all I had to do was leave my front door open. I will soon display your dead body at my front gate, so all will know that my power is mightier than yours."

Michael stared with insolence into the black eyes of the man that could be none other than Sheik Sidi Ahmed himself.

"This meeting is overdue, Turkish dog," Michael snarled.

Sidi moved slowly toward him, a cruel smile curving his thin lips. "You have the insolence of your father, but I believe the time will come when you will beg for death to release you."

"I will never beg you."

Sidi snapped his fingers and motioned for someone to come forward. "Turn the insolent Inglizi's face to the wall and remove his robe."

Two guards immediately complied. Michael's face was ground into the slimy rock, and he felt his robe being ripped from his back. He yanked against the chains, straining his muscles to get free, but the chains held fast.

"Every man has something he fears—every man has vulnerability," Sidi taunted. "I wonder how long it will take me to find yours? I have yet to find your father's, but I shall before he dies."

Michael only laughed. "Do what you will and be done with it. If you can't break my father, you can't break me either. Get on with it, or do you intend to talk me to death?"

Sidi's voice came out with the intensity of the whiplash. "You are as uncooperative as your father, but I'll find your weakness, and then his."

"I think not."

"I will ask you questions, and you will answer."

Michael merely straightened his shoulders.

"Where is my nephew going to strike, and when?"

"Why would I know? I don't even know your nephew."

Sidi's voice was silken. "Do you play games with me? I know my nephew, Prince Khaldun, is your champion. I've had you watched since you saved him from death on the ship from England."

"Your cutthroats are bungling fools." Michael sneered. "It's to be hoped that the rest of your soldiers have been better trained than those I've met thus far."

Sidi's voice had an edge to it now, and Michael knew he'd struck a raw spot. "What do you mean?"

"You sent your men to kill Khaldun on board the *Iberia,* and they failed. They later tried to capture me and failed in that. You even attempted to abduct Lady Mallory and blundered there, too. It's hard to fear anyone who is so incompetent," Michael taunted.

With an angry yell, Sidi uncoiled his whip. Before Michael could say another word, the lash snaked out and cut into his back. The pain ripped through his body, but he closed his eyes, and he thought of how his father would expect him to resist.

"Insolent dog!" Sidi said as he lashed out at Michael once more. The sting of the whip forced the very breath from Michael's body, and he clamped his teeth together to keep from crying out in pain.

He tried to think of something that would make him forget about the pain. He opened his mind to the vision of a pair of blue eyes. He reminded himself of the softness of Mallory's skin, as the whip continued to cut through the air.

"Cry out!" Sidi said, his voice coming out in an angry hiss. "Beg for mercy and I may spare you." His voice rose in volume. "Beg, you son of a desert sheepherder!"

"Never," Michael whispered, as his knees buckled from the force of the whip.

Again and again the whip cracked through the air.

"Ask me to stop," Sidi's voice became more insistent.

"May God damn your soul to hell," Michael said, biting his lip so hard it drew blood. He tried to hold onto the image of Mallory's blue eyes, but they were slipping away as pain became the only reality. The whip cut deeply, and he slumped forward, into a bottomless black abyss.

Mallory sat in the garden beneath a shade tree, impatiently waiting for Fizal's return. He'd been gone for hours, and it was almost sundown. Suppose something happened to him, she thought frantically. What if he was captured and was now in prison himself?

She heard the sound of soft footsteps, and glanced up to see Fizal's aunt approaching with a tray of food. The woman smiled at Mallory and offered her the tray.

Smiling and nodding in return, Mallory lifted the glass to her lips, finding it was fruit juice. "Thank you. It is delicious."

The woman placed the tray on Mallory lap. After she'd returned to the house, Mallory nibbled on a piece of cheese. She tore off a bit of *kishk*, the flat Egyptian bread she had become accustomed to, and ate it with relish. She hadn't realized how hungry she was. Evidently Fizal's aunt and uncle were very poor, but they gladly shared their fare with her.

Fizal's aunt and uncle had retired for the night, leaving Mallory alone in the small room they used as a sitting room. The candle burned low, and still she waited for

Fizal. When the door opened, he stood there looking glum.

Mallory was on her feet. "Did you talk to your cousin?"

"Yes, and he's agreed to help us."

She clasped her hands. "That's wonderful!"

"Not so wonderful, lady. He has asked to guard the tower but does not go on duty for three days."

Mallory's face fell. "That will be too late."

"I fear it will be," Fizal agreed. "I should take you away from the city before trouble comes."

"I will not leave until I know about my husband's father. Has your cousin seen him?"

"No, lady. Jabl will only be allowed to guard the door, and is not permitted contact with the prisoner. He tells me there is one guard at the door and one inside who has the key to the cells. It will not be easy to subdue them both."

"Nevertheless, you must return to your cousin and beseech him to find a way to help us. I fear they will kill my husband's father when the fighting begins."

Fizal saw the circles beneath her eyes. He had come to admire this woman who would not give up, even against impossible odds. "I'll talk to Jabl again tonight, and we will try to work out a plan. But you should rest, lady."

Mallory nodded. "I am weary, but I doubt I'll be able to sleep."

He lifted the candle and placed it in her hand. "My aunt has prepared a bedroom for you. You should sleep now."

"I'll try, but don't forget I will be waiting for your return." She reached out and touched his hand. "How can I thank you for all you have done?"

Fizal smiled, his chest swelling with pride. "I am willing to die for you, lady."

Mallory frowned. Never would she understand the fatalistic attitude of the Egyptians. Never would she forget the loyalty they gave unquestioningly.

Two guards supported Michael's unconscious body between them, while a third guard unlocked the cell. Raile ran forward and slid his arms around his son.

"That bastard!" he ground out, pushing one of the men away from Michael. "Who has done this to my son?"

The guards grinned, shrugged, and left, locking the door behind them.

With considerable effort, Raile managed to carry Michael to the bed, where he gently laid him on his stomach. He felt sick inside when he saw how brutally Michael had been whipped. Each lash mark was like a pain in his own body. Michael's wounds needed attention immediately, so Raile pushed his anger to the back of his mind.

Michael stirred and moaned when Raile bathed his back, but he lost consciousness again and his father was grateful. After Raile had cleansed the lacerations, there was little more he could do because he had no medication. He knew Michael would be in a great deal of pain when he awoke.

Raile paced the floor like a wild animal. He'd been in the cell for so long that he had begun to think there was no escape. But now, he was determined to get his son out of there, even if he had to plead with that devil, Sidi.

Raile kept vigil over his son while anger grew in his heart. Sidi would pay for this—if it cost Raile his life, the day would come when he would have his revenge.

He heard Michael groan in his sleep, and wondered what Kassidy would think when she learned what had happened.

Michael moaned, and Raile rushed to him. Michael gritted his teeth and managed to gain his feet, but he was so unsteady, he had to lean on his father.

"You shouldn't be up yet," Raile told him. "You have been badly injured, Michael."

"I'll not let that man defeat me."

"Who did this to you?"

"Our friend, Sidi." Michael raised pain-filled eyes to her father. "Did he use the whip on you?"

"No. I was not harmed in any way. As you can see, he's allowed me to live in comfort, if you can call being caged like an animal comfort. I'll kill him for what he's done to you!"

"This was his way to strike at you, Father. But I told him nothing."

"What do you mean?"

"He wanted to know about Khaldun and his army, and when they would attack."

Raile's heart contracted. Michael had the same proud spirit of his mother. "So you endured his whip in silence to save your friends."

"I can confess to you that I wanted to cry out, but I wouldn't give that man the satisfaction of hearing me beg."

"He's cunning, Michael—ambitious and dangerous."

Michael's legs almost buckled under him, and his father led him to the bed. "You should rest."

"No. I need to regain my strength."

"Michael, you're badly injured, and we have nothing to put on the wounds. I doubt you could even walk across the cell without my support."

"I have to. Have you another shirt?"

"Michael, you aren't thinking rationally. "You can't wear a shirt with those wounds."

"I must. Bind me so the blood won't soak through."

"The blood would dry and stick to the shirt," Raile reasoned. "It'll hurt like hell when you remove it."

"I can't think about that now, Father. When the battle begins, we have to be ready. I know Khaldun will come for us."

Raile helped Michael sit on the bed, and then went to his valise. "I'll do as you ask, Michael, but I fear we will regret it later."

"I'll endure anything to get us out of here. I have a feeling Sidi will send for you next, and I don't know what he'd do to you now. He's a madman!"

Raile took one of his white shirts and ripped it so he could bind it around Michael. "I wish I had some ointment to put on your wounds."

Michael winced in pain. "Just do it quickly. I can stand anything if it doesn't last too long."

Mallory was sleeping fretfully in the small bedroom at the back of the house. It was oppressively hot, and no breeze stirred the curtains at the window. In her dream state, Mallory imagined she was again the prisoner of the Arabs, and she cried out in distress.

"Lady," a worried voice spoke from the other side of the curtained doorway. "Lady, awaken."

Mallory sat up. "Fizal?"

"Yes, lady. "I have good news to tell you. Hurry, we must make haste."

Mallory shook her head to clear it. "Just one moment, and I'll join you."

She dressed quickly and pushed her foot into the soft red leather boots. When she moved out of the bedroom, Fizal and his aunt were waiting for her.

She looked at Fizal expectantly. "What has happened? Did you find a way for us to get into the tower?"

"Yes, lady. My cousin offered to stand in for the guard on duty tonight. The man was only too willing to agree. Is that not fortunate for us?"

"Do you mean your cousin is guarding my father-in-law tonight?"

"He will be on duty for three more hours, lady. We must hurry. And do not forget about the other two guards. We will have to overcome them."

Mallory smiled at Fizal. "Thank you."

"There is no need for thanks. I do this for you and the great one."

The elderly woman smiled widely and handed Mallory a black burka, saying something Mallory could not understand.

Fizal translated. "My aunt says you are to have her best burka."

Mallory leaned forward and hugged the tiny woman who had taken her into her home without asking questions. "Please express my gratitude to your aunt. Tell her how much I appreciate her kindness."

When Fizal spoke to his aunt, she bowed and touched Mallory's hand. "She says she wishes Allah's blessing on you."

Mallory pulled the veil over her face. "Let us leave immediately."

Chapter 25

The half-moon gave off little light as it hung above the ancient city of Caldoia. The oxcart that carried Mallory and Fizal rolled along with its load of cheese and goats' milk. The streets were filled with frantic people who paid little attention to Mallory and Fizal, but conversed fearfully as they prepared for war.

Mallory sat beside Fizal, her head bent, and her white hands tucked beneath her veil. "I noticed your aunt and uncle were packing when we left. I hope you warned them not to stay in the city."

"They are leaving for the Bedouin camp where my aunt was born. They will already have passed through the gate."

She held her breath when several armed guards approached, and didn't let it out until they rode past.

"Fear not, lady," Fizal said, "no one will question that you are not what you seem."

She bit her trembling lip. "I never thought I'd be so frightened."

"I can yet take you back," he said hopefully.

"Never—we go forward."

The cart creaked and groaned so slowly over the rutted street that Mallory wanted to scream. Her heart was beating in her throat as a group of over fifty soldiers rode past.

"I fear they go to engage Prince Khaldun in battle," Fizal observed.

"I know you want to be with him at this time, Fizal."

"I will join him after we have tweaked Sidi's nose, by taking the great Inglizi out of his grasp."

As they passed a bazaar that was closing for the night, Fizal's voice rose excitedly. "There, lady, look ahead and you will see the tower where they keep the prisoner."

Mallory raised her eyes and was suddenly overcome with the magnitude of the task that awaited them. "It looks so formidable. How will we ever get in there?"

"Put your trust in me, lady. I will get you in—and if Allah is willing, I will get you safely out again."

Michael saw that his father was sleeping, so he turned to stare out the window helplessly. He was beginning to lose hope, but he couldn't let his father suspect. Three days had passed since he entered Caldoia. Surely if Khaldun was going to attack, he would have done so by now. Why was he delaying? He knew the answer to that— Khaldun was giving him more time to get his father out.

He turned suddenly, and pain ripped through his back, leaving him gasping. He clenched his fists and stiffened his body until the pain subsided a bit.

Michael's mind turned to his new bride. They had

known one another such a short time, but she had aroused feelings in him that he'd never had before.

He realized that he and his father would never leave Sidi's lair alive. If only he knew that Mallory was with child, and the DeWinter line would continue, he could die without remorse.

He closed his eyes, but sleep did not come. He had badly bungled his attempt to rescue his father. He had many regrets, but he wasn't sorry he was with his father. If they were going to die, let it be together. But how his mother and sister would grieve—for that he was sorry.

Would Mallory grieve? he wondered.

Fizal halted the cart at the back door of the tower, and jumped to the ground. He banged on the door with his fists, while Mallory waited in the cart.

The door was suddenly thrown wide, and a man in a green uniform barred the way. She watched the exchange between the two men, and it appeared that they were arguing. She surmised that this was not Jabl. The surly look on the guard's face told her that he was none too happy at being disturbed.

At last Fizal returned to the cart and spoke under his breath to Mallory. "Keep your head down." He shoved a basket into her hand. "He knows me as Jabl's cousin, and I have convinced him that you are Jabl's sister, come to bring his dinner."

When Mallory and Fizal entered the tower, bright torches illuminated the large anteroom. The guard gave them a muffled command and unlocked a heavy wooden door which closed behind them. Mallory heard a key grind in the lock. There was no turning back now, they could only go forward.

They moved through a labyrinth of hallways and then ascended steps until at last they came to a room were two men sat at a table playing backgammon. When they stood up, Mallory saw that one man wore a ring of keys at his waist, and she knew the other would be Jabl.

Fizal engaged both men in conversation, and although she couldn't understand them, she knew he was explaining that he was Jabl's cousin and that Mallory was his sister. The man was easily convinced, because he dropped back in the chair while Jabl approached Mallory.

He spoke in a whisper. "You will distract the guard by offering him food from your basket. All you need say to him is *molokhiya,* for that is his favorite meat dish."

Mallory nodded, glad for the heavy veil she wore so they wouldn't see how she trembled with fear. Taking her courage in hand, she moved forward, pronouncing the unfamiliar Arab word over and over to herself. As she approached the guard, he glanced up at her, and she flipped aside the heavy cloth that covered the basket.

"*Molokhiya?*" she asked, hoping he wouldn't notice how badly she was trembling.

He grinned widely and reached inside the basket. Greedily, he attacked the meat-and-rice dish.

Out of the corner of her eye, Mallory watched Fizal approach. With the hilt of a heavy sword, he came down hard on the back of the guard's head and the man crumpled to the floor.

"We have trouble," Fizal said, quickly removing the keys from the belt of the unconscious man and handing them to Jabl. "My cousin tells me that there is a second Inglizi in the cell."

"Bring them both. It doesn't matter who he is, I will not leave one of my countrymen behind," Mallory said.

"It will make escape more difficult," Fizal told her, taking one of the lanterns.

"Nonetheless, you will bring them both."

"We must hurry," Jabl said in Arabic, inserting the key in the lock and motioning for Fizal to follow him.

"Remain here," Fizal cautioned Mallory. "If the guard awakens, call out and I will come to you at once."

Michael heard muffled voices and rose from the cot. He moved to the bars. Two men were looking in all the cells, and he wondered what they were doing. At last, they stopped before him.

"Inglizi?" one of the men asked.

"Yes, I'm English," Michael said in a cutting tone, thinking the men probably had orders to take him or his father to Sidi.

Fizal raised the lantern and stared at Michael. "Akhdar 'em Akraba, I did not know you would be here. We came to rescue only your father."

By now, Raile had joined his son.

"Who are you?" Michael said in a suspicious voice, thinking this must be one of Sidi's tortures.

"I am Prince Khaldun's man."

"I don't know you."

Jabl tried the keys until he found the right one, and the door swung open. "There is no time to talk," he said urgently. "We must leave now."

Raile and Michael exchanged glances, and Raile nodded. "We can't be worse off than we are now."

When Michael moved out of the cell, he almost collapsed, so his father supported his weight. When they reached the anteroom, they saw the unconscious guard and an Arab woman draped in veils.

Mallory could only stare at Michael. How had he come to be in prison? And he seemed to be injured. He was so pale. She lifted her eyes to the man who supported Michael's weight—his father—the duke.

Her first instinct was to run to Michael, but at that moment, the outer door swung open and laughter emitted from the lips of the man who stood in the doorway with two guards at his back.

"So, my birds would have flown their nest. I think not today," an oily voice said in English.

"Sidi, you bastard," Raile said angrily. "So this was a trap all along."

Sidi sauntered in, his dark eyes moving over the faces of each person—they paused on Mallory, and then moved back to the duke. "I would like to take credit for trapping you, Your Grace, but it seems you have friends willing to give their miserable lives to rescue you—first your son—now these poor, unfortunate devils."

Sidi moved to the unconscious guard and nudged him with his foot, but he didn't stir. "You'd have made it too, if it hadn't been for the commotion at the gate. You see, your friends are attacking my city, so I came to put an end to your lives."

Mallory heard the exchange of gunfire and knew that Prince Khaldun had indeed begun his attack. She lowered her head, knowing that she had brought more trouble to Michael and his father. She watched Sidi jerk a gun from his guard's hand.

"Your Grace, how shall I hurt you the most?" he taunted. Shall I simply put a bullet through your heart? Or . . . shall I make you watch your son die before I kill you?"

Michael raised his head. "Do what you will and be done with it. Don't expect us to beg."

"Oh, no," Sidi, said through gritted teeth. "A

DeWinter would never beg, would he? In any case, this is the night you both will die, but not before you know that your friend, Prince Khaldun, is doomed. As we speak, his troops are trapped between the walls of my city and my men who will come up behind them."

Sidi raised the gun and leveled it at Michael's heart. "I think the son dies first."

No one paid the slightest attention to Mallory. She carefully bent down to the unconscious guard, took his gun, and raised it at the Turk. She didn't know if the gun was loaded—she certainly didn't know how to aim, but she prayed she would hit her target. She leveled it at Sidi's chest and pulled the trigger.

Raile watched the surprised look on Sidi's face. Then Sidi stumbled backwards, clinging to a chair for support. His eyes turned slowly to the woman draped in black, who still held the smoking gun in her hand.

"Kill . . . her," he muttered, just before he fell back, his head hitting hard against the stone floor. Everyone knew he was dead.

Mallory dropped the gun and shuddered. She had just taken a man's life. But she'd had to—he was going to shoot Michael!

When the guards moved toward Mallory, she took a quick step backwards. Fizal and Jabl moved between the guards and her, barring their way.

Heated words were spoken in Arabic, and the four men came together in a violent clash. Mallory watched tensely while the men struggled. At last, Fizal and Jabl were triumphant!

Fizal took Mallory by the hand and pulled her out the door, while his cousin motioned for the two Inglizi to follow them. When they were outside, Jabl locked the door and tossed the keys into the night.

Mallory whispered quickly to Fizal. "I don't want my husband to know who I am. I don't want him to know what I did."

He lifted her into the cart. "But, lady, he will be proud of what you did."

Fizal had brought only one robe and head covering, and Raile insisted that Michael slip them over his clothing. They both climbed into the cart, and it was apparent that Michael was in agony.

Jabl arranged a large crate of cheese in front of them, so they would not be detected.

By now, the gunfire at the gates was more intense, and the battle was raging fiercely.

Fizal climbed in the cart and urged the oxen along, while Jabl leaped in the back.

"Where do we go?" Raile asked.

"I will take you to my aunt's house," Fizal told him. "You will be safe there until we can smuggle you out of the city."

From his hiding place, Raile watched the man expertly guide the cart through the chaos. "How can we ever thank you for what you have done for us?"

"There is no need for thanks. I was honored to help."

"Does your wife speak English?" Michael inquired.

"No," Fizal lied hurriedly. "She does not speak Inglizi."

"Will you thank her for saving my life?"

"She needs no thanks, great lord."

"I don't know why the three of you would risk your lives to save us, but my father and I shall see that you are rewarded."

Mallory lowered her head. She trembled to think what would have happened if the rescue had not taken place tonight. She laced her fingers together, wondering how she would ever live with the fact that she had taken a man's life.

As the cart moved along, Michael struggled to sit up. "I have to open the gate, Father. You heard what Sidi said, Khaldun and his men are trapped in a cross fire. I will not abandon them."

"I'll do it," Raile said.

Michael slid off the cart, and doubled over in pain before he could stand upright. "You can't, Father. You don't even know how to find the front gate."

Raile called for Fizal to stop, and when he halted the oxen, Raile walked back to his son. "Michael, be sensible. You can hardly stand, let alone make your way to the gate."

"I have to, Father. My friends are depending on me."

"Then I'll come with you," Rail said.

"No. You wouldn't make it to the gate. Everyone would know that you're English. And, if I had to worry about you, I would surely fail in what I must do. Please understand that my friends are dying on the other side of that gate, Father."

Raile looked into his son's eyes and stepped back. The father in him wanted to go with Michael, and make sure that he would be safe, but the man in him knew that Michael must go alone.

"Where will we meet afterwards?" Raile asked.

Jabl moved to stand by Michael, and said something in Arabic.

"My cousin says he will go with you, lord," Fizal said. "He can walk among the enemy without them being suspicious, and afterward, he will bring you to his parents' house, where I now take your father."

Mallory wanted to cry out for Michael not to go, but she dared not. She could see that he was in pain. How would he make it to the gate?

Michael motioned for Fizal to leave.

As the oxen slowly moved forward, Mallory turned to watch Michael until he melted into the shadows. By the time the cart reached the corner, he had disappeared completely.

Mallory glanced back at the duke and she saw the concern on his face. She could only imagine what torturous thoughts were going through his mind, because she herself was so frightened for Michael.

The night sky lit up with the flash of gunfire, and the cannon atop high walls boomed out, echoing in Mallory's ears.

She thought of Prince Khaldun, and her heart saddened—he and his brave Jebeliya were facing those cannons. Michael *was* their only hope.

Mallory knew this would be the longest night of her life.

Chapter 26

ichael and Jabl made their way toward the main gate. Many times, Michael was overcome with weakness and had to stop for a moment until the weakness passed.

When the pain became too bad, Michael thought about his friends being cut down by enemy fire, and that gave him the strength he needed to keep going, and he moved forward, ever closer to the gate.

At last, it was in sight. Michael paused, leaning against a building so he could assess the situation.

"What shall we do, lord?" Jabl asked in Arabic.

"My friend, I don't even know your name," Michael answered him in the same language. "I don't know why you want to help me, but if we are going to die together, I believe we should call each other by first names. I am called Michael."

"I am called Jabl, lord."

"Michael," he insisted.

"Michael," Jabl repeated, grinning. "I know you only as the great Akhdar 'em Akraba."

Michael grimaced at the sound of the appellation. Was he to go through life with that cursed name? "The one thing that is in our favor, Jabl, is that Sidi's soldiers are so busy watching their front, they won't think to look to their back."

"That is so."

"What I want you to do is walk among them, spreading the word that Sidi has been assassinated. That news will surely demoralize them and make them less eager to fight."

"I will do that, Michael."

"Remember to keep your head down. I don't want anything to happen to you."

"Would it not be better if you let me open the gate? You are hurt, Michael."

"No. You will better serve our cause if you can create chaos in the ranks. Leave the gate to me."

"May Allah walk at your side," Jabl said.

Raile, alone in the small garden, watched flashes of light from the artillery illuminate the night sky. His distress was plainly written on his face. When the veiled Arab woman appeared at his side, offering him food, he waved her away.

"I can't eat, not while my son's in danger."

Mallory merely nodded and was turning to leave, when Raile spoke to her. "I know you don't understand English, but I owe you so much. You saved my son's life. I wonder if you know what that means to me? It must have been difficult for a woman brought up in your religion to take a life."

Mallory's eyes were tear filled, but she shrugged, pretending she didn't understand what her father-in-law was saying. She could see that Michael looked very like his father. They were the same height. Their features were very similar, and they were both handsome. Their eyes were not the same, though—the duke's were dark, while Michael's were like emerald fire.

The sound of cannon blasts shook the ground beneath their feet. Raile's eyes were troubled as he looked toward the explosion. "I don't even know where the damn gate is. I feel as if I should go to my son." He swung around to face Mallory. "I fear you may have saved his life only so—no . . . I won't think about that."

Raile sat down on a bench and buried his head in his hands. "Sidi used a whip on my son, did you know that?" He glanced up at Mallory. "Even though you don't understand what I'm saying, it feels good to put into words what I'm thinking."

She approached him and handed him a cup of strong, sweet Arab coffee. He took a drink and leaned back against the bench. "My God, the world is falling apart all around me, and I'm sitting in a garden sipping coffee and talking to a woman who doesn't understand a word I'm saying."

Mallory looked into the distance, where several buildings were burning. Gunfire split the air, and cannon fire continued to shake the ground. She, also, was frightened for Michael, and she needed the comfort his father could give her, but something kept her from revealing her identity.

"My son is the pride of his mother." Raile looked up at the silent woman. "You would like my Kassidy—everyone does."

Mallory sat down on the bench as the duke continued

to talk. She needed to be near him, to hear him speak about normality, because she was so frightened.

"I have a daughter, Arrian. She's sweet and gentle, not fiery tempered like her mother." He was quiet for a moment, and when he spoke, it was with deep feeling. "Michael is married, and I haven't yet met his wife. He is the last of the DeWinter line, you know? His mother and I wanted to see him settled down with a wife. We wanted many grandsons to inherit the lands and title."

Mallory could listen no more. She stood up and held her hand out for his cup. When he gave it to her, she started for the house, but stopped when he spoke.

"I apologize for talking so much. If I knew the words in your language, I'd ask you to forgive me."

Mallory nodded, and walked away.

Fizal met Mallory at the door and took the tray from her. "You did not tell the great one who you are?"

"I could not. Promise me you will never tell Michael that I was with you tonight." Her voice took on an urgency. "I don't want him to know that I was there, Fizal. And I don't want him to know I killed a man."

Fizal nodded. "He will not hear it from me, lady. This I swear."

She followed him into the tiny kitchen. "The fighting is getting closer, isn't it?"

"I believe so."

"Are we in danger?"

"I will do all to protect you."

She felt true friendship for this young man who had done so much for her. She touched his arm. "I will always feel safe with you nearby. But could you not go in search of my husband? I fear for him."

"I will go, lady. You will be safe with the Inglizi here to protect you."

*   *   *

Michael moved cautiously toward the gate. When he encountered a group of foot soldiers carrying cases of ammunition, he joined them, lifting one of the cases on his shoulder. The pain he felt was so bad that he had to clamp his lips together tightly so he wouldn't cry out. As they moved toward the ladder that led to the battlements, he slipped into the shadows.

Overcome with dizziness, Michael dropped the case of ammunition. "Not now," he said aloud as beads of sweat gathered on his upper lip, and he fought off lightheadedness. "I can't lose consciousness now."

From the sounds of the battle, it appeared that Prince Khaldun and his Jebeliyas were taking a pounding.

Michael gritted his teeth and stumbled toward the gate. Amazingly, with the battle going on, no one took notice of him. Using all his strength, he shoved the wooden bolt aside, and the heavy gate creaked slightly open.

He could hear the sound of cheering as he pushed against the gate and it opened wide. Michael dropped to his knees, too weak to move out of the way. All he could see was the charging horses riding toward him.

He closed his eyes, waiting for the impact, but instead, he felt a horse brush against him as if he were being shielded from the onslaught. He blinked and looked up into the smiling face of Prince Khaldun.

"You did it, my friend. You did it!" the prince cried. He turned to a man behind him. "Bring another horse. We shall ride into the city in triumph!"

It was all Michael could do to climb into the saddle. But they did indeed ride into the city at the head of the victorious army.

There was nothing to fear from Sidi's troops. Those

who had attempted to take the Jebeliya from behind had been vanquished, and those who defended the city threw down their weapons and surrendered when word reached them that Sidi was dead, and that Akhdar 'em Akraba had magically opened the gates of Caldoia to welcome the conquerors.

Now, as Prince Khaldun's army rode through the streets, the people of Caldoia appeared subdued and frightened. In the distance, only sporadic gunfire could be heard, and even that soon stopped.

The victors waved their guns above their heads and cried out a chant. "Sheik Sidi Ahmed is dead! Long live Prince Khaldun!"

Hakeem joined Khaldun and Michael, his eyes dancing with elation. "We have done it, my friends! We have defeated the Turk!" Heartily, he clapped Michael on the back. "Praise be to Allah that we had Akhdar 'em Akraba on our side."

Michael slumped forward as blackness engulfed him. His last conscious sensation was of falling . . . falling . . .

Khaldun leaped from his horse and lifted his friend's head, not knowing what had happened to him. "Someone make a litter, quickly. Lord Michael has been injured."

Fizal came forward and bowed to his prince. "If Your Highness will permit, the lord should be taken to my aunt's house. His father waits there for him."

"Then his father is alive?"

"He is, Highness."

Khaldun looked into Fizal's face, and when he spoke it was in a stern voice. "It was my belief that you were escorting Lord Michael's lady to Cairo. Why is it that I find you in Caldoia among my enemies?"

Fizal found it difficult to lie to his prince. "I have done as I was told. I am here because my aunt and uncle live here, and because I thought I could help with Lord Michael's father. As it happened, Lord Michael was also a prisoner."

"You rescued them?"

"With the help of my cousin and . . . his sister."

Khaldun's attention was drawn to the men who were carefully placing Michael on a litter, and Fizal was relieved that his prince had no time to question him further.

"Take Lord Michael's horse and lead the way to your aunt's house," Prince Khaldun commanded. "I will follow. I want to see his father for myself." He turned to his father-in-law. "Hakeem, have someone find my physician and send him to me."

Khaldun walked beside the litter and was soon joined by an army of men. It was a quiet procession that wound its way through the city. The hero of the day was gravely ill, and no one knew how seriously he was hurt.

Raile was the first to hear the murmur of voices. He flung open the door and saw the procession that stopped in front of the house. He ran forward to the figure on the litter, knowing it would be his son.

Mallory would have run after him, but she stopped herself just in time. It would appear suspicious if an Arab woman showed too much interest in Lord Michael. Instead, she stood in the doorway, clasping her hands, not knowing if he lived or if he was dead.

Cairo

England's consul to Egypt sipped tea with Her Grace, the duchess of Ravenworth, and her son-in-law, Lord

Warrick Glencarin. He was very aware of the importance of his guests.

"Your correspondence was not forthcoming," Kassidy said with veiled anger. "So I decided to come to Egypt myself. Tell me, Lord Geoffrey, what exactly are you doing to locate my husband and my son?"

"Your Grace, I can assure you that we have searched extensively for His Grace. Even now, we are following every rumor, and there have been many. As for your son, my assistant tells me he warned Lord Michael repeatedly not to go into the desert."

"It would seem that too many people just disappear around here, Lord Geoffrey. Doesn't it seem odd to you?"

"Your Grace," Lord Geoffrey said in a shocked voice. "Surely you can't blame me for your son's disappearance. I was in England while he was here in Cairo. I never even met his lordship."

Lord Warrick said, "You speak with Her Majesty's voice here in Egypt. What do you suggest we do, my lord?"

The consul tapped his fingers on the arm of the chair. He was more interested in trying to distance himself from blame for whatever had happened to the duke of Ravenworth and his son than in putting forth an answer to Lord Warrick's question. "His Grace should never have gone into the desert without an army escort. If he had asked my advice, he never would have disappeared, and we wouldn't be having this conversation."

Kassidy's eyes snapped with anger. "I'm sure my husband thought his mission for Queen Victoria would take precedence over any warning you might have given him." She shifted in her chair impatiently. "Tell me everything you know that might help my husband and son, and tell me now."

The consul cleared his voice. "I have heard only bits of news that keep filtering in from the desert. It seems there was a fearsome war that broke out between several Bedouin tribes and the Turk, Sheik Sidi Ahmed, who was slain. As it turns out, he was the man who was supplying the guns and inciting war. At least that problem is taken care of, Your Grace."

"Do you think he was the man who captured my husband?" Kassidy asked.

"The rumors say an Englishman was held captive in Caldoia, which was Sheik Sidi Ahmed's stronghold, although I cannot say for sure."

"Didn't you investigate?" Warrick asked.

"It takes a long time to run down every rumor that filters in from the desert. But it was something I was going to explore, eventually," Lord Geoffrey assured him.

Warrick was losing patience. The man seemed to talk a lot, but say nothing. "The only thing you seem to be sure of, Lord Geoffrey, is that you aren't sure of anything."

The man coughed and sputtered. "I have done my best with the communications being what they are in this primitive country."

Kassidy placed a restraining hand on Warrick's arm. "You must understand that we are desperate. I have no intention of leaving Egypt until I have my husband and son with me."

The consul shifted some papers around. "As it happens, a Bedouin brought me a letter from Lord Michael only three days ago. And it's addressed to you, Your Grace."

Warrick's eyes gleamed dangerously. "Why didn't you say so in the beginning?" He took the letter from Lord Geoffrey's outstretched hand and gave it to Kassidy.

She quickly read the scribbled message. She glanced up at Warrick with a strange expression on her face. "Warrick,

Michael says he's married!" She turned to the consul. "Are you acquainted with Lady Mallory Stanhope?"

"I've not had that pleasure. But I do know her parents."

Kassidy looked shocked. "I've never heard of any of those people. How could Michael have—" She realized she was discussing private matters before an outsider. "Warrick, Michael goes on to say that he believes he knows where Raile is being held and he was leaving to find him."

"It seems to me," Warrick said, "that our search should begin at the city of Caldoia. I believe you should remain here, Kassidy, and I'll go into the desert."

Kassidy's jaw set stubbornly. "I'm going with you, Warrick. I haven't come this far to remain in Cairo while my family needs me."

Warrick had known that Kassidy would insist on going with him. "Very well," he relented. "We will leave first thing in the morning. I'll see to what supplies we'll need."

"I'll send a company of soldiers with you," the consul said, glad that he could offer some assistance. "And you will need servants. I can provide you with some that you can trust."

Kassidy stood, holding her hand out to Lord Geoffrey. "I'll take the escort, but we have our own servants. You will forgive me if I was ungracious. You see, we are a close family, and when one of us is in trouble, the others rally around."

"I don't suppose I can talk you out of going?" Lord Geoffrey asked.

"No. I want my family back. Warrick and I won't stop until we are all reunited."

Warrick glanced at his mother-in-law and smiled. "You had better listen to her, your lordship—we all do."

Chapter 27

*M*allory hovered near the bedroom where Michael had been carried, knowing she could not enter as the Arab woman she pretended to be.

The duke, Prince Khaldun, and Fizal stood near the bed, with worried expression on their faces.

"Who has done this monstrous thing to my friend?" the prince inquired in anger.

"Sidi," Raile replied, worriedly watching his son. "But he paid with his life. Do you know of a doctor that can treat him?"

Khaldun looked at Michael's father, and saw the image of the son in his face. "My physician will arrive as soon as he has been located. I assume he is with my wounded."

Mallory made certain her veil was in place before she boldly entered the room. Michael needed attention now, and she would help him no matter what anyone thought.

She gasped when she saw Michael. He was lying on his stomach, and the back of his shirt was a bloody mess. She wanted to run to him, to fall on her knees to him and help sooth his pain, but she dared not.

"Who are you?" Prince Khaldun asked Mallory, grabbing her hand and holding her firm. "Tell me at once—what do you want in this room?"

"Please, Highness," Fizal said quickly, drawing the prince's attention. "She is known to me and would be a good nurse for the lord."

"I trust her with my son, she is the one who saved his life," Raile said.

Khaldun studied the draped woman. "Is it not against your religion to help with a man who is not of your family?"

Again Fizal answered for her. "Highness, she is not of the Islamic faith."

The prince nodded. "Then I will permit her help."

"We can't wait for your doctor," Raile said grimly. "We will need water to soak the shirt so it won't stick to the skin. Fizal, please ask the woman to bring us these things."

Mallory quickly disappeared into the small kitchen. Her hands were trembling so much that she had to clench them together to steady them.

Fizal appeared beside her. "Lady, why do you not tell them who you are? Then you can be with your husband without being questioned."

She picked up an empty jug and handed another to Fizal. They both moved out the door, and had reached the well before she answered.

"No, they must not know who I am. But I fear they will soon begin to question you about Lady Mallory, since you were supposed to escort me to Cairo."

She dipped the jug in the water, handed it to Fizal, and

then filled another before she reached in her pocket and handed a letter to him. "Give this to Lord Michael, and it will explain everything."

Fizal, as always, was perceptive. "Lady, you are going away, are you not?"

"Yes. As soon as I know that my husband is in no danger."

"But, lady—"

"We must hurry with this water. I still have to heat it."

Fizal took both jugs and walked beside her. "Where will you go?"

"To Cairo, and then to England. You will not tell Lord Michael about me. You promised you would keep my secret."

"I will not break my word." He glanced up to see a man dismount before the house. "Look, it is Sheik Hakeem and the physician. Now the lord will have help."

It was in the early part of the morning, when the rest of the house slept, that Mallory sat beside Michael's bed holding his hand. His back had been cleaned and healing ointment applied. The physician had decided it would be best to leave the back exposed so it would heal faster.

It was oppressively hot, and since everyone else was in bed, Mallory pushed her veil aside.

Michael slept fretfully, often groaning in pain. At those times, she'd wet his lips with a damp cloth and hold his hand, talking in a soft voice until the restlessness passed.

Once he became delirious and began to talk in broken sentences. "She warned me . . . the Gypsy. Betrayal . . . friendship. I will . . . not marry . . . no . . . Samantha."

Mallory pressed her hand on his cheek. "Sleep," she

said soothingly, not wanting to hear any more about some woman in England that he was to have married. "I will not leave you, so you can sleep."

"Must find my father. . . ." He tried to move, but he winced in pain. "I will not tell, you Turkish devil. Kill me . . . I will not talk."

Raile was unable to sleep, so he dressed, thinking he would sit with Michael. He pushed the curtain aside and was about to enter the small room when he paused, stunned by what he saw. The woman who sat beside his son was not the Arab that she would have everyone believe. Her face was lovely in the soft candlelight. Shimmering red hair spilled about her shoulders and he could see tears glistening on her cheeks.

Raile watched her take Michael's hand and raise it to her lips. "Sleep, Michael, you are safe now. You will be better soon, my dearest. You will be on your way to England, and all your troubles will be over."

Raile lowered the curtain and stepped back into the shadows, where he could still observe her without being seen. Now he understood why the woman had shot Sidi to save Michael's life. He knew the red-haired beauty was Michael's wife, Mallory. But why was she keeping her identity a secret?

Raile listened to her speak soothingly to his son, and he could see why Michael had married her, for there was kindness and compassion in her words. He saw love shining in her eyes when she looked at his son. She must have her reasons for hiding behind that veil, and he would not betray her.

Quietly, he returned to his bed. Michael was in capable hands.

*   *   *

Kassidy and Warrick rode into Caldoia, escorted by twelve British soldiers. There was still evidence that there had been a fierce battle in the city. Burned-out buildings stood like ghostly reminders of the conflict, and the streets were scattered with debris. There was a nervousness in the air.

A mass of people crowded the bazaar as residents clambered for the food that had just arrived by caravan.

Warrick called a halt and asked questions of several merchants, until he found one who spoke English. He was told where he could find the Englishmen.

Kassidy had to curb her impatience to race her horse through the crowded streets. She didn't even know if the Englishmen would be her husband and son—she didn't even know if either of them were alive. She held her back straight and gripped the reins. In only moments, she would know their fate.

Michael was well enough to sit up, and Raile watched while the veiled woman fed him. Hearing the sound of several riders, Raile looked out the small arched window, expecting to see Khaldun's men.

"That's strange," he commented, turning to Michael, "It's British soldiers. I'll just go and see what they want. They may be here to escort us back to Cairo. No, wait! My God, it's your mother, Michael!"

Warrick placed his hands about his mother-in-law's waist and lifted her to the ground. "Kassidy, don't get your hopes up. These men may be strangers."

"I—" The door to the small house was flung open, and Kassidy and Raile stared at each other for a long moment. Then Kassidy ran to him, with tears running down her face. "Raile, oh, Raile!"

He caught her in his arms, holding her tightly against him. "Kassidy," he whispered, "my dearest, how did you know I needed you?"

She raised her head, not caring that they were the object of many curious glances. "I couldn't stay one more day in London, not knowing if you were alive or dead." She touched his face lovingly. "Oh, dearest, you look tired. What has happened to you?"

"It's a long story, Kassidy."

"Then we will speak of it later. Everything will be all right now that we are together."

"There were many times in the past months when I thought I'd never see you again."

By now, Warrick had joined them. "It's good to see you, Raile," he said with genuine affection in his voice.

Raile gripped Warrick's hand and smiled. "I understand Arrian has given me another grandchild."

"Yes. I'm the proud father of a beautiful little girl named Kassidy. Arrian wanted to come with us, but the doctor forbade it."

Raile eyes softened as he looked at his wife. "It wouldn't surprise me if Aunt Mary came riding up on a camel."

"Raile," Kassidy said, her brow furrowed in a frown, "why isn't Michael here?"

There was a heavy silence as Raile looked into worried green eyes. "He's in the house, Kassidy."

When she would have rushed past him, he caught her arm. "Before you go in, I want to prepare you."

Her face drained of color. "What's wrong with my son?"

"The man who held us prisoner used a whip on him.

He was badly hurt. You must gather your courage before you see him."

Kassidy buried her face against Raile's chest. "What a monster!" She raised her eyes to his, her lips trembling. "How badly is he hurt?"

"He will heal in time, but he will need a lot of care. He's in great pain, and will be for some time."

"I'm ready now, Raile. Take me to Michael."

"Not before I explain some things about him. You will be so proud of him, Kassidy. It seems your son is something of a hero to these people."

Michael frowned at the veiled woman and pushed the spoon away. "I don't want any more." He ran his hand through his tousled hair. "I haven't shaved, and I don't want my mother to see me looking like this."

Mallory took the bowl and was about to leave, when Kassidy burst into the room. She brushed past Mallory to get to her son.

Dropping on the bed beside him, Kassidy took Michael's face in her hands.

"Oh, Michael, my son, I'm here, and I'll take care of you now."

His hand moved about her shoulders. For a moment, he was like the young boy who had needed his mother, but then Kassidy saw a transformation. There was about him an air of suffering, and of knowledge.

"My dearest son, I've come to take you home."

Mallory saw that the duchess had the same green eyes as Michael, and it was apparent that there was a great love between the mother and son.

When the duke entered the room, he was accompanied by a stranger, whom Michael was glad to see. It soon became clear that the man was Michael's brother-in-law, Warrick.

As the DeWinter family gathered around Michael, Mallory realized that she was no longer needed. His mother would take care of Michael now. It was time for her to leave. She would go in search of Fizal so that he could escort her to Cairo.

Michael was drifting in a dreamlike sleep. He was feverish, and in his dream, he felt Mallory put her cool hand on his brow and speak to him in her soft voice. A great fog seemed to swirl between them, and she slipped away. He called to her, but she didn't answer. He reached for her, but she was not there.

"Lord," Fizal called from the doorway.

Michael's eyes opened, and he realized he'd been dreaming. But he could have sworn that Mallory had been with him several times since he'd been ill. How could a dream seem so real?

"Lord," Fizal called again.

Since Michael still had to lie on his stomach, he couldn't see the door. "Come in," he said, "and sit in this chair so I can see you."

Fizal sat on the edge of the chair, his dark eyes cast downward, lest the lord be able to read the deception in his eyes. "I have this from your lady," he said, handing Michael the letter Mallory had given him.

Michael would read it later, when he was alone. "I'm glad to have this time to talk to you. I have heard that Prince Khaldun has made you master of his elite guard, and that he's given you your own house."

Fizal grinned. "Yes, lord. It was because you praised me to him that he so rewarded me."

"You deserve all that you get, and more. I would also like to do something special for the woman who saved my life. Perhaps you could tell me what she would like."

Again Fizal cast his eyes down. "She will take nothing from you, lord. She will be going away today."

"All the same, I'd like to do something for her. I'll ask my mother, she'll find an appropriate gift to give an Arab woman."

"Lord," Fizal said, trying to turn the conversation, "it was a fortunate day for my family when you came to Egypt. My cousin, Jabl, has also been honored. He will remain here in Caldoia as liaison between Caldoia and Kamar Ginena. My aunt and uncle are to be given a larger house and a pension for the rest of their days."

"Even that is not enough, Fizal. How do you repay someone who saved your life and the life of your father, at the risk of his own? It is I who am indebted to your family. Most of all, I'd like to tell Jabl's sister how much I admire her, and to express my gratitude to her for nursing me while I was so ill."

"I am taking her away now, lord. It is not permitted for you to have contact with her now that you are well." He stood up so Michael couldn't question him further. "I wish you long life and good health, lord. I was told you will soon be leaving for your own country."

"Yes. But when I think of Egypt, I'll think of you and your family."

Fizal left hurriedly, leaving Michael to ponder his strange behavior. The veiled woman had shot a man to save him, she had tended him when he was so ill, and yet he would never be allowed to see her face. He would never forget that she had put herself in danger to save him.

* * *

Prince Khaldun moved through Sidi's palace, watching his own steward make an inventory of what remained of the Turk's furnishings. Many items had been stripped away and burned in a hugh bonfire, to symbolize the Egyptians' distaste for all things Turkish.

Mallory, still veiled, walked two steps behind Fizal as they approached the prince.

"I ask a word with you, Highness," Fizal said, bowing.

The prince smiled at his faithful captain. "What is it I can do for you?"

"I know you expect me to return to Kamar Ginena at once, but I beg leave to escort this woman to Cairo."

Khaldun glanced past Fizal to the woman that stood meekly behind him. "This is the woman who slayed Sidi?"

"Yes, Highness."

"I would have a word with her."

Fizal glanced quickly at Mallory. "She does not understand, Majesty. She is shy, and would be too frightened in your illustrious presence."

Khaldun frowned, and his gaze dropped to the woman's hands that were clasped in front of her. They were white, delicate hands—English hands. He suddenly knew who she was. "Walk with me, Fizal, I want to ask you about something. The woman can remain here until we return."

"Yes, Highness."

Khaldun led Fizal into a room where three servants were rolling up a carpet. He ordered them to withdraw, and then turned to Fizal. "I am proud to have you in my elite guard, Fizal, for I feel you demonstrated that you are fearless and can be a leader of men."

"Thank you, Highness."

"There is one other requirement that I always ask of

my commanders, Fizal. They must be honest with me."

Fizal looked into Prince Khaldun's eyes. "I will always be truthful with you, if I have not already sworn secrecy to another."

"You know to what I'm referring?"

"I do, Highness—the woman."

"We both know who she is, don't we?"

"Even if you strip me of all my honors, I cannot betray her, Highness."

Khaldun seemed to look inward for a moment. Then he smiled. "You would have forfeited every honor I have given you to help Lady Mallory. That kind of loyalty is exactly what I want in the commander of my guard."

"How did you know it was she, Highness? I hope nothing I said gave her away."

"No, you kept your promise to her. I once had an occasion to study those hands with great admiration. It is clear to me that only someone who loved Lord Michael would have killed Sidi to save him."

"Have I your permission to escort the great lady to Cairo?"

"But why is she being so secretive, Fizal? Why has she not revealed herself to Lord Michael and his family?"

"Her reasons are her own, Highness. I do not question her."

"Then take her safely to Cairo, and I will meet you in Kamar Ginena when you return. Take everything you need to make her journey comfortable."

Fizal bowed. "I will discharge this duty with all haste."

The prince watched the black-draped woman walk away, remembering a time when he had desired her. Now all he could think about was finding the proper man to put in charge of this city, so he could return to his beautiful Yasmin.

Still, it would be a long time before he would forget blue eyes and red hair.

Chapter 28

My Lord,

I know you will understand when I inform you that I am releasing you from our marriage. After having time to think about our situation, I realized that we acted in haste. I'll be returning to England, but do not be concerned that I will contact you or make any demands on you. I don't intend to tell anyone about our marriage. Since it wasn't a Christian wedding, I doubt it would even be legal in England. I know you have been ill, and I hope you will have a speedy recovery. I will always wish you well.

Mallory Stanhope

Michael reread Mallory's letter, trying to make sense of it. What did she mean, their marriage wasn't legal? What did she mean that she was returning to England without him?

"Mother," he called out in frustration. "Mother, will you come here?"

Kassidy came running into the room. "What is wrong? Are you in pain?"

"I want my clothes. I'm going to get dressed and go after my wife."

Kassidy stood over Michael with a determined look on her face. "You aren't going anywhere until you are well enough to travel. When I feel you're ready, then we'll leave, and not before. Besides, we are going to stay together until we are back in England."

Michael groaned and carefully lowered himself to his bed. He was weaker than he'd thought. "If I wait until then, it may be too late. Mallory will already be gone."

"Turn over, so I can apply ointment to your back while we talk about your wife." She said in a voice that told him she would have her way.

Kassidy applied the soothing medicine while he winced in pain. "The wounds are beginning to heal, but you still aren't well enough to ride, Michael."

"I must get to Cairo. Mallory is planning to return to England, and I want to talk to her before she leaves."

His mother closed the ointment jar and handed him a cool glass of water. "I want to hear all about her. I confess I don't know anything about the Stanhope family."

He took a sip of water and handed the glass back to her. "Actually, I know little about her myself."

"Where did you meet her?"

"On the voyage coming over. Actually, our first encounter happened just before the voyage. It seems my carriage splashed mud on her as she was crossing the street. She wasn't too happy with me at the time."

"Oh, Michael, you didn't?"

"It wasn't my fault, and I didn't even know we'd splashed her until weeks later. But that isn't the worst of it. When two men were swabbing the deck of the ship, one of them didn't see Mallory, and threw water on her. I grabbed the bucket away from him, and all she saw was me with the evidence in my hand. I admit I did look guilty," he said with a grin.

Kassidy frowned. "I don't find any of this amusing, Michael."

"Neither did Mallory. I can tell you she snubbed me for a long time."

"But you overcame your differences and fell in love?"

Michael looked uncomfortable. "I don't know how I feel about her, and I certainly don't know how she feels about me."

Kassidy was trying to understand. "If you didn't love her, why did you marry her?"

"I felt I owed it to her—at least, I think that's why I married her."

"There's something you're not telling me, Michael."

He sighed. Even as a child, he had never been able to fool his mother. "Also, I was coming here to search for father, and I didn't know what was going to happen to me," he admitted. "Mallory is from a good family, and I . . . well, this family needed an heir in the event that I didn't return."

"Ah, I begin to see. You used that poor girl as a receptacle for the next generation of DeWinters. How could you do that, Michael? I'm not surprised she left."

"It's not the way it appears, Mother. Before the war started, I sent her to Cairo so she would be in no danger."

"Michael, it seems to me that you have misused the poor girl. It's no wonder that she is running away from you. What were you thinking?"

"Even if the marriage started off badly, I won't let her go."

"I should think not. It will be up to you to convince her to remain your wife."

He held the letter out to her. "Read for yourself."

"No. I will not read your private correspondence."

"There's nothing in the letter that you can't read, Mother."

Kassidy quickly scanned the page and handed it back to Michael. "It appears to me she's giving you your freedom because she thinks it's what you want. The only thing that troubles me about her is that she knew you were injured and didn't come to you."

"Something strange happened the first night I was in this house. I know now I was dreaming, but I could have sworn she was with me. I saw her—she talked to me and took care of me. Once before, when I was wounded, she took care of me. I suppose I got the two incidents confused."

"What are you going to do about your wife after you find her, Michael?"

"As I said, I won't allow her leave me."

"Then you have only to convince her that you want her to stay."

"She can be the most maddening woman. I never know what she's thinking, and I certainly don't know how she feels about me. I never realized how a woman can complicate a man's life."

Kassidy looked at him for a moment. "I always thought that you would marry Lady Samantha."

"I had decided I would offer her marriage when I returned to England," Michael admitted. "At the time, she seemed the sensible choice."

Kassidy smiled. "Oh, Michael, you are more like your father than I thought. I can't wait to meet this new daughter-in-law of mine. She may just save you from yourself."

"What do you mean?"

She bent to kiss his cheek. "Never mind, you wouldn't understand. You must rest now. The quicker you heal, the sooner we can get your bride. Perhaps we will arrive in Cairo before she leaves for England."

Raile entered Sidi's former palace, and Prince Khaldun greeted him with a welcome smile. "Thank you for coming, Your Grace. I have many things I'd like to discuss with you. But first of all, may I introduce you to my wife's father, Sheik Hakeem."

Raile exchanged greetings with the sheik.

"I have a strong liking for your son, lord," Hakeem told him. "I would not be ashamed to call him my son, and I have on occasion."

"Michael speaks highly of you also." Raile turned his attention to Khaldun. "I want to thank you for being my son's friend."

"It was he who first befriended me. Did he not tell you how he saved my life?"

"No, he didn't."

"That's like Michael. Will you sit with me?"

Raile sat in the chair that Khaldun indicated. "The palace looks quite different from when I saw it last."

Prince Khaldun smiled. "That is because my father-in-law detests anything Turkish, and he will be occupying the palace from now on."

"Not a prospect that I'm looking forward to, great lord," Hakeem grumbled. "My daughter's husband would make me into a city dweller, while I enjoy the simple life. I have lived too long roaming about in the desert, and he would confine me in this palace."

Khaldun laughed, knowing the old sheik really meant what he said. "I can think of no man who is more capable of restoring Caldoia to its past glory. You are a fair man, and will rule the people with wisdom."

Sheik Hakeem grinned. "What he means, great lord, is that I have lived too long by my wits, and he wants me to turn respectable now that I am allied with his family. I am too old to change. He puts me in charge of the treasures, when he knows I would rather find a way to relieve the people of those treasures than to guard them. Being respectable is a burden that a man of my talents should not have to endure."

Raile smiled. He knew why Michael was so fond of the old sheik.

Prince Khaldun stood. "Your Grace, will you walk with me? I have something of a personal nature to discuss with you."

Already Hakeem had moved into the hallway, berating the men who were laying a rug. "No, you sons of sheep dung, I don't want red in this hallway. Have I not told you that I want blue here?"

Khaldun smiled. "He is a man of colorful language, but a man with honor, though he would have you believe otherwise."

"Then you made a wise choice." Raile and Khaldun stepped into a huge anteroom.

Raile looked about the room. "I confess I will be glad to leave this city. It holds no pleasant memories for me."

"I understand that. Will you be going to Cairo before you leave?"

"Yes. My ship, the *Nightingale*, is docked in the harbor there."

"What I want to ask now may seem strange to you. I have many ears in the desert, and I have come upon something that I feel I should share with you. You can decide what you want to do with this information."

Raile had been looking at the high domed ceiling, and he dropped his eyes to Khaldun. "I would be interested to hear what it is."

"How much do you know about Michael's wife?"

"Only what little he's told me. I don't even think he knows much about Lady Mallory himself."

"What would you say if I told you that Lady Mallory had been with Michael in Caldoia from the beginning?"

"Tell me what you mean."

"I happen to know that Lady Mallory was the one who arranged your escape from Sidi's prison. She's the one who shot Sidi when he was going to kill Michael. And, for the first days of Michael's illness, she was the one who nursed him."

Raile nodded. "I went to Michael's room one night and came upon her unveiled. I knew then that the woman who pretended to be an Arab was indeed my son's wife. I have said this to no one, especially not to Michael. Do you know why she kept her identity from us?"

"That is known only to Lady Mallory, but she loves your son, and he loves her. Is it not right that they should be together?"

"I know Michael is determined to reach Cairo in time to prevent her from returning to England, and I believe he will be able to travel within the week."

The two men shook hands. "I was leaving for my home today," Khaldun said, "but I have decided to remain until Michael is well enough to travel, so I can ride some of the way with you. It will be a sad day for me when I must part from my friend."

"I'm glad you decided to share what you knew about Lady Mallory with me, your Highness. I will discuss this with Michael's mother, and we'll decide whether we shall tell Michael."

"They started their marriage under difficult circumstances. May Allah guide them to a life together."

Mallory stood before the doorway of her parents' home, but before she knocked, she turned to Fizal. "There is no need for you to remain. Thank you for all you've done for me. "I shall miss you, my gentle watchdog."

He looked at her with admiring eyes. "If ever you are in trouble or you need me, no matter how many years have passed, I'll come to you, lady."

She smiled and held her hand out to him. "I'll remember that."

She watched him ride away, feeling lonely.

She knocked softly on the door, and Safwat soon appeared. "My lady, I have been so worried about you. It is good you are safe."

"Have my parents returned?"

"Follow me, my lady, and I'll take you to them."

When he led her into a small office, Mallory stared at the two people who were packing boxes with Egyptian artifacts. They looked up only when Safwat cleared his throat.

Lord Tyler glanced at Mallory, and then angrily at his servant. "I thought I told you we weren't home to anyone tonight."

Mallory felt his words like a slap on the face. Her own father didn't even know who she was.

"Don't blame Safwat," she said, studying her father's face dispassionately, and then looking at her mother, who stared back at her coldly. "He thought you would want to see me, since I'm your daughter."

"Mallory?" her mother asked.

"So you returned," her father replied. "We didn't know what to think when we found that you had been here and then left. It was thoughtless of you not to leave word of where you were going."

But she had been abducted, and Safwat knew it. Why hadn't he told anyone? Mallory watched the two strangers walk toward her. Why had she expected a warmer welcome? She should have known better, after all these years.

"I envisioned you as a small girl until I went into your bedroom and saw your clothing," her mother told her. "You are quite lovely."

Her father looked her up and down. "That damned red hair! It comes out every so often on your side of the family." Neither tried to touch her or show any affection.

Mallory wanted to run away, to escape from these people. In that moment, she realized that Cousin Phoebe had protected her from their indifference all of her life. They were even more unfeeling than she had expected.

What did it matter? Mallory had been through harder in the last weeks; she could certainly endure this. "Did Safwat not tell you that I was abducted?" She had to know.

"He did rave on about some ridiculous tale of abduction and enemies sneaking into the compound. But he's always been one to exaggerate, and we didn't believe him," Lady Julia said.

Lord Tyler's voice was hard and held hidden meanings. "Don't go telling anyone some wild story about abduction, Mallory, for no one would believe you, either. Our work here is very important, and we can only stay as long as we don't offend the government."

Her mother tried to be more diplomatic. "The natives wouldn't dare touch an Englishwoman. It was more reasonable to tell everyone that you got lonely and returned to England."

Mallory was too angry to cry. She didn't know these people, and it was obvious that they didn't want to know her. "In any case, I won't be staying," she said. "I've decided to go back to England."

"A wise decision," her father agreed, nodding his head. "This is no place for a young woman of marriageable age. We would never find you a suitable husband in Egypt."

Mallory was weary, and she felt as if she'd swallowed half the desert. "If you will excuse me, I will go to my room. I just want to bathe and go to bed."

Her mother stepped before her. "I can't believe how beautiful you are. You were such a homely little thing, who'd have thought you would turn out so well?"

"Her eyes she gets from my side of the family," her father said, taking a closer look at her.

"If the two of you will excuse me, I will wish you good night. I'll try not to intrude on your lives any longer than is necessary."

After Mallory left the room, her parents exchanged glances.

"Phoebe should have taught her better manners," her mother said. "She seemed to have a rather cold nature, don't you think?"

After Mallory had bathed, she slipped into bed, planning her departure. The next day she would make the long voyage down the Nile and take the first ship for home. She would go to Cousin Phoebe and ask if she could live with her.

It had been a mistake for her to come to Egypt. She thought of Michael, and turned her face into the pillow, crying bitter tears. If she had remained in England, she would not have fallen in love with a man who would never love her in return.

She fell asleep clutching the signet ring that Michael had placed on her finger when they stood before the holy man. This was all she had left to remember him by. This ring was hers, and she would keep it with her always.

Chapter 29

$\mathcal{I}$t *was early morning as Mallory* dressed in her plain gray traveling gown. She counted out her money and sighed with a heavy heart. There would be enough to pay for her passage to England, but she doubted that she would have enough left to take a public coach to Cousin Phoebe's house. She would have to put her pride aside and ask her father for money.

Mallory hadn't expected to find her mother and father awake at such an early hour, but they were in the dining room having breakfast when she entered.

"Good morning, Mallory," her mother said, indicating the chair near her. "I'm glad we have this time together. Will you breakfast with us?"

"Yes, thank you."

Lady Julia spooned thick porridge into a bowl and handed it to Mallory. "That's a ghastly gown you are wearing. I suppose it's one Phoebe chose for you. She never knew anything about style."

Mallory became angry at their criticism of her cousin. "Cousin Phoebe managed quite well on the money you allotted her."

Lord Tyler took a sip of coffee, then turned to his wife. "You see how disrespectful your daughter is? I told you we should have sent her away to school, but you insisted your cousin could look after her."

Mallory came to her feet, her head held high. "I'm leaving today. But I find myself short of funds. I'm loath to ask you for money, but I have no choice."

Her father ducked his head, and she could see that he was embarrassed. When he looked up at her, his eyes were sorrowful. "Some people just shouldn't have children, Mallory. I know we haven't been good parents to you, but we had a life we loved, and you just didn't fit into it."

Mallory shook her head. "I don't know either of you, and I don't ask you to know me. All I want is to leave. If you'll assist me, I'll have Safwat drive me to the docks."

He stood. "I'll get the money from my office."

When he left, Mallory looked at her mother. "I apologize for any inconvenience that I may have caused you. I can assure you that you will never again be bothered by me."

Her mother stood up and moved to Mallory, but didn't touch her. "I have many regrets in my life, and one is that I never knew my own daughter." She shrugged. "If you had been born the son your father wanted, it would have been different. You can't understand what pride a man can have in a son. They like to boast about their son's accomplishments and—"

"I understand," Mallory said, moving to the door. "I've always known what a disappointment I was to you."

"Would you like us to accompany you to the docks?"

her mother asked, as if that would make up for some of their neglect.

"No, if you don't mind, I'd prefer to go alone."

"Your father and I will be criticized if you travel without a chaperon."

Mallory looked at the stranger who by birth was her mother. Her mother's only concern seemed to be what people thought. "I will keep to myself and give no one the least reason to blame you for my behavior."

Lady Julia looked doubtful. "I suppose there's nothing else we can do."

By now her father had returned, and he handed Mallory an envelope. "This should cover all your expenses. I have been more than generous with you. When you get home, buy yourself a new wardrobe."

"Thank you." She turned to the door. "I must hurry because Safwat is waiting to take me to the docks."

They walked with her to the front door. "You wouldn't have enjoyed life with us, Mallory," her mother said. "We travel so often and don't really have a place we call home."

"You have a home in England that is suffering from neglect," she reminded them.

"We feel no kinship with Stoneridge, since it will pass to a distant cousin on your father's death."

Her father patted her shoulder, and her mother pressed a stiff kiss on her cheek.

Safwat helped Mallory into the buggy, and she didn't look back when they drove away. There was nothing for her here; there was nothing for her in England, either.

She could see herself becoming a spinster like Cousin Phoebe, and ending her days alone and friendless. But she'd had one glorious night of love, and no one could take that memory away from her.

*   *   *

A long line of riders wound its way across the desert. Michael and his family stayed abreast with Prince Khaldun, while British soldiers rode beside Bedouin tribesmen. When they came to the Nile River, they followed it toward Cairo. Just before they reached the outlying vicinity of the city, Prince Khaldun called a halt.

"This is as far as I go." He and Michael dismounted and embraced. Khaldun's eyes were sorrowful. "When friends part, it is like losing a part of one's self, but when those friends are like brothers, they will never lose that friendship."

Michael nodded. "We will meet again, Khaldun."

Michael knew that he would never know a better friend. "Yes, we shall meet again. Good friends shouldn't be apart too long."

Michael mounted his horse and allowed his eyes to run down the line of Jebeliya warriors. He'd come to know so many of them. He had eaten their food and fought at their side. A part of him would always be Akhdar 'em Akraba. He raised his hand in a silent salute, and turned his mount toward Cairo.

When Michael topped a sand dune and turned to look back, Khaldun and his soldiers had disappeared. Even their horses' hoof prints had disappeared in the shifting sand.

Lord Tyler and Lady Julia were packing crates of artifacts to be shipped to the British Museum when Safwat entered the room.

"There are very important people wanting to see you," he said, bobbing into a bow. "Very important."

Lord Tyler laid an ebony statue aside and looked up in irritation. "Who is it this time, Safwat?"

"Very important," he repeated.

Lady Julia patted her hair into place. "I'm weary anyway, Tyler. We'll see who it is, but don't offer them tea. We don't want to be late for Lady Mangrem's dinner. She always has the most interesting guests."

Michael glanced around the small sitting room that seemed more like a museum, looking for anything that would prove Mallory was there. But there was nothing that was hers.

Raile picked up a small Egyptian statue of Osiris and turned it over in his hand and then handed it to Kassidy. "Fake," he said distastefully.

"You've a good eye for authenticity," Lord Tyler said, entering the room with his wife. "Most people are deceived by that statue."

"I'm surprised it would fool anyone since it's made of black marble, a substance not available to ancient Egyptians."

"That's right," Lady Julia declared. "But not many people are aware of that." She looked curiously at the four people in the room. The woman wore an emerald green riding habit that could only have come from Paris. The three men were obviously wealthy, and of great importance.

"My servant failed to give us your names," Lady Julia said by way of apology.

Michael stepped forward. "These are my parents, the duke and duchess of Ravenworth, and my brother-in-law, Lord Glencarin. I'm sure your daughter had told you about me—I'm Michael."

The Stanhopes were clearly impressed by their guests. But they were also curious.

"Well," Lord Tyler said, "I have certainly heard of you. Who hasn't heard of the DeWinter family? But Mallory didn't mention that she was acquainted with you."

Michael looked stunned, and then annoyed. "Perhaps if you would ask Mallory to join us, we can clear up everything. Where is she?"

Lady Julia offered them a seat. "Would you like tea?"

Kassidy could see that her son was displeased that Mallory had not told her parents about their marriage, and she was afraid of what he might say, so she intervened. "That would be nice, thank you. We can't stay long though, because the captain of our yacht told us that we must get under way before sundown. We only came for your daughter."

Lord Tyler looked confused. "What do you want with Mallory?" Then he became suspicious. People such as the DeWinters would not be interested in his daughter unless she had done something to displease them.

"I know we English should behave in a way that is a credit to queen and country," Lord Tyler said, "so, let me assure you that you don't have to be concerned about Mallory's actions any longer, since she is on her way back to England."

"When did she leave?" Michael demanded harshly.

"Please don't concern yourself," Lord Tyler said. "And I want you to understand that Mallory's misconduct has nothing to do with her mother and me. She was raised by my wife's cousin, and we saw little of her. If her actions seem unconventional, I pray that you will consider her youth and her lack of guidance and not blame us."

Warrick looked quickly at Kassidy, knowing that Lord Tyler had said the wrong thing.

Raile placed his hand on Kassidy's arm, hoping to calm her, but she shook his hand off.

Kassidy's eyes were blazing. "I can no longer allow you to malign your daughter, Lord Tyler. While I have not met her personally, I have come to admire her greatly. She has courage and character that many of us lack. Rather than condemning her, you should be glad that you are blessed with such a daughter. I can assure you that this family has every reason to be grateful to her, and we shall cherish her as you obviously haven't."

Lady Julia moved forward to support her husband. "Just what did our daughter do that you think is so wonderful?"

Raile spoke up before Kassidy could inform them. "Perhaps we should let our son tell you," he said, looking pointedly at Kassidy.

Michael felt no better about these people than his mother did. "Not only did Mallory save my life and that of my father, but she did a great service for her country, as well. My father plans to advise Her Majesty of Mallory's actions, so she will be justly rewarded."

He looked at Mallory's mother, who could only stare at him in amazement. She had to sit down when she heard his next words.

"Apparently Mallory hasn't told you that she is my wife."

Lord Tyler and Lady Julia looked at each other in stunned silence. Then the significance of Michael's announcement struck them.

"Your Grace," Lady Julia said, turning to Kassidy. "To think of it, our families united by marriage. I can't tell you how happy this makes me. We should intercept Mallory and bring her back. We'll have a grand party. Perhaps the viceroy himself will attend."

Once again, Raile thought it best to intervene before Kassidy could find her voice. "You will excuse us if we seem impatient. But we are on our way to England."

Lady Julia could see all her grand plans dissolving. "But surely you could remain for a few days longer? I'll send Safwat to fetch my daughter. Perhaps her barge hasn't yet sailed."

"Thank you, no," Michael said emphatically. "I will find my wife without your assistance." He turned to leave, his anger smoldering.

Kassidy and Raile followed after him without a word.

Warrick, enjoying himself, smiled politely as he paused in the doorway. "I don't believe we'll be staying for tea after all."

After their guests had departed, Lord Tyler and Lady Julia exchanged glances. It was Mallory's father who spoke first. "We deserve no better than we got, Julia. We have cut Mallory out of our lives, and now she has a new family. I can only imagine how cold and heartless we appeared to the duke and duchess."

"Oh, Tyler, we have treated our daughter badly. I wouldn't blame her if she never wanted to see us again."

"It's strange, but I find myself comparing my behavior to that of Henry the Eighth. Like him, I wanted a son desperately. And like King Henry, when I found myself with a daughter, I rejected her. His daughter, Elizabeth, was the greatest monarch England has ever known, and similarly, our daughter has distinguished herself with no help from us. She will one day be the duchess of Ravenworth. We, I fear, will not be a part of her life."

"Nor do we deserve to be. For the first time, I'm ashamed of myself. She needed me as a mother, and all I could do was criticize her. It's no wonder she didn't tell us about her marriage."

"I can't even be angry that Lord Michael didn't ask my permission to marry Mallory. Why should he—I've never been a father to her."

"Oh, Tyler, what have we done?"

Chapter 30

*T*he Nightingale *dipped her* sails as a signal for the cargo barge to come about. Since a British flag waved above the yacht, the captain of the ship called out in English, "What is your business with us?"

Captain Norris called back to him. "This is the ship of the duke and duchess of Ravenworth. Their daughter-in-law is aboard your ship. Her husband wishes to board you to get his wife."

"Come ahead," the Egyptian captain called back, thinking only an Inglizi could lose his wife.

Mallory's eyes came open with a start. Had the ship stopped? Most probably they had put in at some port to take on cargo. She turned to her side, wanting only to reach the headwaters of the Nile so she could board a ship that would take her to England.

Tears gathered in her eyes. She was not the same

woman she'd been when she came to Egypt. She had known happiness, and she had known sadness. She had fallen deeply in love and she had killed a man. How could she take up her old life as if nothing had happened?

She buried her face in the pillow. She would never be happy again.

The door of her cabin flew open, and she jerked her head up to see Michael standing in the doorway. Light from the corridor poured into the small quarters, and she could see that his features were etched in anger.

"Don't you think it's a bit usual for a wife to leave her husband without asking him?"

She sat up slowly, not knowing what to think about his sudden appearance. "H-how did you get here?"

"Never mind that." He reached out for her and lifted her into his arms. "You will not leave me until I tire of you." His green eyes probed into her blue eyes. "And I have not yet tired of you."

"Michael, I—"

"Be silent! You have already caused me no end of trouble. You are coming with me, and I will hear nothing to the contrary."

Mallory thought her heart would burst with happiness. He wanted her, or he would never have come after her. "Yes, Michael."

He reached for the gown that she had folded neatly across a chair. Expertly, he pulled it over her nightgown, turned her around, and laced the back.

When Mallory would have spoken, he silenced her with a glare.

Lifting her in his arms, he carried her up the dimly lit passage to the upper deck, where curious onlookers watched with smiles.

"Thank you, captain," Michael said. "I'll just have my man load my wife's belongings on my ship, and we'll trouble you no more."

"Yes, Excellency," the Arab captain said with feeling. "You should beat your wife often, as I do mine. Then she will think before she leaves you."

Michael's eyes gleamed as he glanced down at Mallory. "Perhaps I'll take your advice. This woman is a most disobedient wife."

Mallory buried her face against his chest, too happy to speak.

Without ceremony, Michael flung Mallory over his shoulder and climbed over the railing and down a rope ladder to a waiting longboat, where he plopped her onto a seat.

She saw the huge ship just a few feet away. "Where are you taking me?"

"To my family's yacht."

After her trunk had been brought aboard the longboat, they were under way. Mallory searched Michael's face. "I thought I wouldn't see you again."

He glanced, not at her, but at the *Nightingale.* "My parents wait to be formally introduced to you. I believe you will understand when I say they are very curious about you."

She looked down at her simple gray linen gown, feeling embarrassed at how shabby it was. "But I'm not dressed properly to be presented to your family."

He turned to stare at her. "Perhaps you would prefer a long black gown and a veil over your face?"

She lowered her gaze, wondering how much he knew about the role she played in Caldoia. "No, I will never again wear the clothing of an Arab woman."

He was aware that they were being observed from both

ships, so he merely took her hand. "What am I to do with you, Mallory?"

"You could have allowed me to reach England, then I would have troubled you no more."

His eyes swept her shimmering hair that seemed to capture the dying rays of the sun. "No, I couldn't do that. Like it or no, you are my wife."

She had no opportunity to answer because they were approaching the *Nightingale.*

Once Mallory was on board, she was surrounded by Michael's family. The duchess took her hand and led her down the steps of a companionway into a brightly colored sitting room, while the rest of the family followed.

When they were away from curious eyes, Kassidy hugged Mallory and then stood back to look her over from head to foot and smiled. "I can see why my son married you, my dear. You are lovely."

"It's my turn," Raile said, taking Mallory's hand and raising it to his lips. "My son is fortunate indeed. Welcome to the DeWinter family, Mallory."

Mallory hadn't expected such kindness. Her eyes were shining with tears when Lord Warrick came up to her and brushed her cheek with a kiss.

"I know we must be a bit overwhelming to you," Lord Warrick told her. "I once stood where you are now, and was enfolded into the circle of this extraordinary family." He glanced at Michael, who had just entered, after directing the men where to place Mallory's trunk. "This family is fortunate indeed, for all our women are beauties."

Michael pulled Mallory into his arms. "What do you think, Father, did I choose well?"

"I'd say you found a rare jewel, Michael," his father said.

Raile opened a bottle of wine and passed glasses around. "I'd like to drink a toast to my new daughter-in-law. Without her, I wouldn't be here today, and neither would Michael."

Mallory turned to Michael. "You know what I did?"

"I didn't at first. But I should have known you could not be trusted to go to Cairo as I instructed. I should be angry with you for putting yourself in danger."

Now, in spite of her attempt to hide her tears, they spilled down her cheeks. "I will never forget that I took a man's life. I can't get the look on his face out of my mind."

Kassidy came to her and enfolded her in her arms. "You aren't to dwell on that. Think only that you saved my husband and yours. From what I've heard, Sheik Sidi Ahmed was an evil man and deserved to die."

How comforting it was to put her head on the duchess's shoulder. Mallory had never known a mother's comfort before now. "I . . . will always see his face."

Kassidy held her at arm's length. "No, you won't. After today, you will not give that man a thought." Kassidy reached into Raile's breast pocket and withdrew his handkerchief, dabbing at Mallory's cheeks. "My dear, if you cry another tear, you'll have me crying with you."

"This is to be a happy evening," Raile said, trying to introduce a lighter mood. "To my family. No man was ever more blessed by his women, or more cursed by them," he said, winking at his son.

Kassidy laughed. "Mallory, I think my husband is referring to us and my daughter, Arrian. You see, my dear, we must always keep them guessing about what we are going to do—that way they won't come to think of us as commonplace."

Mallory smiled, feeling the warmth of the DeWinters surround her. But when she looked at Michael, she could see the brooding light in his eyes. He was quiet now, almost subdued, and she didn't know why.

Mallory followed Kassidy into the spacious cabin, where her feet sank into a thick cream-colored rug.

Kassidy didn't understand why her son had asked her to put Mallory in separate quarters.

"This is my daughter, Arrian's, bedroom," she said. "I hope you'll be comfortable here. I suppose I should have had it redecorated after Arrian married and moved to Scotland, but I kept it the way she had it. I suppose I'm sentimental."

Mallory looked around the room, at the powder blue and lemon yellow furnishings. There was a narrow bed with silken bed hangings and coverlet. There was a yellow couch against one wall, and another wall had a long dressing table.

"Arrian chose the materials herself on her twelfth birthday."

"It's lovely."

Kassidy smiled. "I know you are feeling somewhat overwhelmed by all of us. But I want you to know how happy I am that Michael had the good sense to marry you."

"But you don't know me."

"I have always been gifted with great perception. I know you will make my son very happy."

"Your Grace—"

"I don't suppose you'd consent to call me Kassidy, would you?"

"I will try, but you are a duchess."

She touched Mallory's hand. "Someday I'll tell you how I came to be a duchess. I'm Michael's mother, and I want to be someone you can come to when you need a friend. You know, Mallory, one day you will stand in my place."

"Oh, Your Grace, I hope not for a very long time."

Kassidy laughed as she looked into earnest blue eyes. "Let us hope so." Then she became serious. "Michael's room is just across the companionway. He thought you would be more comfortable in here."

Mallory lowered her eyes, but not before Kassidy saw sadness reflected in the blue depths.

"It is but a short distance across the hallway. Perhaps you should take the first steps, Mallory."

Mallory turned away and closed her eyes. "I will not do that, Your Grace."

Kassidy knew something wasn't right between her son and his new bride, but she would not interfere. They must find their own way to one another, she could not help them in this.

Mallory sat beside the duke, listening to the light banter exchanged at the table. She had never known a family with such warmth and kindness toward each other. She watched Warrick as he spoke of his wife, Arrian, with love and respect. Clearly, he missed their children and her.

It was apparent that the heart of the family was the duchess. All three men appeared to defer to her, and their eyes softened when they looked at her. Mallory was not allowed to feel like an outsider. They included her in the conversation, while asking about her life.

Kassidy's eyes saddened when she heard the unspoken loneliness of Mallory's childhood.

"Tell me, Mallory, what do you think of the *Nightingale?*" the duke asked.

"I never knew a ship could be so luxurious, Your Grace. It reminds me of a floating palace. Does the name have some significance?"

Raile's and Kassidy's eyes met, and they smiled.

Warrick laughed. "We would all like to know the significance of the name, Mallory. But Raile and Kassidy keep it as their secret."

Kassidy placed her hand lovingly on her son-in-law's. "I'll leave you a note in my diary, to be opened in the event of my death, telling you about the *Nightingale.*"

Raile caught his wife's hand. "I think not." He raised her hand to his lips. "That's our secret. It will die with us."

Mallory looked at Michael, aching inside to have him look at her the way his father looked at his mother. She wondered if this family knew what a rare gift they had—yes, they knew, and they treasured it.

As the *Nightingale* moved from the Nile into the flow of the Mediterranean Sea, moonlight cast shimmering reflections across the dark water.

Mallory stood at the railing, feeling on the fringe of something wonderful. How she wanted to be a part of the feeling of togetherness she felt in this family.

"I wondered where you disappeared to, Mallory," Michael said, coming up beside her. "I looked around, and you were gone."

"You were playing chess with Warrick, and I didn't want to disturb you. Who won?"

"I did this time. But my brother-in-law is good. Most probably, he'll win next time."

"Congratulations."

He looked down at her. "So you like the *Nightingale?*"

"I never knew anything could be so wonderful. You must love this ship."

"Yes, I do, but wait until you see Ravenworth. That's the family's real love."

She shivered from cold, and he pulled her into the warmth of his arms. "That's your ancestral home, Michael?"

"Yes. You know, it's strange, before I came to Egypt I thought little of my heritage, and even less of my future. Now everything seems so clear, as if a door has opened and I saw the secret of life."

"That's because you are one of the fortunate ones who had your life set before you were born."

A wisp of her hair blew across his face, and he ran the silken strand through his fingers. "I met your father and mother."

"What did you think?"

"That you have had a lot of loneliness in your life. I intend to change that."

She looked up at him, her breath caught in her throat. "What are you saying?"

"That you belong to this family now, and we will take care of you."

She dropped her gaze to the gold button on his shirt. "Oh."

He smiled, not knowing that she was hurting inside. "How would you like to take the helm of the *Nightingale?*"

Her eyes suddenly gleamed. "Is that allowed?"

"Of course." He pulled her forward and led her to the upper deck.

"Mallory, may I present Captain Norris? Captain, my wife, Lady Mallory."

The captain grinned. "Pleased to meet you, your ladyship. I never thought his lordship would settle down. After meeting you, I can see why he has."

Mallory liked the captain and the easy way he spoke to Michael. "I'm happy to meet you, Captain Norris."

"Mallory, Captain Norris taught me all I know about sailing. He's the only captain the *Nightingale* has ever had."

"She's my only love, m'lady. I know every bolt on her, and I guard her jealously."

"I'll relieve you for a while," Michael said, taking the wheel.

"She's running smoothly, m'lord. When you're ready to go below, just have MacNab take the helm." He touched the brim of his hat. "Have a pleasant evening, m'lady."

When the captain had gone, Michael pulled Mallory to him and placed her hands on the wheel. "Do you feel what I do when you take her helm?"

"What do you feel?"

"That she's somehow alive. She's like a lady that will respond to my every touch."

She smiled up at him. "I'm sure there were many ladies who would do just that."

He pressed his hands over her, helping her guide the wheel. "I was speaking of the ship."

"I like your family, Michael."

"They like you."

Suddenly he tied the wheel off, and turned her to face him. "Why did you leave me?"

"I . . . had much to think about. I had killed a man. That is a difficult thing to live with."

"I have killed many men." There was regret in his voice.

He outlined her face with his finger. "It was you who nursed me the night I was so ill, wasn't it?"

"Yes."

"I felt it was."

"Michael, I wanted to give you your freedom, because we married for the wrong reasons. Seeing your parents and Lord Warrick, I know I don't belong with you. I have nothing to give you."

He touched his lips to her forehead. "On the day when you can give me what I want, come to me, and I'll be waiting. Until then, I will be patient."

"I don't understand."

He smiled sadly. "More's the pity."

He turned her back to the wheel, and for over an hour they steered the ship.

Mallory felt as if she were part of the wind, as one with the sea, and her heart was beating wildly because Michael was pressing his body against hers. She remembered their wedding night, when he had made love to her, and she ached for him to take her to his cabin and make love to her again.

She tossed back her head and found him watching her intently.

"Michael, I want to be your wife."

"Why, Mallory?"

She stood on her tiptoes and pressed her lips against his.

Taking a deep breath, he pulled her tightly against him, deepening the kiss. Suddenly, he released her and called out. "MacNab, you can relieve me now."

When the crewman came on deck, Michael led Mallory to his cabin. It was dark inside as he took her in his arms and pressed a burning kiss on her trembling lips.

ichael ran a stroking hand down Mallory's hair. "So soft, so alive," he murmured in her ear.

"Michael?"

"Yes, Mallory?"

"You said that you wanted something from me that I have not yet offered. I gave you my body, and then I gave you freedom—what else can you want from me?"

"Don't you know?"

"No. I have thought about it, and I have nothing of value that could possibly interest you."

"Why did you leave me in Caldoia?"

"For many reasons. Because I'd killed a man and didn't want you to know about it. Because . . . because you called out another woman's name when you were ill."

His hand slipped up her arm, and he paused at her soft shoulder. "I did?"

"Yes, you did. I believe that when a man calls out a

woman's name in his delirium, he must love her."

He tried to think whose name he could have uttered. "Will you tell me the name?"

"Samantha."

His smile was hidden by the darkness. "And just what did I say about Samantha?"

"I didn't understand it, you weren't lucid. You said something about a Gypsy . . . love and betrayal. I don't remember exactly."

Michael's arm slid around her shoulder, and he brought her against him. "Dare I hope you are jealous?"

She wanted to melt against his warmth and experience again the awakening of passion, but she dared not. "I have no right to be jealous, Michael."

He brought her closer to his bed, the only place in the room that was illuminated by the moon shining through the porthole. "And you want your freedom?"

What she really wanted was to stay in his embrace forever. "I . . . yes, I do."

His lips brushed her neck. "Why?"

"I . . . can't think when you do that."

He gripped her around the waist. "Oh?"

She twisted out of his arms. "Why are you doing this to me?"

He took her hand, kissing each finger. "Doing what, Mallory?"

"Michael, don't torment me. You know I'm not accustomed to—"

He bent down, his lips brushing hers and then settling into a long, drugging kiss. All the while, he was unfastening the back of her gown.

He kissed her throat, her cheek, and nipped her ear while she collapsed weakly against him. "Now do you know what I want from you, Mallory?"

It suddenly became clear to her, and with that realization came pain. "You want a son," she whispered.

She couldn't see the disappointment in his eyes.

"I want many sons, Mallory, will you give them to me?"

"That's why you married me so quickly," she said as her mind began to clear. Why hadn't she seen it then, it was there before her eyes. "You didn't marry me to save my reputation, you thought you might die, and you wanted to get me with child."

His voice was deep as he slipped her gown off her shoulders. "Does it matter why I married you? I wanted you then, I want you now."

"I'll give you your son, Michael. I suppose I owe you that much."

His lips brushed the hollow of her shoulder, and he laced his hands through her hair, untangling the curls. "And I, sweet Mallory, what shall I give you?"

"A family," she said as he lifted her into his arms and settled her on his bed. "I want to belong to this family."

He came down beside her, his hand trembling as it slid over her hips, pushing her underclothing aside. "Then come to me." He settled into her softness, and his body shook with emotions he couldn't understand. "Come to me, and I'll fill you with sons, Mallory."

"Michael, I—"

"Shh," he whispered, "don't deny me. I will have you every night, and when we dock in England, you will be carrying my seed."

He wasn't saying the words she longed to hear, but his hands burned into her flesh, and his mouth was draining her of denial.

With a forward thrust, he robbed Mallory of her reasoning. With his hands, he guided her hips so that she met his sensual movements.

Oh, how she wanted to have his son, to carry within her that part of him that no other woman could give him, a legitimate heir.

"Fiery little redhead," he whispered, "you do take my breath away."

She felt a building pressure and gasped when her body trembled and quaked. Wave after wave of wild sensations exploded within the deepest core of her body, and she clutched at Michael, trying to hold on to him. In her mind, she touched the sky, the stars, the moon, before she settled back into the bed.

He rubbed his mouth against hers. "I chose well for the mother of my sons. You have fire in your blood, Mallory. With you I could spend my life in bed."

Her mind was slowly clearing, and she realized she was just an instrument to him—a receptacle to carry his seed and give him sons.

"There is one more thing I want from you," he said, pulling her head into the light and staring into her softened eyes. "And this one is the most important."

"I can't imagine what that could be, Michael."

"When you know, you will tell me."

He was a mysterious man with great depth, and she doubted she'd ever understand him. Her hand moved over his back, and she felt the scars there. With tears in her eyes, she kissed the scar that ran across his shoulder.

He pulled her to him and stared into shimmering eyes. "Do you weep for me?"

She turned her head away. "I cry for innocence lost, Michael."

"Yours or mine?"

"I wonder if you were ever innocent."

"Perhaps more so than you know. If only we'd met before Egypt, you would know how I've changed."

His hands were again moving across her body, sliding delightfully, arousing, pulling her beneath him. His kisses were drugging, and he knew just what to do to make her want him.

Mallory willingly gave herself to her husband. As long as he needed her, he would keep her with him. She wouldn't allow herself to think past the day she gave him a son and he no longer needed her.

Kassidy removed her gown and draped it over a chair while her husband reclined on the bed, watching each movement. "Raile, something is wrong with Michael and Mallory. They don't act like two people in love."

He watched her unpin her hair, and a curtain of gold fell to her shoulders. "Not everyone is as fortunate as we are, Kassidy. And don't forget, you didn't love me when we were first married."

She backed up to him so he could unhook her pearl necklace. "It's more than that, Raile. Mallory is so sweet, but she never smiles. And Michael—well, he's not the son I raised. Sometimes, when he thinks no one is watching, I see such . . . remorse in his eyes. What could it be?"

Raile dropped her pearls on the bed, and pushed her hair aside, his lips brushing against the nape of her neck. "Must we talk about this now, Kassidy?"

She sat on the bed, her eyes troubled. "Yes. I want to know what happened to my son in Egypt. I don't mean about the beating he took from Sidi. I see cynicism and a hardness in his eyes that wasn't there before."

Raile had been dreading this moment, for he had known his wife would begin to question the change that had come over their son. A man could better understand what Michael had been through—war, fighting, killing.

Did a man ever forget the faceless, nameless men he'd killed in battle?

He took her hand and laced his fingers through hers. "Michael has faced death, Kassidy. He's killed men—he'll never be the same. As his mother, you should never ask him about what happened in Egypt. If he wants to tell you, that's another matter, but don't ask him. Our son is strong, Kassidy. Stronger than even I had imagined. He did the impossible and won, but not without it taking something out of him. He will need time to put all this behind him."

"And we'll give him that time, Raile. But one thing that worries me is that I don't know why he married Mallory. Poor child, we know she hasn't been cherished by her mother and father, and I'm not sure that Michael loves her. I am growing fonder of her every day. She seems so alone at times. I want to assure her that we want her in our family. But it's Michael's love that she really needs."

"She's stronger than you think, Kassidy. And why wouldn't Michael love her? She's sweet, lovely. She has all the qualities a man would look for in a wife."

Kassidy smiled and slid her arms around his neck. "And just what did you look for when you took me to wife?"

He smiled against her hair. "Lovely, for certain—sweet, I don't think so, my hot-tempered little hellion."

"Raile!"

"What other woman do you know who would sail to Egypt, trek across the desert, and prepare to take on any enemy?"

"Mallory, for one. Only she went farther than I—she actually rescued you and Michael." Kassidy rested her face against his chest, comforted by the beating of his heart. "On, Raile, what would I have done if anything had happened to you?"

He clasped her to him, and neither spoke—there was no need for words between them. Their lives were so tightly interwoven that one could scarcely breathe without the other taking a breath.

Raile touched his lips to hers and pulled her against his body. Kassidy would never know the weakness he'd experienced in that prison. He would have lost his mind if he hadn't known that he'd hold her in his arms again.

There was a full moon, and Mallory lay on the soft bed, watching reflecting patterns of the ocean sparkle on the ceiling like breaking waves. How glorious it was to bask in the luxury of her surroundings.

Since the night Michael had taken her to his room, she had remained there. The next day, the *Nightingale* would sail up the Thames to London, and the voyage would be over.

The cabin door opened and Michael entered. He was silent as he moved to the porthole and then back to the door. Restlessly, he paced back and forth.

"Michael, is something wrong?" she asked, sitting up and pulling on her robe.

"No," he said, pausing near the door. "Go back to sleep. I'm sorry if I disturbed you."

She belted her robe and moved to stand beside him. "I wasn't asleep." She reached her hand out to him, placing it on his shoulder. "Can I help?"

He shrugged her hand off and moved back to the porthole, staring into the night. "I'm not fit company, Mallory. Perhaps you might want to consider sleeping in Arrian's cabin tonight."

"If that's what you want." She moved to the door, but he grabbed her hand and kept her from leaving.

"I don't know what I want, Mallory. I suppose I've been away from civilization so long, and tomorrow it's going to come crashing in on me."

"I don't understand, Michael."

"I'm not sure I do either. I knew who I was when I went away, and now I realize I can't go back to the life I had before I went to Egypt."

"I'm sorry, Michael."

He tugged at an errant red curl. "That's not true of you, is it, Mallory? You know who you are, don't you?"

"No, Michael, not anymore."

"You're my wife."

"I'm not sure of that."

"Are you still fretting because you didn't understand the marriage vows?"

"Yes, I suppose so."

He cradled her in the crook of his arm and rested his chin on the top of her head. "It's a husband's place to make his wife happy, and your doubts I can do something about, Mallory."

"But, I don't see—"

"Go to your cabin and wait. I'll come for you shortly."

"But—"

He led her across the hallway and opened the door for her. "Smile, nothing is ever as bad as it appears."

She watched him disappear with a frown on her face. What was he talking about?

It was dark inside the cabin, but she didn't bother to light a lantern. She sat down on the couch and waited for Michael to return.

Michael was banging on the cabin door. "Mother, Father, wake up. I need to talk to you."

Raile lit a lantern, while Kassidy pulled on her robe. "What time is it?" Kassidy asked in alarm.

"I don't know. After midnight." Raile opened the door and found his son smiling. "Michael, do you know what time it is?"

"I don't care, we're going to have a wedding."

"What?" Kassidy said. "A wedding? Michael, what are you talking about?"

"Father, I've already asked Captain Norris to perform the ceremony. He's authorized, since he's a captain and we're at sea. Mother, will you help Mallory dress? I don't know what you have to make her look like a bride, but knowing you, anything's possible."

"Michael, what is this about?" his father demanded. "Weren't you and Mallory already married?"

"When Mallory and I were married in Kamar Ginena, the man who performed the ceremony spoke no English. You know how women are. Mallory doesn't feel married."

Kassidy smiled and clasped her hands. "Oh, Michael, what a romantic thing to do. I did so regret that I didn't get to see either you or Arrian married. Imagine, a wedding at sea!"

She threw open her trunk and rummaged through it, throwing clothes and petticoats on the bed. At last she came to what she'd been looking for—a white lace mantilla that had been her mother's. She held it lovingly in her hands. "Yes, this will do nicely."

Raile looked at his wife and his son as if they'd both lost their minds.

"I have a white silk gown that will be perfect," Kassidy continued enthusiastically.

She gathered up her bounty and rushed out the door. "I'll just help Mallory dress."

Michael looked at his father. "What is it about weddings that makes women react in such a manner?"

"I don't know, son. But take my advice—give them what they want—they'll get it anyway, and this way, you can look generous instead of a fool."

Chapter 32

ne of the crew members had gathered all the blooming plants from throughout the yacht and placed them in the formal sitting room, where the ceremony was to take place. Dozen of candles had been lit, and their glow gave an ethereal atmosphere to the room.

Captain Norris, looking very distinguished in his white dress uniform, thumbed through a book, nervously reading over the wedding ceremony.

"I never married anyone before, m'lord," he told Warrick, who was dressed formally for the occasion.

"Since they are already married, Captain, you have only to go through the formalities. But the words are the most important part to Mallory, I believe."

"I want this to be a solemn occasion, because I've known Lord Michael all his life. But I never thought I'd have the honor of conducting his wedding."

Lord Warrick glanced over the captain's shoulder. "Be certain and emphasize the part about love and obey."

Kassidy placed the lace mantilla on Mallory's head and handed her six white silk roses she had taken off the shoulder of one of her other gowns.

"You look lovely, my dear." She brushed Mallory's cheek with a kiss. "Michael told me about your wedding, and I can understand why you would want to be married in an English ceremony."

"I . . . never thought Michael would—"

"Be so sentimental?"

"Yes, that's it."

"Men are much more sentimental than they would have us believe. A woman just has to pretend to be soft and demure. A man likes to think that he is the all-knowing wise one of the family—and if a wife is all-knowing and wiser, she'll allow her husband to keep his dream."

Mallory laughed. "I hope I can make Michael as happy as you've made his father."

"You will. I'm sure of it."

Michael actually felt tension in the pit of his stomach. He hadn't been this nervous at the real wedding ceremony. He looked at Warrick, who could only smile.

"Your sister never had a formal wedding either, Michael. When she hears about this, she'll probably demand that Captain Norris marry us."

Michael glanced at the crew members who had dressed for the occasion and were standing at attention at the back of the room. Suddenly the door opened and his mother entered, beaming and looking beautiful in an emerald green gown. There was a catch in his throat as his father led Mallory forward.

As Mallory walked slowly toward him, her eyes locked with his. She was shimmering, all in white, and the lace mantilla made a perfect foil for her flaming hair. Never had she looked so beautiful, and he felt his chest swell with pride that she belonged to him—and would be twice tied to him.

As their hands met, Michael led her to Captain Norris. As the age-old words were spoken in the captain's clipped tones, Mallory stared straight ahead, fearing she would cry because of the beauty of the ceremony.

She felt Michael's hand tighten as he slipped a beautiful emerald ring on her finger. She could only suppose the ring was his mother's.

Raile and Kassidy stood with hands clasped while Kassidy remembered her own wedding. Michael and Mallory seemed so right for each other, she thought, and what a handsome couple they made.

Mallory's eyes were swimming with tears when Captain Norris proclaimed them husband and wife.

Michael turned Mallory to him, and his eyes probed hers. She caught her breath and her lips trembled beneath his.

Suddenly Mallory was pulled from his arms, to face a smiling Warrick. "I claim my right to kiss the bride," Warrick said, brushing a kiss on her cheek. "You know, Mallory," he told her with a teasing light in his eyes, "you can never deny that you were married to this man, because you have an entire ship's crew as witnesses."

Raile took Mallory's hand and hugged her to him. "A flaming-haired daughter. I warrant you'll lead my son a merry chase—I pray that it's so."

Mallory already adored the duke, but in that moment,

she felt closer to him than she'd ever felt to her own father.

Kassidy hugged her son, and whispered so only he could hear. "How kind it was of you to do this for Mallory, Michael. Many men would have thought it frivolous, but you are sensitive and loving."

At that moment, she saw something that pulled at her heart. What was it—agony? Uncertainty?

"Loving, I'm not sure I know what that means, Mother. I merely wanted there never to be any doubt that any child of mine is legitimate."

Kassidy frowned. Could this be her Michael, or some stranger? No one else seemed to notice his mood. Michael said the right things, smiled at the right time, appeared to be in a festive mood. But Kassidy watched him closely, wondering if he would ever be the man he'd once been.

Wine was poured for everyone, and many toasts were made to the happy couple. At last, Michael led his bride to their cabin and closed the door behind them.

Mallory came readily into his arms, her mouth opening beneath soft, probing lips.

"Michael, it was wonderful!" she said, trying to catch her breath.

"Happy?"

"Oh, yes. I can't imagine a more beautiful wedding."

She moved out of his arms and gently removed the lace mantilla and folded it carefully. "This was your grandmother's, you know."

"No, I didn't."

"Your mother's mother."

"And the dress?"

"Your mother's. Michael, your family is so extraordinary. Your father pretending to be gruff, but his eyes give him away. And your mother is the kind of mother every girl would like to have. Warrick, so handsome, but I could see the loneliness in his eyes. He told me tonight that he misses your sister and the children. I can't wait to meet Arrian. Will she like me, do you think? Will the children like me?"

Michael laughed and took her in his arms. "Come here, you little magpie. I have something on my mind besides talk."

The *Nightingale* came into harbor under full sail. Captain Norris brought her expertly into port and ordered her sails to be lowered.

Mallory stood beside Kassidy, watching the loading and unloading of other ships in the harbor.

Suddenly, Kassidy's eyes lit up, and she waved excitedly toward the crested coach.

"It's Arrian!" she cried. "Now, how could she have known we'd be arriving today?"

Raile came up behind them, also waving at his daughter. "Nothing deters our daughter when she wants to know something. She's probably had someone watching for us this last week. And look, Aunt Mary's with her."

Lady Arrian raced across the dock and hardly gave the crew member time to swing the gangplank in place before she came aboard. First, she ran to her father and was encircled in his arms.

"Oh, Father, you're home." She touched his face and buried her face against his chest. "I was so frightened for you."

"How could anything happen to me with a daughter like you waiting for me?" he said, looking down at her tenderly.

Arrian kissed him soundly and turned into her husband's waiting arms. Warrick held her for a long moment. "I missed you, Arrian."

She raised her face to his. "And I missed you. I don't think I'll ever allow you to go away without me again."

"How are the children?"

"Wonderful." Arrian's eyes met her brother's over Warrick's shoulder, and she went to him. "Oh, Michael, I heard what happened to you. Are you all right?"

He smiled down at her. "I stand before you, the image of health."

She stared at him, knowing there was something different about him, but not knowing what it was. They were closer than most brothers and sisters, and she sensed something was very wrong.

"I wouldn't allow anyone to write you about Mallory. I wanted to see your face when you met her."

"Who?"

Michael caught Mallory's hand and brought her forward. "Arrian, this is Mallory, my wife!"

For a moment Arrian was too stunned to speak, but she quickly recovered. "Did you say . . . I'm sorry, what is your name?"

Michael couldn't keep from laughing. "This is the first time I've seen you at a loss for words, Arrian."

The two women looked each other over carefully. Mallory was the first to smile. "I'd heard you were beautiful, and you are."

Arrian took her hand. "I know nothing about you, but you must be very special indeed if you caught my brother's attention." She laughed and hugged Mallory. "Michael married. He finally came to his senses. I want to hear all about you. We'll talk for hours when we get to Michael's town house."

Lady Mary chose that moment to come bustling aboard, grabbing the railing to steady herself on the swaying ship. "What's this about Michael?" she asked. "Did someone say Michael had come to his senses?"

Kassidy hugged her daughter and clasped Aunt Mary's hand. "Yes, dear Aunt Mary, Michael has finally come to his senses."

"Come along, everyone," Arrian said happily. "Cook has prepared all Father's favorite food. We have so much to celebrate tonight."

"Yes," Kassidy agreed. "Your father and Michael home safely, a new daughter, and a new granddaughter. I'd say we have much to be thankful about."

The town house was filled with laughter as everyone gathered in the formal salon. The meal had been superb, and afterward, the children were brought in and everyone had played with them.

Mallory held the new baby, looking down at her in awe. "She's wonderful."

"Uh-hmm," Arrian agreed.

Soon the nanny took the children upstairs and they were tucked into bed under their mother's watchful eye.

Now the family had congregated in the informal sitting room.

Mallory moved to the window and surveyed the DeWinter family. She could feel the love in this room. She smiled at something Aunt Mary had said about Michael having to buy a bigger town house or tell his sister to stop having babies.

"This was where Raile spent his bachelor days, Mallory," Kassidy explained, coming to sit beside her on the window seat. "When Michael came of age, we gave the town house to him. You may find it a bit cramped." She looked wistfully at her son. "Of course, there's always Ravenworth. If you so desired, the two of you could have the west wing all to yourselves."

Michael stood with one booted foot propped on the hammered brass fireplace ledge, his dark hair falling carelessly across his forehead, his riveting eyes on Mallory. "I believe this house will suit us for the time. I'm not yet ready to retire to country life."

"Well, I am. We're going home tomorrow," Raile announced. "I've been too long away from Ravenworth. Warrick, are you, Arrian, and the children going with us?"

"Yes. I believe we should give Michael and Mallory some time alone."

At that moment, all eyes went to Mallory, and she knew they were thinking about the heir she would one day present to them. Mallory could have told them that she was already with child, but tonight was not the time. For now, it was enough to celebrate the duke's and Michael's homecoming.

"Well, in any case, I'm going home," Aunt Mary said, rising to her feet and steadying herself on a silver-handled cane. "I've had enough excitement for one day."

She came to Mallory and squeezed her hand. "My great-nephew made a wise and charming choice in you. I never did care much for Lady Samantha Taylor—she's too flighty, and her voice begins to grate on my ears when I've been with her for a whole evening."

Mallory blinked, not knowing what to say. "It's been a pleasure meeting you, Lady Mary. Michael has told me so much about you. He's very fond of you."

Lady Mary patted her hand. "Call me Aunt Mary. And I'll be dropping in on you from time to time."

"That would be lovely," Mallory said, a bit overwhelmed. "Perhaps you can help me find my way around London."

Lady Mary's eyes lit up. "Indeed I shall, child." She glanced down at Mallory's plain brown gown. "I think I should show you the dress shops first."

Kassidy came to Mallory's rescue. "You mustn't mind my aunt, Mallory. As you can see, she has a difficult time speaking her mind."

Lady Mary raised her head and looked at each person in the room. "When you get to be my age, you can speak the truth without people taking offense. Everyone excuses me because they just say I'm in my dotage, when actually, I'm far from it."

"You'll be making witticisms when we're all dust," Michael said, walking his aunt to the door.

"See that you're good to her," Lady Mary told him, offering her cheek for a kiss. "She's too good for the likes of you."

He kissed her, his eyes taking on a distant glow. "You're probably right, Aunt Mary. You usually are."

week had passed since Michael's parents had departed for the country. Michael was gone most of every day, and some evenings he didn't arrive home until Mallory was in bed. He still came to her bed each night, and she knew she should tell him about the baby, but she kept her precious secret to herself.

Mallory was alone again. She stood at the front window, gazing out on the park across the street. She watched as several carriages passed, hoping one of them would be Michael's—they weren't.

She ate a solitary meal in the formal dining room, thinking this was little different from when she was alone at her father's house in Cairo. After thumbing through several books in the library, Mallory decided to retire.

She was already dressed for bed when she felt the strangest sensation within her stomach. At first, she thought she might have imagined it, but no, there it was again. She could only liken it to the flutter of butterfly wings.

The baby had moved!

Too excited to sleep, she pulled on her blue robe and walked to the small office Michael had given her as her own. She sat down at the desk, took paper and pen, thinking she would write Cousin Phoebe and tell her of her marriage, and about the baby.

She had left the door open so she would hear Michael when he arrived. The letter was almost finished when she became aware of voices downstairs. She assumed Michael had returned and was talking to the servants. She put her letter aside.

She was so excited—she would tell Michael about the baby and that she'd felt it move tonight!

She hurried to the stairs. The voices were coming from the sitting room, and Mallory could hear the butler talking to Michael.

She rushed into the room, her eyes bright, her hair streaming down her back. "Michael, the most wonderful—"

She stopped, her eyes falling on her husband, who was seated on the couch next to the most beautiful creature she'd ever seen. There were several other ladies and gentlemen in the room, but she was hardly aware of them.

"Michael," Lady Samantha said, looking Mallory over with a critical eye, "who is this woman? She can't be one of the servants, or she wouldn't have addressed you so familiarly. Her robe is at least ten years out of date, and tattered besides. I can only say that if she's your doxy, then you were in the desert too long."

Mallory's lips trembled, but she raised her chin, her blue eyes flashing dangerously. She was humiliated, and she was outraged. "And who are you?" she demanded, although she already knew it was Lady Samantha.

"Michael," Lady Samantha said with a pout on her lips, "surely you aren't going to allow her to speak to me in such a manner?"

Michael came to his feet, staggering slightly. "I admit I've had too much to drink, Mallory. But this isn't what it looks like. I was at my club with my friends when a servant informed us that there were ladies below in a coach, asking to see us."

Mallory didn't flinch. "So you brought them here?"

"They're my friends."

There was no accusation in her voice, only hurt. "And you haven't told them about me?"

"Why should he?" Lady Samantha said, pulling up her elbow-length gloves. "Women like you are seldom introduced to respectable people."

Michael was aware that Samantha put her hand on his arm, and he shook it off.

"Michael, I will not discuss this in front of strangers, but when they have gone, you'll find me in my room." Without another word, Mallory turned and left.

"My God, Michael, who was that beauty?" Lord Grussom asked. "If you don't want her, I'll take her. Where have you been hiding her?"

The look in Michael's eyes made Lord Grussom take a step backwards.

These people weren't his friends anymore, Michael thought with distaste. He'd been trying to recapture his life as it had been before he left England, but he'd realized tonight that it was useless. He didn't want that life anymore.

"Get out of my house, all of you. Don't you know a lady when you see one? Not a one of you is worthy of my wife."

There was stunned silence in the room. At last, Lady

Samantha spoke. "Your *wife!*" she cried. "No one told me that you were married."

"I should have told you, but I wanted to keep her to myself. She's not like us—hard and unfeeling. You hurt her tonight, Samantha, and I allowed it."

"I waited for you," Lady Samantha raged. "You led me to believe we would one day be married. You did, Michael—you know you did."

He shook his head, trying to clear it, while all he could think about was the stricken look in Mallory's eyes. "If I did, I apologize. You should have listened to the old Gypsy. Everything she's predicted has come to pass." He turned to the butler.

"Show them out."

Mallory sent the upstairs maid for her battered trunk that had been stored in the attic. When the maid returned, Mallory could see pity in her eyes, and that hurt almost as much as Lady Samantha's insults.

"Have a carriage made ready for me, and then have someone come for my trunk. I'll be leaving almost immediately."

"Yes, m'lady." The servant quickly withdrew, and Mallory tried not to cry.

When Michael entered the room, she didn't even look up, but went on cramming her belongings into the trunk, not caring if they became wrinkled.

"You aren't leaving," he said, bracing his back against the door.

She paused and glared at him. "Yes, I am, Michael. I have tried not to be demanding and encroach on your world, because I knew you needed time to become accustomed to having a wife. But I would never have believed you capable of deliberate cruelty. You humiliated me tonight, Michael, and in so doing, humiliated yourself as well."

"It wasn't like that, Mallory. I told you that I'd had too much to drink."

She stamped her foot. "And I hope you have the damnedest headache in the morning."

He dropped down on the bed. "I won't let you leave."

"You have nothing to say about it."

His head seemed to clear as he looked at her. "I don't want you to go."

"Shall I stay so I can be the butt of jests, and endure your friends' hateful remarks? You don't know me very well if you think I'll live like this. I've never had a real home, and I thought—no, I hoped, I would have one with you. I know now I was mistaken."

He stood up and gripped her by the shoulders. "I know it's my fault tonight, but it started out in innocence."

"That may be, but the pity is that you would rather be at your club with your friends than at home with me."

"I did try to go back to my old life, but it wasn't the same. I've changed, Mallory, and my friends haven't. I'm older in experience, and I'm not one of them anymore."

"And I don't belong with you anymore."

"Mallory, won't you try to understand?"

"I'm trying. If I hear you correctly, you want me to understand that you were bored with your friends, bored with me, and looking for something that wouldn't bore you."

His hand tightened on her shoulder. "No, damn it, that's not it at all."

She moved away from him and closed the trunk, securing the leather straps. "I'll be waiting in the coach for my trunk."

"Where are you going?" Michael asked.

"I'll let you know."

He watched her leave, feeling helpless to stop her. Until this moment, he hadn't known how much he wanted her. It was too late. She'd never believe him now.

Mallory entered the waiting coach, half hoping that Michael would come after her. When he didn't, she settled into the seat and rested her head on the high leather back. "Take me to Ravenworth," she told the coachman.

It was midafternoon when the coach stopped before the massive doors of Ravenworth Castle. Kassidy had been cutting flowers when the coach arrived. When she saw Mallory, she dropped the flowers and hurried to her daughter-in-law.

"My dear, what a wonderful surprise. If I'd known you were coming, I would have planned something special." She hugged Mallory to her. "Is Michael with you?"

Mallory met her inquiring eyes. "No. I'm alone."

"What is wrong? Has something happened to my son?"

"No, Michael is all right. I . . . Michael . . . I didn't know where else to come, so I came to you."

Kassidy looked into eyes swimming with tears and put a protective arm about Mallory. "If you don't want to talk about it, you don't have to. This is your home, you can come any time you like."

Mallory collapsed against her, and Kassidy called for the coachman to carry her upstairs.

Mallory opened her eyes as a cool cloth was placed on her forehead. She caught at Kassidy's hand. "I'm sorry to cause you distress."

"Nonsense. Does my son know you're going to have a baby?"

"No," Mallory said, not even surprised that Kassidy had guessed her secret.

"I see."

"You won't tell him?"

"No. That will be for you to do." Kassidy moved to the door. "When is the last time you had something to eat?"

"Yesterday . . . I'm not sure."

"You rest now, while I get you something light. It's always better to have something on your stomach when you are expecting a child."

Mallory caught her hand. "I don't want you to think Michael did anything wrong. I . . . he . . . cannot help it if he doesn't love me."

For the first time in her life, Kassidy was angry with Michael. "Did he tell you that?"

"Not in words." Tears spilled down Mallory's cheeks. "I came to you because of the baby. I know how important this child is to the DeWinter family." She wiped her eyes. "But you should know this. I'll never leave my baby, as my parents left me. This is my child, as well as Michael's."

Kassidy closed her eyes, feeling the young girl's pain. "I don't know what happened between the two of you, and I don't want to know. But you are as welcome in this house as Michael. And he will not bother you here, if you don't want to see him."

"You are so kind."

"Not at all. Actually, I've been lonely since Arrian and Warrick took the children back to Scotland."

"You must think badly of me."

"Not at all. You are exactly what I would want for my son. And I know, better than you think, what you are feeling. There was a time when Raile was like Michael. But have hope, because where there is love, there is hope. And Michael does love you—I believe that."

"I don't believe that love is what he feels for me. But I don't want him to worry. If you would have someone notify him that I'm here, I'd be grateful."

"I'll do that."

Mallory was so exhausted that her hand fell across her chest. "If I could rest for just a bit, I'll feel better."

Kassidy pulled up a chair and sat beside Mallory until she fell into a restless sleep. Oh, yes, she knew so well how this sweet girl's heart was breaking. There had been a time, when she and Raile were first married, that she had thought he didn't love her, and she had never forgotten the hurt.

She left the bedroom in search of her husband. It was time Michael became a man and accepted the responsibilities of being a DeWinter.

Michael had slept little since Mallory left. He worried that the coach had been in an accident. When the coach did return, he was on the steps waiting for it.

"Where did you take her ladyship?" he asked the coachman.

"Why, m'lord, I took her to Ravenworth."

"Was she all right—I mean she didn't seem upset or—?" He broke off. One didn't question the servants about one's wife.

"I have a letter from His Grace," the coachman said, reaching onto his coat pocket. "He said I was to deliver it into your own hands."

Michael took the letter with his father's seal on it and hurried to his office. He closed the door, ripped it open, and read.

Michael,

This is to let you know that Mallory arrived at Ravenworth without incident. It is at her request that I contact you, so you will not worry. She and your mother have become very close, and I've come to love her like a daughter. Let us hear from you soon.

Michael ran into the hallway and up the stairs, calling for William. "Pack my clothing, we're going to Ravenworth."

"Very good, m'lord."

"Hurry, William. I want to leave within the hour."

Mallory opened the bedroom door in response to Kassidy's knock. She smiled, shaking her head when she saw the two maids carrying armloads of what looked like gowns.

"What have you there?"

"I had the seamstress make you several gowns. I noticed you are beginning to fill yours out, and I wanted to surprise you."

Kassidy instructed that the gowns be placed on the bed, and when the servants left, she picked up a powder blue one and held it up to Mallory.

"Just as I supposed, blue is a good color for you."

Mallory touched the light gauze fabric. "It's lovely, and how cleverly it was made to disguise the baby."

"I haven't given you a wedding present, so, after the baby comes, you and I will go to London and I'll give you a whole new wardrobe."

"I would love that."

Kassidy picked up a pale pink gown, then frowned, and tossed it aside. "Not with your red hair."

Mallory touched her stomach. "I feel the baby move almost every day."

Kassidy's eyes glowed. "I can't tell you how excited I'll be to have a baby in this house again. Arrian's children are wonderful, though they are being raised in their Scottish heritage, and rightly so, but this baby will be a DeWinter."

"I hope it's a son. Michael seems to be driven by the need to have a son."

"As was his father." Kassidy sighed. "I was always sorry I couldn't give Raile more children."

"You gave him two."

"Actually, Arrian was the child of my sister and Raile's half-brother. Abigail died giving birth to her, and Raile and I took her as our own daughter. She has been as dear to us as if she had been born to us."

"I would never have guessed she wasn't your daughter." Mallory was quiet for a moment. "Do you suppose he'll come?"

Kassidy knew she meant Michael. "Oh, yes, he'll come, if not today, then tomorrow."

allory moved through the picture gallery, looking at portraits of long dead dukes and duchesses of Ravenworth. She could only wonder at the pride that ran deeply in this family. Had she not seen that pride in Michael?

She stopped beneath a portrait of the present duke and duchess. Raile with the proud tilt to his head, stood with his hand on Kassidy's shoulder, while Kassidy, looking beautiful in a frothy white gown, had a slight smile on her lips.

Mallory moved down the hallway looking at portraits of many generations of DeWinter wives. She wondered if her portrait would ever hang there. She doubted it would.

Mallory had basked in the kindness of the duke and duchess. Raile was particularly solicitous, inquiring about her health as a father might inquire about a daughter. He was an amazing man, and she was in awe of the power he wielded in the village of Ravenworth. But if they respected the duke, the villagers loved their duchess, and surrounded her whenever she went among them, the children holding out bouquets of crumpled flowers for her.

The people had been curious about Mallory at first, but now they smiled at her and wished her a good day when she accompanied Kassidy to the village.

She paused at a huge portrait of Michael and Arrian as children. She looked into the eyes of the boy her husband had been and saw something she had not seen before. Life seemed to pulsate from him, and the smile on his lips was a smile of one who was contented, and certain of the future.

"Our portrait will hang here. Would you like that, Mallory?"

Breathlessly, she turned to see her husband. There was no arrogance on his face, no haughtiness. Was that uncertainty she detected in those green eyes?

"Michael, you have come," was all she could manage to say.

"You should have known I would, Mallory." He took a hesitating step toward her and paused, his eyes looking back at the blank wall that was reserved for his portrait when he became duke of Ravenworth.

"Imagine, years from now, some young wife will stand where you are now standing and look up into your face. She will wonder at your beauty, and her husband will say, 'That's my great-grandmother. Was her red hair not glorious to behold? Was not my great-grandfather the most fortunate of men?'"

Mallory's throat closed off with emotion because the

look in Michael's eyes was soft, and she could see love shining there.

She rushed into his open arms and cried against his shoulder. "Oh, Michael, I love you so desperately. And I have missed you so dreadfully."

His grip tightened on her. "Oh, Mallory, Mallory, how long I've waited to hear those words from you. Do you remember that I once told you I wanted something from you?"

She nodded. "I remember."

"I was waiting for you to love me."

Happiness burst from her heart. "I love so much. I never knew it was possible to love this deeply, and to hurt so badly."

Michael's eyes swept her face. "The last person in the world I'd ever want to hurt is you, Mallory. That night you left, I feared I would never see you again."

There was earnestness in his eyes as he paced back and forth, trying to find the words that would make her trust him. "You must believe that nothing happened between Samantha and me. She means nothing to me, and never has. Please say you believe me."

"I have found you to be an honorable man, Michael. If you say that nothing happened between you and Lady Samantha, then I believe you."

"You are wise beyond your years, Mallory. I pledge to you this day, before my ancestors, that I will never in any way dishonor you or the vows we took"—he smiled—"twice."

She searched his face. "Michael, you haven't told me how you feel about me."

"Don't you know? How could you not? I believe the moment I first lost my heart to you was when you thought I'd just doused you with a bucket of water. There you were, dripping wet, your eyes flashing with anger." He took her hand. "Come with me, so we can be alone. We have much to talk about."

At that moment, Raile and Kassidy entered the end of the hallway, unobserved by Michael and Mallory. When Raile would have called out to his son, Kassidy took his arm and led him away.

"I wanted to talk to my son," he protested.

"Not now, dearest. They need to be alone so Mallory can tell him about the baby."

Raile nodded. "You're right, of course. Did you see the way he was looking at her?"

Kassidy nodded, her eyes filled with tears. "Young love, and first discovery, is beautiful to behold."

Raile took her hand and led her to the garden. It was a glorious day. The sun was shining so brightly that it was almost blinding, while birds were singing in the huge oak tree at the far end of the walk.

"There's also something to be said for love that has aged and mellowed, and grown until I don't know where I end and you begin."

Kassidy moved into the circle of his arms. "Oh, yes, my dearest husband. What we have is love in its purest form. This is what I want for our son and Mallory."

Michael held the door open so Mallory could enter. "We won't be disturbed here." He removed his coat and tossed it across the bed. He looked at Mallory, thinking how lovely and fragile she looked. Her cheeks were flushed, and her flaming hair fell loosely about her lovely face.

"Now, where was I?"

"You were going to tell me how you felt about me," Mallory prodded.

She watched him push a hand through his tousled hair and noticed that his hand was actually shaking. She smiled to herself, knowing how difficult this was for him. But she wasn't going to make it easy. There was no doubt in her mind now that he loved her, and her happiness was boundless.

Relenting, she went to Michael and took his hand. "What, the courageous Akhdar 'em Akraba, who faced dozens of armed enemies and laughed in the face of Sheik Sidi Ahmed, and yet you are frightened of one unarmed woman?"

"Scared? I'm petrified. I've never told a woman I loved her before."

Mallory unhooked her gown at the neck. "I'm glad to hear that. A wife likes to believe she's the only woman her husband has loved."

Their eyes met, and Michael laughed. "You have me just where you want me, don't you?"

She smiled coquettishly. "Not yet." She nimbly unbuttoned his shirt. She wanted to tell him about the baby, but had decided it would be fun to allow him to discover it for himself.

His eyes gleamed as she pushed his shirt off his shoulder and pressed her lips against his neck.

He closed his eyes, trying not to think about what her soft body offered. When she ran her fingers through his hair, he grabbed her hand. "If you continue to entice me, I'll never finish what I'm trying to tell you."

Mallory moved back and stepped out of her gown, kicking it out of the way. "Some things are better experienced than said, Michael."

His body trembled with anticipation. "You little vixen, don't tempt me beyond my control."

She unfastened the laces across the bodice of her petticoat, and slipped it off her shoulders, allowing it to fall at her feet.

Michael came to her, picking her up in his arms, his hungry mouth devouring her soft lips.

"Oh, you do so sorely tempt me, my lady." He placed her on the bed, his eyes raking her soft body.

He looked puzzled for a moment. Her breasts were fuller than he remembered. He dropped down beside her, his hands roving at will over her soft hips.

"I love you," he whispered against her ear. "I love you so much it's . . . like . . . pain."

"I know," she said softly, turning to her back and taking his hand and placing it on her rounded stomach. She smiled to herself, wondering how long it would take him to discover that she was going to have his child.

His lips were hot against her throat, his hand moved over her abdomen, his thoughts were clouded by the satin-soft skin. He paused, frowning. He moved back, his eyes moving from her full breasts to the roundness of her stomach.

"Mallory?"

"Is something wrong?"

He hesitated to mention what he was thinking. He was new at being a husband, but he was wise enough to know it wouldn't be prudent to tell Mallory she was putting on weight. "No, it's just that . . . nothing."

She could read confusion on his face and decided to help him. "I have a new wardrobe. Mine didn't fit anymore."

"Uh, didn't fit?"

Mallory laughed and reached up, pulling him down to her. "My wonderful, innocent husband. Don't you see the weight I've gained?"

"I . . . didn't want to mention it."

Again she laughed and took his hand, pressing it against her stomach. Nature was kind, because the baby chose that moment to kick.

Michael pulled back his hand as if he'd been burned. He opened his mouth to speak, but no words came out. With his eyes shining, he touched her breasts ever so lightly, then bent and touched his lips to her stomach.

"My God," he said in a choked voice, "a baby. My own baby!"

He tenderly took her into his arms. He was too filled with wonder to say more.

"I have come to know, Michael, how much this family cherishes its children."

He drew in a ragged breath. "Have you also noticed how we cherish our wives?"

"Oh, yes, Michael, I have noticed that."

He pulled her body against his, reveling in the swell of her stomach that pressed against him. "When next I'm in London, I want to seek out a certain Gypsy woman and reward her properly."

Mallory looked puzzled. "Surely you don't believe in fortune-tellers?"

"This one I do."

He cupped her face and stared into her eyes for a long moment. "This is what I've been searching for without knowing it. You, my dearest love, are what has eluded me for so many years. I looked for you in every woman I met. Little did I know I would find you in the least likely place."

Mallory threw her head back and allowed him access to her lips. He spoke her name with reverence, and she hugged him tightly against her. She had never dared hope this wonderful, complex man would love her.

"Mallory, you will never leave me again?"

"Never," she answered breathlessly.

As he touched and stroked her, she felt every shadow of loneliness fall away. She would never be lonely again.

It was a cold December day, with the snow falling and the tree branches bending beneath the onslaught of the north wind. But inside Ravenworth Castle, warm fires had been lit in the hearths and there was a bustle of activity as if something out of the ordinary was happening.

The servants worked quietly at their duties, while often casting anxious glances to the grand staircase.

In the upstairs sitting room, Raile handed his son a glass of brandy and smiled because Michael was so pale.

"Babies have been born since the beginning of time, Michael, and this one will be no different."

"I've heard it's painful."

"Of course it is."

"Why did I put her though this?"

Arrian entered the room, her face glowing. She linked her arm through her brother's. "What a wonderful Christmas this will be." Her eyes danced with merriment. "Father, if this baby doesn't come soon, we'll have to have the doctor tending Michael."

Michael moved to the window, still clutching his glass of brandy. He stared out at the bleakness of the day, his face a mask of misery. He suddenly panicked, wanting to rush down the hall and hold Mallory in his arms. She was going to die—he just knew she was. He knew that death often came to the women in the village during childbirth.

At that moment, a cry could be heard, and Michael stood petrified. Raile, knowing well what his son was feeling, went to him, smiling.

"It's a lusty cry. It must be a boy."

Michael took a deep swallow of his brandy. "Do you think Mallory is all right?"

"Of course. Didn't Dr. Worthington assure you many times that Mallory is built for bearing children?"

"Yes, but—"

Kassidy entered, carrying a tiny bundle in her arms, her eyes shimmering with happy tears. She passed her husband and her daughter, and went right to Michael.

"I'm happy to tell you that Mallory is doing well, and she wants you to meet your son."

Michael thought he would feel awkward with a baby, but when his mother placed his son in his arms, he could only stare at the tiny face. There was wonder in his eyes as he touched the soft hand, and he was awed by the perfectly formed fingers.

"A son," he whispered, raising the child to his face. Then his voice rose in volume as he looked at his father. "A son! I have a son!"

Kassidy and Arrian were hugging each other and crying with joy. Raile took the baby from Michael and beamed at the tiny bit of humanity as if it were the most precious possession. "Another DeWinter is born."

Michael hurried out of the room, content to leave the baby in loving hands. He pushed open his bedroom door and went to Mallory.

He was surprised to find her looking so well. Her red hair was tied back with a white ribbon, and she was propped against several pillows.

"Do you think long-dead DeWinters are smiling today, Michael?"

She held her hand out to him, and he clasped it tightly, then he softly kissed her cheek. "I'm sure of it—the line continues."

Epilogue

he reception the duke and duchess of
Ravenworth gave to introduce their daughter-in-law to London society was held at
Lady Mary Rindhold's spacious mansion. Hundreds of
invitations had been hand delivered, and it was reputed
that Queen Victoria, herself, would be making a brief
appearance to honor Lady Mallory for distinguished service to the Crown.

The members of the DeWinter family were all present,
and stood near the door to receive their guests. Lady
Mary was first, and Raile and Kassidy were beside her.
Mallory and Michael were next, with Warrick and Arrian
standing at the end of the receiving line.

Michael looked at his wife with pride. Mallory looked
beautiful in a shimmering blue silk gown trimmed with
flossed silk fringe.

Mallory greeted each guest with a warm smile. So far,

she had met a prince, three princesses, several dukes and duchesses, and numerous marquesses and earls and their ladies.

Suddenly Kassidy took her arm, bringing her to the front of the line. "Mallory, your mother and father are here. I believe we should include them with the family. Do you have any objections?"

Mallory was stunned. "No, of course not." She hadn't heard from her parents since leaving Egypt, but then she hadn't expected any contact with them.

Her father awkwardly kissed her cheek, and her mother clasped her hand. "We had to come when we received the invitation from Her Grace," Lord Tyler explained.

"Thank you for coming," Mallory said, wishing she could feel warmth toward her mother and father, and wishing she could think of anything else to say to them.

Lord Tyler and Lady Julia stood at the end of the receiving line, knowing it was their fault that they would never be included in their daughter's life. They were aware that they had been invited only because the duchess of Ravenworth wanted to present a united family to the world for Mallory's sake. They watched Mallory as she was received by the elite of London society.

Warrick spoke to Lord Tyler. "What do you think of the baby?"

Lord Tyler looked puzzled. "What baby?"

"Your grandson. I can tell you, he's the pride of this family."

Lord Tyler looked at his wife. "A grandson. Imagine, one day he'll be the duke of Ravenworth."

Mallory's eyes lit up when she saw Cousin Phoebe enter the room. She rushed forward and embraced the little woman, and after introducing her to Michael, she insisted her cousin stand between them in the receiving line.

Phoebe was overwhelmed by the honor, and she beamed when Mallory introduced her to Raile and Kassidy. "I'd like you to meet my cousin, Phoebe. Actually, she's more like my mother, since she raised me."

Lady Julia watched Phoebe Byrd laughing up at her daughter, and she felt pangs of jealousy. It should be she who stood where Phoebe did, but she had given up that right. What a mistake they had made. She looked into her husband's eyes and knew he felt the same.

When there was a gap in the line, Phoebe leaned close to Mallory. "You cannot imagine what has happened to poor Sir Gerald Dunmore."

Mallory hadn't thought of that odious man in a very long time. "Something unfortunate, I hope."

"You might well think so. Poor man had an accident. He says he had a fall from a horse, but I heard he fell out of a woman's bedroom window when her husband came home unexpectedly and caught him."

Mallory smiled. "How dreadful."

"Indced," Phoebe said, trying to look rueful, but her eyes danced with mirth. "Pathetic creature broke his back and is laid up for an indefinite time." She leaned in even closer and lowered her voice. "But don't be concerned for him, I understand he is receiving devoted care from his wife. It is said she is his constant companion."

Mallory met her cousin's eyes. "May she make his cvery day as miserable as he's made others."

"She's had years of neglect and mistreatment from that man, so I'm sure she shares your sentiments." She clasped Mallory's hand. "I can see that you are happy, child."

"Yes, I am."

"It shows. I am so glad, Mallory. Later, I want to see your son."

"Cousin Phoebe, are *you* happy?"

"I keep busy."

"How would you like to come to Ravenworth Castle and look after my son? He has a nurse and a nanny, but I would feel better if you directed his care."

Phoebe's eyes misted. She knew Mallory was only being kind, but she also knew she could be useful. If the child was anything like his mother, he'd need a firm hand to guide him. And he would probably have brothers and sisters who would need the same.

"We'll talk about this later, but I won't let you say no," Mallory assured her. "At Ravenworth, you won't be treated like a poor relation. Everyone will give you the respect you deserve as the woman who raised me, and as my only true family."

"I would like that above all things, Mallory. I've missed you. I would like to care for your son the way I cared for you."

Michael took Mallory's elbow and turned her to face the door. "Here comes another surprise for you."

Mallory smiled in delight as she saw Prince Khaldun and Princess Yasmin, who were making their way slowly down the receiving line. The prince looked handsome in his white-and-gold uniform. Yasmin was dressed in a bright yellow silk gown and headcovering, with only her eyes showing behind the veil.

"I can't believe they are here!" Mallory exclaimed.

"Try to appear surprised when they present you with Egyptian medals from the viceroy," Michael murmured.

She clasped his hand tightly. "This is the happiest day of my life, Michael."

"I promise," he told her, "if it is within my power, you will always be as happy as you are today."

Dear friends, I want to make an urgent plea for you to wear your seat belts every time you get into a car. Even if you are only going to the corner grocery store, strap up—it only takes a moment of your time, and it could save your life. Over the Thanksgiving holiday, my daughter, Kimberly, and my three granddaughters were in a terrible six-car pile up. All of them were wearing their seat belts. My daughter sustained only minor injuries. Caitlyn and Courtney, the three- and four-year-olds, had only burns from the seat belts, and five-week-old Cameron didn't have a scratch on her. The police informed my daughter, that had they not been wearing seat belts, they would have all been killed. So please, buckle up—it could save your life.

COMING NEXT MONTH

STARLIGHT by Patricia Hagan
Another spellbinding historical romance from bestselling author Patricia Hagan. Desperate to escape her miserable life in Paris, Samara Labonte agreed to switch places with a friend and marry an American soldier. During the train journey to her intended, however, Sam was abducted by Cheyenne Indians. Though at first she was terrified, her heart was soon captured by one particular blue-eyed warrior.

THE NIGHT ORCHID by Patricia Simpson
A stunning new time travel story from an author who *Romantic Times* says is "fast becoming one of the premier writers of supernatural romance." When Marissa Quinn goes to Seattle to find her missing sister who was working for a scientist, what she finds instead is a race across centuries with a powerfully handsome Celtic warrior from 285 B.C. He is the key to her missing sister and the man who steals her heart.

ALL THINGS BEAUTIFUL by Cathy Maxwell
Set in the ballrooms and country estates of Regency England, a stirring love story of a dark, mysterious tradesman and his exquisite aristocratic wife looking to find all things beautiful. *"All Things Beautiful* is a wonderful 'Beauty and the Beast' story with a twist. Cathy Maxwell is a bright new talent."—*Romantic Times*

THE COMING HOME PLACE by Mary Spencer
Knowing that her new husband, James, loved another, Elizabeth left him and made a new life for herself. Soon she emerged from her plain cocoon to become an astonishingly lovely woman. Only when James' best friend ardently pursued her did James realize the mistake he had made by letting Elizabeth go.

DEADLY DESIRES by Christina Dair
When photographer Jessica Martinson begins to uncover the hidden history of the exclusive Santa Lucia Inn, she is targeted as the next victim of a murderer who will stop at nothing to prevent the truth from coming out. Now she must find out who is behind the murders, as all the evidence is pointing to the one man she has finally given her heart to.

MIRAGE by Donna Valentino
To escape her domineering father, Eleanor McKittrick ran away to the Kansas frontier where she and her friend Lauretta had purchased land to homestead. Her father, a prison warden, sent Tremayne Hawthorne, an Englishman imprisoned for a murder he didn't commit, after her in exchange for his freedom. Yet Hawthorne soon realized that this was a woman he couldn't bear to give up.

Harper **The Mark of Distinctive**
Monogram **Women's Fiction**